ROSETTA 6.C

What is the mystery of
the rose cinquefoil?

How can it save America?

James Atticus Bowden

Cover art by Christina Van Oss

© 2006 James Atticus Bowden
All Rights Reserved.

No part of this publication may be reproduced, stored in a retrieval system, or transmitted, in any form or by any means, electronic, mechanical, photocopying, recording, or otherwise, without the written permission of the author.

First published by Dog Ear Publishing
4010 W. 86th Street, Ste H
Indianapolis, IN 46268
www.dogearpublishing.net

ISBN: 978-159858-219-2
Library of Congress Control Number: 2006934762

This book is printed on acid-free paper.
This book is a work of Fiction. Places, events, and situations in this book are purely Fictional and any resemblance to actual persons, living or dead, is coincidental.

Printed in the United States of America

We have now sunk to a depth at which the restatement of the obvious is the first duty of intelligent men.
—George Orwell

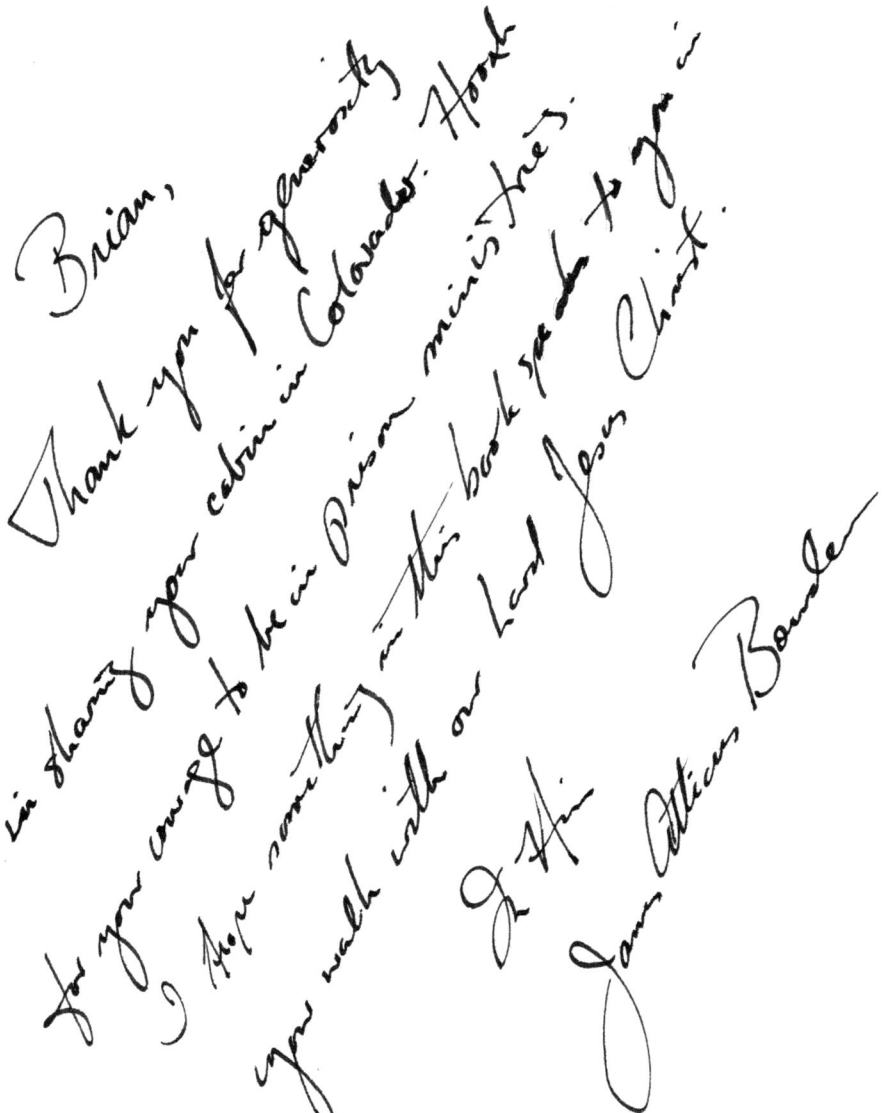

Dedication

To Atticus W. League, James Albert Bowden Sr.,
Edith Henderson Bowden.

Grandfather, Father, and, especially, Mother taught me
the subject of 'courage'.

They lived courage by the chapter and verse of their lives.

Preface

The motivation to write *Rosetta 6.2* began on a snowy Bradley Fighting Vehicle gunnery range, Range 214 at Grafenwoehr, Germany, on the ides of March 1987. I had an extraordinary experience, an answer to seven years of prayer, where I was told, "You will read and write." I finished this book, for the last time, 18 years later.

It's a long way from March 15th, 1987 to January 7th, 2005. I don't know if I was too slow or the Lord was taking His time to make sure I did 'right' in His Will. My prayer from the first time I put pen to paper through the publishing of *Rosetta 6.2*, is that this work in my hand be in His Will, not mine. Consequently, whatever is good about *Rosetta 6.2* is to the glory of my Savior, Jesus Christ, and whatever is wrong is mine, James Atticus Bowden.

In March 1990 I had two years to go to U.S. Army retirement but it was time to get on with the reading and writing after duty hours. I asked God what should I write specifically. From that moment on, I never had writer's block. The ideas and words just came to me. Sometimes it was hard to keep up and get the thoughts on paper as they flooded into my mind. I wrote the book in my head, made a detailed outline, and created a large file of scraps of paper with ideas, dialogue, and key events between March 1990 and December 1992.

In the first week of December I found in my daily Bible reading what I took as my personal covenant for my life, Isaiah 59:21. Armed and energized, I began composing *Rosetta 6.2* from front to end on my new PC in January 1993. It took me six months to finish Chapter One, writing in the hours after children's bed time and before sleep overtook me. Over the years I took lengthy diversions to read about different subjects, like illegal drugs, computer science, the Koran, Islam, Jesuits, Martin Luther, etc. And to think. And listen.

Some of the ideas that seemed like science fiction in the early '90s became science facts. I imagined computer programs flowing on common electronic current and facial visual identification software. I read about optical computing and imagined the nano-technology for the rose cinquefoil computer chips. Interactive voice navigation systems, software 'spiders', and personal communicators like today's 'blackberry' came to my imagination for fiction before I learned, years later, they had become real.

I projected the future global, ideologically-based struggle from my job as a military futurist. In the Army After Next (AAN) war games, playing the enemy 'Red' team, we discussed using commercial airplanes against targets in the United States. I developed an international, non-nation–state enemy based on Islam, like Al Qa'ida, for the AAN 1997 Fall War Game. I participated in an intitial 'Homeland Security' seminar in 1997 to prepare for the AAN 1998 Spring war game. I expected an attack before 2010, so I was surprised only at the timing of the attack on 9–11–01.

I wrote in earnest throughout 1998 until I finished in June 1999. My first draft had too many details and distractions. I've rewritten the entire book three times.

Rosetta 6.2 morphed over the years from dealing with the one evil of drugs to the conjunction of the evil of drugs and Islamist terrorism, simultaneously, within the Great U.S. Culture War. The Culture War is known as ACW II (American Civil War II) in the op eds I write. I came upon the idea of illegal drugs and Islamist Terrorism serving as the catalyst to bring ACW II to a head. My first op ed, a response to 9–11, 'One Front: Two Wars' (www.americancivilization.net), suggested how our unity would evaporate over time. So, it has.

I finished up to the last chapter by Labor Day 2004. I waited for the outcome of the election of '04 to decide if I would use a real politician as the 2012 Presidential incumbent in *Rosetta 6.2* or a fictional one. 2005 and 2006 were given over to an agent to get published and to develop my art concept for the cover. I think it was a time for *Rosetta 6.2* to lie fallow. After enough time passed I had the distance to look at the words for one last time before printing and edit the last. I pray it went well in His plan.

If *Rosetta 6.2* serves properly, someone will come to know the

Lord or someone will find a deeper, personal relationship with the living Jesus Christ. Other insights, if they happen, are merely interesting. I understand the suffering drug abuse and Islamist terror cause and write against them. I've seen the power of prayer to save and heal. I give praise to Lord Jesus, because God is good, all the time—no matter what.

Chapter 1. Discovery

Hampton, VA
September 3rd, 2012
Monday

Will they ever fix the gears on these stupid road teeth? Jack watched the lifting bar slip off another broken spoke on the giant gear and crash down to the next spoke. The huge half-barrel cam rotated ten tons of steel barricade down into its hole like a troll sliding back beneath his bridge. The sharp, serrated fangs set across its forward edge spanned the whole width of Wythe Creek Road to intimidate a vehicle of any size. The road teeth fell smoothly for one foot and shudder-dropped the next. The herky-jerky ratchet intrigued him as an engineer even as it frustrated him.

The city is strapped just to pay the guards for these checkpoints. They'll never upgrade the infrastructure until every gear in these road teeth break and the road is impassable. Then it'll be months of detours through big crime country.

Jack scanned the darkening horizon for any sign of danger before he obeyed the guard's impatient wave. There was nothing to fear in the wide marsh of the serpentine Back River, but the safety habits important for survival become second nature.

He breathed the night air deeply and smiled. The natural scent of southern marsh basting in summer's heat is a hot, humid fetid rot. It was perfume to Jack because he declared this place, Tidewater Virginia, home. As the last blue hue of twilight shadows deepened to black, he sensed something in the air changed. Autumn is coming. He loved autumn. He even loved the name 'autumn' because it has more dignity than fall. Soon enough the daylight won't linger as today, Labor Day. The crushing heat gives way to pleasant warmth. Jack tasted the anticipation.

If I had my old convertible, I could just feel the air wash over me and drink the night in. Jack smiled pridefully at his poetic thoughts. *But nope, no way today.* He sold his red baby at quite a loss several years ago just as the Terrorist and Criminal Incentives Act became law. He looked at each point of the intersection ahead for a carjacker ambush.

That Act outlawed convertibles. Convertibles were too easy a target for terrorists to carjack. Not that they ever would, but they could. Anything a terrorist could do, however remotely, was forbidden as a matter of Homeland Security. The security geeks just had to dream up the possible, earnestly declare it plausible, and then they could regulate it for the safety of us all. Convertibles presented too much of an incentive for punks desperate for drug money. If the incentives were too great, then the criminals could not be blamed for their actions. So, the Nanny State banned convertibles. It was up to the good citizens to not invite terrorists or provoke crime.

When did it all get so screwed up? Jack asked his memory. *First, there were the Islamist suicide bombers murdering in malls, schools, sports events. Second, the drug lords and Islamists joined up together. Then, ah, two thousand ten, the year that designer drugs went wild. When crime got so out of control. When fear became paramount. Was that Nathan's Year? No, my precious boy was born three years before. What do I call this year past? The Government's been cracking down harder on Homeland Security.* He let his mind roam for the precise word to label the year properly.

Every year of his conscious life fit completely on one side or the other of the demarcation line of September, exactly at the Labor Day weekend. Summer and the old school year fell to the rear. Autumn and the new school year stood, waiting, on the other side. Even a dozen years of work since college could neither blur the distinctions nor dampen the need to divide, label and catalogue the year. Except, of course, for September 2001 when the 11th divided life as it divided the world.

Jack recalled a year like pulling a book from a library shelf. He smelled the dust, the ink, and the paper of the year as he ran his hand on the binding. He felt the weight of the names of the past few years. *'Baby Mary's Year'* was also the *'Year of Last-Child-because-Maude-insists'*. *'Frustration Year'* was before that. Maybe I'll call last year *'Quiet Desperation'*. Jack sensed if the words fit or not, like a foot wriggled into a new shoe, feeling it for itself.

"Next year may be something else," Jack liked the sound of his own voice. "If I can crack the code on the computer from this creep Ishmael, I'll be doing all right." He imagined the immediate promotion ceremony with his cubicle inmates in the Security Systems Directorate, National Aeronautics and Space Administration (NASA) applauding. *I've gotta find out what's Ishmael's connection to the Narco-Terrorists. Maybe there'll be a clue tonight. Maybe there's a domestic terrorist connection...*

The security bulletins associated with Ishmael—the discrete access codes: ASSASIN, APOCALYPSE, BUGS and EUREKA— definitely were tied to the new, super secret Omni system. *What's the link?* He was in his mind, not behind his eyes, driving prudently, passing the heavily guarded entrance to NASA, tucked in and housed at Langley Air Force base, parking, setting the car security system, entering the long, low office building with a handprint screen biomimetics test and facerecognition[1] system once over.

When he arrived at his office, he snapped back into present tense focus and carefully entered the security code with one finger. He half-cocked the doorknob to the left before he jerked it back to the right and bumped his shoulder against the door. The temperamental lock opened after two shakings. He swung his briefcase deftly between his legs to wedge the door open. A few minutes of ventilation before the door sensors started beepingly to complain would be wonderful. *I'm going to get a lot done tonight all alone on a holiday evening.*

The office air hung stale and thick from a long weekend of old coffee and rotting fruit fermenting in the overflowing trashcans. Eight workstations crammed the room, giving the office the permanent look of confusion. Before he started a small pot of coffee to keep company, he casually leaned over his fax/phone unit, hit 'Power' and typed in his password: "rosebud.96d". Jack kept his computer voice recognition off because background voices violated

---

1. Visface and Facerecog are the names of families of computerized face recognition surveillance systems.

his cubicle. The cursor fluttered and prompted, "RE CODENAME". *Odd.* Jack typed "rosebud.96d" again. As he turned his head and stepped away, he saw the cursor flutter again out of the corner of his eye. It was as faint as a butterfly testing its wings. An inner voice, unspoken but something still undeniable, told him to panic and flee. Danger! Danger! Danger! There was an odd whining noise.

He lurched forward a couple of steps just as his computer exploded into a perfectly symmetrical cone of metal, plastic and flame. The death cone blasted his chair right where the base of his neck should be. The force and fire expanded until it rent itself against the far wall and ricocheted around the room. Jack fell forward as the concussion slapped his head to the floor. The room filled with flame and smoke.

He was disoriented. Yet, he crawled to the door. His briefcase holding the door open made good his escape. The room became an inferno. The door slammed shut behind him. In rapid order each of the other computers exploded. The shrapnel careening inside the room made uneven noises, like very loud popcorn. His head throbbed. He pushed and propped himself against the wall to gain his feet. He staggered down the black corridor lit at long intervals by firelights.

"*Help!*" Jack thought, "*What happened?*" He was at the rear emergency exit, not at the front where he entered. Jack leaned on the emergency exit bar with his right side. His left arm was numb. He knew that something was hurt.

Jack stumbled out. He was sure he would throw up and faint at the same time. He fell back against the red brick building. The power was blacked out everywhere. Two cars sped to the front of his building from the darkness. One of them looked like a 'NASA Security' vehicle. Jack tried to call, but he struggled to breath in shallow gasps.

Something was wrong. The six men who sprang from the vehicles and rushed towards the entrance carried late model Russian assault rifles and German laser-designated automatic pistols—the weapons of choice for the Narco-Terrorists. All wore combat helmets with full-face mask protection and built-in vision photonics[2]. Jack gasped. He felt another intense wave of nausea.

---

2. Headgear for the U.S. Army Land Warrior 21 found its way to commercial markets with multi-spectral sensing devices for super-enhanced vision and hearing

"This is a hit!" he thought. *"Oh, no! Why me?"* He felt a terrible urge to wet his pants. His car was fifty shadowy yards away and only a few feet from their two cars. *They're going to kill me.* He felt a cold emptiness in the pit of his stomach. Again, he was sure he would vomit.

Jack swallowed hard. He wanted to cry. Instead, he crouched and ran as fast as he could to his car. He held his keys and security remote in his outstretched arm like a magic icon. At every step he listened for the gruff voice or the crackle of fire aimed at him. He winced, expecting to feel the pain of high velocity fleshettes piercing him. He trembled as he gunned the engine in reverse, spun backwards and out of the parking lot. Only then did he dare look towards the building. The roof over his office vented letting flame and thick black smoke billow into the night sky. There were more explosions. He saw no one.

Coming towards him a swirl in their lights and sirens, two fire trucks and another sedan raced to the fire. Jack sped up as the road swung around the end of the runway and along the perimeter fence. When he got to the gate, the Air Police were looking beyond him and over the tree line at the growing explosions and fire at NASA. Jack eased past the distracted guards. *Maybe they're paid off too.* He passed the traffic baffle, turned right and stepped on the gas for home.

"Why?" Again, *"Why me?"* Then he remembered the security bulletin he had read recently. Four people were killed at their government computers in the past six weeks. He recalled the locations.

- Joint Staff, the Pentagon, Washington, DC
- National Security Agency, Fort Meade, Maryland
- FBI Training Center, Quantico, Virginia
- Drug Enforcement Agency, Washington, DC

Another fifteen people died in the ensuing explosions and fires.

Jack remembered the last fellow. He was in the middle of a tandem test for complex virus gremlins used in Total Information Awareness. The video camera caught in the twinkling of an eye an extraordinary code query (RE CODENAME) and a pulsing prompt, a flutter, before the explosion. *Ah.*

Jack grasped the analysis intuitively despite the fear choking his thoughts. A new and very powerful hunter-killer virus was loose. For this virus to strike Jack's computer, it had to alter his special computer defense instructions. That meant it entered at the standard language component level, simultaneously muted his virus alarms, and countered his anti-viral inoculation.

"Some virus," Jack whispered as he slowed for the City of Poquoson South checkpoint with the noisy road teeth. Poquoson ran checkpoints for the only two roads that lead onto this little peninsula on The Peninsula of Virginia. Local homeowners ran the other five. The guards knew him well.

"Uh, Sir, what happened?" asked the young guard. His mouth fell agape as he looked at Jack's forehead.

Jack felt the weight of the swelling press down on his left eye. "Muggers," he stated matter of factly. One guard could be corrupted as easily as another.

The guard nodded vigorously and said, "You might need stitches." Nothing more needed to be said. Another guy was attacked. No big deal.

Jack grunted, "Yeah." The road teeth lowered in spasms again. He pulled slowly across them and turned left up Cary's Chapel Road.

Who wants to kill me? Is this Ponce de Leon? Ishmael?

He needed to hear his thoughts out loud, "They must know there was a strike and they will find out who works in the office and which machine took the first hit. They'll know it's me. It'll be easy to find out the rest." He groaned, "I gotta hide Maude and the kids."

He slowed down for the last checkpoint. The neighborhood security association, Yorktown Road Homeowners, operated this checkpoint for three years, since the Supreme Court ruled that "properly licensed public and private roadblocks for safety on public roads is not un-Constitutional."[3] This guard, too, cautioned him to get stitches for his forehead.

Trying to compose himself, he made the turn at Powhatan Drive and aimed for the non-descript brick rambler he called home.

---

3. The U.S. Supreme Court and lower Federal and State courts ruled for many restraints in public transportation, access, and assembly. In each case the Supreme Court made up reasons for more security and less freedom. The Courts were especially keen on finding reasons to allow roadblocks on public roads, etc. for neighborhoods that could afford for the personal security services.

He slowed down and looked for anything out of the ordinary. No. The well-kept yards and tidy houses rested in the warm night. Jack gave himself a mental checkmark for being cunning. 'They' could already be at his home.

He hurried inside and quickly locked the security system. He was reassured by the very normal chatter of children and the discordant blare of a TV turned too loud.

"Maude, come here!" he strode past the outstretched arms of his toddler son, Nathan.

"Oh, you come here," she retorted. She walked in carrying a full laundry basket, "Take this." She thrust the basket at him and gasped, "What happened Jack? Oh, your head!"

Jack cut off her interrogation, "Listen. My computer exploded at work. Someone is trying to kill me. We've got to take the kids and get out now," Jack held her at the elbows and glared into her eyes.

He knew her next questions. "They could be coming here right now to get me," Jack paused, "and all of us." He nodded towards the children. He tightened his jaw and lowered his voice. "We can talk in the car. We've got to go right now. Maybe we can go to Kathy's."

Maude read Jack's face. She trembled. Nathan walked to his mother in the same "hold me, hold me" stance he had offered Jack. Maude swooped him up and settled him astride her hip. Despite her fear, she reasserted herself, "Jack, you just…"

He cursed and cut her off, "Maude! I know about security. This is my business. The Narco-Terrorists are after me. Now get packing! Right now!"

She was startled to hear him yell. Her voice dropped and softened, "Why Kathy's? I want to go to home."

He looked at her hard, "They found my computer and made it blow up. Now, they will find our home. After they find our home, they'll find your parents and look for you there. There's no electronic audit trail to Kathy. I need to know that you and the kids are safe. I'll leave you there and go sort this out. You haven't called her lately, have you?" His voice rose again. This time it was for effect.

"No," she said meekly, "we don't even email, except at Christmas. I've been meaning to call since Tom and her…" Her voice trailed off. Her best friend from high school, Kathy, recently divorced. She moved back from California to nearby Isle of Wight

County across the James River.

"I'll get the bags. You put everything to pack on the beds. Hurry!" said Jack. Maude heard the order.

The children moved to Maude like ducklings to mother duck. They clung and whined for reassurance and, yet, were so full of wonderful childish curiosity. Maude started to cry. She looked at the sweet heads around her. Thomas was an amazing five-year-old. Mary was a precious three. Nathan was her newest darling baby at eighteen months. Maude gathered herself. She smiled at the children as she wiped tears from her cheeks with the back of her hand. She asked, "Who can help Mommy the most?"

Jack scouted out from the window every other minute. His head and arm throbbed. He felt speechless and disbelieving. *We're running for our lives.*

The drive to Kathy's was surreal. The children sat snugly in their safety seats, clutching their favorite sleepy bye stuffed animal, waiting for signals like puppy dogs. Jack asked over his shoulder, "Hey, how do the wheels on the bus go?"

"Round and round, all over town!" Jack lead the chorus. The children's glee cleansed the air.

"I can't believe this, honey," Maude put her hand on Jack's thigh.

"The children on the bus…"

"It's a precaution, babe. A really important one." The traffic seemed normal, not sinister.

"The driver on the bus…"

"But, you work for the government. Can't the police…"

"Maude, that's exactly why we're running. Narco-Terrorist money buys anything. Anybody. We need to hide before they find us."

"The baby on the bus…"

"But, the children, Jack. How long will this be? What do we do?"

Jack's chest felt tight, "Darling, it's the children we have to hide. You wouldn't believe what I read at work."

"I hear the news."

"It's a lot worse than the news. Just trust me. We turn here for Kathy's don't we?" As they drove, every minute crawled.

There was a moment of anxiety as to whether Kathy would shelter them. Kathy was scared, but she nodded her head in assent and urged Jack to hurry and go. Jack's eyes filled with tears when he clutched Thomas, Mary and Nathan in turn and kissed their checks and forehead. His tongue got too thick to speak, except to mumble, "I love you. I love you so."

He held Maude and kissed her passionately. Her body thickened all over in the past year or so, but her figure was still nicely curved. He tried to hold their kiss, but she turned her head and said, "Jack."

Jack waved back from the car, because he couldn't talk at all now. Maude stood at the door with the children clustered around her. She waved, smiled bravely for a second, and then, holding her face in her hands, turned to Kathy. Her shoulders shrugged in sobs. Jack memorized the moment and headed away out into the night.

Newport News, VA
September 4th, 2012
Tuesday

It was past midnight when Jack drove across the long low causeway and bridge that is the James River Bridge to Newport News, Virginia. *Where do I go?* He looked out across the broad black water; the James dressed for night, at the moonlight playing across the short, choppy waves. He sighed and took a nice cleansing breath. *Okay, let's just take this problem one step at a time. How do I throw them off the trail?* He let the thought look for an answer. Nothing. *How do I lose them for just right now?*

His lips pealed back in a broad grin. *I'll dump the car so it'll be found. I'll leave a cold trail. No trail. If Maude stays off the phone, they won't find her either. Oh, she had better do what I told her to do.* His smile faded by degrees. *Oh God, make her remember.* Strange to call out to God, but it seemed necessary.

Jack's grin grew back. *Yes! The Colonial Parkway doesn't have a stoplight or a checkpoint. There shouldn't be any LiveCam or TrafficCam. No informants watching. I can hike to Williamsburg. A ride anywhere out of there will be good.*

Jack was tight-lipped when he passed the Colonial Parkway warning "TRAVEL AT YOUR OWN RISK DUSK TO DAWN DAILY" sign. He searched where to abandon the car. He strained under the growing tenseness, like driving in a down-pouring rain on a busy road. When he crossed the reedy mouth of Felgates Creek emptying into the York River, he saw a car and a few figures in the roadside park. The edge of his headlights caught a quick glimpse of a woman, a man, and a little child. Like a robot, he slowed the car and pulled a U-turn.

The woman saw him. The old man called to her, "Darlin-darlin, that fella is turning back. Now you'n Lil' Bit get in the car."

She answered, "Coming, Daddy. Come here Lil' Bit!" She stepped forward to grab the boy peeing designs in the tall grass.

"No, Mama, I do it! Let me zip!" He ran away from the car.

The Grandpa was well up in years. He drew himself up and stuck out his chest. He stationed himself by the rear door. An elderly woman huddled two girls in the back seat next to her flour sack bosoms like chicks under her wing.

Jack pulled up. Mother and son emerged from the grass. Jack got out quickly, "Excuse me. Excuse me. I'm sorry, but, I, uh, I, uh, I…" He stood in front of his headlights to show them he meant no harm. His own shadow hid their faces from his reading.

"I don't mean to bother you, but I need some help." They listened like stone. The boy tried to squirm free of his Mother's grasp. "I need a ride, please. Please!"

"You just drove here. Why do you need a ride?" demanded Grandpa.

Jack looked to the sky and shook his head like he was caught in a great practical joke. The old man's accent was hillbilly. Look who he turned to for rescue. Jack's shoulders slumped in surrender, "Jeez, that must look so stupid! I drive up and ask for a ride! Jeez."

"My name is Jack Tillman. I work in NASA Security," He held out his security badges clipped to an office geek neckstrap. "Tonight my computer exploded and almost killed me. It was a hit. That's how I got this," Jack leaned forward and pointed to his swollen forehead. "I need to get away. I've got my family hidden. I need a ride, please."

"Why don't you go to the police?" asked Grandpa.

"I have reason to believe they're in on it." The silence grew.

"The corruption. You know. I just need a ride."

"Daddy, it'll be okay," the woman said.

"Naomi! We've got no business doing this. Fella, you step back now."

"Daddy, this man can ride with us. We'll be good Samaritans." She handed the squirming little boy to the old man. "C'mon Mister. We're heading home. We stayed late at Busch Gardens. We just decided we're gonna drive home tonight, but we got turned around. Maybe you can help."

Grandpa, breathing a bit hard, secured the boy in the back. Jack slid in after Grandpa in the front seat.

"Where to, Mister? And where's the Interstate?" she asked.

Jack felt all eyes in the back on his neck. The Grandpa stared ahead with his chin stuck out and his lips pursed.

"Oh," Jack paused. He looked at the Grandpa. *Bubba.* His co-worker friend was almost Grandpa's age. Good, old reliable Bubba would help him. "Uh, Ma'am, I'd like to go to Poquoson, if I may. I'll show you the Interstate from there."

The mother laughed, "Never heard of it. Where in the world is this Pah-COH-sin?"

"It's less than thirty minutes from here. I'll show you," said Jack.

"Now Daddy, I know there's nothing to be so worried about. This's right. Besides, it's His Will." She sighed. "I know it is."

"We'll see Naomi. We'll see."

"Now you children snuggle up with Grandma Winona and close your sweet eyes. Ruth, Sarah, Joshua, I love you precious, precious, and precious." The woman named Naomi sang lullabies until the children were asleep.

"Thanks," Jack whispered after a few moments of silence. He leaned back in the seat. His eyes welled with tears.

At the final checkpoint, the Hunt's Neck Neighborhood Association post, Jack leaned across Grandpa to show his face and NASA identification to the guard.

"We're going to Bubba Holland's."

The guard looked at him sideways and said, "At this hour we'll just call."

Jack recalled visiting Bubba's place earlier in the summer for a security section office picnic. He loved the old farmhouse that stood like a New England lighthouse on a tiny point of land. It bravely thrust itself between the Chesapeake Bay and the broad marshes of Robert's Creek. The house, the land and the water captured Jack's imagination like no other place in Tidewater. Jack dreamed of such a place to bring harmony to work and love and all the other discordant notes in his life.

Bubba waited on the wraparound porch as they drove up the long neck of driveway. His big dogs ran down the stairs barking to inspect the visitors. Bubba's thin gray hair and round face shined by the porch light. He strolled over and stood straight-backed with his arms crossed over his broad chest. He smiled under a thick brush of a salt and pepper moustache. "Well, young Bubba, has Maude sent you packing?" He liked to call any man he pleased 'Bubba'. His inflection made it a sobriquet of endearment or of scorn—just as he pleased.

Jack hopped out and talked across the roof of the car, "My computer blew up at work tonight. Bubba, it was a hit. An intentional hit on me."

"It wasn't a very good hit. They didn't get you," Bubba breathed deeply. "I know all about it Jack. You and me are out of an office. It's all burnt up. I spent most of the night there. In fact, I just got home. We had a section recall to try and sort this out. You're the only one missing. I went by your house, but you, Maude and the kids were already vamoosed."

Jack felt weak again, "Bubba, they're trying to kill me." He looked left and right and whispered hoarsely, "It was a Narco-Terrorist hit. It's something to do with the Omni. They've got a new computer virus that's a killer."

"I figured it was something like that. Tell me, do you know an Agent Jones with the FBI?"

Jack shook his head. "Nah, I don't."

"In all that inter-agency work you've been doing you didn't meet an agent in the Richmond or Norfolk office named Jones?"

"No, and I met most of them."

"Well, Jack, I met Agent Mister Jones at your house tonight. Actually, he was in your house. He said that he knew you."

"I'm sure I don't know an Agent Jones."

"Seemed odd for someone from the FBI to be there so fast. Also, he was alone. I thought the FBI only worked in pairs like Mormon missionaries. Jack, are you sure that your family is okay? You know they're using the Patriot Acts to round up political enemies—especially the Evangelical Christians."

"Yeah, sure. I think."

"You need to come in and rest and then we'll sort all of this out. These folks with you probably need to rest too. Uh, who are they?"

"They gave me a ride," Jack recalled the woman's words, "like good Samaritans."

Bubba looked at Naomi and held out both of his hands, "Won't y'all come on in?"

Naomi shook her head 'No'.

"Missy, you can't get into many places at this hour. Come in and rest." He squatted to bring his face to eye level with the window. He nodded towards a very bleary-eyed Grandpa, "Y'all need some rest. We've plenty of room. We had room for five kids. Course, we've run most of them off by now. Y'all come on in."

Jack spoke into the car, "You can trust Bubba. We work together. He's really okay. It's too late now for you to travel safely."

Naomi looked at her father and saw how tired he was. She saw through the windshield Jack's full face for the first time. His eyes were honest and kind. She turned to Bubba. Even though he wore round gold-rimmed glasses she saw the twinkling light—the brightness of ice blue eyes. She nodded softly, "Thank you, sir. Thank you kindly. Daddy, you go on. I'll get the kids with Mama."

"I'll help," volunteered Jack.

In a few minutes the children, their mother, and grandparents were tucked under clean, crisp cotton sheets in comfortable rooms. Jack was shown his room, but he waited in the hallway to explain himself to Bubba. Bubba waved at him from the utility box at the end of the hall. He spoke in a stage whisper, "Go to bed Jack. We'll talk in the morning. Sleep well. You know I need to get my beauty rest."

Jack waved weakly from the wrist. He watched Bubba flipping switches and taking readings from a high-speed security system. *If anyone has a super system for home security it'd be Bubba.* Barbara

Holland called Jack into the kitchen.

She cleaned Jack's wounds with stinging disinfectant. Jack thanked her profusely. He went to his room and undressed awkwardly. He laid down to review all that happened so fast to reason some sense of it all. His arm and head boomed painfully. Surprisingly, he felt the pain letting go to sleep.

Poquoson, VA
September 4th, 2012
Tuesday

It was very bright when Jack awoke. He smelled fresh coffee brewing. *Ah, there is bacon frying, coffee, and something else, really good, cooking.* The bed with clean sheets felt like such a refuge. Then, last night's drama pushed clarity of frightening thought over his moment of lingering. He rose quickly, washed, dressed and followed his nose to the kitchen.

It looked like a family reunion. The women worked, standing at the counters and the stove. Grandpa sat at the table with Bubba. Huge mugs of coffee stood curling up steamy wisps among the empty place settings. The children clustered around a game in the adjoining family room.

"Hi Ho!" called Bubba. He rose for his guest. "Want some coffee? How about some surgery for that eye?" The wound formed a large blue-black sock over his eye. His arm was one large bruise and very sore.

Mrs. Bubba, Barbara Holland, wiped her hands on her apron and gently touched around his forehead. She examined his arm.

"Hmm," she stood back and smiled, "You've superficial contusions and abrasions. No surgery. No stitches needed."

"That's not what the road teeth guards said," Jack answered.

"That's my considered medical judgment. I'm a registered nurse and the absolute chief physician in this house! It just looks terrible, Jack."

Everyone laughed at how Barbara said it.

Introductions were made all around. The angel of roadside mercy was a tall, dark-haired woman in her mid-thirties—Naomi

Tolley. Her mother noted, "Naomi Acord Tolley. Acord's after my people." Her parents, as Bubba graciously introduced them, were Mr. Arnett Greathouse and Mrs. Winona Acord Greathouse of Beckley, West Virginia. The children were Sarah, Ruth and Joshua.

Bubba kept conversations going through breakfast like a stadium crowd bounces big balls above their heads. No one mentioned what happened the night before. Jack waited to explain. Yet, despite his anticipation, he enjoyed the warmth of the moment. The kitchen was bright and polished. Except for the Irish Blessing (May the road rise to meet you, May the wind…), all the framed cross-stitch messages were Bible verses. A set of French doors offered the waters of the Bay stretching to the horizon.

When the meal was done and the table cleared, Barbara left to help Grandma Winona watch the children. Naomi, Arnett, Bubba and Jack sat down with their refreshed coffee. Bubba smiled from the head of the table, "Ok, what's up, Bubba?"

Jack cleared his throat, "First, what about work? They know something is going on with my family and me. Why aren't you going to work this morning?"

"Well, Mr. Tillman, I called in sick today because I was up too late last night for an old man. Also, the fiery destruction of our dear workplace was just too much for this old bureaucrat to take." Bubba's smile swept back underneath his wiry whiskers.

"You see, my good man," Bubba mocked an upper crust British accent, "I reached an early conclusion in this sordid affair that you were involved. Furthermore," he puffed himself up, "you are *not* guilty, but decidedly dealt a very sticky wicket!"

"In other words," Bubba changed to a Southern cop's patois, "you in a heap of trouble, boy!" Bubba quit his funny accents and grew grim, "Jack, I think that you're going to need all the help that you can get. I know that you're a good man. You'll be all right, son. Now, why don't you tell us a story?"

Jack blushed at the compliment, "What about these folks?" He made a small circle with his hand.

Bubba said, "Not to worry. They risked their necks giving you a ride last night. You could've been some terrible Narco-Terrorist. I reckon they deserve to hear your story. Besides, they won't tell. They're one of us. They're Christians. Now, your story, Sir."

Jack didn't get it. *Like almost everyone else isn't Christian? Aren't eighty per cent of Americans Christian?* Jack gave a chronological account from opening the door to the office, "I think this hunter-killer acted upon a single codeword after a specific user identification code. That means the virus can hide, wait, and query to find the right victim."

"That requires incredible sophistication," said Bubba.

"Maybe it was one of the newer viruses which flows with common electrical current like data move through the telecommunications grid. Maybe this hunter-killer virus sent a message to cause the power surge."

"Uh-huh, then the hunter-killer virus flipped the switches at all the power transfer nodes, over-rode the logic and actually guided the surge of power that comes boiling towards a computer."

"Exactly, the computer virus shapes the energy into a cone at the point of release," said Naomi.

"What is your techie background?" asked Jack. He almost lost his concentration when he looked into her eyes. They were large, brown pools. A man could fall into those eyes.

"That's what I do for a living. I'm a software systems manager for the United Mine Workers. You know, the Union."

Arnett piped up, "She's the best. She makes their entire system spin like a top!"

"Yes, Daddy, I make everything spin around until someone gets sick to their stomach! That reminds me of yesterday. I don't care if I never see another ride as long as I live. Or at least until the kids cry next year to come down here."

Bubba pushed his chair back from the table, "If y'all will join me upstairs in my study, I think I can explain some of what's going on." His guests raised their eyebrows at one another and followed.

Bubba's attic was finished in polished hardwoods that invited the hand and soothed at the touch. He put in a high ceiling with great stretches of glass that fixed their gaze on the Chesapeake Bay. It was a solarium-on-the-sea. Jack loved it. *Wow, it would be so peaceful here.*

Bubba brought him out of his daydream. "Jack, what was the last address you were using for the interagency network? Not the bulletin board, the interagency network security patrol."

Jack's mouth dropped, "How do you know about that?"

"Wait and ye shall know the truth and it will set you free, heh, heh," Bubba fixed his gaze on the computer screen. "What's the address?"

"InNetSec. Then, ping 145.876.124. That should get you in the front end of the netswitch. But you'll need to choose a communications protocol to go out the other end of the net switch."

"I got it," said Bubba. His hands moved across the computer keyboard with the flourish and the authority of a performing concert pianist. "We're in and looking around. It'll take a few minutes. My electronic snoops gotta lift up some software laying about, look for evidence and set it all back so no one knows that we've been there."

"Bubba, I was working to see how the Narco-Terrorists tried to penetrate us in the past year." Jack hesitated, "It was the Pablo Ponce de Leon drug cartel stuff. Plus that junk with Ishmael. Very classified. You know what I mean. How will you get to that from here?"

Bubba responded, "Let me tell y'all a story. I've been the Systems Administrator for the Security Directorate for twenty-eight years. I've installed, de-bugged and maintained every software system for all of those years. Early on I learned about a strange phenomena, a corollary of Murphy's Law. Nothing was going to go wrong during the workday. Everything that would be really important to screw up would go buggy or crash at night or on weekends. So, I started to upgrade my hardware and communications devices bit by bit." He grinned impishly, "When I got the panic calls, I would mosey up here and do ninety-five percent of the work here at home. I worked better without the pressure of some guy standing behind me. Besides, if I needed a break, I could chase Mrs. Holland around the house."

"While the kids were home?" asked Naomi with a lilting, almost musical, question in her voice.

"Well, I could at least go chase her for a squeeze and a kiss! Then, when I did get in to the office, finally, I'd rub my jaw and scratch my head and give a few 'Gollydangs, I don't reckon I've quite seen *that* before'. And, I'd fix the problem in nothing flat."

"Bubba, how could you work from here? This isn't a secure system," asked Jack.

"Name me a system that hadn't been compromised," countered Bubba. "This system is more secure than anything we've got at NASA Langley. Besides, no one can track spiders back to here."

"Spiders?" asked Arnett. "You hate spiders, Naomi."

"Yes, Daddy, spiders," replied Naomi. "These spiders fix software problems like spiders mend their web."

"What do they look like?" Arnett grasped.

Naomi smiled lovingly at her father's concern and replied, "They don't look like anything, except the front and back of a long email message. They're just packages of instructions looking at every branch of executables in billions and trillions of lines of code." Arnett looked back blankly. "Daddy, if software has a failure rate of less than one thousandth of one percent a day, then for a billion lines of code, there's ten thousand errors to fix every day."

"Ok," said Arnett.

Jack added, "These spiders are just software programs that have toolkits to eliminate bad code, like eating a bug. They write new code, like spinning new strands of web. If the spiders can't solve a problem, they send an error message to the system administrator."

"I get hundreds every day, Daddy."

"Jack, you were working on the spiders to see if they could spy for us in other systems. You wanted to see if they'd look through someone else's communications node," said Bubba.

Jack looked stunned.

"Uh-huh," mumbled Bubba, then, "Uh-oh. I want to look at the message traffic before and during your episode last night. But, something… is… not… right. The file came up and went right down. Now…," he whistled inadvertently. He tapped the mouse and pulled up an inset screen. He expanded it to cover the monitor. The screen printed a column faster than the eye could read. Bubba typed and another small inset screen came up with speeding lines, "ping 143.224.157, ping 143.225.168, ping 143.226.171, ping 143.227.173, ping 143.228.195."

"Goodness!" Bubba exclaimed, "Somebody's backtracking and trying to find me!" He changed screens to an electronic plumbing diagram of flashing, colored 3-D icons. "Uh-Oh! They're only one node away!" His hands flew across the keyboard. The screens changed like hummingbird wings. There was a flurry, a whirring of motion and the screen went black.

"Somebody's really good!" Bubba, huffing hard, looked at Jack. "Just now I went into our system a few miles away at Langley. For security I routed through the weather station in western Australia and more. Somebody found my spiders reading the commo log and worked my path backwards. I've got good multi-level security here. That's about impossible to track back through encryption!"

They looked at the floor, the ceiling, each other, and out the magnificent window. Nothing was said until it seemed that something must be said. Jack rose from his seat and motioned to the whiteboard hung from a built-in bookcase. "Mind if I use this?"

"Sure. Markers are beside it on the book shelf," said Bubba.

"Okay. Let's write what we know and what we don't know and what we need to find out. We know that someone is interested in the interagency system. We know that there is a hunter-killer virus that can look for a specific codeword on one box in one system. We know..." Jack spun out the details they knew. "Okay, where does that leave holes?"

Bubba suggested, "We need to get into the interagency security net and find out what's so important and who's so interested. But we need to do our detective work from a different system. They almost 'kotched' me as brer rabbit would say. We could use the system I installed at my church." No one offered a different solution.

Bubba said to Jack, "You and me need to go on over to Emmy-us."

"Where?" asked Naomi.

"Emmy-us. It's spelled E-m-m-a-u-s. But it's pronounced Emmy-us Baptist Church at the end of Emmy-us Road right here in Pah-COH-sen." Bubba smiled slyly. "Didn't you know that all of Christendom says Emmaus? But here in Pah-COH-sen, good old Bull Island, it's pronounced properly as Emmy-us. You gotta talk Tidewater. That's the phonetic litmus test we give to see if you're a local or a move-in. Course it still don't prove if you're a native. You've got to be at least five generations 'Bull Islander' to be a native."

"And they say West Virginians have accents!" said Naomi. "I'd like to help, but I need to tend to my kids."

Bubba drove Jack on the winding roads to Emmaus. He waved to the muscular young men taking down a large banner from the columned portico of the brick church. "Revival week ended Sunday. We had six people saved."

Jack stared back silently. They walked behind the two story Sunday School building and through a large athletic center and upstairs to a small corner office. "Sancta Sanctorum," said Bubba.

"I'd have thought that would be back at your place," said Jack.

"Well, you're right. But here is the place for the Lord's work. So it must be sanctified, I reckon. Anyway, I've done my part in the community of Christ in this little room. I've moved a lot of electrons," Bubba said as he gestured to the shelf of carefully stored disks.

The two men separated by a generation and a belief system and other things tangible but indescribable, pulled up chairs to work together, knee-to-knee, at the computer. There were few words. Occasionally, one or the other would offer, "let's try…" The work was slow, tedious and disappointing. They came close to being found out several times. The day waxed and waned. They grew mentally exhausted from the tense concentration. They succeeded in reading the communications logs in hurried glimpses. It was like reading the morning paper through binoculars while walking around the kitchen table. Their spiders found addresses that were obvious fronts for Narco-Terrorists. A few addresses were real mysteries. They couldn't find anything that looked like provocation for the hunter-killer virus attack last night. Odd references to 'Ishmael sends, I-note, and Ish Gram' on government commo logs baffled them. Bubba stood up and stretched.

"Jack, what do you think is going on?" Bubba took a long pull on his coffee.

"I don't think that my work on the interagency net is the issue. It was good, though. We were keeping people out." Jack looked to Bubba for approval. "The real issue is that someone is chasing someone else trying to get in…" His voice trailed off. "I dunno. I keep hearing about the Omni because of the Presidential election and this candidate, you know, Maggie Kyle who is going to do something different against Narco-Islamist Terrorism. I don't get much on Omni officially. And I hear that Hillary will never give up the Presidency.

You know. The power. Election or not."

Bubba looked out to the West and setting sun. He was so still and seemed so far removed from the room. "Let's go home. We're done here."

"Ok," Jack felt the word 'home' sting. *I want to see my family. I miss them. I'm afraid for them. Oh, I wish it was like it was before the hit. I want to go home and back to normal. I can't believe this is real.*

Jack was surprised to see that the family of his roadside rescue had rested and stayed the day at Bubba's.

The whole ensemble of the Holland elders, the Tolley and Greathouse tourists and the bruised fugitive, John James Tillman, enjoyed a huge supper with lots of fresh vegetables from Barbara's garden. The family-at-rest, a family-at-home, atmosphere felt like an old sweater. Bubba talked in tales and joked non-stop. The elderly Arnett seemed enraptured by Bubba's constant chatter. After supper clean up they resettled at the table with bowls of hot apple brown betty a la mode and large tumblers of sweet iced tea.

Bubba brought everyone up to speed on the progress of the afternoon and what still needed to be done. They shared in the spirited discussion of what to do next. A consensus shaped that a larger network of computers was needed.

Naomi offered, "Why don't you come to Beckley? We can do this on the UMW[4] systems."

The conversational smile fell from Arnett's face, "We've done quite enough help here. We need to get back home."

Naomi looked at him squarely, "Daddy, I know what worries you. But, consider that they can't possibly work down here. This man," she motioned to Jack, "needs to get away from here anyway."

"If you know my worries, then why," Arnett's eyes narrowed, "would you put yourself and your sweet angels at such risk?"

"Because, when Saul fled to Taurus for his life, he didn't quit preaching the Good News. When he was needed, he went to Antioch. When the dearth struck Jerusalem, he returned there with material help from the Gentile Christians from Antioch. And that was just the beginning. When did he reckon that he had "did enough" and go live safely? How many shipwrecks did he survive?"

---

4. UMW is the Union for the United Mine Workers.

Arnett set his jaw, "You aren't the Apostle Paul. Young Lady, you should honor your father and obey. This's wrong." He looked to Jack, "Even if our brother is in need. I'm sorry. I'm truly sorry."

Naomi set her jaw as firmly as her father, "Daddy, as much as I love you and honor you, I know what is right. You show me where it says to stop doing good for fear of evil, or to stop being righteous because of persecution or whatever, and I'll consider it in prayer."

"All right then. You're too much like me," scowled Arnett.

"I'll go, too. I can take Jack and help with the computer work when we get there," said Bubba.

Barbara said, "No, sir, you don't need to be gallivanting off. You've a lot to do here at Langley. It'd raise suspicion, wouldn't it? They will really need you here putting things back together. No one else can do it. It's your duty."

"Oh, Bar," Bubba whined, "you don't understand. This's really important."

"No sir! James Cox Holland, don't tell me what I don't understand. You may get your old fool self killed. Now I understand that!"

"Uh-oh, she's called me by my whole name. Old sweet mama-tama is upsot!" Bubba got up to hold her. She ran from the room making little, halting sobs.

"She's a dear. She'll be okay. But, I'm going. I'll take my overdue comprehensive leave to go fishing in West By God Virginia. Y'all excuse me, please."

The others cleaned the kitchen in respectful silence and called it a night.

Poquoson, VA
September 5th, 2012
Wednesday

Barbara Holland served up another large breakfast. Everyone gave their respects and loaded cars. Bubba threw his fishing gear in the back of his pick up truck and said, "Maybe we can finish early and I can use this to as good an effect as I am trying to use it for affect now, eh?" Barbara stood on the wide porch compulsively drying her hands in her apron. Bubba bounded up the steps. He grabbed

Barbara in a great bear hug and kissed her firmly on the mouth. She laced her fingers behind his thick neck and clung.

"Oh, baby, don't go. Please don't go," Barbara cried. "For me."

"Oh, sugar, don't cry so. I'll be back in two weeks. No big deal. I've been gone longer."

"Baby, baby. I love you."

Bubba pried her hands loose and held her wrists as he kissed her again. Her round face was wet with tears. He jogged to the pickup truck. He blew her a kiss and said, "Don't cry, pretty. I'll be home soon enough. I love you!"

"I love you!" She waved and called long after they drove away and out of sight through the far stand of pines.

The lead car was filled with the excitement of children. The pickup following was silent for awhile. Bubba broached the quiet to discuss Jack's fugitive status and pragmatic problems. The conversation shifted to untying the Gordian note holding the answer to the hunter-killer virus. They turned over the same ideas like so much mulch turned over the day before. The conversation drifted in and out of quiet times. Jack fiddled with the radio and CDs.

Outside Richmond, Bubba asked, "Didja know that I commuted to Richmond for two years?"

"No, did you know that I commuted for a year?"

"Yes, I remembered. So, you and I shared the same prayer road, huh?"

"The only prayer I did is that I wouldn't get killed by some maniac driver or some road rage nut."

"I prayed that too," Bubba chuckled. "But there was a lot more for me. Didja enjoy the change of seasons on the road?"

"Some. Not much. That was a pretty intense time. I was just out of the Army. The only job I could get was online sales. It was a lousy pyramid scheme. I hated it. I just marvel that there's so much woods still between Jamestown and Richmond. It's been settled here for over four hundred years and the place is still woods."

"I call that progress!" said Bubba.

"Progress is New York and Boston and Philadelphia," Jack deadpanned.

"That's progress I can do without."

"Spoken like a man of the Tidewater," said Jack.

"Let me explain prayer road, John-James. When we drive down the highway we see the same road, blue sky, same clouds, same trees, same cars and people. We appreciate the scenery the same. We love the same seasons. We look at the patterns of light as they change minute to minute in the day—just like we both love late, late afternoon.

But, there's a difference, John-James. When you're driving down the road, you're thinking about your life. I'm driving the same road and I'm talking to the God Almighty. He and I are talking about what I see—together. I'm telling him, 'Lord, what a great day! Thank you for this day. I can't breathe a breath without You. I just want to thank You for everything You've done. Thanks for bringing Jesus in the world and creating the life everlasting for us. In all things and all ways I give You praise. Oh Lord, I love You. I worship and adore You. I love my family so much. Oh, please, Father God, watch over them. Oh, Precious Lord put Your arms around them and hug them. Oh, please, Dear Lord, bless and keep my family. Hold them up. Hold them lovingly.' Then, I try to shut up and listen. It is so great because I can feel His peace," Bubba took a breath and looked at Jack. Jack chose the window.

"So, John-James, your real world itn't my real world. I'm living in communion, in conversation, in fellowship with God almost all of the time. I wish it were all of the time. My thoughts are constantly, constantly, turning to God. I talk with Him. It's a real relationship. The most real one there is."

"Bubba, you should've been a preacher. I'd no idea that you were so religious," Jack tried to put a nice face on his discomfort.

"John-James, John-James, I'm sorry. Not to worry. I won't froth at the mouth or anything. Besides, Christianity itn't about religion, its about relationship with God."

Jack looked back, finally. "Everyone is entitled to their own opinion. You can have yours. It's in the Constitution."

"I know, I know," said Bubba. "It used to be in the Constitution."

The old individual seat air conditioning couldn't quite keep Jack cool. Jack's eyes grew very heavy. He let his mind roam as he often did in the netherworld of falling asleep. His thoughts, daydreams, began in crisp images, then they blurred, and the story line wandered. In his mind-plays the lines for streets and hallways strayed and bent like a Salvador Dali painting.

And in the waning seconds before sleep he considered, again, his own death. The Narco-Terrorists were going to kill him sooner or later. The moment of death wasn't too hard to script out and feel. Jack knew pain from his experience with broken bones, other injuries and illnesses. Once, an Army physical therapist warned another therapist before an exercise session to make Jack be careful because of his remarkably high tolerance for pain. Jack felt like he was awarded a medal.

It was the moment, the second, after the pain that troubled. Death, then what? He disabused himself of notions of Heaven when he was a young man. It was too neat, too clean, and way too self-serving. All of biology pointed to humankind as a higher animal with an ego. Man, alone, could contemplate his death. Immortality was only a concept, a mental construction for humans. But, the question nagged. *Could humans have anything beyond the living awareness of a conscience? Can anything about the human be immortal?*

First, he imagined his body losing life, like when he blacked out from shock. His strength and then his breath swept out from him. It moved from his toes and fingers to his head. Consciousness would be cleaned out by a powerful wave washing his body. It was irresistible. He was totally powerless. Then there was nothing but darkness. Jack felt it all. He took small gasping, gulps of air.

But what if the darkness came and he never woke up? Some people took comfort in the notion of eternal sleep. He would agree if you woke up. The sweetness of sleep only comes with the awakening. Or some liked to say, "remember what it was like before you were born? It will be the same". That would be terrible. He remembered nothing before he was born and he desperately didn't want to become nothing. His heart beat faster.

The terror in death for him was the nothingness. How could he become nothing? How could his life have such rich detail and his mind have such exquisite awareness and all of it become nothing?

Jack shook his head violently and leaned back open-mouthed. He felt like he couldn't get enough oxygen from the deep breaths he took. He was a little faint. *Anxiety attack.* He closed his eyes. *I will not give in to the Fear. Come on, you monster, make me pass out or kill me with a heart attack. I shall keep my eyes closed and you will go away.* As he rested, he sensed Bubba watched him. His pulse raced, making him light headed, but he knew that he wasn't going to die in the next five minutes. *I'll be okay.*

Bubba said, "You all right? Getting sick?"

"Nah, just a bit uncomfortable."

"We could open the windows, but that just means moving hot air."

It was mid-afternoon when the family car up front took Beckley's Harper Road Exit and tooted its horn gaily. Both men in the truck grinned. "They're happy to be home," said Bubba.

Home was only a couple of stop signs and turns away in a neighborhood of modest well-kept houses. Their's was a long low brick framed by magnificent trees. The screen door swung open for a big man in a flashy suit. Peter Tolley was home early this afternoon.

The children raced to him all a-chatter. He smiled and pulled all three up in a bear hug. Naomi walked up to him, offering her cheek for a quick kiss, and shooed the children inside. Pete caught her by the elbow and asked, "Who're these guys?"

"They're company, Pete. Let Daddy introduce you. Be nice."

Arnett paused at the steps. Winona said pleasantly, "Miss us, dear?"

"Something terrible," said Pete. He checked out the strangers. Pete flashed his best sales grin and shook the men's hands just a little harder than they did.

Pete was at least six foot two and was once a powerfully built man. A spare tire of stomach sagged so much that it couldn't be sucked in. He combed his thinning black hair straight back and fluffed it up.

As the family Tolley unpacked, put up, cleaned and cooked, Jack and Bubba made themselves as useful as they could driving the grandparents home and running to the store. Naomi and Pete had a long conference alone in their bedroom. A few times their voices were loud enough to hear them down the hallway. Naomi emerged and said, "Tomorrow we can go to my office. We can work out some access for y'all on our computers. Tonight, you're welcome to stay with us." She gave a heavy emphasis on "tonight".

Bubba spoke up quickly, "No thank you, ma'am. We can't impose. Thanks, though. We'll go back to one of those motels we passed coming into town." A polite argument ensued like the squabble over an expensive restaurant bill when it is absolutely clear who is the host and who is the guest. Both sides know how it will turn out.

Jack and Bubba shared one room at the motel in a stab for more security. Bubba telephoned Barbara Holland. When it was time to turn out the lights, it amazed Jack to see burly Bubba get down on his knees beside his bed and softly say his prayers like a little boy.

Beckley, WV
September 21st, 2012
Friday

Two weeks came and went without solving any of the riddles surrounding the attack on Jack. It was time for Bubba to go home. He couldn't extract himself just yet, so he got an extension on his leave from his boss and a fierce reprimand from his beloved wife. Bubba and Jack worked with Naomi at a place in uptown Beckley in the United Mine Workers office. It was a renovated Depression Era slate gray office building guarding the square of the Raleigh County Courthouse. Uptown in Beckley literally means perched 'up' on top of a steep ridge.

The days were interesting, stimulating and tiring. At times it was too stimulating, like walking in the middle of a freeway. Their computer spiders suddenly stopped at unforeseen security checks. Occasionally, they actually watched a message header for a known hunter-killer virus scroll across the screen and then disappear as computer death appeared on their screen and faded to take its quarry.

They built a routine into their lives. They rose in the morning for a country breakfast buffet with large biscuits, pan gravy, applesauce, and mounds of bacon or sausage. They worked through the day at their large, flat screens. Often, they took brain breaks and walked up and down hilly Kanawha Street. They looked over their shoulders a lot. In the evening they went to the Greathouse's small tidy house with the tall brick wall on Woodlawn Avenue. They played bridge and hearts and spades. They walked long miles on the exercise machines. They communicated safely along a very circuitous deception to spouses Barbara and Maude. All was quiet at home and in hiding so far.

Late in the afternoon Naomi met with Jack and Bubba to figure out how and where to proceed.

"Okay," Naomi said as she crossed her legs, leaned back in the chair and laced her hands across one thigh. Her movements were as natural and casually athletic as they were appealing—even though Naomi never meant to entice. "The only connection for any organizing principle is the special access codes. Jack found this from the beginning. Someone is going into every compartmentalized and supposedly secure systems there is. That someone has a connection to the Omni software developers or the Ponce De Leon drug cartel or both."

Bubba added, "Also, this guy Ishmael is involved somehow."

Jack added, "The one anomaly, which creeps up with increasing regularity, are these messages with an association of a colored rose. So far, I've identified red rose, black rose, yellow rose and green rose."

He scribbled on the whiteboard. "They read, like this:

- green rose:grow/weed
- red rose:build thorn/prick thorn
- black rose:prepare/green
- rose/red rose/exec
- yellow rose:copy/send/keeper."

"And these appear in odd places in other messages, protocols, and even in machine code?" Bubba answered his own question.

"I think…hmmm," Naomi hesitated. "Why don't we send some routine traffic and see if we can pick up when a rose passage is inserted? Then…" she stopped again to put words to her thoughts, "maybe we can figure out how to capture a rose passage. I know that's easier to say and harder to actually do."

Bubba brightened "Yes ma'am, it 'tis hard, but they're several techniques we could try. Tell me more what all you think this rose passage is. Maybe, we can get a better handle on what to do about it."

"We need to consider the rose passages as several possibilities. First, they may be virus fragments left over from clumsy attempts to attack. Another possibility is that they may be the header or trailer for some other instruction we can't see. Orrrr," she rolled her 'r', "they may be symbolic language for something much more complicated. Maybe they're a keyword for spiders to do something."

"Yeah," said Jack, "the rose passages could be codes for other software. When it reads, say, 'yellow rose' it knows to do something. Yeah, there're a lot of things these roses could do."

Bubba said, "But then is not a rose, just a rose and a rose by another name?"

"Yuck, that's terribly pun-ny. You shouldn't stop taking your medication!" Naomi smiled and shook her head in mock disgust.

"Now why would I, good doctor of laughter, take medicine? I prescribe laughter as the best medicine."

"With your lousy jokes you prescribe it in very small doses, Doc," smirked Jack.

"I've got what is good for what ails y'all and y'all know it," retorted Bubba

"Ok, Ok. We can set up surveillance of communications grids and see if we can capture something on these roses. There's one other subject," Naomi paused, "security."

"That's my line," said Jack.

"I asked our security manager to do some checking on the fire at your office. I used the excuse to get any lessons learned by the government employees union. I was able to get a complete security report. It's pretty interesting."

"Do you have it here?" interjected Jack.

"It's back in my office," Naomi motioned with her thumb. "The security report cited very suspicious origins. But, in the Ongoing Actions Section you, Jack, were listed as a missing person, not as a suspect. That means the Feds aren't looking for you."

Jack was visibly moved, "Yes, it usually means that you are not being actively pursued. Really, though, it can be the cover for an operation to smoke you out."

"Maybe, but I also got a copy of the latest fugitives bulletin and the close-hold, eyes-only version. You're not on either list. But, you may be on a domestic terrorist list. The secret Homeland Security list somewhere. Hillary's Hit List."

"But, the Narco-Terrorists are still looking for me. I'm on Pablo Ponce de Leon's death list. Or Ishmael's." The room darkened with the shadow of the implications.

"We suspected it was them all along. If it isn't the Homeland Security guys," said Bubba.

"Our own government?" asked Jack.

"Yeah, the ones that're spying on conservative political opponents, raiding offices and arresting folks. Making lists of Christians who quote the Bible in public about homosexuality. Getting the IRS to audit preachers, churches, pundits, even bloggers. Having the Federal District Attorneys prepare charges of conspiracy to commit hate speech. That U.S. government and 'Blue' state and local governments too."

"That's not happening."

"Yes, it is. The news is suppressed."

"You can't suppress the Internet."

"Wanna bet? You can come close. I can name names of people questioned, arrested and a couple disappeared."

"They can be beat. There's greater powers than them. There's greater powers than any man," said Naomi. Her brown eyes bore through both men.

"Amen," said Bubba.

"Let's call it a day and a week. Do y'all want to come'n eat at my parents and go to the movies with all of us? They're finally playing a 'G' one," said Naomi.

Jack and Bubba rode together to the movies after supper. A strong, crisp breeze rocked through the truck at a stoplight. Jack put his cheek closer to the open window to try to catch another breeze as it happened.

Bubba said, "Great sleeping weather itn't it? Mr. Miller said the Raleigh Shopping Mall was the first in Beckley to be open to 'Members Only'[5].

---

[5]. Most shopping malls around the country are 'Members Only' because of the long litany of terrible crimes committed in and around shopping malls despite enormous increases in "security". Advances in computing made the Closed Members Only Shopping possible.

"Thanks," Jack enjoyed the rest of the night drive to feel and smell the Autumn darkness.

Once they were inside the mall, Jack said, "The face recognition at the entrance to the building was pointed too high. If it'd been properly calibrated I'd have been in a fix."

"Funny, I forgot to check. I didn't even remember that your face was hot property. Sorry."

"No problem. I do enough worrying for the two of us."

The children broke free of restraining hands and ran for the large fountain. The commotion with the children continued from the fountain to the ticket line through the concession stand. Jack watched and longed to see his own kids.

Inside the theater the children jockeyed for their favorite places by their Mama, their Papaw and Mamaw. Pete couldn't come because he had what he said was a very important business dinner at Flat Top Country Club. When the whimsical chairs ended Jack found himself sitting next to Naomi. Lil'Bit squirmed in and out of her lap.

Jack enjoyed the smell of her cologne. It wasn't Maude's. It was a husky scent like the one his true love when he was at West Point had worn. He breathed deeply and remembered lost love. He saw Naomi with her arms wrapped around Lil'Bit. She rocked and kept kissing the crown of his little head. She nuzzled his soft fine curls. Lil'Bit stared intently at the movie screen. Jack saw the picture of himself sitting side by side with this woman. It was a little strange, because it felt really good. He let go of his awkwardness and enjoyed the closeness to her.

Massive data base management made it easy to draw a list of enough shoppers with the right spending profiles to insure profitability for the entire shopping mall. People bemoaned the passing of fast access, drive-in and drive right out, parking lots. But they soon adjusted their time schedules for a new reality of inconvenience, just as they had adjusted their personal freedom for a new reality in public safety. Enough of the elites in America were scared stiff. They created the right semantic cover and wrote new legislation to keep the "closed" malls open. The judges took care of the rest.

Beckley, WV
September 26th, 2012
Wednesday

A week of computer seek, hide and seek folded into the next week without a seam. Jack marveled how networks are physically no more than plastic boxes connected to other midsize plastic boxes and to smaller, nondescript communications boxes by cables and thin air. Our naked senses only detect the mild electronic hum of this cybernetic world. Yet, life teems in a passionate struggle in the invisible places. Like the world of tiny animal and plant kingdoms visible only to the microscope and God. As the unseen bacteria can kill a person in the prime of life, so the unseen batch of software can wreak dire results on highly complex systems. A few wavelengths of electrons traveling at near the speed of light can destroy hardware and humans alike as the old plagues past. The killing is different, but the consequences are severe when an economy collapses, or military systems fail in combat, or rioting mobs are falsely hyped.

The rose passages were definitely coming out of the Washington, D.C. area. A better breakdown showed a number of inquiries about rose passages, astonishingly much like their own inquiries (but a little less technically elegant) coming from Georgetown University in Washington.

Jack, Bubba and Naomi worked together at screen-side making inquiries where a yellow rose passage imbedded itself in the routing instructions for the National Military Command and Control System. They tried to see how the yellow rose passage reacted when different questions were asked of the host communications node. They got a quick note on the screen.

"Rose war:\havoc.check."

Then their system crashed. Naomi bolted from the room and ran to the systems administration workstation. She feverishly shut down the entire UMW system. "Thank you, Lord," she breathed heavily.

They gathered at Naomi's office. She called her boss and then the president of the UMW. "You gentlemen will have to work at my alternate site."

"Alternate site?" asked Jack.

"Yes, I'll show you. Let's make sure that everything's down, and I mean everything, before we go. The alternate site is in the church where I got baptized and married. It's the Temple United Methodist Church."

Without another word they did her bidding.

They drove all together in Bubba's truck to the church. Naomi explained why she had an alternate site for her computer systems like Bubba did. The UMW went through a purge a few years ago. Maybe they had read about it. That purge brought a rank and file member to the presidency. The president, Gordon Miller, was a born-again Christian. He was the real thing. He wasn't a "professional" Christian like so many politicians and businessmen.

"So what has this to do with the alternate site?" demanded Bubba.

"Mr. Holland," she said putting on southern airs. "Ah am surprised at your rudeness. Just who do you think you are speaking to? Your wife?"

"No, but you're starting to drag on your stories like her," Bubba smirked.

"Power corrupts men. And women. Our union people deserved that the truth be preserved in our records."

"Jeez, I can't believe we spend so much time in churches working with computers." said Jack. They walked through the side alcove where the bridegroom would wait to enter the sanctuary. The September late afternoon was bright and warm.

"What's wrong with that?" asked Bubba.

"Nothing if you're a Sunday School teacher, I suppose."

"I am a Sunday School teacher," said Bubba.

"So am I," said Naomi.

"I guess it is okay then," said Jack with a resigned shrug.

"Tomorrow, I'll be putting our systems back on line," said Naomi. "You gentlemen can use this system to see why we crashed."

"Your crash came from our work, don't you think?" asked Bubba.

"Yes, we can count on that," replied Naomi.

"That crash worked like your standard Information Operations defense. I've seen this before," offered Jack. "The Rose messages are connected to the Omni and National Military Command Center. I'm sure of it."

"Okay. Well good luck sorting it out," Naomi said. She lead the way out.

"Feels like a nice house for God. Very pretty," said Bubba as they headed out.

"Well, what'd you expect?" Naomi asked with one eyebrow raised.

"I don't know. But you have done real good for a bunch of lightly sprinkled Methodists who are wannabe Baptists."

"Oh, right." She raised her chin to just the right haughty angle to look down her nose at Bubba. "Do you know the difference between Baptists and Methodists?"

"Sure, Methodists are afraid of water immersion and can't sing," Bubba changed his tone. "They almost lost their church to the liberals, the sissy Christians."

"Perhaps," she allowed the start of a smile. "The real difference is that the Methodists know how to read."

They laughed. As they stepped outside onto the sidewalk Naomi caught sight of a group of young men walking towards them fast.

"Oh My Lord, Doctors[6]!"

Eight young men strutted in highly starched white doctor's gowns. Their hands were thrust well into the deep pockets so their shoulders rolled forward. They walked with their necks thrust out like the vultures they could be. They were only a few yards away.

---

6. The Doctors are gangs of criminals. They take their manner of dress and nicknames, like Docs, Doctors of Death or Pain or Love or their initials DD, DP, DL, mocking the medical professionals who deal in drugs. The doctors' gowns are excellent for concealing their wares and odd assortments of weaponry. Sometimes a crew of doctors would stand in a circle and hold up their gowns like capes. The curtain created is effective cover for the retail drug transactions or violent crime, as it suits them. The gowns prevent eyewitness accounts. Some gangs modify the gowns to carry their colors or logos. The drug Docs hurt people. Yet, they can attain the wealth and the neighborhood status, like real physicians, if they live long enough. That is the real mockery, because they could never compete in school to even dream of going to college, let alone medical school. The gang members delight in addressing each other as 'Doctor' this or that. Nationwide, they gain notoriety for the cruelty of their assaults.

They were druggie 'Doctors' all right.

Naomi froze. Jack quickly stepped to put his body between her and the Docs. Bubba moved up closely to her side. The Docs brushed by them. The Docs spat out curses mixed with racial epithets. The Docs kept their attention on something down the street. As the Docs rushed by them, they realized that the Docs were a full head shorter than they were as adults.

Bubba exclaimed, "Those little jerks are just kids. They're practicing to be Doctors!"

"Goodness gracious, they liked to scared me out of a year's growth. I thought they were Doctors. We do have them, Drug Doctors, in Beckley, you know."

"Whew," Jack blew out a long breath. "I'm glad they're not grown up."

"Me too, John-James, me too," said Bubba.

"Thank you kind gentlemen for standing beside me," said Naomi. She noticed how Jack had moved so quickly to protect her.

"You're welcome," Jack blushed.

Beckley, WV
September 28th, 2012
Friday

Naomi worked all the repairs to the UMW system, while Jack and Bubba labored on the system at the church. The men made glacial progress. It couldn't be seen with a casual glance, but it could be measured over time and it was important. They narrowed their investigation to the main library of Georgetown University. Jack thought someone was using the inter-library loan system as the conduit for rose passages.

Bubba went deftly into the files of the main office of the library. His thick figure hunched over the keyboard for hours as he tenaciously went to each computer and broke in like a thief picking a lock. He had extraordinary problems getting into the computer in a private study carol. The building directory placed the carol some three floors below ground in the bowels of the library. Finally, Bubba pushed back his seat with both hands.

"Sugar!" He stood up and stomped around the small room. "This fool computer makes me mad enough to cuss. And, then I really get mad when I do cuss. I pretty well gave that up years ago."

"Gave up cussing?" asked Jack.

"Felt it didn't ennoble or enrich. Just didn't need to anymore."

"If I gave up swearing, I feel like I'd give up a large part of my vocabulary," teased Jack.

"It did almost make me mute. Only for a while. But there's times when mute is better than trash mouth. Like always."

"No argument, but sometimes it is so *damn* therapeutic to really curse and to curse creatively," Jack moved over to Bubba's blinking terminal. "Mr. Holland, let me try to sneak in here."

Bubba gave a slow blink and shrug of his shoulders, "Go ahead."

Jack probed like a good upstairs man as if Bubba hadn't already tested the doors and windows to this house for the previous forty-five minutes. He started some standard communications pings to see how the computer linked with communications modes. That was easy enough. The computer had broad-based up and down links including a dialup to the Library of Congress and special access-by-ID-only to a commercial auto trans medium serving that neighborhood in Washington. The neighborhood included the State Department and White House communications.

"Sure are a lot of high-powered communications links for a study carol in a library," Jack murmured. *Gotta steal some "borrowed" time on the super computers from the good old National Security Agency.* It was one of his favorite tricks in the security trade. He cherished his knowledge. It was like being in a secret fraternity. The super computers at NSA analyzed billions of messages and sorted them daily. "I'm going to see if I can analyze this commo log at NSA."

"Looking good, John-James," Bubba said. Jack was in and out of the NSA machines fast. "We'll have an answer in about five minutes."

As Jack spoke, he absentmindedly called back to the target computer and tried to log on. He got several rebuffs using computer icons for the police, Internal Revenue Service, NASA and the Department of Defense. Most computer security systems would open for these icons and give access to the database. Exasperated, Jack typed in his former code word—"rosebud.96d".

The computer countered. "Password expired. Use new password."

Both guys sat up abruptly. "What was that?" exclaimed Bubba.

"I'll be!" Jack caught the curse before it left his mouth. "Somebody had my password! How could this guy have my password? Did he get my password from my system?"

"What's your password?"

"Rosebud dot ninety-six D."

"Anybody could use rosebud. Why'd you?"

"The movie Citizen Kane of course."

"Of course. Maybe this guy likes Citizen Kane too. If he is a real fan, he may have kept the rosebud password or taken something else from the flick."

"Try rosebud star star."

Jack typed. The screen responded.

"ACCESS DENIED."

Bubba massaged his forehead, "Try Rosebud star star police icon[7] and whatever the official Georgetown icon is." Jack pulled down a Georgetown icon window. Bubba's combination didn't work.

"Keep that icon window up right here," Bubba said pointing to the corner of the screen. He put his hand hard against his cheek with the thumb down and breathed loudly through his nose into the palm

---

7. Iconic language: Highly symbolic language, software shorthand and icons, captures more and more complex expressions that impute full meaning immediately upon recognition. Consequently, language spoken and written by humankind comes full circle from the symbolic language of cave paintings. The symbolic language in cave art and the early writing forms, like cuneiform and hieroglyphics, expressed simple, commonly understood concepts to small homogeneous audiences. Advances to the lettered alphabet created open-ended opportunities for very complex, expansible expression in the spoken and written word to larger, heterogeneous audiences—sharing one language. Yet, the reading and listening audience must be attentive to follow, understand and react. The symbolic language, specifically a iconic computer language (a very advanced HTML), used on computers is understood at sight. The iconic language can be translated from icons to words in any language using the automatic translators available in most computers. Strides in iconic computer language are on the verge of closing the loop to bring most of the world to the fireside of single cave.

of his hand. He gave directions to try different icons and combinations. Jack invented more on his own.

The NSA super computer beeped them that their analysis was complete, transmitted and waiting in their external data buffer. The guys took a quick peek and saw it was huge. It was going to take a lot of time to read it all. They returned to the icon list.

"What's this?" asked Bubba, pointing to an icon with the letters 'MRC' next to it. The icon was a stylized graphic picture of a man in robes holding an empty bowl in outstretched hands before him. His head was bowed forward showing his distinctive tonsure. It looked like an Olympic logo for a Catholic monk begging for his bowl.

Jack read from the directory's fine print. "The MRC icon is shorthand for 'mercy'. Hey, look, the icon means a request from a member of a religious order. And the appeal is made in the spirit of brotherhood and mercy. The appeal is to fill a need to nourish the body, the mind, or the soul. Hmmm ..."

"Modifiers?" Bubba couldn't read such a small font.

"The icon can be modified in many ways," Jack paraphrased. "Arrows indicated relationships to other icons. Shorthand modifiers to MRC can be prefixes or suffixes. This icon is a request. This MRC, aka, 'mercy' is different from the empty purse icon, the hungry child icon, the battered child icon, the father with family begging icon, and blah, blah, blah." Jack knew the icons had a potential union of shape and meaning far beyond the language of Japanese and Chinese characters. The simplicity of communication made iconic sign language easy to understand like American Indian sign language.

"Try rosebud MRC icon," said Bubba.

Their eyes widened to see the internal prompt pulsing before them. They were in.

"Ask for a directory," urged Bubba.

"My thought exactly," said Jack. For the next hour the guys rummaged through file after file of research notes and bibliographies to no avail. They found some communications logs, but, like the analysis from NSA, the message archives were huge. There were many references to the mysterious 'Ishmael, Isaiah and Ish'.

The door lock buzzed a warning as the code was pecked in. The door flung open and Naomi burst into the room. She was breathless and nervous, but not terrified.

"Fellas, there's some trouble."

"What?" They turned from the computer.

"There are some strangers in town. They're probably looking for you."

"How do you know?" Jack was incredulous. Bubba was a rock.

"We've got very good security people, Jack," Naomi replied. "Listen, our people keep a close watch on this town. They've lots of means to do this. I help with the automated aspects of surveillance and reporting."

"You're a security snoop, too!" Jack exclaimed. The guys smiled.

Naomi cocked her head, "Well, okay, if you want to call it that. Let's say that I'm very involved in all computer operations. And as I was saying, gentlemen," she took a breath that was almost a sigh. "We know that these four fellows came to town yesterday. They came from Cleveland like they were back here in the hills visiting kin. The police and us UMW thought they might be here for a local drug deal. Or, maybe as the advance men for a more important meeting or something. But, they brought hardware to electronically clean buildings. They're doing some pretty sophisticated searching."

"If the cops know this, then why can't they bust them?" asked Bubba.

"First off, these guys haven't committed a crime, yet. There's no probable cause to make a bust even though they've got a bunch of weapons. The Beckley cops aren't supposed to know what they know. Besides, the police Chief thinks that some of his force is dirty. They'll tip these guys off."

"Why would he tell you all this?" demanded Jack.

"He's in my Sunday School class."

"This's not good," said Bubba.

"Not good at all," confirmed Jack.

"It itn't too bad," Naomi advised. "We'll know how many times they blink. UMW security can act fast. But we can't be too visible in stopping the druggies. It'll draw way too much attention. Gordie Miller has gone a long hard way to clean up our membership. But he knows not to go mess with drug lords. Besides, he has to worry about the Feds abusing the Patriot Acts against him and the other outspoken Christian leaders."

An urgent, incoming message blinked to be opened.

<<Greetings and peace be with you.>>

They looked at each other in amazement. Bubba clicked on the voice recognition system to answer faster.

<<Good afternoon to you, sir. Who are you?>>

Oddly, the reply came back in scrolling script—no voice.

<<Brother Pablo. I have an urgent message for you. You are in great danger! They know where you are and are coming to get you.>>

They exchanged a worried set of looks. Bubba quickly typed back, <<Who is coming? Do you mean they are coming to this location, right here?>>

<<Yes. They have you fixed at the Temple United Methodist Church.>>

<<How can they know? How can we know about you? Do you have a personal communicator so you can fax some id?>>, replied Bubba.

<<Understand you. No. You have no time! Run! I'm a Jesuit brother and an Assistant Professor here. Trust me. You know my computer location—contact me here later, when you are safe, and we will chat. Hurry! Hurry!!!>>

Bubba punched the off button, "We gotta go. C'mon."

They rushed out of the office. Jack went ahead and waved to them to come on. He desperately wished that he had a weapon like when he was in the Army. Jack jumped into Naomi's van. Bubba followed in his truck.

As they pulled up to Arnett and Winona's house Jack noticed a large sports utility van with silver gray one-way windows. He pointed it out to Naomi. Her face visibly relaxed, "That's ours. Oh, thank you, Lord Jesus."

They went to the kitchen immediately. Winona was slow cooking the last of the snap beans she didn't can. The large tureen was at a slow bubble. A hunk of fatback gave it a nice aroma. As usual there was a pot of coffee ready. Winona and Arnett hovered nearby. They were too agitated to sit and be part of the discussion.

Bubba began, "Can you believe that feller said the druggies were a-coming for us and then la-ti-da we could 'chat' when we got the chance? What was all of that? I didn't see any bad guys. I didn't even see our friendly dwarf doctors." Everyone mustered the best brave smile possible.

"That Pablo guy had our position pegged. He knew an awful lot," said Jack.

"I'll call our people to see what is what," said Naomi. A muted telcon followed. She looked ashen. "The NTs broke into the church. The NTs just missed us!"

"Lord Jesus," Bubba said shaking his head.

"We need to get out of here. Maybe I can get help in D.C.," said Jack.

"I know my way around NoVa and D.C. I'd like to find out what the fellow three stories down in the library knows," said Bubba.

"What about going home?" asked Naomi. "Your job and your family?"

Bubba lowered his head. He looked up and turned his eyes upon each person in the room. The blue of his eyes shone like ice on a bright winter's day. "I'll send a note to my boss and tell him as much of the truth as I can. I'll have my sons and son-out-laws augment the security NASA might provide and the security my church brothers will provide."

"You'll need more than that. More than 'prayer cover' you talk about," said Jack.

"Hey, my brothers in Christ, John-James, are Christian soldiers in every sense of the word."

"You've already done enough," said Jack. *Barbara Holland needs you home.*

"Thanks, John-James, but duty itn't over until it is over. I'm going."

Naomi spoke up. "I know you won't like this, but," she looked at her parents. "I feel a calling to go. I knew when we met Jack on the road that it was the Lord's Will and I really feel it now." Winona started to cry. Arnett bit his lip.

Bubba said softly, "Why don't we pray about it?"

Naomi got up and led everyone into the tiny living room. She fell to her knees before the coffee table. Bubba, Arnett and Winona followed suit. Jack copied them and took a place next to Naomi. They held hands. Naomi began a long rambling prayer about God's Will in our lives and the desires of our heart being in His Will. Jack felt intensely uncomfortable.

Long silences, except for Winona's sniffling, were interrupted by even longer prayers. Jack knew they all kept their eyes closed because he peeked. It seemed that each person was asking their own questions and expecting some kind of an answer. Once he was sure that they were not going to do anything really weird, Jack felt a sense of warmth. He heard them say so many times how much they loved 'You, my God, Father, Lord, Lord Jesus, Jesus, Sweet Jesus'. It was like they were really talking to someone in the room with them.

Quiet reigned for a time. Then, Naomi let go of his hand and stood up. They all stood up. Jack had the only dry eyes in the room. Naomi hugged and kissed her parents. Her father told her to be extra careful. Her mother told her to hurry home. Jack gave Bubba an inquisitive stare.

"It's decided. She's going," said Bubba.

"What?" asked Jack.

"We know what we're doing. She's going," Bubba gave Jack a paternal bear hug. "Someday you'll understand."

There was an uproar in the Tolley house that night. Naomi was adamant. Pete looked into her eyes and said, "How would it look if you go out to do something dangerous and I stay home?"

Naomi was shocked. She saw fear in his eyes. It wasn't the concern that her father might have for her. It was plain fear.

"Well?" he asked again.

She couldn't answer him as she felt the certainty that her man, her husband, father to her children, partner for life, lover, was a coward. Naomi was ashamed of herself for being taken in all of these years.

Beckley, WV
October 1st, 2012
Sunday

Sunday was an Appalachian postcard day. The chill in the air spoke of apple cider and pumpkins, haystacks and colors too beautiful to ignore. The color pageantry made the humblest neighborhood or hollow spectacular. High clouds swirled in the blue skies as the finishing touch to the Master's living canvas. Bubba and Jack waited by the truck. Arnett and Winona gathered the children around them. Pete popped the back of the SUV and got Naomi's large traveling bag out. Sarah, every bit as perceptive as her Mama, was the first to notice something was going on.

"Mama, where's your bag going?" she asked.

Winona started to cry again. Arnett stood ramrod straight looking at his daughter with the unconditional love aged over almost four decades, while two silent lines of tears coursed down his cheeks. Pete's face was distorted with anger and frustration. Naomi started to choke as she spoke.

"No, precious, my bag isn't just going somewhere. Mama's got to go for a little trip," Naomi kissed Sarah and stroked her hair. She gently touched the pink barrette in her soft brown hair. Sarah was alarmed. Ruth got upset. When her mother kissed her she lunged for her. Ruth cried to Naomi, "Don't go, please don't go, pul-ee-ease don't go."

Wide-eyed Sarah asked, "Mama, are you getting a divorce?" She had seen divorce break the hearts of a few of her little friends.

Naomi smiled, "You precious darling, we're not getting a divorce. Mama," she paused to get the words out, "has to go help these men go do what's right."

"Why doesn't Daddy go?" asked Sarah. Joshua took in everything like radar. He bolted for the SUV. Naomi scooped him up in her arms. She kissed his cheeks, his forehead and neck. "I love you Lil'Bit. You be a very good boy."

He bucked his body to get free. When Naomi set him down, he called out as he ran, "I get my cars and go with you, Mama. Wait for me!" Naomi treasured every moment she watched him from the kitchen window play with his little cars in the dirt.

Pete kissed Naomi on the cheek and brusquely pushed her towards her parents. She hooked their necks in her arm. She kissed them on their tear-stained cheeks. "I have gotta go," she pleaded. Arnett took Sarah by the shoulders and stood behind her. Winona took Ruth into her arms. The little girl buried her head in Winona's neck.

Pete stood at the open SUV door to make sure that Lil'Bit didn't get out. Lil'Bit tried to push himself under Pete's arm. When he was stopped, Lil'Bit leaped into the driver's seat and threw himself against the window. His little pudgy hands pressed against the window.

As Bubba backed the truck out of the driveway, Naomi saw her innocent baby boy pound the window with his hands. His eyes were wide with fear. His little white-shirted chest heaved with rapid breathing. He screamed with all of his voice, "No! No! No! Mama! Don't leave me! Wait for me! Wait for me! Mama, Mama, Mama!"

Naomi couldn't wave. She sat between the two men with pain etched on her face. She stared out at her loves with her mouth slightly open. A groan came up from deep inside her as a great pain struck at her very center. How soft was that terrible sound.

As they headed out of town Jack heard Naomi mumbling. Rapidly, very hushed and under her breath, she recited the Lord's Prayer and the Twenty-Third Psalm as the tears flowed. Bubba patted her knees a couple of times. Jack wanted to put his arm around her. After awhile on the road, Bubba reached his old bear arm around her shoulders. Tenderly he said, "Little sister, little sister." Naomi collapsed against his chest, closed her eyes and wept more.

Chapter 2. Connections

Near Staunton, VA
October 1st, 2012
Sunday

The cab of Bubba's truck grew cozy over uncomfortable. After a couple of silent hours of steady descent from the Appalachians to the rolling floor of the Shenandoah Valley, Bubba opened his lively chatter box. Often Naomi closed her eyes. Her lips moved but there was no sound. Her face changed from pain etched stone to smoothed clay as the potter's hand wiped away every hard crease and wrinkle except her happy crow's feet.

"Listen to this voice," said Bubba. He asked his automatic navigator some questions on directions. Then, he switched channels to information and asked for some historical site questions. "Some voice, huh?"

"Sounds about so," said Jack. Naomi nodded dry-eyed.

"And a very pretty voice too. Sultry. I love playing this when Barbara is riding with me. Just to get a rise out of her!" Jack and Naomi smiled politely.

Jack's red-bricked Virginia went by with each house by field by hill, holding his imagination until it fell behind his window post. Since he was a boy, he wanted to live in 'The' Valley or just across the Blue Ridge to the Piedmont. Jack drank in the charming mixture of town and country, history and wilderness, and flowing waters framed by mountains. When he left the Army, life's simple circumstances—no job—excluded him from another dreamy desire. The Valley still looked nice from the road. You couldn't see the ugly sores of crime, corruption and senseless, unremitting violence from the road. Also, the hidden simmering in people's minds with the seething fear and resentment of Liberal Puritans for believing Christians and Jews and vice versa. Liberal Puritans had a special deep dread of the Christian base of Conservatives coming back to presidential power after Hillary. The Christians couldn't wait.

Arlington, VA

After rolling by mile after mile of Northern Virginia sprawl they exited the crowded highway corridor. Naomi gave directions through busy streets.

Jack said, "Hey, this my old neighborhood! I can't believe it! Back to Arlington." Arlington, Virginia was the childhood 'home' to Jack. Jack's Army officer father served three tours in the Pentagon and retired there. Last year at this time, his mother followed his father in death to Arlington National Cemetery.

"We're coming up to my house. Up there," he pointed, "Sycamore Street." Jack choked on the lump in his throat. This was the house he cleaned and closed after his mother died. Jack emptied the house of every belonging—those things which made so many different places look like the same family home—so his parents were truly no more. Jack strained to look up the gentle rise through the graceful curtain of trees draped over the street.

"Hey, don't pull in here," Jack said suddenly. "Naomi, call this security fellow and tell him to come outside where we can see him from Sycamore as we drive by. We shouldn't go into any place blindly. No matter what."

Naomi turned on the phone in her personal communicator. She insisted the Security Chief come outside. Her face brightened, "Ooh, there's Tommy and he looks put out."

"Tough," said Bubba.

The Security Chief, Tommy Schultz, showed them to their condo in gruff and grumbling tones. Tommy was fiftyish with a very large watermelon belly. He built a thick neck and stout arms as a laborer before he moved up in union management. He made the point, several times, that he knew his area better than "any blankety-blank body" and Mrs. Tolley knew that nothing was going to go wrong here or anywhere that he worked. He fussed more, cursing casually, about how it was safe enough for his family to live here.

The condo was nicely appointed. It layered three bedrooms on four floors. The tiny back yard held a patio and a tall fence for privacy. The upper rooms' rear windows overlooked the parking lot for the East Falls Church Metro station. The refrigerator was well stocked. Bubba begged off from meeting just yet for a short nap first. He slept for almost three hours.

Naomi and Jack puttered until it was time to eat. They prepared a Summer meal of salad and fruit. They chatted along themes they developed in West Virginia—family, work, information technology, weather and music. Naomi remembered all the words to nearly every song she ever heard and sang rather nicely. Jack remembered only the tunes and sang poorly, but loudly. They played 'Name That Tune' and shared light laughter as they cleaned and chopped.

Bubba joined them for supper. He looked very pale. The big question was how to make contact with this Brother Pablo at Georgetown.

"I hope that Tommy 'Sunshine' knows his security," said Bubba.

"Me, too," said Jack.

"Me, three," said Naomi. They smiled at one another. "We've dealt with a lot these past years. You know, assassination attempts on Gordie. Stuff like that."

"How comforting to know that your life is in the hands of a man like Tommy," sneered Jack.

"I've seen Tommies all my life," said Bubba.

"Yeah, and I worked for too many," said Jack. "Shakespeare said to 'not suffer fools gladly'. Well, I've worked for fool upon fool and those fools did not suffer me gladly."

"Y'all may be right, but there's times when fools do their bidding and fetch and hew as needed. We need to hope this poor fool can do things right. Bless his heart. We'll be real careful too. He's still one of the Lord's children, so we gotta love him. Right now, we need him."

Bubba thrust his chin out like he was going to spit, "I really do hate it when you're always right. You're just like Barbara." He lowered his glasses to the end of his nose and spoke in his best Oxonian English. "Of course, I never let her know that she's always right. It would be impolite to let that 'ver-e-tay' become one of the foundations of our relationship. I quite prefer to keep the 'is-see-u' of who's right or wrong in healthy contention."

"Quite so," said Naomi.

"Okay then, so we're just gonna go downtown and use the computers in the UMW office. We follow UMW security procedures to get in and out of cyberspace?"

"Uh-huh," Naomi and Bubba nodded.

"How long do you think we have before we're found out?" asked Bubba.

"I don't have much experience with this cops and robbers thing. My security experience is more with information security," said Naomi.

"We may've already been found out," said Jack.

"Here?" asked Naomi.

"The enemy pinpointed us when we were working at the church. That's a pretty tight fix on where we were. Not only that, but remember it was reported that they were looking for somebody—us—before they broke in." Jack read their faces.

"Also, this Brother Pablo, whoever he really is, had an incredible fix on us and them! So, at least two sources knew exactly where we were in the time and space continuum down to the nearest minute and square meter. Look, they certainly know who I am since they tried to kill me. The goons in Beckley most likely have figured out the connection to Naomi through the UMW and the church. They probably put out enough talking money. If they made any kind of surveillance before they moved out, then they got a positive ID on all three of us. I'd bet real money, if I had it, that they know exactly who we are and where we are."

Jack saw intensity instead of anxiety. He continued, "However, they don't necessarily know where we're right now. Not, exactly. Yet. They'll work a process of elimination for UMW and NASA connections. They'll check out our personal connections to see if we're hiding with family or friends. They look in all the usual good hiding spots like in any game of hide 'n seek. Except this one is for keeps."

Bubba and Naomi stared.

"They can check almost everything unobtrusively. These guys have incredible resources. They can bounce a microwave off the windows at night to get a profile of everybody inside based on how they breath in their sleep. Nobody is safe if the NTs want to hit."

"Do you think they used these things against us in Beckley?" asked Naomi.

"Dunno. They might have. But, it doesn't matter. They could spot us as early as tomorrow or as late as a week or ten days. That's as good as I can guess."

"Should we move?" asked Naomi.

"No, not yet. It depends on how good your passive defense is here. That's what we have to find out in some detail from good old Tommy Schultz. He really does have our lives in his hands for awhile."

"You give me the security questions and I'll get the answers," said Naomi. She patted Jack's forearm.

"John-James, I knew that. It's just a matter of time until we're located here," said Bubba. "I'd thought it'd take longer."

Jack read something new in both pairs of eyes. There was no fear. *What's this? Determination? Hmm, no, resolution. It's all resolved, all over, for them.*

Arlington, VA
October 2nd, 2012
Monday

October morning broke Jack's sleep. The sun was high enough early enough to catch the window of his room. Light pierced through sleep before the heavy veil of fatigue lightened and lifted on its own accord. Jack hurried downstairs to face the day. He gulped a cup of coffee and reached for an instant refill. *I've gotta make this security work right.* His stomach knotted. *I don't know what to worry about.*

There was a loud knock at the door. They all flinched together.

Tommy and a young man in a trench coat walked in before Jack could undo the lock. Tommy said, "Never mind, Buddy." He opened his hand to display a small control device.

"You've got a remote to our security system?" asked Jack.

"I've got a remote to *my* system. We're in a hurry. Get your jackets and let's go." Tommy gave them the plan, "We'll take the Metro and walk to and from the UMW headquarters downtown. There's so many cops there you gotta really ante up for a hit."

"Oh, jeez, run and grab the vests!" His young assistant left his post at the kitchen window and hurried to fetch the armored vests.

"Okay, listen up folks. We're going with the 'shadow and light' bodyguard technique. My assistant is the light. He'll stay close. They gotta see him. The average creep will leave you alone. The pro will try to take him, the bright light, out first before going for the marks. That's you guys. I got another guy who is the shadow. Nobody but me knows who the shadow is. As we move, our shadow will change but will always be with us. There may be more than one guy and they may swap out along the way. The shadow is what counts." They strapped on the thin vests with expert help.

When Jack stepped outside, he felt the day. A rain last night put a chill in the air and washed the streets and combed some of the leaves from the trees. Leaves lay wet and matted to the street and sidewalk like so many colored strands left in the hairbrush. The wet smell was strong. The low flying tufts of cotton ball clouds raced below and ahead of the brightening overcast. *I'd like to love this day. So Autumn. But jeez. I can't. Where's the shadow? Where are the bad guys?*

Washington, DC

They arrived downtown at the Farragut West metro stop with disarming ease. Walking the few blocks to the new UMW office on 16th Street, they passed a row of uniformed officers standing like a police picket fence. If a fire broke out, the cops could make an old-fashioned bucket brigade from the Lincoln Monument past the Capitol. They shared a collective sigh of relief and group smile when they got to the seventh floor security office and took off their armored vests.

The rest of the morning was briefings. The information network for all UMW Washington operations was described in detail. Soup, sandwiches and salad were delivered to the conference room for lunch. The union Vice President for Washington operations joined them. Mr. Frank Jablonski was pleasant and solicitous through all the meal's small talk.

"Some security issues require first class coverage. Tommy's the person for that," said Frank.

Tommy gave a thumbs up and said, "Right, Chief."

"Is there any special consideration that he should know about?" asked Frank.

He doesn't know the whole deal why we're here, thought Jack. He said out loud, "No. I think you've got it all covered. We just need to get to work."

The trio rose from lunch with pleasantries. They were shown to their computers in a small, windowless room next to the telecommunications center of the building. The doors had special access locks with Visface and retinal/handprint screen checks. They were left alone inside.

"Looks like a cell," said Bubba.

"How would you know?" asked Jack. He started arranging the work space to his liking. "Have you spent time in prison?"

"Not in this city. I'm not even wanted in many states anymore this side of the Mississippi. I can go into a Post Office and not see my picture any more," said Bubba.

"Oh, Bubba," smiled Naomi.

"Ah'm not wanted by the law yet, right here. But, we're sure wanted by somebody."

"I hope that greasy Vice President and fat Tommy do their best to save our skins."

Naomi winked, "Don't be silly, we know how important this work is for the UMW. Let's just see how these systems work." After a few minutes she walked to the table in between Bubba and Jack's work stations. She set a piece of folded paper down and tapped it with her forefinger. It read: LOOK FOR BUGS!

"Ai-yi-yi yi," Bubba slapped his forehead. "We really need to check out this great opportunity we've got here. These guys sure know how to run their own show."

"I think there is too much for us to do here from what I can see," Bubba spoke slowly with an exaggerated emphasis like he was speaking his lines, badly, in community theater. "Let's see if can get some good pings at the right places and then call it quits early. Anyway, I'm not feeling so well. Come here and watch this."

"Certainly," said Naomi. Jack came over too.

Bubba started a series of standard commo log-ins. He stuck his present location and the local identifier code for the UMW in the format for the preamble to all the messages. Naomi and Jack looked at each other behind his back and exchanged question mark faces. Bubba "pinged" and said "hello" with an electronic handshake to the UMW in Beckley, to an older, stand-alone PC in Temple United Methodist Church, the Systems Security Directorate at NASA Langley, and the library services public access line for Georgetown University. Suddenly, he said, "Okay, that's a wrap. Let's shut it down and boogie."

Naomi and Jack rolled their eyes in disbelief. Jack used the outside security wall phone to announce that they needed to go. He asked for whatever special instructions were required.

The trip back was faster. The going in carried the weight of anticipation. Their return was lightened by relief. When they were in the condo, Bubba called out, "I need to check something I set up last night with security."

Naomi went to the kitchen and started a pot of tea. Jack double-checked the door to see if the lock and security system engaged properly. It looked okay, so he stood by the window. He looked out on the sidewalk, decorative trees and parking lot. *It didn't happen. I'm still alive. Nothing is ever as bad as I fear. Just like always. So, why do I still get scared? What is it?* The sky was graying with thickening clouds. *Oh, God. Death is so...*

"Okay-dokay, we're finer than frog hair. That tea sure smells good. Thanks Naomi," Bubba strode into the kitchen and reached for a cup. "That was, as they say in West-By-God-Virginy, 'thoughty' of you." Naomi smiled and leaned back against the kitchen sink. Jack joined them. He looked at Bubba with expectant, arched eyebrows.

"I wanted us to hurry back, because we gotta talk," Bubba smiled. "I saw lots of bugs and some major tampering with the code right away at the UMW. That made me more and more worried and then I thought, 'Why should I be worried? I've done nothing wrong!'"

"I've done nothing illegal or shameful. But, they're some

really bad people looking for me," Bubba nodded, "us." His blue eyes carried intensity like a weight. "We don't know who is hunting us for sure," said Jack.

"Dodn't matter. Islamist Totalitarian. Secular Humanist Totalitarian. They're allies when they need to be against the Christians and Jews. Narco-Terrorists and the Drug Lord bosses are just their tools."

"Huh? Liberals fight Islamists. Liberals fight drugs. Sorta, except what they want legalized. At least they work to increase security."

"Don't you see? This is wrong that I'm the hunted one. I'm hunted like a criminal by the criminals. Whatever their name is. This's wrong that I'm hiding and looking over my shoulder. You can say that is the way it is, but that's not good enough. There's no reason why I, the good, upright citizen, should be ever put into this situation. So, it's time that we fix it." Bubba hit his fist into the opposing open palm. "It's time to go from defense to offense!"

"Mr. Holland, if we take the stand, how'd we do it?" asked Naomi. "Which enemy?"

Bubba spun around on his heel and paced, "When I got agitated at the incursions into the UMW system and outraged at our predicament, I started to pray, 'Oh Lordy, Lord, what are we to do?' Then the thought came to me, 'fight, fight—fight them here'."

"Oh geez, Bubba," said Jack, "you made those commo pings because you heard voices?"

Bubba's red face turned two shades more. But, in the instant of time that he took a step forward, his face relaxed. He said, "There were no voices, John-James. When I turned my thoughts to the Lord, the thought came to me. And I just knew." He cocked an eye towards Naomi.

"You just know," said Naomi.

"Come on! You know what? Those commo pings are like waving a red flag to come get us. And, they will come get us. Then what? What will you know then?" He shook his head 'no' more than Naomi nodded 'yes' to Bubba. "Will you know something when they come and kill us? Will you know that you're a dead duck?"

Bubba clasped his hands together, intertwined the fingers and drew up the praying fist below his nose. He stretched out his index fingers together and pointed to Jack's chest. "Listen, Son, I know thoughts like this don't come every day. When you know, you know. The only way to fight the bad guys is to stand up and fight. Since I don't know where their lair is, I had to get them to come get us. You haven't heard me out. On the ride back here I got some more ideas. Here's what I think. The UMW isn't safe. It isn't even safe to let them UMW fellows know how unsafe and compromised their system is. So, trying to keep the UMW as a safe and secure workplace is just stupid. No offense, Miss Naomi."

"None taken."

"Trying to stay hidden even for just a week is futile. We need to get our enemy out where we can see them. Whichever enemy it is, let'em come get us. So, I let the cat out of the bag. I sent an alert message to the best good guys I could think of, my friends, to watch the pinged stations and set a trap. We'll see ourselves if and when the UMW gets hit one-way or the other. That's where I need your help John-James to think about all of the options. Naomi, I need you to grade what we two fools come up with."

"Come up with what? What are these other ideas?" asked Jack.

Bubba opened his hands palm upward, imploringly, towards Jack, "Right now, I just know that I'm supposed to get the bad guys to make a move. I'm sure that the calling them out to fight is right. I know it. I don't care who it is. Pablo, Ishmael, Hillary."

"This is too unbelievable," Jack signaled 'stop' with his hand. "You're calling out the freakin' Narco-Terrorists or some Islamist or the President of the United States to fight and you think you have some ideas on what to do when they show up. The whole, stinking country is corrupted by their money. There's bloodstains everywhere from the dead people who got in their way. Everybody is afraid of their power. And you, you—Bubba, are calling them out. It's unbelievable! You're unbelievable!"

"You're right. It may not just be the Narco-Terrorists we're bringing out in the open. Ishmael probably is an Osama Bin Laden wannabe. President Hillary may have Homeland Security suppressing the People. We're a going to find out."

"So unbelievable."

"Oh, I see. I see it now. Jack, you just answered why Bubba did what he did. You just said why we have to fight here and now," said Naomi.

"Huh?"

"If the whole country is corrupted and bloodstained, then… Oh, what was the other word you used about being scared?"

"Everybody is afraid."

"Right, if everybody is afraid to stop corruption and murder then it's gone way out of control. Then something must be done. We've got to do it."

"You're nuts too! Don't you get it? They're bigger than us and we can't defend ourselves. Nothing will stop them if they decide to get us."

"If there's no way to defend, then we must attack! We need to get them. The time is now."

"You're both speaking gibberish. It's like all of your religious… stuff. I don't mind that you talk about God and Jesus all the time. That's your right I guess to speak in private. But, you can't believe that, that stuff has anything to do with what's going on in the real world. We're dead meat."

"Jack, everything we say is very real. It's not real because we believe that it is real. It's the real, whole truth," said Bubba.

"Right, the one true religion, the only God. C'mon, it is the same story in every culture. Blah, blah, but get real. What're we going to do right now?"

"Jack, we know the truth and don't want to argue about it. Someday, you will ask and we will tell what we know and feel about the Word. That's a separate issue from fighting drug lords like Pablo Ponce De Leon. Or Narco-Terrorists like Ishmael. Or the Diversity Police[1]. You should see that you're arguing, right now, *for* what Bubba's done. If everything is so bad and if we're doomed, then we ought to not stand idly by like so many chickens. We need to fight."

"You're a mother of three kids and you want to fight? With what? What will your kids do when you are gone? Aren't you people supposed to turn the other cheek?"

"We turn our cheek to insult, but we stand up to sin and evil. If the country is as bad as you say and we know it is, then I'm no

---

1. Diversity Police. The name applied to any police officer or administrator enforcing 'hate speech' laws making it a criminal act to speak against protected classes of persons. Speaking 'against' persons became more and more broadly interpreted to say anything a protected person or Liberal Puritan didn't like, including historical references.

account of a mother to leave such trash to my children. Their lives are just going to be terrible. So, if I'm gone it won't matter much. Better to die trying to do right to give them a good life."

"You don't believe that," said Jack.

Naomi answered with silence.

"I know she believes it. Listen up, you don't know as much about us as you think, John-James. Nobody loves their children more than I do, but I'll risk my life, and maybe theirs, if it has to be done. How do you think our ancestors lived on the frontier fighting the Indians? No different now basically. 'Cept we got electricity," said Bubba.

"So, how do you know when some stupid thing or the other has to be done? What's worth all the risk? I don't get it. Really, I don't."

"Why John-James, you young West Pointer, you're asking me when something of self is more important than 'Duty, Honor, and Country'? Something is worth the risk when it is right. How do I know? I …," Bubba paused, "we all knew that you were worth it a few weeks ago back in Poquoson. You still are. Like I said, when you know, you know. You risk it all."

"Amen," confirmed Naomi.

"Fight. Not flight, huh?" Jack was silent as he walked to the window. He pulled the curtain aside to see more of the darkening sky then turned to his friends across the room in the kitchen. "I guess you're right. We gotta do what we gotta do, but we need a plan." *I just shortened my own life. Oh God, I want to see Maude and my babies. I want to live. I wanna go home.* The growing wind whipsawed the tree in the tiny patch of front yard.

Arlington, VA
October 11th, 2012
Thursday

Day after day the NTs didn't attack. Neither did anyone else. The drumbeat of the days was long work and short rest, long work and short rest. The long hours at work produced two photonic memory wafers with a program and a set of data to attack the enemy computers. The short evenings of rest were tuned to the election of 2012. It was a political Super Bowl frenzy. The stoking, smoking fire of conflict smelled like revolution about to burst into flames.

"What's the big deal about this stupid election?" Jack asked over a delicious late night desert treat. Bubba said Naomi cooked "tenderly" and the food appreciated it.

Naomi and Bubba looked at each other and smiled. Bubba made a hand bowing gesture with his desert spoon and said, "Ladies first, me lady."

Naomi took in a deep breath as she squared her shoulders. She looked like a finalist in the middle school recitation contest, "Jack, what do you believe is at stake in this election?"

Jack thought of an answer quickly, "Who'll run the government for four years. Who will be in and who will be out. Usual BS."

"True, but what's at stake?"

"The usual. Liberal versus Conservative. I'm a middle of the road guy. Not a lib. Not Religious Right."

"Who woulda guessed?" said Bubba more as a fact than a question.

"Okay then, let me ask you this … what has happened since you graduated from West Point in 2000 to make this election such a big deal?" Naomi prompted him.

"Let's see. 9–11 was in '01. The Taliban in Afghanistan got kicked out in '02. Saddam Hussein was taken out in '03. The economy came back. Bush won the election in '04. Iraq just went on and on and on. Small stuff at home. Some bombings like before 9–11. Hillary won in '08. Then, in '09 and '10, it's like it all went nuts. Everything. Crime and drugs. Illegal immigration. The designer drugs went wild. Got your Sin^2 drug going. Islamist attacks. Suicide bombers here. Culture War protests. Homeland Security[3] went crazy too. Everything's still in an uproar. The Diversity Laws[4] were passed. Cops, the stinking Diversity Police, really enforced the PC rules. Domestic Terrorism is an issue. Your guys in the Christian Right are on the hot seat too for your Ten Commandments civil disobedience and other stuff. Especially, the homophobia hate speech. Wearing Christian symbols at work and school. You know."

"Why?" Naomi topped off their coffee cups.

"Why what? The uproar or what?"

2. SIN. The ultimate designer drug is an authentic aphrodisiac. The new designer drug the street named 'SIN' seemed so transparent a joke but it was too potent to laugh long. The drug 'SIN' fulfilled the alchemists' dreams for ages. The chemical cocktail was refined to hit all the right receptors in the brain and hypothalamus to release a torrent of hormones and chemical signals that created a mild euphoria and a powerful lust. All the appropriate bio-chemical changes in the body made it super ready for sex. There was a pink pill chemically constructed for women and a blue pill designed just for men. The drug made every man or woman ready, very willing, able and driven to have sex.

Sudden death occurred in one out of every ten thousand uses. The victim could be a first time or thousandth time user with a healthy profile. A single use created an almost insatiable desire for the drug. Internal bleeding and severe depression were side effects too. But, over time a sinister implication, one which was hotly debated as urban myth or conspiracy theory, was the fact that the drug stopped having the desired effects but trapped the user in the desperate grip of desire. The scientists called this the plateau stage of the drug. The plateau could be reached as early as the hundreth use of the drug, even though some people seemed to go on and on without hitting the plateau. The drug was profoundly unpredictable. The drug was controversial immediately. SIN meets the desires of instant gratification at the most common, powerful biological level in humans. It felt incredibly good for a little while. The user sensed power, desirability, excitement and joy. It made the humdrum of daily living pale in contrast and recede from consciousness. Once someone had SIN, that is all they wanted until it killed them or crippled them. Even then, hating what had happened to their bodies and lives, the user could not consider life without a hit of SIN everyday. When SIN dominates the lives of its users, it demands their very being. Few thoughts can crowd out thinking about SIN. So, the presence and concentration of the mind so necessary to make one's way in the world as an individual is lost. As the user's mind goes, jobs and relationships go away. Some users with exceptionally hardy constitutions claimed they could control SIN, and perhaps they could limit SIN in their life for awhile, but the press of SIN over time was like the build up of pressure as one descends in the ocean depths. The light fades, the known world falls up and behind, artificial substances replace the natural breath of life, and finally at some great depth, the pressure crushes everything.

3. Homeland Security. Refers to the activities of the Homeland Security Office, a cabinet-level position. The series of Patriot Acts gave extraordinary police and judiciary powers to the Homeland Security Office and other Federal agencies like the FBI, DEA, ATF, Secret Service.

4. Diversity Laws. Laws protecting groups of persons because they add 'diversity'. These protected groups include all non-white races and ethnicities, non-Christian religions, homosexuals, lesbians, trans-gendered, bi-sexuals, midgets, dwarfs, giants, disabled and handicapped persons, foreigners, illegal aliens and anyone else a judge imagined should have been covered as a compelling object of state-sponsored diversity for protected classes of persons.

"Why so many troubles from '09 to '12? We're the only world superpower. What's up?"

"I'm not sure. The designer drugs went wild for sure. President Hillary got government in gear."

"It's more than that."

Bubba said, "You've heard it said that the War on Islamist Terror is a World War and it's one war with two fronts—one overseas and one at home."

"Yeah, the War on Terror we do every day at work."

"Well it spilled over into the Great U.S. Culture War in '09. And this Culture War, I like to call ACW II for American Civil War II, bled over into the War against the Islamists."

"You're so politically incorrect, Bubba, to say Islamists all the time. Ok, you got two wars mushed into each other. What? Like the perfect storm we've the perfect war now?

"Something like that," said Bubba.

"Jack, its really the complete war. Too many Christians stayed out of the '08 election because the Republicans let them down. Too many Republicans went wobbly on the Marriage Amendment after Bush won in '04. They wouldn't fight and get all the real conservative judges appointed. They got some good judges, but not nearly enough. Not conservative enough. The judiciary just got worse. They are oligarchs. Black-robed tyrants. The judges culturally cleansed the country of the Ten Commandments and our God. CHRISTmas. You name it. Hillary Rodham Clinton won. She ran as a 'moderate' Christian who was just conservative enough to not be scary liberal. She had to win a couple of Red States like stupid Iowa. And she did. She's been tightening the screws since on us. But, the borders are wide open to illegal aliens and more voter fraud. She's not going to lose this election. No matter what."

"How's that the complete war?"

"We are fighting for freedom against foreign and domestic enemies. Just like your oath to the Constitution," said Bubba.

"The President, even if it's Hillary, can't be the enemy," said Jack.

"You don't see her using this Homeland Security apparatus to suppress Christians?"

"She's a Christian, Bubba. She's a Methodist like you Naomi."

"No, Jack, not like me. That's like saying Hitler was a Catholic," said Naomi.

"Hitler was never excommunicated."

"He excommunicated himself. So did Hillary."

"What do you mean by suppress Christians? Aren't the Christians causing the confrontations? Especially in the South?" asked Jack.

"They're using all the snooping powers that were intended for Islamist terrorists to gather information on Christian activists."

"So? What's wrong with information if you're not doing anything illegal? And what do you mean by an activist?"

"They've used the arrest authority to pick up Christian leaders. Even bloggers. Outspoken people, writers, radio people, columnists, you know. They hold them for a long time. They are charged with Hate Crimes for Hate Speech. You know, for quoting the Bible. They're going to have secret trials next."

"No way."

"It's true, Jack," said Bubba. "That's why the Omni is so important. Whoever has control of it will rule. Don't you get it? Even if Hillary loses the election, she can use the Omni to make it look like she won. It'll change the voting machine totals."

"How do you know this? You never talked about the Omni like this before."

"I know what I know about Omni. I know a lot more about Hillary. I know a whole lot about this election. The Omni will do what ham hounded ex-commies did in the Ukraine in 2004. But, you'll never know. No one will ever know."

"What?"

"Since before '06 the drug lords and the Islamist terrorists have been working hand in glove. Each side thinks its using the other for short term gain. Each thinks it will unload the other and take them out when the time is right. We call 'em Narco-Terrorists like they're one group. But they're separate allies."

"I'll buy that."

"Liberals, the real zealots among them, think they can use both the drug lords and the Islamists terrorists—the Narco-Terrorists—as political tools to beat the conservatives. Really, that's code for crush the Christians and Jews—the believing practicing ones.

Everything that goes wrong is the conservative's fault. And they're using the Homeland Security laws against political enemies. They'll sneak in more and more socialism in the name of public security."

"I can see some of that. But, the liberals aren't conspiring with those other bad guys. And they can't go too far in abusing the laws. The courts won't let them."

"The courts? Ha, the courts! They're as much the domestic enemies as anyone. They're the biggest enemies the People have!"

"Nah."

"Not all of them, but way too many of them. High priests of political correctness. Pagans, nearly all of them. Jack, they're just as much the enemy as the Islamists. They'll just kill the country in a different way. Connect the dots."

"You connect them for me," said Jack. "You seem to have it all figured out."

"Okay. Drugs went wild in this country because the new ones are just too good, too powerful and hook you in a heartbeat. We don't have the will to fight the drug war like a real war. The drugs keep coming in too because we don't have the will to close the border and enforce our own immigration laws. That's connected to our multicultural sabotage by the liberals," Bubba drew imaginary lines with broad strokes.

"The drug lords in Latin America rule the drug connection countries. Either they run things in the open or under the table. They want the United States to lose power so they stay in power. The Islamists want to destroy us as the Great Satan. Pushing drugs, using drug routes for terrorists and weapons, and financing their own operations is a deal. So, drug lords and Islamist terrorists become Narco-Terrorists. With me so far?"

"Yup."

"No one, including the Republicans, had the guts to close the border. The immigrant invasion made the voter fraud in '08 colossal. Now, finally, the public outcry against the drugs, crime, and fear of terrorists gives the government a green light to solve the problem. But, the liberals don't have the will to solve it—to fight like it's a war and win. They take away freedom here to build and preserve their own power—the rule of elites—for our own safety, for security, for the children, for feel-good legislation. They appease overseas instead of fighting. If they win this election, their voter fraud will be institutionalized and they'll never lose again. The Republic will be over. Except, Hillary's met her match in Maggie Myriah Kyle. Iron Maggie's got the will to win."

"We've been praying for a leader, a David. Maggie's our David," said Naomi.

"King David of the Bible?" asked Jack. "You want a king?"

"We want a leader with God's spirit on her. We don't want rule by politically correct and pitifully corrupt judges. We want Gideon's Army," said Bubba.

"I've heard of Gideon, but can't place him."

Bubba smiled, "It was like the first Army Rangers. They started with many thousands of soldiers and pushed them until fewer and fewer were left. The hard core. Gideon lead these couple of hundred guys to defeat a whole army of thousands. God did it."

"And you want God to win this election?'

"We want God to bless us with a leader to win these wars," said Naomi.

"Onward Christian Soldiers," said Bubba.

"I see the dots you're connecting, but maybe there's another way," said Jack.

"Listen to Maggie Myriah Kyle," Bubba turned up the TV. "See for yourself if she open the eyes of your heart."

Much later than usual for them, they put away the dishes and prepared for night and a new day. Jack heard bits and pieces of the prayers Naomi and Bubba offered in their nightly prayer time, kneeling, at the coffee table. He overheard, "And let our dear friend, John-James Tillman, come to know You and …".

Arlington, VA
October 12th, 2012
Friday

Late the next day Frank Jablonski barged into their room at the UMW headquarters.

"What's wrong Frank?" asked Bubba.

"Next time knock," added Jack.

Frank glared at the two men, but he re-shaped his grimace into a plastic smile. "I've got an important package for you." He smiled at Naomi. His eyes quickly fell to her breasts, back up and then gave her full body a once over. "The package came from Gordie, hisself."

"Why, thank you," Naomi took the package and set it down.

"We should open that and log it in as a secure document," Frank replied in his matter-of-fact monotone voice.

"*'Personal For'* documents aren't security items," said Jack.

"Maybe not at NASA, Mr. Tillman, but all closed documentation that's stamped UMW Secret like this one here is required to be properly registered at the facility of receipt," said Frank.

The trio exchanged raised eyebrows. They never told Frank that Jack worked at NASA.

"I'll take the risk," said Naomi. "I'll send Gordie an email and let him know how well you handled his package with your personal concern."

Frank looked uneasy. "Well, thank you ma'am. I, uh, I'd better get going now. And, youse make sure that if you need anything at all, anything, youse let me know. I'll make sure that this national headquarters makes it happen. Be careful, now."

The door closed and the last internal lock clicked shut. Naomi hummed loudly as she picked up the package and cradled it in her arms like a baby. She held it out at arm's length and danced a slow, swirling step around the room.

"I bet he could spit!" said Bubba.

Naomi raised her eyebrows in warning and hummed louder. She sang, "Later, later, I know what this is. You'll know too, but later, later. Let me send that email to Gordie and we can wrap it up here for another day." Naomi let her voice fade up and away with the wisp of smoke that was her thought a second ago.

They shut down their work for another day.

Naomi sneaked the package out under her coat. On the Metro ride home Jack was sure he recognized people. *Were those two middle-aged guys at the same spot in the same stop?*

At the condo, Naomi sat down and looked up slyly. In her affected Southern belle speech she asked, "Mr. Holland, would you be ever so kind as to get me a bite to eat? I swear I am so famished. Ther're some hors d'oevres in the fridge you can nuke in the microwave. Mr. Tillman, would you be ever so kind as to get me a glass of tea with just the tiniest twist of lemon? I could just perish from thirst."

The men hurried and took their seats at her side. Naomi took a leisurely bite to eat and a slow sip of drink. She sighed, rolled her shoulders, and stretched her arms out in front like a cat stretching its front paws, "You know, gentlemen, I could become used to treatment like that. Why, it seems to me that you've a certain curiosity about this envelope. Well, let's just take a look!" The men grinned like excited little boys at a birthday party.

Naomi opened the layers of special magnetic tape. The magnetic field established by the tape prevented most intrusion devices from working properly. Naomi snatched the note attached to the thick folder. "Oh, that Gordie! What a kidder!" She crumpled the note and put the wadded ball in the small side pocket of her sweater.

She slowly opened the file. On the left flap was a stack of photographs. The top photograph was a full-face photo of a man in his late twenties. The right side was a thick notebook neatly color tabbed and divided. A photonic wafer disk was secured along the seam in a special magnetic-safe pouch.

"So, this is Brother Pablo? This is the guy who saved our butts in Beckley? Boy, he looks so young!" Bubba said what they all thought.

The face smiling at them from the glossy photograph was a very handsome man with huge brown eyes and jet-black hair cut in simple shocks. Strong Hispanic features looked like the model for a 'Visit Mexico' advertising campaign. His clerical collar added a sense of dignity and reservation to the face of carefree youth. Pablo Cervantes exuded vitality even in this old-fashioned flat portrayal. His holograph, the next item under the cover photo, was a completely convincing picture of young vigor.

Naomi slowly turned the pages of the dossier. The men huddled close by her shoulders. Jack smelled her perfume. He tried to breath deeply without being noticed. As they read each item, they took turns "umming and hmming".

"Hmm, he's well down the path to full priesthood as a Jesuit," said Bubba.

"Studied at Harvard and Columbia before going to Georgetown," said Jack.

"His father was a laborer and died young. His mother raised a family of six children in Bakersfield, California. There's so much stuff here. Look at this financial data cross-referenced with the files for every purchase using electronic medium for the past seven years by date, by type of purchase, by location, and by electronic carrier card. Look how complete this record of Internet 'cookies' is," said Naomi.

Jack's small personal communicator played the photonic disk with even more personal information including video footage. The unusual montage of recent film clips from electronic tellers, cash registers, the Department of Motor Vehicles and his medical plan ID tapes were supplemented by candid video and some zoom-ins through crowds at a surprisingly large and diverse number of events. *How did all of this information get gathered from so many disparate sources and get put together? If this is all just from legit sources, what do the Narco-Terrorists know about me and my family? What do the Homeland Security guys know? What can Omni do?*

Washington, DC
October 29th, 2012
Monday

Two more full weeks of work passed planning a computer attack on the Narco-Terrorists. Their enemies didn't hit them first. There was no word from Brother Pablo. Days started slowly and before Jack could grasp it, each day gathered speed and came to a close. Time raced through sleep and all waking until it slowed briefly at sundown each day as it paused to catch its breath.

Jack was tired. He was ready to go out in the waning day and go home. He wanted that daily break to think. The email icon flashed at his workstation. The whole time they had been working there Jack hadn't received any email until now. "Hey, Bubba, Naomi, come here and look at this!"

He steered Naomi by the elbows and pointed her away from the blinking icon.

"What's this?" asked Bubba.

"Look. This flutter. It's different…" Jack hesitated, "before at

NASA... He clicked on the icon with his mouse. The voice recognition light turned bright. The rich baritone of the software voice read the message out loud:

<<Understand you are looking for me. Many apologies. Please call me at the circulation desk where you left a message for me. Pablo>>

"What the...?" said Jack.

"Let me check the diagnostics. Who this is really." Bubba took a red disk from his white shirt and inserted it into the drive. He tapped on the keys. The whirring and humming punctuated the digital pings and tonal cadence counts. The printer kicked in across the room with column upon column of coded gibberish. The last page printed a bold, 'Brother Pablo Jesus Cervantes'.

"Pablo sure is something. I can't figure it out. Where's he been for weeks?" Jack said.

Bubba massaged his chin with one hand. He looked at Jack, then Naomi and back to Jack again. "I don't know either, son. But I suppose we should just move out and contact him and set up a meeting. Don't you?"

"Yes, let's do it. Go directly to him. Jack, where's the best place to meet him?" asked Naomi.

A long pause squatted among them. Jack said, "We should have him come to a public place where your friends, Bubba, and the UMW security guys can check it out and cover us. We should have him come over to somewhere in Arlington. Let's see if he's online now. Maybe we can get this Pablo to answer us in realware voice."

"Yes, this is Pablo. How do you do?" The voice was young, clear and precise. He had no regional accent.

"Uh, fine, thank you," said Jack.

"I'm so sorry for not staying in touch," said Pablo. "I saw that you avoided the danger in West Virginia. Just after that, I started some very serious work and lost track of the time. I forgot to call and then I misplaced the note you sent, and then I really forgot to even remember I was supposed to call. So, I'm so truly sorry. Uh, how are you doing now?"

"We're fine, thanks again. But we really need to talk. May we meet you?" asked Jack.

"Sure, I have some more things I have to do tonight, but we..."

"Not tonight we need to set up a meeting."

"Well, sure, okay."

"Could you come out to Arlington tomorrow?"

"Yes, I don't see why not, I can get our car … I am confident. That should be fine."

"Do you know Lee Highway in North Arlington?" asked Jack.

"The road near Bishop D. J. O'Connell High School?"

"Yes, do you know the intersection of George Mason and Lee Highway?"

"I think so."

"Ok, does your car have a Universal Locator?"

"Oh, yes! But, I've never had to use it, since I know the few places I go."

"Then, just hit the dialogue key. It'll get you anywhere. There's a restaurant right on the corner."

"Yes, I've stopped there after my classes. You know I teach some evenings and weekends at the High School. In fact, now that I think of it, I may have stopped there last month. Very nice salads."

"Okay. How about five o'clock tomorrow? Is that okay?" Jack mouthed, "still daylight" to Bubba and Naomi.

"Yes, I don't see why not."

"Ok, then," Jack looked at Bubba and Naomi to see if they had anything to add.

Bubba whispered, "Will he contact us tomorrow? Where? When?"

Jack nodded, "Will you be in contact tomorrow?"

"I'll email in the morning. You know we could all meet over here at Georgetown since you are in the city."

"Yeah, uh…We've been advised not to do that. We can have a security sweep out here without raising too much attention." Jack made it up as he went along.

"Oh, that might be so. How ironic here in security city, but probably true. Arlington it is then. You won't need much of a security sweep for me. But you should certainly do one for them."

"Excuse me?" asked Jack.

"They're not far from thee or me, according to my calculations. So, we should be seeing them soon enough."

"Huh?"

"Yes, Jack?"

"Uh, what do you mean we are about to see them?"

"We can chat about it at supper. We need to keep it brief right now, but my analysis indicates that the Narco-Terrorists are only one firewall from my systems. They broke through the others, so even if I create a new one, then they will breach it in very short order. I am fresh out of ideas on how to create a new firewall anti-penetration logic. So, I expect they will find me fairly soon. I'm not sure where they are with you, but I found you easily enough."

"Yeah."

"So, supper it is then. I'll see you in Arlington. Peace be with you!" said Pablo. Jack reached over and turned the phone off. He leaned back and breathed out a great breath.

Once again a long pause filled the room. They studied each other's faces. Then, as if on cue, they all smiled softly. At least they knew something definite now. The long weeks on the emotional tightrope made them a high wire trio bound to each other by need. They defied death, like circus professionals taunt gravity, with their teamwork.

Bubba spoke softly, "Pablo said they will find him fairly soon. That must mean they know where we are by now, and are choosing not to act. I wonder why and what we'll find out from Pablo."

"I wonder too. I think Pablo can explain some of the why's. Like 'why' we're targets. Really. I don't expect too much more," said Naomi.

"Yeah, but I hope he'll also tell us more about them. We need to do more than we're planning now. Our attack programs are ready, locked and cocked. Maybe we can make them better before we launch them," said Jack.

"We can't take too much time to make them too much better. Time's a-wasting, Jack. If we knew why they haven't hit at us, then we might know how much more time we really had. As it is, we only know one day at a time. We should launch as soon as we can. Like immediately, after we meet with Pablo," said Bubba. Naomi nodded her consent.

Arlington, VA
October 30th, 2012
Tuesday

The following morning broke without a care to their concerns. The condo flooded with light. The Autumn air held just a hint of extra warmth and humidity. It was a glorious day to anyone who took the time to relish it. They were too busy preparing for their meeting, finally, with Brother Pablo to notice. They drove by the restaurant to check it out closely. Bubba laughed at how easily he accessed, remotely, the security cameras in the restaurant. Also, he got into several places of business near by. The systems feed sensor readings of visual, motion, heat, smell, sound—you name it—to a local security provider. The system spilled its guts to Bubba's electronic questioning.

Before it seemed possible, Jack looked at his watch and said matter-of-factly, "Gotta load and go in five minutes." Time stopped. "I wish I had a weapon," Jack said.

"Mr. Tommy Schultz has the on-site detail," said Bubba. "Besides, my old buds will be there too. But, you won't see'em."

"I hope those two groups don't fight each other," said Naomi.

"Nah, no way, Naomi," Bubba said assuringly. "These guys are all professionals."

"So are the Narco-Terrorists," replied Jack.

"Trust in the armor of the Lord, John-James and these armored vests," Bubba smiled back as he tapped his chest.

"We'll be fine, Jack," said Naomi, "I know it." She curled her soft sweatered arm in the crook of Jack's to let him escort her to the car.

"Then, let's go," said Jack.

Their truck pulled into the parking lot at precisely 4:55 p.m. Jack walked to the restaurant. Bubba kept the engine running. Naomi sat beside Bubba and looked at the sensor display in a page size, flat panel, remote unit. It was an Army Future Combat Systems command display the UMW picked up somehow. The display had several little two inch by two inch live video inputs. A large array of icons on tool bars were color-coded, flash-coded, and alarm-coded to make any threat obvious. Jack came out of the restaurant in a few minutes and waved to Bubba and Naomi.

Jack knew this restaurant as a child, as a teen and as a young man. The building held his memories of special people, emotions, words and feelings better than any video ever could. The delicious mixture of smells took him to every moment he cared to recall with a clarity that made time disappear. The restaurant knew and felt nothing. Yet, Jack loved seeing it, just like an old friend. He had to wave away the memories to sense any danger that might await them. *I gotta focus.*

When they sat down, Naomi asked, "Is this okay? Shouldn't we wait for Pablo?" In the booth next them a Middle Eastern family, the women wearing robes and head coverings, talked loudly.

Bubba said, "We just don't know how this is gonna go. Let's order now so we can talk fast."

"There's always something, huh?" Naomi.

"Yes, ma'am," Bubba's voice warmed up. "But, the longer it takes them to figure out that all of their fish will be in one barrel, the less time they have to make a decision to act and give the right orders.

"And all that security you mentioned?" Naomi asked.

"That ma'am, is as good as it ever gets against these Narco-Islamist-Terrorist guys. We just have to go with what we have," Bubba replied.

"Okay," said Naomi.

Bubba looked up as the waitress walked over to take their order and saw a young man taking a long look around. He was modestly dressed and about 30 years old. His black hair was parted neatly with one thick shock falling to the center of his forehead. His brown eyes looked warm and intelligent, even at a distance, as he searched the room. A bright white clerical collar accented his brown skinned neck. When Bubba stood up, the man gave a flash of recognition and smiled broadly. Brother Pablo Jesus Cervantes walked over and extended his hand over the table to Bubba.

"Peace be with you," Pablo smiled sincerely. The anachronistic greeting seemed so modern and natural.

"Hello," Bubba stammered, "finally." He gave quick introductions. Each person around the table held the other in their eyes for a few seconds. Pablo scooted in between Bubba and Naomi. He murmured a prayer below hearing, crossed himself and bathed each person again with his warm eyes.

After they ordered their food, Bubba softly recounted their story from the blow up of Jack's office at Langley. "Uh," Jack started to interject, but Bubba flicked his fingers up in a half wave and continued. He was far more precise than usual and left out his usual attempts at humor. *I wonder how long Bubba practiced this? Odd way to say 'hello'.* Pablo nodded and smiled as Bubba spoke.

Bubba paused as he started to get into the technical details of where they were heading in their work.

"I'm sure that we have many questions of each other," said Pablo, "but first, I must apologize for how intermittent and inconsistent my contact was." They stared back blankly. "It's a weak excuse, no, it's no excuse, but when I get into my research it is like I go into a cave." His smile was full of satisfaction. "Actually, it is a cave of sorts, my study alcove could be called a grotto. It's so far underground in the stacks of the library." His voice projected a slight nasal hollowness and his speech played the polished precise tones of a very well educated man. "You know I found you while I was doing my research. It was all quite by accident."

Everyone perked up a bit more.

Pablo continued, "I was working on symbols of the Renaissance. You know, I was taken by the image of the cinquefoil and was intrigued to find its use in modern iconic computer code. Well, that is when a number of interesting things happened."

"Excuse me, what is a 'sink—foil'?" interrupted Jack.

"Oh, it's a design of five joined foils." Pablo pulled a pen from his pocket and drew on a paper napkin. "It dates to the 14th Century. It comes from the French, and before that, Latin for five leaves. Today, of course, it's the name of a genus of herbs and shrubs of the rose family with five-lobed leaves and five-petaled flowers." Pablo drew five small clockwise circles. Together, the five leaves created the overall shape of a circle. It looked like a five-leafed clover. He added a thin-lined circle around the five leaves to enclose them. He made another circle to surround it all. His hand was steady as he drew the rose foils with slight flourishes.

"I found several cinquefoil icons in some very incongruous places on government Web sites. There was one at NASA Langley," Pablo smiled knowingly at Jack and Bubba, "that took me to the computer security directorate and some odd documents." He winked at Naomi. "You wouldn't believe how many also connected to the DARPA Cyberspace Network Operations Center[5]."

"I thought that Center was in the Pentagon. It's Department of Defense," said Jack.

"It's in the Pentagon and its DARPA and DoD," said Pablo.

"I found the cinquefoils in late May. Since then, they have changed substantially. They changed in their locations and in the content."

"Content?" Bubba hung on every word.

"Yes, contextually and substantively, the cinquefoil icon is quite different. Actually, the cinquefoils went away. They disappeared for about a month or two. In August they started popping up like mushrooms. But they don't do the same things," Pablo paused to eat a bite.

"What're they doing? And what did you say about the cinquefoil and roses?" Jack asked.

Pablo smiled indulgently. He set down his fork and pushed away his plate. "The cinquefoil icon was color-coded when I first noticed them. They were hypertext icons, but they weren't all blue like normal hypertext. Regardless of color, the icon would zap like regular hypertext and jump across the World Wide Web. It was remarkable. You would be amazed, really, at what happened and how it happened when you tried to access one of the icons. You would double-click on the icon and then you would be skimming through all sorts of links of no rhyme or reason that I could figure out. Then you were dumped in an almost empty Web site. Each Web site was different. Each had very little information on it."

"What kind of things where there? What did they look like?" asked Naomi taking a bite of her salad.

"Well, each Web site had background graphics that were the

---

5. DARPA Cyberspace Network Operations Center. The Defense Advanced Research Projects Administration, DARPA, co-sponsored with the Department of Defense (DoD) the project, initially, to use the Carnivore System to gather, collect and interpret data as part of the Total Information Awareness to counter terrorism.

color of the cinquefoil. The backgrounds were all different, red brick, white parchment, green marble, whatever. The text, as I said, was sparse. It really looked like a lot of controller code. And each site had a huge set of hyperlinks. Most of the links went to databases. The controller code looked like the execute files for many, many programs."

"Did the cinquefoils look like real roses or," Jack motioned to the napkin drawing, "like these rounded circles?" Jack asked.

"They looked like the stylized cinquefoils. But many of the commands at the Web site had colored roses in the execution files."

Jack snorted. His checks pulled his tightly pressed lips into a thin smile, "The roses, Bubba, the roses. We *knew* there was a connection."

Bubba nodded, "Yup, Pablo, we knew there was something to those rose words we kept findin' in the code. But what do you think these Web sites were supposed to do?

"I'm not sure," Pablo paused like it was awkward for him to speak the name, 'Bubba'. "I think the Web sites were the locations of a lot of beta code. This was the test model for something really big. You should see the execution instructions and the database links, and the routing and security files."

"*Was* the test model?" asked Jack.

"Yes. I downloaded everything I could in May and early June. Habit of mine, you know, to just download and look at it later. Research paranoia I suppose," Pablo grinned shyly. "But, as I said, in July the cinquefoils disappeared. When they came back, they weren't in the same places. Also, when you double-clicked on them almost nothing happened. You went to some place wholly in keeping with the subject matter. No more mad dashes across cyberspace. And, definitely, no more Web sites related to the colored cinquefoils."

"When can we see what you have?" pressed Jack.

"Now, sure," said Pablo, "we could do that now. I recommend that you come to Georgetown to the library."

"Could you bring it to another office in DC?" asked Jack.

"Hmmm, no, I don't think that would work unless you have terrific capacity, like the library. You need something huge."

They looked at him blankly.

"You see, when you reach a Web site and do anything, even

scroll the page, let alone open an execution file, the code starts to expand."

They stared with disbelief.

"I'm not kidding. Once you enter the Web site, it starts working. Hypertext starts to print on the page and it goes on and on and on. It's all hypertext too. Not a word of normal print. The Web site spews out this hypertext prose like a random number generator with a fast printer can punch out digits."

"Wow!" said Jack.

"Then, windows of information start popping open and close. It's like watching something out of control, but very creative. It's visually impressive."

"So, what is it then?" asked Naomi.

Pablo's face tightened. For the first time he looked up and around at his surroundings. He lowered his voice to a conspiratorial whisper, "I think it's the code that controls a lot of different programs. It reaches more programs than you can imagine. I think it is meant to put together something really very important and secret."

"For the Narco-Terrorists?" Naomi winced.

"No, about the Narco-Terrorists," Pablo kept his voice low. "Have you seen references to 'Ishmael'? The NTs really want to know about the cinquefoils and this guy Ishmael, if there is such a person. That is why they are after you. The Homeland Security Office is looking for you too."

"They think we know? I thought Ishmael was a NT, an Islamist for sure," said Bubba.

"They don't know what you know, but they want to find out."

"Ah," Jack looked sad, "That's why they haven't killed us yet."

"Do they know about you, Pablo?' asked Naomi.

"I think that they are trying to get to anyone and everyone who's been checking the rose cinquefoils. But, they don't know it is me, yet. Regardless of that, there is another issue with this Ishmael character."

Suddenly, big flush-faced Tommy Schultz barreled in, "Time to go folks. C'mon with me." He waved brusquely. The urgency in his eyes added to his out of breath sternness.

"Pablo, come with us," said Naomi.

"I've got a guy for him," said Tommy.

"We'll leave a message for you at the library to meet us in town tomorrow."

Bubba quickly shook Pablo's hand. Jack turned to escort Naomi. She impulsively grabbed his hand. The trio rushed out of the restaurant behind Tommy.

Once they were in the truck and speeding away, Naomi looked down at the sensor board in Jack's lap. It blazed in flashing colors. A couple of black sports vehicles roared past them going the opposite way on Lee Highway. She shivered and pushed back into the seat.

Jack listened through the chatter of broken messages. He hunched his shoulders forward, leaning almost to tipping over and stared hard ahead. "Turn left," Jack gave directions curtly through the hours it took the rabbit to lose the hounds.

Arlington, VA
October 31st, 2012
Wednesday

At breakfast the trio agreed to press on with their work. Last night was too much, too fast, to assess. They saw nothing else to do, except to hide in the closets and cringe. The pressing question on everyone's mind was what did Pablo know and how could they use it in their own cyber war attack. They agreed the earliest date they could launch their D-Day, or E-Day, as Bubba preferred, was November 6th. They would hit the Narco-Terrorists as hard as they could the day after the election of 2012. So be it.

They called Pablo at his library carole as soon as they got to work. He agreed to come right over to the UMW, but insisted on gathering everything he had on the cinquefoils before catching the Metro.

Bubba paced like a caged animal.

"What's wrong, Mr. Holland?" Jack asked.

Bubba gave him a quick sideways glance. Even in that split second, his blue eyes pierced, "Nothing, really, I'm trying to sort out this fellow Pablo."

"What're you having second thoughts about?" Naomi offered.

"Know it, just can't say it yet, ma'am. Sometimes my understanding of something is on the tip of my tongue and if I can just wrap my brain around it tight enough, the words will drip down to my lips. If I can say the thought, then I understand it and it's mine."

"Uh-huh, sort of like what happens when I smell freshly baked chocolate chip cookies and start salivating?" Jack deadpanned.

"I know what you mean," said Naomi.

"If I can say the thought, I understand it and then I own the idea," said Bubba as he looked up at the ceiling not hearing anyone, "or the feeling. I almost have Pablo."

"Have?" asked Jack.

"Hmm," said Naomi.

"First, Pablo is on our side. Second, Pablo is sincerely one of us, a believing Christian," Bubba started slowly.

One of us Christians? I'm one of us? Jack listened carefully.

"Third, Pablo is an intellectual. He really is one, not a pretender or a pseudo-intellectual. He lives in a different world in his mind. Fourth, Pablo is going to lead us to things he doesn't even know about. He knows more than he comprehends."

"What?" asked Jack.

"He hasn't put it all together yet, but he has enough disparate and different data to fill a lot of holes in the tapestry we've been trying to see."

"Tapestry?" smiled Naomi.

"Poetic, huh?" Bubba's eyes blazed when he let the love emit from them. "Yeah, Pablo is going to help us solve the puzzle or most of it at least. Puzzle, tapestry, whatever."

"How do you know all of this stuff? We just met the guy," asked Jack.

"I'm an old man. I'm a wise old man," Bubba chortled softly.

"You have the gift of discernment, don't you?" asked Naomi.

"No, I don't have spiritual discernment. Few do and mostly it's women. I just know people, especially men, well enough to figure things out," said Bubba.

"Hope you're right about Pablo," said Jack.

"Right about which part?" teased Bubba.

"Solving the puzzle, completing the tapestry, answering the mail, cutting the Gordian knot, tickling the itch," Jack laughed, "making my day, floating our boat…"

"I'm right about all the parts," said Bubba. "I got Pablo right."

"Hope you do. Hope you do," said Jack.

"I know you do," Naomi patted Bubba on the back.

The yellow 'door opening' warning lights flashed. Pablo entered. "I am so glad you are all okay!" Pablo was exuberant.

"Glad you could make it," said Bubba, "We're sorry that our supper was interrupted last night. Did they take care of you all right?"

"Oh yes, that," said Pablo, "I was fine. They hustled me out and escorted me over to the High School and then home. I never thought I'd rate a motorcade."

"We really look forward to spending some time together. Glad you could make it today," said Jack.

"Yes, we're so glad that you're with us," said Naomi.

The coffee was poured all around as they took seats at a conference table to chat. Jack brought his ubiquitous writing pad and pen.

"Cinquefoils," said Bubba expectantly.

"*Bien sur*," smiled Pablo. He took a cleansing deep breath. "The cinquefoils are icons for macro instructions to beat all macros you have ever seen in your life."

All eyes widened.

Pablo continued, "Most macros, as you know, are the grouped instructions for common and repetitive tasks, but these macros act as controllers. A single macro activates start or stop commands."

"The rose messages?" Jack interrupted.

"Yes, exactly! The rose messages are embedded in the rose cinquefoils. Artistic, don't you think?" Pablo asked rhetorically. "Moreover, it looks like these rose messages reach every system everywhere."

"Everywhere?" asked Naomi.

"Yes," said Pablo.

"No way," said Jack. "Literally everywhere, meaning every communications node, every computer system on the Internet of the World Wide Web, and every system that uses commercial or government communications, is billions upon billions of places."

"Everywhere," nodded Pablo to the affirmative.

"No way," repeated Jack.

"Yes, way. Everywhere. And the cinquefoils are specifically tailored to interoperate with the omni-code for the new Omni computer."

"How do you know that?" asked Bubba.

"It's common knowledge that the Omni is supposed to come on line in April 2013. All the politicians are fussing about it in this election," replied Pablo. "The Omnivore makes the old Carnivore[6] system look primitive."

Bubba interrupted, "It's a state of the art optical computer with an unprecedented ability to cross-index, query, evaluate and package information for presentation. It makes the Narco-Terrorists vulnerable. It makes citizens, everyone, transparent to government. Information that was too tough to collect, collate and evaluate will be nano-seconds away from the forces of the government. Financial dealings, anywhere, will be cross-referenced to communications from all media, anywhere, to physical movements of persons and things, anywhere. Money laundering will be almost impossible. Nothing can be hidden. No one can hide either. But, it's the speed that is so decisive."

"Bubba, you never told me how much you know. Holding back? Why?" asked Jack.

"Time and place for everything, Jack. Everything," said Bubba.

"It makes me nervous," said Naomi. "I actually agree with the civil liberty Liberals, Libertarians and hard core Conservatives that the Omni will have too much capability. It might be the Omnivore for data management. But, it could be used by a one world government to enslave the People."

"Omni code is backwards compatible to speak to other systems, but will not respond to anything but Omni instructions. That is why these cinquefoils are so important," said Pablo.

"Congress shrouded the Omni in the special security language of the appropriations for Homeland Security. The Act specified severe limitations of executive oversight of the details for the Omni," said Bubba.

---

6. Carnivore System was designed by the Federal government at the turn of the century to improve information sharing across Federal agencies. It was un-funded and stopped in mid-development because of civil liberty concerns from Liberals and Conservatives alike.

"Let me show you something," Pablo pulled a disk from his pocket.

Jack showed him to the machine where he saw the 'butterfly wings'. As Pablo sat down, they drew up chairs in a semi-circle around him.

Pablo inserted the long thin plastic disk that looked like a confectionary's wafer to go with coffee. He gave a tentative click on the mouse and looked at what screen came up. He lifted his chin and looked down his nose like an older man with fading near vision perusing a new book. He performed a couple of perfunctory security checks after Jack gave him the log-on codes for the stand-alone system, the local network and the worldwide access server.

"Ok, then watch closely, my friends," Pablo said. The gentle word 'friends' came out naturally. "Let's scan this network we are on right now to see if we can find *une jolie cinquefoil*." Pablo's long fingers floated across the keyboard.

"First, we go to the UMW security system for this local area network's server connection to the outside world. Aha, we see our way blocked," said Pablo. The screen blinked back unmoved. A warning message flashed as a trailer across the bottom of the monitor.

"Hmmm, if we note the address for the security program on our network and return to our system for a second," Pablo worked so deftly the screens open and closed almost as fast as the eye could ascertain their image.

"And, we take a message from our email and put a cinquefoil icon from my handy dandy disk in the header, hmmm, right about here," Pablo paced his speech to synchronize himself with what happened on the monitor. "Then, we re-launch this innocent little email with our icon stuck in the routing address of the header. And, *voila!*" He leaned back in his chair and extended his slender arm full length to point to the monitor. Something very odd took place.

Screen after screen popped open like frantic parachutes. Quickly, the computer multi-tasked itself to splash over a hundred screens open. Each screen showed a cinquefoil icon blinking on the address line.

"The security program for the UMW. Your home system castle keep is right here."

"I still don't get it," said Bubba.

"The cinquefoil is inserted into all of these programs or the cinquefoil opens all of these programs?" Naomi asked.

"Both, huh, Pablo?" nodded Jack.

"Both," said Pablo. "The cinquefoil was inserted first. I don't know exactly how that happened frankly. I don't know—yet—that is. But, I believe that after the cinquefoil is inserted then a follow on cinquefoil comes in and gives instructions. The first is to open everything up."

"Instructions? How do you know there are more than one?" asked Naomi.

"I find that there is a dynamic of change operating. I can print the screen as is and print the code level underlying it and I'll find that a few minutes later it is different."

"How different?" asked Bubba.

"Different at different times. It's hard to explain. At the minimum there is a counter that is part of the cinquefoil embedded in the host program," said Pablo.

"So, someone knows how many times the cinquefoil is activated," surmised Jack.

"I think so and more. When I said dynamic, I meant that I find that the cinquefoil is doing things on its own. It's giving instructions. It's moving data and passing it on."

"It's not a virus, then. Have you read the code level file for a cinquefoil?" added Naomi.

"No," Pablo looked chagrined. "It's written in something I've never seen. That's why I think it's Omni Code. I didn't get to look long enough before it just vanished. When I tried to read the code under the icon, I never get it long enough to print. It opens and—poof—is gone. Just like that," Pablo's chagrin turned wry. "The speed of light is fairly fast but I saw something. It just wouldn't print."

"You've figured out something, Pablo. Congratulations," Jack smiled. "You've figured out that someone, using new, perhaps impenetrable code, created an icon that embeds in programs and then acts in programs surreptitiously. Also, that icon might just be able to get into every computer it can reach in the entire world. That's really something. Hooah!"

"Who do you think it is? Doing this?" asked Bubba.

"As I said before, it isn't just the Narco-Terrorists," said Pablo. "They're trying to figure it out. Actually, they are trying to kill it. No, it's not those bad guys." He looked wistfully at the screen again. "I think it is this Ishmael character. You know the 'Ish sends' stuff in messages. Maybe, it's an intelligence agency or some part of Homeland Security."

"Which one?" asked Bubba.

"I don't know. But I've got a lot of information stored on this," Pablo said as he retrieved his disk.

"Some storage, Pablo. There's a terabit of data in every cubic centimeter," Bubba edged closer to look at the wafer disk.

"Yeah, this puppy has its own internal chip. It's a one micron job," Jack added.

"What does the chip on a data disk do?" asked Naomi.

"Anything you want it to do. Most chips manage the data storage and retrieval on the disk itself. You can use them to run the disk like a message center instead of acting like a shelf of dead books," explained Bubba.

"I read about them at the trade Web sites, but I hadn't seen one yet," said Naomi.

"I really must get back," said Pablo.

"But we haven't gotten anywhere yet," said Jack.

"You know more about the cinquefoils than any other living person, I'll bet," said Pablo. "That is, if I were a betting man, which I'm not."

"Why must you go?" asked Bubba kindly.

"I have a research deadline to meet," said Pablo. "It has nothing to do with this."

"What should we do?" asked Jack.

"I copied my cinquefoils into your machine. Actually, your machine made a copy without my permission when I booted my disk. You can work with the cinquefoils for awhile. I think there is enough for a few days," said Pablo.

"A few days? Then what?" asked Jack.

"The election! Who wins really matters for the Omni project!" interjected Bubba. "Right, Pablo?"

"Yes, that is my thought," replied Pablo.

"So much for our plan," said Jack.

"We'll be better prepared. What does a few days more matter?" asked Naomi.

"The Narco-Terrorists are looking for us hard. Everybody's looking. That's what matters," said Jack. "They're probably looking harder than the government guys."

They made their farewells. The group of three puttered tentatively with the cinquefoils on Jack's computer for the rest of the day. Eventually, they decided to call it a day and went home resigned to their usual routine.

Arlington, VA
November 3rd, 2012
Saturday

Thursday and Friday consumed themselves in the detailed work preparing the cyber-attack. Jack found a way to attach their attack viruses to the cinquefoils. Perhaps they really could hit every information system, PC, communications device, and bit of financial data the Narco-Terrorists touched. If the cinquefoils did the target identification right, it might just work.

Jack didn't want to take a break on the weekend, but Bubba and Naomi insisted. *Maybe they figured out something in their prayer sessions.* Saturday was a day of bright crispness. It was one of the several prototypical November kinds of day that frequent the East Coast each year. The blue-sky contrasted with the browning gold of a harvested cornfield for a hunting dog calendar photo shoot. Jack was restless. When it became too much for him, he went out for a walk despite Bubba and Naomi's protests. Next door, Tommy hustled to get some guys on a roving area surveillance.

Jack walked to tire his anxieties. He turned his face to the wind and let the air lift his forelock and flop it back and forth across his forehead. As he walked on and on, he felt a building energy. He began to exult in his body. His legs felt strong. His arms swung loosely like an athlete's limbs. *Good.* His heart pumped hard but didn't pound. He felt no flutters, no tightness, no queasiness, no hateful weakness anywhere in his body.

The trees were loud with their tossing 'shush' and rustle. The leaves and limbs collided rapturously as the correct accompaniment to the autumn wind. He looked up at the absolutely cloudless sky. *Can I talk to You, God?* Jack paused as he pondered the answer to his own question. *Nah.* The palette of blue sky blended its blues from pale baby blue, Infantry blue, on the horizon to the deepest of blues directly overhead. Beyond was the blackness of space. *Could anyone capture these colors—this moment?* Much as he wanted to write, and for his writing to matter, he knew his words could never box this beauty on a page of paper.

I want more days like this. He felt like a stallion prancing and snorting great frosty breaths across an open field.

They can try to kill me now. Come on, monsters. I'm ready to fight. He wished he could share his courage with a woman. *But not Maude.* She would just find something to criticize or mock. Sad, pathetic Maude who couldn't love beyond herself except in short, fleeting moments.

He felt wild enough to risk his life in the next second of his being with nothing to fear or care about except the next step forward. Maybe it was like the imaginary leap from his ship to the rigging of pirate vessel with cutlass and pistol in hand. *Ah, my friends, the shows in my mind.* Jack looked at the blue sky again and again. He wanted to drink it in and never turn away from its beauty and power.

He would make this his defining moment. *From this moment on, I fear not.*

Bubba and Naomi seemed so grateful to see him return. Jack didn't let his natural shyness get in the way of his thirst for drinking up their attention. They had a wonderful meal ready for an early evening repast. He felt how really chilled his face and hands were as he pulled off his sweater. The house was warmed a bit beyond comfortable, as Bubba liked it. It felt so cozy to come 'home' to this condo and be greeted with such enthusiasm.

When Jack sat down he noticed that Bubba and Naomi looked like they were going to explode with excitement. It was like his parents and sisters used to be on his birthday when they were thrilled with the presents they would give him after supper.

"What's up you all?" Jack dragged out the 'you all' to mock it.

"You go ahead, Mr. Holland," Naomi giggled.

"Okay dokay," Bubba's eyes twinkled. "We're going to win John-James. We're going to win!"

"Huh, win what?" asked Jack.

"The election! We're going to win. Yee-hah!" Bubba reached over and slapped Jack on the back like a teammate.

"Praise the Lord Almighty!" said Naomi.

"How do you know?" Jack reverted to kind. Analysis first, emotions maybe later.

"The polls are breaking our way," said Bubba. "And we just know. There's an arising. They can't cheat their way to win this one."

"I thought you were down by five," Jack countered. "You said Hillary'd cheat enough to win."

"We were down," Naomi shivered with excitement. "But the shift is moving and the break on undecided is going our way three to one. Or better. She can't cheat enough on this one. It'll be even better, way better, than 2004."

"A lot could happen between now and Tuesday," said Jack.

"Yeah, we could get even more votes!" said Bubba, "And make it a landslide. Let's eat!"

They are really happy. Wow. All together they watched political news until much too late in the night. They lingered past the call of fatigue, because it was so nice to share the space and time in that room together. Leaving was like getting up from a warm fire on a cold night in the woods. It's so hard to pull oneself away from the warmth to go out into the cold even if a warmer sleeping bag beacons.

Arlington, VA
November 5th, 2012
Monday

Monday broke grayer than Sunday. Yet, Bubba and Naomi were perky all day. Jack grappled with too many important things to think clearly. He preferred to consider just one issue at a time that seemed big enough to wrestle. Today was cinquefoils. Jack kept the thought with him during the day as he went about his daily business and returned to the thought whenever he had time for it. Jack kept his highest thinking on things—one at a time—which really interested him. The day passed in small, hurried events that distracted him from what he wanted to concentrate on.

This election eve their candidate, Maggie, ran a last minute nation-wide appeal live in primetime. The program opened in her living room. The screen subtitle ran 'Falls Church, Virginia'.

"Hey, that's right near here!" hooted Bubba.

"Just up Lee Highway," said Jack.

"Shhh!" said Naomi. She set a tray down on the coffee table. Three bowls of steaming, hot apple cobbler and vanilla ice cream beckoned.

The TV showed a room filled elbow to elbow with her family and key supporters. Maggie Kyle began, "My fellow Americans," and her eyes sparkled as genuine loving kindness brightened her face. The cadence of her voice started softly, but ever so slightly picked up a rhythm of resounding emphasis.

"Every politician tells you that every election is about life and death. And, of course it is about life and death—of the politician if he or she wins or losses. But elections are rarely about life or death, peace or war, feast or famine. Elections are usually tacks on the wind for the ship of state to move left or right a bit from the steady course being directed by the winds of change."

"Yet, I stand here before you to say this election is an epochal choice," Maggie's pause was pregnant.

"Tomorrow's election is a vote between peace and war. If I am elected, the United States of America will go to war against the Narco-Terrorists. The United States will open a new front against the Islamists. Illegal immigration will stop. Period. We will establish, maintain, and control our borders. We will be sovereigns of our own state," Maggie's sharp look pierced the camera.

"The so-called War on Drugs has been a sham for over forty years. The open border for illegal immigration is an open highway for illegal drugs. The War on Islamist Terrorists has sputtered for four years. This administration is abusing the Patriot Acts to persecute political rivals and opposing, very ordinary, citizens. It will all stop. Elect me and we will actually wage a war, a war without surrender, a war without end until the scourge of drug abuse, terror, crime and political oppression is over. Destroying the Narco-Terrorists and hunting the Islamist terrorists go hand in hand. D-Day for the American People is tomorrow at the polls."

The commentators started sputtering, interrupting her closing.

Naomi said, "Listen to them. That's why I don't think much of politics. It's dirty business. But, Maggie'll do right."

"So what is the UMW if not political? Isn't that why the UMW has offices up here, to play politics?" asked Jack.

"Yes sir," said Naomi, "Unions have to be in politics because that's where the power is. The power is necessary to help the miner— the little guy and his family. The dirty politics is when someone is after the money."

"I think it all becomes the same," said Jack.

"It has in the past," Naomi nodded as she finished a bite full of cobbler. "But, again that's the point. If you're corrupt, then you're corrupt. It's still important that men and we women of good will work for the little guy. They need to stick together or get it stuck to them."

"So, they're another interest group."

"You wouldn't say that if you were from West Virginia. There's powerful reasons why people joined the unions," said Naomi.

"She's right. My great-grandfather joined the railroad union for the same powerful reasons," agreed Bubba.

"Gotcha. Politics for a noble reason is less political," said Jack.

"No, John-James, if you wrestle with a pig, then you both get muddy and the pig loves it. Politics is for pigs. It's up to the people," Bubba gestured with his spoon as he swallowed, "and the unions to butcher a pig now and then. Hah!"

"So the whole nation of the people are going to join us soon? Hope it's soon enough."

"Me too. But, it won't be the whole nation. Maybe fifty-two or fifty-three per cent. Legal votes out of the whole mess will be over fifty, but not by much," said Bubba.

"I wish I could vote tomorrow," said Naomi.

"Me, too," said Bubba.

That night, as Jack lay waiting for sleep to carry him away, the thoughts of dying and death and the possibility of violent death the next day came back again to take away his breath. As he lay on his stomach with his head turned and an arm crooked to hold the pillow, he felt the anxiety and fear and frustration boil threw him. *I'm still afraid.* Breathing deeply, he dressed and went downstairs to watch some mind-numbing TV until he fell asleep without thinking.

Washington, DC
November 6th, 2012
Tuesday

Election day dawned with the promise of showers, but teased as to the exact hour of rainfall. The grey cloud shadows of darkness and patches of light inter-played like a fast moving puzzle overhead. The air was so humid it smelled fetid. Stiff breezes promised to purge it. During the day they watched the news from their work area with awe. Early returns placed Maggie out front and pulling away. The trio worked late into the dark of night half-listening to the TV droning.

They were in good spirits when they trudged around the corner into the gated parking lot for the condo. Jack noticed that the front door to Tommy Schultze's place was open and the light was on as well. A step further showed him that the front door to their place was open and the light was on. *Something's wrong.* Jack stopped and elbowed Bubba. Bubba reached for Naomi's sleeve and stopped her. He nodded towards the open doors. Jack felt the sudden rush of alertness that he experienced when his computer blew up at NASA-Langley. Their escort scooted ahead.

"Bubba, take Naomi and see if the truck is secure. Start the engine and let Naomi take the wheel. I'm going into Tommy's place first," said Jack.

"Gotcha," Bubba said taking Naomi's hand. As Jack reached the stairs, two men bounded past him from around the corner. A young man and a heavy-set middle age man brushed his shoulders. He got a glimpse of their anxious faces. The younger one had a weapon drawn at the ready, while the older man kept a hand stuck inside his trench coat. *Tommy's security guys*.

When Jack stepped into the doorway, he saw a huge blood stain on the wall. It looked like a full can of red paint splattered against the wall. Just to the side of the dripping spray, Mrs. Schultze's body lay on her side at odd angles like a broken doll.

The middle-aged security guy was in the dining room shouting into his cell phone, "Authenticate my butt! This report isn't bogus. I'm at Tommy's right now! We got two dead. Mrs. Schultze and Tommy's boy, Frank."

"Tommy's here! He's dead too," came a shout from upstairs.

Jack looked at the bloody pulp of a dog lying on the carpet in front of him. *They killed the whole family.* Jack shivered. He walked up the stairs to see Tommy for himself.

He looked in the teenaged boy's room. The young boy lay face down on the bed. Jack didn't want to see his face.

Tommy's body was sprawled out in the third floor bathroom. His weapon was on the floor beside him. His head, or what was left of it, was in the tub. Jack froze looking at the horror.

"I'll get them for this!" the young guy said through clenched teeth. He cursed again. Jack found himself downstairs where the older security agent kept yelling for back up. Jack headed to his own condo. Jack was well into the living room before his mind cleared with the cold wind of fear. He realized that he was alone and unarmed. The place was wrecked. Every computer and appliance was gone. *Anything with a computer chip in it is gone.*

Naomi honked the truck horn. Jack ran out.

"Go, go, go," urged Jack.

"Where to?" asked Naomi.

"DC. Head towards downtown," said Jack in hard breaths. "Bubba, do you have your phone?"

"Sure. Here."

"See if you can get Pablo," said Jack.

"This isn't secure."

"It doesn't matter now."

"Hello?" Pablo answered with a tone of distraction.

"Pablo, this is Bubba," Bubba spoke fast. "They hit our place and killed Tommy Schultze and his family."

"Tommy? Oh, no! Are you all right?" asked Pablo.

"We're okay. But, we're coming to your place," said Bubba.

"We think they're looking for a chip or disk," said Jack to Bubba. Bubba repeated the message like an agitated robot to Pablo.

Jack grabbed the communicator from Bubba.

"They may be coming for you now. We're gonna help you get away. Take whatever you have on the cinquefoils and get it on disks," Jack stated his conclusions as facts. Bubba and Naomi nodded as he spoke.

"Okay. Come into the main entrance of Launinger Library at Georgetown and take the elevator down to the stacks. I'm on level sub-five. They're four study carrels here. I'll be in the only one lighted. You will see. Bye."

Washington, DC
November 6th, 2012
Tuesday

The security officer at the library entrance waited with passes for them. Courtesy of Brother Pablo. The guard amicably pointed out the elevator to them. As they walked to the middle of the room, a reference computer on a table near the elevator suddenly exploded in a brilliant cone of flame and plastic and bits of metal. They were too far away to be hit by debris, but the blast shocked them. Then another reference computer exploded, and another. As the guard ducked down behind his desk, his computer blew up. A low moaning came from behind the desk. The few students on the main floor on this election night fell prostrate on the floor in silence. Some cringed under desks screaming. Jack reached for Naomi's hand and moved forward towards the elevator in a crouch like a combat infantryman in battle. Bubba crouched, too, and moved at his side breathing very heavily. In the long seconds it took the elevator doors to open, every last computer on the floor exploded. Smoke filled the room.

Naomi stopped at the elevator doors and said, "There's fire in the stairwell, too."

"Not a normal fire. We'll be okay. We gotta get Pablo outta here," Jack gasped.

The elevator descended for an eternity in those few seconds. Jack lunged out towards the light shining from a carrel door. The door was locked. Jack banged on the thin metal with his fist. The clanging of the metal door rattling its metal cage echoed through the dark floor of the library stacks.

Pablo opened the door and returned to his computer. The study carrel was a twelve by twelve room that could have been roomy enough for one person to spread out books and papers. Pablo jammed it so full of books and stacks of papers that it looked like a stuffed box. Three computers sat silently with their large screen luminescent eyes blinking as they worked. Some scenic posters of California, Mexico and Italy were taped onto the edges of the dry marker whiteboards covered with Pablo's scribbles.

"I am trying to download what I can. Are you okay?" asked Pablo.

"Unplug!" urged Jack. "The computers are exploding upstairs just like they did at NASA." He looked hard at Pablo, "They must know you're here. They could be here any minute. We gotta go, Pablo."

"I'll be just a second. I need to send my research to a back up. And I'm downloading a directory of locations where I have my private information. I need to add some stuff to the cinquefoils I have here." Pablo patted the photonic disk in his shirt pocket. "My computers won't blow up, Jack."

"Your computers could explode now," insisted Jack.

"It will not be long. I promise. If they were going to blow, they would have blown up by now. Don't you see?"

"Do you know where we could go?" asked Bubba.

Suddenly, loud footsteps on the concrete floor pounded towards them. They looked at the unlocked door just as it burst open. A man followed through his kick against the door to a squatting combat ready position. The targeting red laser of his automatic weapon played across each of their foreheads in turn. His face was covered in black combat masking gauze. His Kevlar helmet, body armor, uniform and boots were black. He moved to one side. Another black combatant stepped in front of him.

"Come with me," he commanded.

They stood staring.

"Come with me, now!" he growled. He expertly reached and grabbed the back of Jack's collar. Before Jack could twitch a muscle, he was pulled up and forward. He was shoved along in front of the combatant and hustled towards the stairs. Other men quickly stepped in and grabbed Pablo, Bubba and Naomi in turn to brusquely move them along.

"Who are you?" asked Pablo.

"Shut up," said the big man in a black helmet.

The men hustled them up the stairs to the third sub-basement stack. As they went down a long, dimly lit hallway, Jack tried to grasp what was happening. He couldn't think to sort out anything.

No, no, this is too fast. No, no, please, no, please, this can't be it.

Two more armed men flung open the door ahead of them. A black van waited with the side door open in the underground garage. Their armed escorts pushed down on their heads and dumped them into the van. The rear compartment was closed from the driver. Two more armed figures sat waiting inside. The door slammed shut. Someone rapped twice on the door and the van lurched away fast.

"Be quiet," said one of the armed men.

Jack sensed Naomi's body trembling next to him. He reached for her hand in the darkness. She grabbed his hand with both of hers and held tightly. The van sped through the night.

Chapter 3. Plan

Washington, DC
November 6th, 2012
Tuesday

The van raced through the night, tumbling Jack against Naomi with each abrupt turn. *Oh God! Oh, God! Oh, God save me!* Jack's heart pounded.

Finally, the van fairly stood on its head screeching to stop. The second everyone whiplashed back into their seats, the van door slammed open. An armed man leaned in and said, "Let's go folks. Please continue to be silent. It's real important." He wasn't wearing a face gauze. Jack looked into his eyes for a dead soulness. The man's eyes were an alert green. The warrior looked relieved.

More armed men escorted them through the parking garage. The bare walls kept the building location nameless. The group dared to make eye contact. Their eyes screamed at one another.

They passed through two security entrances with the works: visface, hand scanners, firing ports for security personnel, ubiquitous cameras, you name it. They ended up at a door labeled 'Director' and waited. The silence became uncomfortable. A light above the door flashed yellow then green. The door opened from the inside. They entered a small conference room. It was starkly decorated with a very large table dominating the room. The door closed and high security interior locks whirred and clanged shut behind them. A lone pole light provided the indirect lighting for a man in a dress shirt and tie seated at the far head of the conference table. His blackness provided all the more contrast to his bright white shirt. His hair was short, receding in the front and gray on the sides. His tortoise shell half-frame reading glasses looked professorial.

"Call me Ishmael," the man said in a deep gravely voice. He waited a second, then two for the words to fly to the other end of the room, alight on the four anxious people standing there and sink in. Then, his smile worked his lips apart and spread across his face. He approached with an arm outstretched from a well-muscled shoulder. He was six feet tall, but he looked bigger.

"Ishmael Ali Akbar Shabazz. Mrs. Tolley," He shook her hand. "Mr. Holland. Mr. Tillman. Brother Cervantes." His handshake was strong.

Jack watched Ishmael size everyone up. Ishmael was so black his skin looked purple black. *This guy isn't an Islamist. Whoever he is, he's testing our reactions to his blackness. Seen that before.*

"You may wonder why I have called this meeting," said Ishmael with a long pause for effect. "Seriously, I'm sure you have many questions. Let me to tell you what has happened, give you a briefing on what we're doing, and then let's chat about what we need to do."

"First, I know you are in shock about the Schulze family. I deeply regret that we weren't able to prevent that tragedy. We were moving to pick you up, believe it or not, and the bad guys hit before we could get there. I am really, truly sorry. I apologize for putting you through this questioning now, at this time, but we can't wait until morning."

"We are the Drug Enforcement Agency. The DEA. I'm the Director of Futures for the DEA. Our work on a project of national significance, which is highly classified, lead us to you," Ishmael paused. Everyone made stone faces.

Ishmael continued, "We watched you for the past month. We know that you are doing freelance work in Counter-Narco-Islamist-Terrorist Information Warfare[1]. You don't have the authority to do what we saw you do. We need to know everything that you're doing." The stone faces didn't crack.

---

[1] Information Warfare. An expanding body of warfare that is ancient in some functions, like deception and psychological operations, while adding brand new capabilities, and counter-capabilities, based on the emerging computer-based Information technologies.

"It's an issue of national security. We figured out that the Narco-Islamist-Terrorists—and I call them NITs on purpose, even though they're worse than nits that make lice—the NITs are looking for you. They're seriously looking for you. Obviously."

"Mr. John James Tillman, NASA wants to know where you are. And they want to know how you are so sick, Mr. Holland, that you won't have any visitors or take calls or answer email at home," Ishmael turned and gave Jack his full focus. "So, why did you leave NASA-Langley, Mr. Tillman, after your building blew up?"

"How do we know you are who you say you are?" Jack controlled his voice to keep it low.

"I am who I say I am. You want to know who I work for—really? Huh?" Ishmael locked his eyes with Jack. A slight scowl formed at his mouth. "What evidence could possibly be sufficient?"

Jack's jaw tightened rhythmically in the growing silence. His face reddened. "Show us someone we know. Show us to the head of the DEA," Jack grasped, "In front of public witnesses."

"You want a press conference?" asked Ishmael.

"No, but we could meet in a public place, like a cafeteria," said Jack.

"You don't want to be in public. Nowhere. Not for a second. Believe me. It's going to be hard to keep you under wraps for as long as I think we must."

The room drew silence like a pulling a curtain across the window. Ishmael leaned back and looked at the ceiling for an answer. Suddenly, he snapped himself forward. He reached back to the small of his back and pulled out a small, flat automatic handgun. Faster than the gasps of breath erupted around the table, he palmed back the return on the top of the gun and let it slam a round forward into the chamber. Ishmael flipped the safety off with his thumb and slid the weapon across the table to Jack.

Jack caught the caroming weapon in his hand. But, he didn't pick up the weapon. His hand closed around the pistol grip. He looked around the room for cameras or firing ports in the wall. Ishmael leaned back and crossed his arms on his chest.

"Hold on to that for security. Now, let's talk about why you're here. The Narco-Islamist-Terrorists are looking for some information you have. They need it sooner rather than later. As you know, they're willing to do anything to get it from you. Do you know what that information is?"

They all shook their heads "No".

"I disagree. Feel better, Mr. Tillman?" asked Ishmael.

"Yeah, a little," said Jack. "Verify, then trust."

"Right!" Ishmael pushed a button under the table and a screen lowered in front of the wall to his right rear. A small section of the table directly in front of him flipped open to cast a slide projection onto the screen. Ishmael pulled a small remote control from his jacket and flipped on the first slide. It was the seal of the DEA.

"As I said before, we are the DEA," he clicked for the next slide. The next slide was a list of dates and a lot of fine print.

"The lawyers always make us put this in here," said Ishmael. The fine print on the slide was a litany of lines from specific authorization laws and executive orders. The bottom of the slide banner proclaimed: 'TS SCI[2]: Special Authorization for DEA Actions'.

Ishmael grilled the group about their actions since Labor Day and Brother Pablo's work for far longer. After an exhaustive review, he asked Brother Pablo why he broke the laws on Internet privacy.

Pablo said, "I knew what I was doing. I took all thoughts into my prayer closet. When I thought about going directly to the authorities it didn't seem right. I asked what I was to do and was told to keep working. I was compelled to keep at it."

"Asked whom? Compelled why?"

"God."

"God?" Ishmael's eyebrows accented the question.

"Yes, God. God speaks in a feeling or in a thought. He even speaks in a small, clear voice you hear in your head. But, actually hearing the voice with your ears, not your mind, is very rare indeed."

"Praise the Lord. Does anyone else at Georgetown know about your work?"

"Yes, my superiors know," replied Pablo.

"They approved?" demanded Ishmael.

"After prayer, they did, reluctantly. They gave me the resources to do what I needed as I asked. But, they were worried about it all the time."

---

2. SCI is a designation for highly classified information. SCI is Special Compartmentalized Information. A person has to be 'read on' with a need to know SCI information.

"They should have. You got their library blown up tonight. How long have you been working on this extracurricular activity?"

"Four years and three months," said Pablo.

"Hmm, that is pretty good to not get caught until tonight."

"I was unobtrusive. I never interfered. I just gathered information."

"I have some guys I want you to have a mind meld with. We're interested in how you did what you did. Also, we would like to know where you keep all of your files. So, where were we? Did you do anything differently before the second of October than you did after that date?" asked Ishmael.

"No, sir. We've been pretty steady in what we are doing," said Naomi.

"At first we thought you were an NIT info operation. Then, we thought you might be a diversion, a front, for them. Then, we considered the darnedest thing. We thought you might be planning an attack on the NITs! Imagine that!" Ishmael laughed with his whole body.

"We were, Sir."

"Ish, Ish, Ish, call me Ish," Ishmael laughed. He seemed to enjoy the act of laughing as much as the joke itself. "We're going to be together for sometime. You see, you are number two, three, four and five on both the Drug Lord and the Islamo-Fascists' Most Wanted List." He caught his breath. "I am number one."

Ish looked at his watch. "Let's go over some more details and then bed you down for the night. Old Ish is going to keep you folks alive for a couple of weeks more while we sort out our plan here."

They looked blankly at Ishmael. "The plan for the sensitive national security project. The slide showed you that we have special security authorizations. You can help. C'mon. Don't bull me. You know what I am talking about—the Omni."

"What about after the plan?" asked Naomi.

"Then you are on your own. Sorry, just kidding, we'll work something out. We have a protective custody that is better than your old witness protection. If our project is successful, then you'll be safe. If not, then may God have mercy on us all. Oh yeah, Mr. Tillman, I need my weapon back."

Jack silently handed the weapon back to Ishmael with the gun butt first.

Ish ushered them to a large office with a waiting room full of couches. Security guards accompanying them pulled blankets out of a closet. "Good night. I'm sorry for all that happened tonight. But, I assure you that we will make it as right as we can. We will need your help to do that. Armed security will be behind these doors," said Ishmael.

When the guards left, each person sat on his own coach. The coaches formed a cozy box in the center of the room.

"I can't believe it," Jack shook his head.

"I am so sorry for Tommy and his family," said Naomi.

"Is this guy the Ishmael we're lookin for? Is this the enemy?" asked Bubba.

"I don't think so. I can't believe that this is our Ish. But, how many Ishs can there be?" asked Pablo.

"Are we under surveillance here?" Jack looked around the room for some clue.

"Yes, but you're not going to see it. I'm ready for some rest. Let's pray good night together," said Bubba.

"Sure," said Naomi.

"Gladly," said Pablo.

Bubba knelt and the others knelt facing him. Jack wanted to join them, but felt stupidly awkward.

"Jack, want to join us?" Pablo extended his hand. Jack knelt between Pablo and Naomi. Naomi's smile looked sweet yet shy.

"Oh Lord," began Bubba. They held hands. "Oh, Father God, please hold the Schulze family in your embrace in Heaven. Love them, love them, love them," Bubba fell silent. Tears rolled down his red cheeks.

"Lord, lift up their family and friends. Thank you for saving us today, dear Father," said Naomi. "But we are ready to come, when You call us home."

"Dearest Father, thank you for all of your blessings. Show us what will be Your Will. Give us the light to see and clarity of mind to understand what you want us to do," said Pablo.

I don't know what to say. Jack closed his eyes tighter.

"You *are* a great God. We worship You. We praise You always and always," said Naomi.

"Great is Your faithfulness. Great is Your love. Let Your love pour down on us," said Pablo.

"We trust in you completely. We want to obey You completely, but it is hard, help us to trust and obey totally," said Naomi.

"We ask for Your help in everything we do," said Pablo. A rhythm built between Pablo and Naomi. When one spoke the other nodded 'yes, yes'. Their short prayer statements were linked like a chain.

"Show us."

"Guide us."

"Sustain us."

"Lord, we put on Your buckler and shield."

"Your shoes and breastplate."

"Your helmet."

"Your sword."

"Your way."

"Not ours."

"No way, but Yours."

"Strengthen us please."

"Make us strong."

"Make us brave."

"Give us Your awesome power."

"Give us Your righteous power."

"The victory will be Yours."

"Regardless of the cost."

"Take us."

"Take all of us."

"We hold nothing back."

"Take our families if You must, but spare them if You can," Bubba found his voice again.

"Yes, take them if You must, but if not build a great hedge around them," said Naomi.

Wow. Take my kids if you must? Never. Not my babies. Jack listened with his heart.

"Fill the hedge with thorns."

"Let no one through."

"Bind the evil ones."

"Place mighty angels with flaming swords around our people,"

Bubba's voice cracked. "Spare our loved ones if its in Your Will."

"If it is in Your Will, we beg protection for our babies," said Naomi.

Only if it's in Your Will?

"We have faith," said Pablo.

"We have Your Word."

"The Word is the light."

"The Word was made Man."

"The Man lived as we do."

"The Man died for our sins."

"He took them on himself."

"He did it for us."

"He paid our price."

"He bought us for a price."

"He made us the adopted children."

"He took back life, so we could too."

"If we believe, we will not die."

"We begin a new life with You."

"It gets better and better as we come to know You."

"Death is not an end to life but a change of form."

"But, we fear pain and death and loss of loved ones."

"So, you sent another part of Yourself to comfort us."

"Your Holy Ghost physically lives in us."

"He holds our heart gently."

"He is Your indwelling spirit."

"Fill us."

"Fill us completely."

"You give us the peace beyond understanding."

"The peace that knows no bounds."

"You are the best."

"You are an awesome God."

"You are an awesome God."

"You are an awesome God."

Everyone except Jack started singing 'Awesome God'.

"Our God is an awesome God, He reigns from heaven above…"

Jack felt chill bumps on the back of his neck.

"…with mercy, power and love. Our God is an awesome God,

he…" They sang with a cadence that shifted from a slow soft reverence and a loud, almost shouting voice.

Pablo gave the Lord's Prayer in a surprisingly strong deep-throat. Pablo and Naomi squeezed Jack's hand hard. Pablo crossed himself.

What just happened? Why am I going to cry like a baby?

Jack's friends, had tears in their eyes and the widest grins on their faces. Everyone hugged. They returned to their respective couches.

Jack lay awake much longer into the night—even after the emotional wringer of a day drained him of energy and stunned in shock. He felt so tired, but he couldn't get the images of the dead Schulzes and jitters he felt on the back of his neck from the prayer circle out of his mind. *Could a thorny hedge and powerfully armed angels be outside the house where my babies and wife sleep now? It's just too much.*

Washington, DC
November 7th, 2012
Wednesday

Early the next morning, a guard awakened them and ushered them all the way back into the conference room where they met Ishmael the night before. They were rumpled from sleeping in their clothes, but shared an air of camaraderie and confidence as they enjoyed the hot coffee, fresh juices and an assortment of breakfast bagels, cereals and fruits. *We're still alive.*

Bubba pounced on the newspapers spread out on the table. "Maggie Wins!" shouted the headlines.

"Maggie won! Ya hoo! Yi, Yi. Yi!" Bubba danced around the table.

"Praise the Lord!" said Naomi.

"This will be interesting," offered Pablo. Jack just smiled and watched.

"Now, the fun begins," said Ishmael. "We are on Maggie's team. And we have a lot of work to do and little time to do it."

"Maggie's team? She isn't inaugurated until January. You're

supposed to be on the government's team," said Pablo.

"Oh, we are, we are. We're the DEA, just like I said last night. But our special mission is supported by Maggie in a big way and her election will put a real crunch on our work."

"A crunch for you? Crunch on the Omni?" said Naomi.

"Yes. Both. Good crunch. The information you gave us last night gave the night crew a lot to work on. Everything you said checked out. We're on the same team," said Ishmael. He grabbed a bagel and took his head chair. "Remember when I said you were big on the Narco-Islamo-Terrorist top ten list? It's because of the Omni. We wondered what your connection was with them. Now we know. They think you know all about the Omni. They want your information."

"That's why they didn't kill us," said Bubba.

"Probably. Hey, I thought you said you didn't know why they were hunting you!"

"What we know about the Omni is that important?" asked Pablo.

"You know enough from their perspective. Mine too," said Ishmael as he took a large bite.

"I don't see how our information could be that valuable. It was preliminary research as I see it," said Pablo.

"It didn't look preliminary to me or the NTs," said Ishmael.

"It might help them find a way into the Omni. Though we haven't deciphered that yet," said Bubba.

"Theoretically, the Omni could be destroyed from the outside. If the NITs can find the copies of the software and all of the documentation, then they can destroy it. But it's like any book burning. Hard to find everything that offends. So, it's really hard to destroy every copy," said Ishmael. His look of seriousness was accented by the deep furrows of his forehead wrinkles. Ishmael was in his mid-forties. He was truly middle aged because his smiling, laughter made him seem so youthful and his serious frowning made him seem so old. This was a moment of aged severity. "The Omni is most vulnerable from the inside. Like everything, it can be corrupted."

"Ok. Let's find out exactly everything, and I mean everything, you know or guess about the Omni," said Ish.

The day flew by for Jack. The computer security specialists he worked with all day were impressed with his work. As the day came to a sudden halt when the cart of hot food rolled into the conference room, Jack realized why he was feeling so much better. *I'm safe.* This Ishmael guy made him feel safe. *How can I be safe when Maude and the kids aren't?* Jack let worry assuage his guilt.

They finished their coffee and ice cream dessert. Ishmael said, "Thank you for all that you have done today. We learned a lot from you and we'll put it to good use. I'm sure of it. It will all be put to good use. Your living arrangements will be the same for tonight. Tomorrow, we'll move you to a safe house in the evening for better accommodations. We have several safe houses that we will use."

"My boss will be here momentarily. She has several things to go over with you." There was a sharp knock on the door and a short woman strode in the room.

"Ah, ladies and gentlemen, Ms. Weinstein, my boss," Ishmael grinned.

His boss shot half a grin at Ishmael and quickly resumed her no nonsense intensity. She was thin, almost angular. Her thick black hair was cut stylishly, but not too short. Her glasses were gold wire rims. She looked early forties. Her eyes were hooded with eyelids growing heavy with age.

"Thank you for your sterling introduction, Mr. Shabazz," she didn't smile. "I am Ruth Weinstein. I have personal responsibility for the project Mr. Shabazz is working on. He has reported to me about the significant support you've given and the extreme circumstances you've been under for some time. Thank you," she looked each person in the eye. "Now, I have several concerns. You're going to need a high level of security for several months."

"Months?" Naomi gasped. "I thought it was weeks."

"Months. Ishmael didn't tell you what we have to do?"

"Let me explain," said Ishmael, "a bit more. We're going to use your work as bait for the NITs. Let them think you're still freelancing. Use you to feed dis-information, bad info, to the bad guys."

"We already set ourselves out as bait," said Bubba.

"Yeah, didn't you though? The NITs don't know where you are now. They should know that you survived their attack. You're still good to bring them out in cyberspace. And we can contend with them there—out in cyberspace. We do info war," said Ish.

Jack listened to Ish finish his explanations with the confidence born only by subject mastery. *This guy is no schmuck. Of course, I'm no schmuck either.*

Washington, DC
November 14th, 2012
Wednesday

Ishmael picked his guests' minds clean throughout the following week. Jack saw an uncanny ability to ask the right questions. Ish called them the 'aha's' that sparked energy into inquiry. He made the days long but fruitful.

Ish set a holographic model on the conference table. "You've got to see this."

Tiny laser lights zapped from 3-D icon to 3-D icon as the holographic model flashed above the large pool table-sized platform. It was like watching a light bulb pulse. Ish scaled it back to one color-coded light and one set of twelve icons. The icon was the red rose used in iconic language.

"The red rose is a macro. I know you already figured that out. This is a red rose cinquefoil," Ish brought up a 3-D red cinquefoil into the center of the display. It rotated slowly with a shiny metallic luster a foot over everything.

"The cinquefoil connects the red roses. The red roses initiate a large series of commands on their own," said Ish. A tiny red light shot from the cinquefoil to each of another 50 or so red rose icons that popped up.

"The red roses provide feedback," said Ish. A different shade of red light shot back from each of the roses to the cinquefoil.

"Is information being passed now?" asked Bubba.

"No, no!" chortled Ish. "This is demo ware! It just shows a simulation of how it works. I had it built because I couldn't explain what I needed in two-dimensions of a whiteboard. Even when I drew it three dimensionally, I couldn't really get the feel of it using 3-D graphics on the computer. It took a lot to build this model and get it right."

"How does it work?" asked Jack.

"The demo or the Omni operating system?" asked Ish.

"Omni," said Jack. He marveled at the flashing display.

"The Omni mimics the brain. It works like the operating system of the brain which matches unique protein chains, the ones that are altered by each thought and experience in life, to other unique protein chains within the brain to make thoughts, memories and actions happen for the human," Ish paused. The lights flashed furiously.

"The human brain doesn't have neatly organized data like a tally of neurons all lined up like boxes on a spread sheet or clustered naturally like some internal galaxy. The brain holds individual memories and cognition of a word, a smell, a sound, etc. like individual stalks of wheat in a wheat field of billions and billions of stalks. Yet, the healthy mind can find a single stalk of wheat, like the memory of the color 'red', and match it with the word 'red' which is found on a separate stalk acres and acres away. Furthermore, the brain can find exactly the right stalk or stalks, no more and no less, at the speed of light. So can Omni."

"No way," said Bubba.

"Way. And way cool," said Ish.

"Wow! What do you need from us?" asked Naomi.

"More help on getting into places we aren't supposed to be. More help on making sure we got into all the places we need to be. Some help on getting the right answer, not a false positive, that our instructions have been carried out on a system exactly like we want them to do. And pass off phoney poop to the NTs," said Ish.

"Locksmiths make the best cat burglars. Burglars make the best security advisers," nodded Bubba.

Ish took a deep breath, "Right, we need to know that when a rose icon is activated and generates commands that all the commands are carried out."

"You mean when the icon is clicked, that the macro embedded behind it will work like hypertext and transmit commands?" asked Jack.

"Almost. The hypertext term red rose is a macro. The red rose cinquefoil is not a macro. It's more."

"Like what?" asked Jack.

"It generates commands and receives inputs and generates

more commands," said Ish.

"An icon with artificial intelligence. That's new," said Pablo.

"What is the problem on feedback? Every standard email package does that. Message receipt is no problem. Verification of receipt by specific users is not new either," said Bubba.

"We're having problems with establishing one hundred per cent reliability."

"You'll never get one hundred per cent," said Bubba.

"I know. But, we need to have one hundred per cent reliability that the message was sent or that it was a no-go and we send another message."

"I don't see the problem," said Jack.

"If there is too much water for the hose, either turn up the faucet volume or get more hoses or a bigger hose," said Naomi.

"Plumbing works for me to understand information flow," said Pablo.

"Or what else? What could we do?" asked Ish.

"Have you tried all of the above?" asked Bubba.

"More or less. We are bumping up against some parameters in the paradigm," said Ish.

"Nice alliteration," said Pablo.

"Let's look at our model again," said Ish. He fiddled with the remote creating a short humming noise in the model. Suddenly, there was a burst of light above the table as hundreds of cinquefoil icons flashed on their different colors and slowly spun on their vertical axis. They gasped.

"This is the family of cinquefoils. It sends instructions to several billion places as near simultaneously as we can get it. And we have to know that the messages were received and acted upon, before more instructions go out."

"Billions?" asked Bubba.

"Billions. Near simultaneously," said Ish. He turned a dial. Too many lights to count flashed. It looked like billions. They shaded their eyes from the blazing constellation.

"Why so many?" Naomi and Pablo asked together, like they were on cue.

"Hmm, why?" Ish's forehead became waves of horizontal wrinkles. "Why not?"

"That isn't an answer," said Jack.

"Because we have to. The rose hypertext or icons with their modifiers serve as message bundlers. Plus they change the message that comes from the cinquefoil in several ways. We still get queuing problems. I worry about our metrics for effectiveness," said Ish.

"If your cueing defies simple math then the problem is process," said Pablo. "If you have to move a million pounds of dirt then a million persons with a million one pound buckets should do the job in about an hour. Unless, of course, you can only use a thousand pounds of dirt at time and that has to settle for a day or so. Then it will take longer."

"Yeah, like nine women can not help have a baby in one month's time. It always takes nine months for the little buggers," said Bubba.

"Except for the first baby in a marriage. That one only takes four or five months, then all others take nine months," Naomi winked.

"You are right about that, Lady," laughed Bubba.

Ish turned the display back to a couple of hundred flashing lights.

"I think I know what to do," said Naomi. "Let one system send out a million instructions from one source, but have the acknowledgment and assessment loop go around to another location. You can have that location programmed to read the acknowledgements. It'll report by exception to the original sender. You could have the same system that is checking the acknowledgements also diagnose the assessments. Or put a human in the loop or have it go to a different system or whatever you want. Basically, you break the task down into smaller steps and use other systems to work in parallel. Disaggregate, double the systems and more and move the info faster like Pablo said. Like adding more checkout lines at the supermarket."

"Duh!" Ish slapped his ample forehead theatrically. "Basic programming one oh one. I was trying to achieve one hundred per cent. It has to be perfect."

"Nothin's perfect," said Bubba.

"Except Jesus," said Pablo.

"Right, except for Jesus," Bubba shook his head 'yes'.

"I know, I know. But you have to understand this. The task at hand can have no mistakes, no slip ups, no failures," Ish spoke each word slower and with more force. He cut the air with his pointed finger. "We can not fail. We shall not fail. I understand that nothing is perfect, but everything that doesn't go perfectly the first time, will be done and done again until the mission is completed. That is the standard of perfection. All tasks must be completed. And fast."

"We can't fail at what? What's the mission?" asked Jack.

"I'll tell you as soon as I can. Let's talk about how to add these other stops on the info loop."

Washington, DC
November 20th, 2012
Wednesday

"Can you believe it's been two weeks more?" asked Naomi.

"Nope," Jack took a long gulp of coffee.

"Me neither," Bubba ambled over from his workstation.

"On the contrary, it's been longer than a root canal," Ish flipped his PDA shut. The days that run up to Thanksgiving and the time of national pause and gear down shifting were very busy. The development of Omni ran into serious snags. They were the normal problems for new software development that any good developer pads into his plan. Good solutions take time. Great solutions, usually, take more time.

"Worse for pain. But time's going by right fast," said Bubba.

"I could use a shot of Sin drug now," said Jack.

"Don't even kid about that," said Naomi.

"I don't have time to worry anymore about that drug 'sin'. The NTs are making an all out recon for Omni. There's no doubt about it. Last night a cyber attack made it all the way into one of our DEA local networks. We know how far away we are from Omni being operational. It'll be a couple of months at least," said Ish. The conference room was heavy with tension and fatique.

Naomi sighed.

"We need to consider how to finish the job while under attack," Ish continued. "I've asked one of our partners in Omni to help us. They work on a compartmentalized basis, but it's time to shift responsibilities."

"The Department of Defense, good old Dee-Oh-Dee, is coming in at a new level. I invited our point of contact and the DoD executive agent, who is also my old boss in the Army, to come over today. It's time to read him on this program," Ish looked at his watch. "He should be here in a few minutes. He is Lieutenant General Larry Trento. Presently, he is the Deputy Chief of Staff for Operations for the U.S. Army."

"The Army Ops?" asked Jack.

"Yeah," smiled Ish, "the Ops. The very ops 'hisself.' Yes sir, the Army Ops and the future Army Chief of Staff."

"Why the Army?" asked Pablo. "Aren't all of the services and intelligence agencies intimately involved in Information Warfare?"

"Because," Ish chose his words carefully. "Because, at some point the Army will have a large responsibility to carry out. As usual, the Army does the heavy lifting."

The group looked perplexed. Ish would have to leave them that way for awhile.

Lieutenant General (LTG) Lawrence Michealangelo Trento entered after a quick buzz and strode over to Ish. LTG Trento was five foot ten inches tall, but his erect stature, purposeful step and fierce countenance made him seem much larger. His face was thin and hawk-like. His hair was black with silver streaking the sides, but so thick it made him look younger than his early fifties. His eyes were hazel, so they changed with his clothing as much as his mood, but they had a constant brightness, an alertness so keen, that historically-minded subordinates whispered among themselves that had his eyes been blue—he would be another Thomas 'Stonewall' Jackson, the man whose eyes were the 'blue flame'.

Ish greeted Larry Trento with the confidence of a proven comrade. They shared an unbreakable trust.

"You're looking great, Ish! How's it going here?" said Larry. He gave Ish the general officer firm handshake with elbow squeeze from the free left hand. LTG Trento's Army uniform looked brand new and perfectly tailored. His West Point ring, Class of 79, shared a finger with his wedding ring in the traditional fashion of Service Academy graduates.

"Great, Larry. Thanks. Let me introduce you to my team. They call themselves the Amigos[3]. They're my team for this fight," said Ish.

Ish made the introductions. Larry went around the table in an act of practiced humility.

"Coffee?" asked Ish.

"Yes, please, I'm a quart low," said Larry.

Ish nodded to one of the DEA agents in the room. He signaled another fellow by the door. The boxes high on each wall flashed on. "Top Secret/SCI/ SAP4[4]" was in large red lights. The light above the door turned red and stayed on. Ish slid a folder across the table to the general with "TS/SCI/SAP" in large red letters at the top and bottom.

"The first page is authorization for the folks in this room. My Amigos[5]," Ish smiled, "to be in the room at this level of security. They'll be read on formally. But, here is the good-to-go interim clearance."

There was a quick knock at the door. Ruth Weinstein entered. Ish and LTG Trento quickly rose to greet her as gentlemen. Her face untightened for a second as she shook hands with Ish and LTG Trento. Ish offered her his seat at the head of the table.

Ruth got right to business. "LTG Trento, you need to see how the Omni project moves into the execution phase. It demands much more of your resources. Moreover, it places a lot of operational demands. The operational demands will involve domestic combat operations," Ruth's words fell like rocks on the floor.

Bubba gasped involuntarily. Naomi and Pablo knitted their foreheads. Jack felt his jaw dropping. Ish's countenance grew heavier. LTG Trento didn't emote. Even his eyes didn't flicker.

---

3. The Amigos. The disparate group of individuals (Jack, Bubba, Naomi, Pablo) tossed together and forged into a team searched for a way to describe themselves. Bubba suggested a name for them that felt comfortable for all.

4. Top Secret/SCI/SAP is the highest security classification, It stands for Top Secret, Special Compartmentalized Information/Special Access Program intelligence.

"The combat operations will involve active and reserve forces. We anticipate that NORTHCOM[5] will be in charge. You will be the Commander there because of the Army's statutory responsibilties for the defense of the nation."

"What about the Commander now? Why aren't you bringing in the Joint Staff[6]?" asked LTG Trento.

"It's been decided that you will be the Joint Task Force Commander. The Joint Staff will come in when it is time to execute. The Joint Staffs for all the supporting and subordinate commands will fall into their usual places when the plan is activated. We need you, the JTF Commander, to be in on the final planning," said Ruth. "Actually, you'll have enough forces to be a super Regional Combatant Commander[7]. But, you don't get a promotion."

"This we'll defend," Ish quoted the Army motto.

LTG Trento's eyes widened.

Jack's jaw dropped. *No way the three star Army Ops will be the commander of a joint operation over sitting four star generals and admirals.*

"This arrangement is approved by the National Command Authority[8]," Ish pointed at the folder. "The Presidential Decision Memorandum is in the folder. There's one with the current President's signature. And another one for the President-elect to sign on Inauguration Day."

"Who is read on?" asked LTG Trento.

"The Chairman and the Chiefs[9] know there may be an upcoming operation against the NITs and that you will be the JTF com-

---

5. NORTHCOM: Joint Forces Command for all forces in the continental U.S. Headquarters for Homeland Defense based in Colorado Springs, CO.

6. Joint Staff. The high level staff which serves the Chairman of the Joint Chiefs of Staff.

7. Regional Combatant Commander (RCC). Formerly called the CINCs (pronounced 'sinks'), these are the 4-star general Joint Commands for world-wide regional commands.

8. National Command Authority (NCA) is the chain of command beginning with the President who have the legal authority to make decisions of war, nuclear war and peace.

9. 'Chiefs' is the nickname for the Chairman of the Joint Chiefs of Staff and the Chiefs of Staff of the Armed Services.

mander. They know it was a by name selection that they should go along with it," said Ruth. Her tone was slightly menacing. "This room knows. And a very few other people in the National Command Authority know, like the Secretary of Defense."

Bubba blurted out, "Hillary signed a Presidential Decision Memorandum[10] to take down the NITs?"

"The President signed a PDM for future ops as a contingency plan. It doesn't specify the enemy is the NITs. It says 'enemy combatants'. That, as you are aware, is the whole range of foreign and domestic enemies covered in the Patriot Acts. In some minds it could be used to round you and your ilk up, Mr. Holland," smiled Ish indulgently.

"Okay, then why won't she execute it now before the inauguration. She says the election is all phony. Declare a state of emergency and do it? What's stopping her?"

"Because she knows five Supreme Court Justices and the Chiefs won't do it unless there is a real crisis. A new, tough attack."

"Good. So, then how will President Maggie Kyle get to do it?"

Ish put his hand up to say 'stop', "Hold it for now, Mr. Holland. The key point is this. We have the legal authority. It won't happen before Inauguration Day. It'll be when the Omni is really ready after the Inauguration. Rosetta 6.2 is ready now."

Larry looked at the Amigos intently.

"This group of experts, my Amigos, are the only people I trust, right now, to go to DoD and make Omni work. They can serve as the technical liasion we need. They have to know more than I ever wanted anyone to know to make it work right. I know this is odd, but these are strange circumstances," said Ish.

"I accept," said LTG Larry Trento.

"This is all about the Omni. The Omni is a computer," said Ruth, "and a computer language and the software that enables the United States of America to go to war and win the war against the NITs. Finally the war on drugs will be over. All the NITs in our homeland and many foreign Islamist Terrorists will be crushed. These military operations will be briefed in detail to you later by Ish."

"I knew you would be behind this," said LTG Larry Trento.

---

10. Presidential Decision Memorandum, PDM, is a formal policy directive, which may be classified, from the President of the United States of America.

"Questions, General?" asked Ruth.

Larry sat back in his chair. He rubbed his chin thoughtfully as he ordered his thoughts into speech. "I understand that Ish will give me the military operational perspective later, but let's go to the larger military issues. Why is this a military action and not a police action? What is the end state desired? How does this stay on the right side of the law, especially the Posse Comitatus Act?"

All eyes were on Ruth. She said, "Omnivore began its development as a super information system. It was an upgrade of the Carnivore system. That was it. More, bigger, faster information. But, about five years ago as the development progressed, it became clear that the information was not neutral. The speed of the information would make counter-NIT operations orders of magnitude more effective. Speed lead to decisions faster than any enemy could react. Also, the Omnivore could deliver the evidence to make court cases a slam dunk. The Omni was no longer just an information system. It became a warfighting system in the war on drugs."

"You must have learned what we did while building the Future Combat Systems for the Army. The new capabilities put together with the right C4ISR transform land warfare. You're doing the same thing with counter-NIT ops," said LTG Larry Trento.

"Right, the transformation of the battlefield is based on the ability to see first, decide first, act first, act faster, finish decisively. It's centered around commanders. It works. We got that from the Army," said Ruth.

"What's important for us is how Omni changes the NIT threat and so-called War on Drugs from a rhetorical struggle, actually, a cops and robbers parody of war and the suppression of freedom at home, into a real war. Omni enables the government to pursue the enemy to a culminating point. We will actually win the war and bring it to close," said Ish.

"Win against drugs? Against an illegal immigrant invasion?" asked Larry.

"Yes, win to the extent that the problem really becomes an issue of police enforcement and not national security," answered Ruth.

"Tell me more," said Larry.

"Ish, jump in here. It's your plan," said Ruth.

"Ish, I trained you. Don't screw this up," Larry winked.

"The drug problem has a social context in the desire of people to alter their consciousness, to get high. That aspect, like the social context of insurgencies, has to be addressed or that part of the problem never goes away."

"And it won't go away, ever," Ruth interjected. "But, it can be altered significantly. Human behavior isn't rigid. Societies make up rules and modify behavior to extremes. It's not impossible to lessen the demand for drugs significantly. The plan has to be smart enough to work. It will be hard. It will take a lot of effort. It will take some time. But, it can be done. We have a plan for that aspect, the demand, too."

Ish nodded his concurrence and took the floor, "The purely military aspects of supply and movement are key objectives that can be hit so hard, thanks to Omni, that they can be taken out. We can break every link in the chain from production to distribution to where the money goes. And we can break them simultaneously. Or, as you taught me, we can achieve near simultaneity of effects. And, we can secure the border with no excuses."

"How do you achieve simultaneity against the NITs?" asked LTG Larry Trento.

"The target set is finite, boss. It's close to a million, which makes it a big number, but it's still finite. I remember that lesson from Trento target planning one-oh-one," Ish continued. "The combined resources of police authority up and down the federal system from local cops through state to US national is in the millions. So we have better than 10 to one force ratio against on the enemy."

"Who is the enemy?" asked Larry.

"Every NIT from the biggest to the smallest."

"Users too?"

"Users are fellow travelers. They're not targets per se, but they will be touched."

"Every user in the US of A?"

"Omni can do it. Omni can deal with almost any finite problem of information management that we can think of. You said that simultaneity is achieved by breaking big numbers of complicated events into their component piece parts and solving them as little problems."

"I said a lot of things. You started making it up on your own after awhile, Ish. So, why is this still a military problem?"

"Because the policing authorities are too corrupt to lead this. They can execute parts of it. The Command and Control has to be military. Also, outside of CONUS operations, OCONUS, there will be military ops."

Jack sat in the edge of his seat. *Trento doesn't look convinced.*

"There are a couple of other reasons. Once Omni comes on line and operates, it will be compromised too. We know that. When that happens then some of Omni's capability can be used against the national government. We call that a clear and present danger. The National Command Authority agrees with us, so far," said Ruth.

"Use it or lose it?" asked LTG Larry Trento.

"Absolutely," said Ruth.

"Sounds like the Guns of August before World War One. We have to execute all of the plan at once or all is lost forever. So, what if we don't use the military and execute this plan?" asked LTG Larry Trento.

Ruth stiffened, "On the day that decision is made, nothing happens. Not a blankety-blank thing different happens. But every day that passes after that decision and, especially, every day after Omni is compromised, the United States of America slips away into the hands of criminals. We go from a liberal democracy of the people into the clutches of criminals. We will be a façade of freedom. Our institutions will be a shell. And ultimately, the experiment in democracy will be over. Freedom will die in the cynicism. Fear will triumph over freedom. America will be over."

"How does this happen?" asked LTG Trento.

"Easy. The NITs make billions in drug sales. The Islamist Terrorists are part of the team. They corrupt an already corrupted government. The government uses powers designed for terrorists against political opponents."

"I concur," said Ish.

"Millions of your fellow citizens would disagree with your analysis," said LTG Trento. "Besides, won't President Kyle stop all of this with the Omni?"

"They would be wrong. They'll be dead wrong. President Kyle has a couple of months to use the Omni or lose it to the enemy. Then, it's all over."

"Larry, how much longer is the military going to stay out of the NITs hands? What infiltration have you seen already?" asked Ruth.

"What do you mean?" asked LTG Trento.

"The classified report you read yesterday," said Ruth.

"You weren't on the 'eyes only' list for that report."

"I know."

"So, what's the whole plan?" asked Larry.

"The plan will be briefed to you in more detail. Right now, we need to know that you are ready to command."

"I am always ready to command. What's the name of the plan?

"Rosetta," answered Ish. "The current version is Rosetta 6.2."

"Rosetta 6.2?" asked Larry. "Like the Rosetta stone?"

"Yes Sir. Rosetta 6.2" said Ish.

"Let's go back, Ish. Principles of War. What is the objective?" asked LTG Trento.

"The objective is to seize and hold every NIT, their weapons, and their drugs in the U.S."

"Too big, man. Too big."

"No sir, not with the Omni. Not with Rosetta 6.2. It's doable."

"Ok. Got it. For now. What about 22 million illegals?" asked Larry.

"We just close the borders, sir, for now. We will get a better ID on them—by name. All 22 million. But, we don't do anything yet. Not until the border is secure and the campaign against NITs is over."

"Roger. When are you gonna ship the illegals? C'mon, you can tell me, I'm the boss."

Ish smiled broadly. They fixed the time of the next meeting—Monday, November 26th.

Jack felt relieved and exalted simultaneously. *Lazor Larry will rattle the cages of his subordinates. They'll run down the answers to every question burning in his flaming brain. Generals don't like surprises. Can Rosetta 6.2 really work? This is going to be really big. I'm right in the middle. Hooah.*

McLean, VA
November 22nd, 2012
Thursday

Jack put on a light blue sweater, grabbed a huge mug of coffee and went out on the deck outside of the 'Florida' sunroom to sit with the Thanksgiving Morning. He breathed deeply and relished the scent of musty woods on a humid day. Grey scallopped clouds dropped the ceiling of the sky to just beyond the brown branches of trees still holding handfuls of leaves.

West Point was so gray this time of year. So stark by this time in November. The mountains stood forlorn and lonely before the coming onslaught of long Winter. Here at home in Virginia there was the gentle suggestion that Autumn could leave with slow gracefulness. I gotta write down these poetic thoughts like the other stuff I've done. Yeah.

Now it's late November. How about that bracing walk in October at the height of Autumn's bluster? That was great. Autumn is moving on to its logical conclusion. More of the change of seasons is imposed on the world I lived in. Now what of me?

Jack waited for thoughts to come.

So, what's different? I'm still in NoVa hiding in fear of my life. My family is in hiding and away from my touch. I'm working on a fascinating computer program that promises to be at the center of something really big. World history big. I always wanted to be part of something this big. Now, I'm so involved, it isn't at all like I'd thought. The days were focused on details. The drama was drowned in work that wore on his mind and energy. The heroic nature was lost under the cloak of continued hiding and his abject fear of violent death. Jack sipped his coffee. The breeze whipped his hair across his forehead like a cat's tail.

I don't know what will happen tomorrow. I just don't know. I don't know what to do.

Jack didn't hear Naomi come from behind him. She lightly touched his shoulder as she passed him. She turned another deck chair around to sit. "Mind if I join you?"

"No, please do," replied Jack. He answered without thinking.

He was captured by the feeling that her nonchalant hand gave him. *She always touches the arms of people as she talks to them. It means nothing.* Yet, he felt light headed, almost giddy.

"Happy Thanksgiving, John-James. Don't you just love this place? This is my favorite safe house."

"Me too."

"And this is my favorite place."

"Really? I haven't seen you out here much."

"I go when you don't."

"You've seen me come out here?"

"Now, Jack. It's hard not to know anyone's comings and goings in our circumstances."

"I didn't know you spend time out here," Jack mock grinned.

"When you're working on your hand held or with your papers, you don't see much of anything else."

"Right about that," Jack could do nothing but agree with her.

"I'm usually out here in the night. I like to come and just sit with the night," Naomi gave a faraway look to the grey sky hunkered to the tall trees.

"Just sit with the night?" asked Jack.

"Yes," Naomi drank deeply. The scent of aromatic coffee was the perfect offset to the heavy, cool air.

"That is my phrase, 'to sit with the night'," said Jack. His pulse sped up. "I put it in a poem."

"I didn't know that you wrote poetry. What've you written?"

"Just scribbles," Jack blushed. He had sent his very best off to lose contest after contest. Since he was a teenager, he was driven to write. He felt that if he didn't write it out, he would explode. Then, when he did write it out, he was frustrated unto screaming because he would only have a couple of paragraphs, an incomplete poem with one good line or two, a sentence, a midly interesting phrase. The words looked so meager on a page when they meant so much to him. Maude would shout, "You dreamer loser! When are you going to finish something and make money? Your poetry is an excuse for you to go sit up late at night with your stupid pens and paper and the blanking computer when you could be helping around the house."

"C'mon, what've you written?" asked Naomi.

"Mostly incomplete poems. Stuff that's on my mind. Turns of

phrases that appeal to me."

"Can you recite one?"

"No. My mind doesn't work that way. The words come to me really quickly and then they're gone. I've read things that I wrote years ago and I didn't even remember writing them."

"If the words just come to you, then it's a gift from God," Naomi laughed lightly. Her plum turtle neck sweater and skirt were modest, but showed her pleasant curves.

"Many of my poems are love poems," Jack ventured.

"Most good poetry is about love. Isn't it?" Naomi offered without hesitation.

"Yeah, I guess. Do you write poetry?"

"No, no!" Naomi wove her chuckles and smiles into a single fabric of speech. "I do like to read poetry. I like old Robert Burns. And I love the Psalms as poetry. Even though they don't rhyme in English."

"They sound poetic in the King James English."

"You're familiar with them in the King James Bible?"

"Somewhat. In an English course, we studied them as form of poetry."

"English course?"

"Yup, used the Bible as a textbook," Jack saw Naomi's smile fade.

"You should try reading it again. As literature or as life manual, if you read it, it'll speak to you. You can even read the Bible with hostility. Hatred. Many have done it like that. And it spoke to them," Naomi searched his eyes. "Eventually the Holy Ghost will speak to you, if you read the Bible. He'll speak to you in language you can understand. You'll be amazed."

"Uh-huh," Jack was lost in her eyes. He felt a sense of peace, a joyful anticipation, that was like a mild rapture. "I'll have to try it someday."

"Do you have a Bible here?"

"No. But you and Bubba must have a dozen."

"Maybe more!" Naomi threw her head back. "I'll give you a loaner. This's been real nice, but I'm ready for an old fashioned country breakfast. I don't care if it takes me an hour to cook it all. I'm 'a gonna be fixin' some good eats, mister feller," she over-West

Virginia-hill-twanged on purpose.

"I don't care if it takes me more'n 'n hour to eat, ma'am, but ah'll do my part," Jack tried to respond in hillbilly dialect as best he could.

Naomi rose quickly. She patted his shoulder again on her way past him. Jack felt like a child smiling so. *Ah, what a day to sit with.* Jack drained his coffee. He didn't want to get up even though a fresh cup would be a grand companion.

The Thanksgiving Dinner table looked like a Norman Rockwell painting. But, the family gathered around the table didn't look right. There were no children. There was only one senior in his early 60s. There was only one woman. Yet, this Thanksgiving, after all that had transpired, the Amigos felt as close as many a family. Like soldiers, they were bound by circumstances, confidence, and mutual commitment. As they took their seats, the door bell rang.

Jack flipped open his handheld communicator. Security hadn't given him a heads' up that anyone unpleasant approached. He read three names scrolling across the tiny screen, "Ishmael Ali Akbar Shabazz, Emily Shabazz, Ruth Weinstein."

"We've got company," said Jack.

"Happy Thanksgiving!" Ruth led.

"Are we late?" asked Ish. He carried a tray covered with a white cloth. His wife Emily held the door for him. She was a new face for the Amigos. Emily was quite overweight, but still had a woman's shape. Her skin was a coffee color and quite a contrast to Ish's deep blackness. Her smile made her more beautiful.

"How could you be late? You know everything about us," Jack didn't mean it to sound wrong.

"We brought some of the best pecan pie you have ever eaten," said Ish.

"We wanted to share with you how much we appreciate what you have done," said Ruth.

"Thanks for eating with the troops," said Bubba, "but what about your families?"

"They understand," said Emily. She shook each person's hand warmly and offered variations of 'I've heard so much about you and it is all wonderful' with a nice personalized touch.

"We will end up eating again, tonight. Not that I complain about that," Ish patted his thick waist.

Everyone took their seats except Bubba. Bubba said, "Thank you for joining us, Ruth, Emily, Ish. Our thanks are multiplied with your good company. Our wonderful meal is even richer with your gifts." Naomi smiled appreciatively even though their additions were gilding on gold to her cooking.

Bubba prayed, "Oh Lord, our great and awesome God. Giver of the harvest and host of the feast. Master of all and loving friend to everyone. Worthy Soveriegn of the universe and Lord of our hearts. Protector, comforter, refuge."

Bubba's voice quavered, "We give you our every thanksgiving for all that You have done. We give You our every praise for all that You will do. We give You our love for Your lovingkindness showered on us. We worship You with praise, joy and thanksgiving worthy of Your holy name. Please bless this food for our bodies for Your use. This we ask of You, and I ask in my tradition, in the name of the Savior and great friend to humankind, Jesus Christ, Amen."

"Amen," they said.

The conversation ebbed and flowed from topic to topic. Bubba and Ish had a knack for pulling a new thread of thought from the remains of the last fabric of chat. Emily inquired about their living situation with a gentle probing concern. Eventually, the conversation veered into the minefield of their present project. They walked gingerly with their words.

"I am confident that Ish's plan will work," said Ruth. "I know we will win." She was through eating her dieting bird's portion of the plenty before her. Her face was flushed from the double scotch she allowed herself.

"I'm not going to divulge classified information," Ruth looked directly at Emily, who sat there without a security clearance. "But, I can speak from a very, very well informed unclassified position. We're going to win because we have an unbeatable plan that is backed up by the incredibly powerful resources of this U.S. government and all the governments of our federal system. And, then, we have, we will have the power of the people. Nothing can stand in the way of a motivated, well-lead, focused American people."

Everyone waited for her to continue past the long pause.

"We Americans are slow to anger and quick to forgive. We have a unique sense of fairness and equity that stands alone in the world. I have heard different explanations for our sense of our selves. Whatever the reason, our optimism is boundless when it is unleashed and our disappointment is temporary when our hopes are unrealized. Soon enough we dream again and we seek our dreams," Ruth sipped her scotch.

So, it's remarkable that the past two decades have been a meandering in the woods without direction since the end of the Cold War. It is astonishing that the decline in American culture would go unchecked without a countervailing movement for so long. Perhaps, the time has arrived for all of that to change.

No, we know the answer. There is no perhaps. The time is now. The tinder is set. The heavy logs that will burn with great heat are laid. We await the spark. The spark of one fire, the right fire, will arouse the flame of American passion.

That is what we really are about as a people. Americans are a people of a common idea who seek life in personal liberty above all else, until they rise up for the passion of their times. Rise they have and rise they will. When the spark touches the tender, then we will execute Rosetta 6.2 and the American people will rise. God help us if they don't."

"God help us when they do," said Ish.

"God help us when they do," Ruth looked at their faces as question marks sitting around her. "Americans concentrate on the problem as it comes into their home, their neighborhood, their schools or work. And, drugs never come by themselves. Drug money funds the Islamist Terrorists. NTs aid, abet and support the Islamist murderers. Drugs come with crime. They come with divorce. They come with child abuse and pornography. They come with failure in education and then on the job. They come with despair from perceptions of race or class. They come as chic coolness to the unsuspecting child and adult. They corrupt the immigrants and their children. They corrupt like cancer the government of the people," Ruth took another sip of scotch. "In fact they come from Hell. They are part of every spider web of pain in our society."

"But you can never eliminate drugs. Just like you can't get rid of alcohol or tobacco. People will use them," said Jack.

Ish stood up. He leaned on the table with both fists. "People will go to the arena and watch other humans fight to the death and be eaten by wild animals if you let them. People will do anything. People are capable of anything you can imagine. And more. Civilized people put limits on evil. Rosetta 6.2 will set a new barrier to drugs and all the evil they produce."

"To Rosetta 6.2," Ruth offered a toast.

They all stood up. "To Rosetta 6.2."

"To the United States of America," said Ish.

"To the United States of America."

"To the American people," said Ruth.

"To the Americans." They took their seats again. The room filled with quiet anticipation.

"Jack, the Romans who ran the coliseums were the greatest civilization ever when they were so powerful and modern," said Bubba. "But they were a pagan people. Ours is a Christian civilization and a Christian nation. So we must do better."

"Judeo-Christian," said Ruth.

"That's what I meant. Really."

"Some would say Post-Christian," said Jack as he reached for the wine.

"Post-Christian is a new name for pagan," said Bubba.

"Rightly said," added Naomi.

"Rosetta 6.2 is Christian? Or Judeo-Christian? What about the separation of church and state?" Jack felt his wine bravado.

"Rosetta 6.2 is a program developed by the United States of America for the American people," said Ish. "It's fully consonate with the policies of the federal system of government; national, state, and local, provided for in the Constitution. Rosetta 6.2 is as Christian as the Constitution, no more and no less. Because, like the Constitution there's nothing about Christianity in it, but it is built upon Christianity."

"It is as Judeo-Christian as the Constitution. No more and no less," Ruth smiled.

Emily brightened up and commented on how lovely the flowers at the table were. The Thanksgiving meal melted the afternoon away. After they had lingered at the table, they went to the den and lingered longer. The chitchat spoke to small things, but the sincere give and take was warmer than the waning light of the fading sun. The warmth hung in the air of the house long after the farewells and throughout three more days of Thanksgiving weekend.

Washington, DC
November 26th, 2012
Monday

"I don't want to work today," said Jack.

"Why?" asked Bubba.

"I'd like to just see the sun plunge down like it does this time of year."

"Why do you need to know how early it's dark?" asked Pablo.

"Not really. It's about knowing Thanksgiving is over and it's Christmas season."

"You mean the Holiday season?" asked Ish.

"Don't get me started," said Bubba.

"I won't. Hey, Amigos, look at this. Houston, we've got a problem. The NITs have a program that searches for rose cinquefoils and destroys them," said Ish.

"Why is that a problem? You can always send out more messages with rose cinquefoils," said Jack.

"There aren't many complete copies of the rose cinquefoil. You know, all of them," said Ish.

"So you make as many as you want using clip art," Jack seemed perplexed. "It's just a graphic."

"No, Jack, that's the problem. We want to be careful about what cinquefoils are where. Let me show you something about the rose cinquefoil on this machine, please," Ish pulled on Jack's chair to invite him out of his seat. Ish tapped the plastic logo on top of the monitor. The logo read "geo-tech".

"This system can do digital analysis for data from spy satellites. Really any sensors. It has a zoom in and out resolution that goes from a telescope to an electron microscope. We only have a couple of these babies at DEA. But I knew the Pentagon has plenty."

"So, let's look at what Jack is doing today," Ish relaxed a bit as he transformed to his teaching mode. "Ah, Jack is looking at the instructions that come from a green rose cinquefoil. Looking to see how the data is distributed across many computers and can be called up without allowing others access to corrupt it, eh? Look at Jack's last five commands and inquiries."

"Spot on," allowed Jack.

"Okay, look closely at the green rose cinquefoil," Ish put it into 5000% view and centered it on the screen. He leaned back in the chair and cocked his head at his creation.

The icon sat there with the slightest pulse of color. None of the Amigos had really noticed that pulse of color before. Naomi pointed at the screen and said, "Look at the filligree on the petals. I never saw that before."

Ish leaned forward and added another ten times, a thousand per cent, to blow up of the view.

Naomi whispered, "That's simply beautiful." The filigree was indeed beautiful. It swooped and looped in unexpected twists and turns. The lines were simple and clean. Taken as a whole the simple became so complex and intricate. The color pulse was much more evident at this magnification. It seemed to have a rhythm.

"Do you like that?" Ish looked back at the Amigos. "I'll spare you the suspense and show you what's behind this work of beauty." He changed system modes from big blow up of the icon pixels to the microscope mode. The computer tower by the desk hummed.

"It'll be a couple of seconds," Ish said. All eyes were on the screen. The tool bar across the top of the screen changed. A small window numbered "microns". The screen zapped black and then popped back in green. There were green lines filling almost every square centimeter of the display. The design of the lines was unambigious with this exposure in microns.

The green rose cinquefoil design was less than half a micron thick. A micron is one millionth of a meter, or about one seventy fifth the width of a human hair. The eye can only see to sixty microns. The Amigo gasps were involuntary.

"It's a chip!" said Bubba.

"Can't be," said Jack.

"It is," said Pablo and Naomi in unison.

"A chip! It is a computer microprocessor chip! The icon is really a microprocessor!" Bubba couldn't contain his enthusiasm.

"It looks like an advanced design at that," added Pablo.

"What did you expect?" smirked Ish. He was a proud papa for this invention.

"Who did this?" asked Naomi.

"Sorry, no need to know on that," replied Ish. "But I can tell you that DARPA money has gone to some good efforts recently. It was my idea. But obviously not my design. I couldn't design a chip if you held a gun to my head. Just my idea to make it happen."

"And for the functionality too, huh?" asked Naomi.

"Yeah, most of it. But I got some great help once we pulled together the design team."

"Just unbelievable, Ish. Great job," Jack felt a twinge of envy at the genius behind this, "Really. Great job."

"Ish, is this chip really less than half a micron in depth?" asked Pablo. "So what happens when you copy the icon in a normal edit and paste it somewhere? Do the details get washed out by the resolution of your system?"

"No," answered Ish. "Thank you x-ray lithography. You see, we can have the chip designed and cut into a crystal silicon laminide on a glass surface. The chip can actually be behind the screen and look like an icon."

"Huh? How does it get there?" asked Jack.

"This is cool," said Ish. "The rosefoil chip gets inputs from the system it is residing on. It actually exists in the graphic interface of the software architecture. It gets energy, electrical juice, from the electricity that courses through that software, so it is not hard-wired in."

"A micro-processor chip is not hard wired into the system?" Jack was incredulous.

"Yup," Ish was so pleased to express his confidence. "We can make chips so small that they could fit inside a resistor like the floating points in an optical computer. They are kept in place by the magnetic radiation of the device itself."

"I just can't believe it,' said Jack.

"Believe it, Jack," said Ish. "Since the rosefoil chip is in the graphic interface, when a command is given to copy the rose cinquefoil icon, the chip knows it. The chip assembles the detailed instructions that will reproduce the rose cinquefoil chip design wherever the icon is being copied to."

"Isn't that a lot of code?" asked Pablo. "Wouldn't that slow up the copy and paste or send?"

"Not enough to notice," said Ish. "I know it is hard to understand. But the code employs enough macros and 'do overs' to reproduce itself with as few bytes and as little delay as possible."

"It just doesn't seem possible without wiring and trouble shooting that the microprocessor could fit into the system. It's like having a tiny engine reside somewhere on a car engine," observed Naomi.

"You can do that. You can have a little engine on a big engine. It used to be called a 'little Joe' on Army tanks years ago. The little Joe powered a couple of the systems, like the radios and the heat, while the big engine rested and didn't consume fuel," Bubba interjected with some enthusiasm. He could see in his imagination how a rose cinquefoil could work and it thrilled him. He thought little of the complicated technology to achieve the breakthrough, but a lot about how it could be put to use. "You have separate little engines on big engines on ships and aircraft too."

"Yeah but a chip that can be transmitted like email and then work like a chip!" exclaimed Jack. He shook his head in disbelief.

"It works," Ish nodded his head to say 'yes it is so' in affirmation.

"So, is Rosetta 6.2 a rose cinquefoil?" asked Naomi.

"No," Ish spun around in his chair to front her and the whole Group more face to face. "No it isn't. Rosetta 6.2 is a program that consists of many rose cinquefoils and the instructions necessary to link them all together."

"It's an operating system code that includes a bunch of different chips that serve to carry out the instructions?" offered Bubba.

"Close," said Ish. "Rosetta 6.2 is a program that does all the things you saw in the demo. Remember the hologram? It does it using the processing power of chips that are an integral part of the overall program."

"Software that includes its own tiny hardware to make the software work?" asked Pablo.

"Aptly put," replied Ish. He wrung his hands together to make his knuckles pop. The muscles in his arms filled out his white shirt sleeves.

"What makes it work again?" asked Naomi.

"A simple set of instructions can start Rosetta 6.2. The operation of the program is based on the code that links the rose cinquefoils."

"What are the cinquefoils operating in?"

"Omni operating system."

"This is all about the Omni?" said Bubba.

"It always was," replied Ish.

"I think I get it," said Pablo. "Rosetta 6.2 sends rose cinquefoils out and around to many systems. Then, on command, Rosetta 6.2 sends instructions to the rose cinquefoils. Then the rose cinquefoils churn out lots of instructions, queries, messages, you name it, like in your demo."

"You got an 'A', Pablo. Move to the head of the class," said Ish.

"Rosetta 6.2 works off the Omni operating system, so it can not be corrupted, except by an Omni-capable technician," Pablo continued, "So what else is going on?"

"When the chip copies itself and sends itself to another system, it sits as so many lines of code until the graphic image is called up. Then, it is reconstructed as the chip design you see on your screen as an icon. That chip design is given a 'fade to back' instruction, so it is up and operating behind anything on your screen."

"So far so good," said Ish.

"It is sending and receiving instructions from the monitor back to the graphical interface layer of the software in the computer."

"Hard to believe, but okay, continue," remarked Pablo.

"Someone has a program, a killer virus, that finds the icon symbol code in the graphic interface and deletes it. Someone is deleting the rose cinquefoils."

"Like I said, make more," said Jack.

"We have to find a way to make them survivable when we send them," answered Ish. "And we need to make sure that the original designs are not lost."

"How many original designs are there?" asked Naomi.

"Five hundred and twenty three rose cinquefoils," said Ish flatly.

"Five twenty three?" Pablo raised his eyebrows. His slim figure stiffened.

"Exactly five hundred and twenty-three?" asked Bubba too.

"Yes, exactly five hundred and twenty-three rose cinquefoils," Ish started to laugh.

The Amigos laughed together, except for Jack.

"What's so funny?" Jack pleaded.

"Five hundred and twenty three is the number of fish that supposedly were pulled out of the boat," said Naomi. She winked at Jack. Jack shrugged his shoulders.

"When Jesus was resurrected, he appeared on the Sea of Galilee to His disciples. They'd bin fishin' all night and caught nothin'. Jesus called out to them to drop their nets over to one side. They complained, but gave it a try. The fish filled the nets to almost sink the boat!

They came ashore and cooked up some of the fish and ate it with this stranger who had called out to them. Then, suddenly, they realized that the man was Jesus. He told them they would become fishers of men. That is why the five hundred twenty three is significant. The Jews thought at that time that there were five hundred and twenty three peoples in all of the world. So, Jesus told them to go out to all of the world. Take the news to all 523 peoples that He had risen from the grave and proved the truth of His teachings."

"The disciples didn't recognize the master?" asked Jack.

"Jesus was transformed by the resurrection. He had a real body that people could touch and he ate food, but he was different. He would appear and disappear. He looked different, but something of his essence was the same, so people recognized him after a word or two," said Bubba.

"Hard to believe that. Sounds like hallucinations."

"It was hard to believe then, too. But the four hundred plus people who saw him risen from the dead and very much alive, had their lives transformed. They were never the same," said Pablo.

"When his half-brothers and sisters saw him, then they proclaimed him the risen Messiah; the Christ. That just clenched it for me. When his own brothers suffer terrible martyr's deaths and never recant, that says everything to me. I can't imagine bearing so much for a lie," said Naomi.

"Plenty of lies live. They breed. Look at the NITs. Look at drug culture," said Jack.

"Lies don't love. Not real love. Lies don't love through disease, torture, humiliation and death. Lies don't sustain in the darkness. Lies don't spread love person to person year after year. Lies quit, but love never quits. Saint Paul wrote that. Love never quits," said Pablo. His eyes looked so dark, that they looked almost black.

Jack looked uncomfortable with everyone directing their attention to him in instruction.

"Ish, was it really five twenty three on the nose?" asked Bubba.

"Well," said Ish slyly, "Not exactly. It was five hundred fifteen to start. I figured we could find eight more needs that required a rose cinquefoil. And we did."

"Nothing like pushing things to support Christian numerology, eh?" teased Pablo.

"You can't question my motives. Besides, we found that we really did need those extra eight cinquefoils. That seemed like we were lead."

"It always does in hindsight," said Bubba.

"Even when we go astray," said Naomi.

"All things work to good. Even your tinkering, Ish," said Pablo.

"The name for the program, Rosetta, is indicative of the nature of the program. Rosetta ties together many, many other programs. It's the key piece that must be to understand the whole. It's the interpreter from one system to another."

"I had guessed that. I knew about the Rosetta Stone that opened up Egyptian hieroglyphics to translation," said Pablo.

"Exactly," said Ish. "But this program could also be called the keystone, because like the keystone in an arch, it holds the arch up. Rosetta 6.2 holds together many diverse capabilities. It pulls it all together to make it work."

"It?" asked Bubba.

"Yeah, it'll all be revealed, if it hasn't been already, by the work you are doing in the troubleshooting of six point two. Right now, we need to save the icons," said Ish.

"Sounds like a bumper sticker. Save the Icons!"

Ish turned back around to the computer monitor and down sized the chip design until it looked like a green rose cinquefoil icon and nothing more. He explained the problems in order as he saw them. Ish described one fire after another that had to be put out.

"You gotta be an honary Amigo, Ish. You're pulling your load," said Bubba.

"No, he is a full Amigo. I get the final word on anything Amigo," laughed Pablo.

The Amigos spent the rest of the day, separately at their work stations, flying around and around and into the flames like moths. Quickly, the day was consumed by the energy they applied to flaming white hot cyberspace. They returned to the flames every day that week.

Washington, DC
December 7th, 2012
Friday

The Amigos sat at their familiar places in Ish's conference room in the DEA building. LTG Larry Trento and Ruth Weinstein entered before the first cup of coffee could be half drained. Ish squeezed his hands together and stretched his arms.

"The NTs are getting closer. We've narrowed our leak internally at the DEA to three persons. But we haven't closed the noose on any one of them. Meanwhile, the NTs have some sense of the importance of the rose cinquefoil icons. They have programs scouring the nets, and I mean all the nets, looking for the icons and destroying them," Ish took a cleansing breath.

"Our end-to-end run through of Rosetta 6.2 is getting set back every day. We're going back by almost a week every day. It will be several months for sure, no doubt about it, before we can do a full up end-to-end test. If we lose much more time, then we will miss the Omni coming on line. If we miss the mark, then the Omni may be corrupted beyond our ability to fix it."

"They'll get to Omni that fast?" asked LTG Larry Trento.

"Yes, Larry, they will," answered Ish. "They have gotten in way too deep here. They're in way too much, far over our estimates, in your Pentagon."

LTG Trento bristled, "Then why did you send these folks over to work with me?"

"Because they have a job to do. Also, I thought that the intrusions could be contained. Now, I am having my doubts. That is why we are meeting here today," Ish's next words were drowned by noise.

The building shook like a stick in the mouth of a big dog. The noise built for a second before it reached a rising crescendo of shock and blast. Before the building stopped shuddering the lights went out. Only one of the battery operated fire lights turned on to give a flashlight cone of light on one corner of the room and shadows everywhere else. Everyone grabbed the large conference table for stability to keep from being thrown to the floor.

"Bomb!" LTG Larry Trento grabbed Ruth by the elbow, practically lifting her from her feet, and headed for the door. LTG Trento experienced multiple bombs in Iraq. "Follow me!"

"I'm trail, Larry. Go! Go!" Ish lunged to the door and touched each person as they exited the room. When he saw the outlines of their faces, he spoke their name.

"Ruth. Larry. Naomi. Bubba. Pablo. Jack."

The building continued to shudder. Smoke billowed up the elevator shaft and through the gaping doors to fill the hallway. The smoke was blacker than night and acrid.

LTG Trento hurried towards the stairs. He assumed a crouching gait, like he was under fire too. Everyone imitated him. The smoke was pouring up the stairs too, but if he squatted a little lower, he could keep his head under the cloud. A familiar popping sound came from below.

He slammed his body against the wall. He crouched down into a deep squat. He pulled Ruth down with him. "Small arms!"

Ish crawled down to LTG Trento. LTG Trento made an open hands gesture to Ish. Ish pointed one index finger up. Wait. He reached to the small of his back and pulled out his nine millimeter automatic handgun. LTG Trento extended his hand to take it. Ish pulled the weapon back into his chest and shook his head 'no'. "Wait here." Ish crawled down the stairs like a cat. His cat's paw held more death poised by its ribs than any claw could ever bring.

LTG Larry Trento listened intently. The popping sound faded. It came back and faded. Suddenly there was a flurry of popping just below where LTG Trento could see. A bright flash preceded the loud bang of a grenade.

"Yo, General Trento! Larry! Come down. Now, Sir!"

LTG Trento lead the file down the stairs. They moved away from the blood splattered all over the walls. They stepped over the two bodies sprawled on the landing. The men were dressed in business suits. They looked like any office worker in the DEA. One fellow was a young white man and the other one was a black middle-aged man. Both men wore earphones with sleek speaker wires curved around to their gaping mouths.

Ish opened the heavy metal door. That portion of the underground parking was dusty with debris, but not in rubble. Ish saw the general's Pentagon van. The doors were open on both sides. Ish could see the driver, a contract civilian was lying by the front wheel. Ish rushed up to the side of the van. LTG Trento's aide, a young major slumped forward in the front passenger seat. His face was red pulp. The keys were still in the ignition. Jack started the van. "Thank you, Lord," Jack gasped.

LTG Trento ran to the van pulling Ruth by the elbow. He saw his aide as he got close enough. He gritted his jaws to stifle his curses. LTG Trento pulled open the side door and pushed everyone in.

Ish yelled, "Everyone down on the floor." He gunned the engine and sped up the ramp. He crashed through the little barrier gate by the empty security booth. As Ish careened the van around the corner at the entrance he saw the look of surprise in the faces of the men in the three sports utility vehicles waiting as getaway cars.

LTG Trento reached into the pocket of his dead aides jacket. He took the military model personal communicator and wiped the blood off the bottom with his green uniform sleeve. He punched in a code and spoke clearly, like he was ordering pizza.

"Army Ops Center. This is the Ops. Sitrep follows," LTG Trento paused for acknowledgement.

"Army Ops, this is Army Ops Center, roger." The voice recognition software informed the duty officer instantaneously that LTG Larry Trento was using his aide's communicator. The lieutenant colonel duty officer didn't need the high tech help. He knew Lazor Larry's voice anywhere.

"Delta Echo Alpha's attacked by high explosives and small

arms assault. Enemy unknown. My aide and driver are Kilo India Alpha. I am inbound to the Pentagon helipad with additional six pax. Have a bird on the pad and turning when I get there. Over."

"Echo tango alpha[11]? Over," asked the duty officer.

LTG Trento looked up to get his bearings. Ish was heading up into Northwest Washington. "Two zero mikes. Out."

"Willco. Out," said the duty officer.

When the van pulled up to the security gate outside the Pentagon, military guards were ready outside the gate in full urban warfare kit; black helmets with face masks, body armor, elbow and knee pads, metal toed boots. The soldiers waved urgently for the van to enter and not slow down. Ish complied. He saw more armed men by a Blackhawk helicopter with its blades turning furiously. One fellow with orange cone lights beckoned Ish forward. When Ish pulled to a hard stop in front of the fellow, he saw a squad of soldiers on the right drop to their one knee firing positions. LTG Trento pulled open the door and hoped out.

"Let's go," LTG Trento helped them out of the door. He pointed to the crew chief by the side of the helicopter. The crew chief looked like a big bug in his helmet and aircrew uniform. Ish got out of the van and came around to LTG Trento. LTG Trento grabbed Ish by the shoulder to pull him close and speak directly in his ear.

"You guys are getting out of here. I'll be in contact later. Take care."

"Thanks, Larry," Ish shouted and he headed for the helicopter.

Larry pulled him back, "Good job back there, Ish. Good job." Larry patted him on the back and then pushed him towards the helicopter. Larry gave him a double thumbs up and turned to jog towards the Pentagon entrance. Ish saw the gesture from his old boss and replied with a thumbs up behind his back as he crouched forward.

In a flurry the Amigos strapped in, the doors slammed shut. The helicopter pitched forward and upward, then banked sharply and dropped its nose to pick up more speed. Jack leaned forward to tap Ish on the shoulder. Ish set in the middle front senior person seat. He talked to the pilot through his headset. Ish looked tired, but strong.

---

11. ETA is the 'Estimated Time of Arrival'.

"Where are we going?" asked Jack.

"West Point, New York," replied Ish.

"My rockbound highland home," Jack smiled to himself. *The old cadet song. My rockbound highland home.* He leaned over and shared the news with the others.

Chapter 4. Cocoon

West Point, NY
December 7th, 2012
Friday

The flight to West Point was an artful illusion of escape and evasion. The deception deposited the Amigos on the darkened parade field at Camp Buckner. A van raced the twelve miles through the back gate of West Point proper and down to the basement entrance of the massive Thayer Hall. The past filled Jack's present. Every sight and smell shovelled up memories.

They were ushered into a large, odd pie-shaped room with two levels. The room was wedged behind the North Auditorium stage. In the far corner was a tall thin outside window. The balcony walked half the walls.

Their military escort was a lieutenant colonel in the green uniform, black sweater and black windbreaker so common at Metro stops near the Pentagon. He asked them to sit at a round conference table that had seen better days. The lieutenant colonel pulled out a personal communicator and placed it at the center of the table.

"This connects you to me. Just push 'send'. Otherwise, you are to be absolutely incommunicado. Nothing. Nada. Zip. Do not leave this room—under any circumstances. There's a bathroom up on the balcony. I'll be back in a few with some supplies for you. Make yourself comfortable. You're going to be here for awhile I understand," the officer abruptly stood up and headed out of the room.

"Excuse me, Colonel," Ruth summoned with her hand. "I must reach the DEA."

The officer turned and walked backwards, "No ma'am, not now. I've got orders."

"I am the Deputy Director of the DEA!" Ruth clenched her fists.

"I know, ma'am. I know. In fact, I know more than I want to know right now."

"Ruth, it'll be okay. Let's just rest and wait." Ish looked down at the spray pattern of blood on his trousers.

Ruth opened her mouth. Her shoulders slumped.

"Welcome to West Point," said Jack. "I can't believe I'm back in this place."

"This is too weird. We've been attacked, saved and in hiding again. Unbelievable. This is beyond Hollywood. Again," Naomi's words were weary.

"Truth is always stranger than fiction. We're just following a contingency plan," Ish looked at Ruth. "We worked this out a long time ago. This is one of the options we planned. We just didn't plan that we would be the evacuees."

Ruth motioned for Ish to sit. Ish and Ruth took chairs facing each other. Knee to knee, they leaned forward whispering.

Bubba, Pablo, and Naomi formed their prayer circle with the old office chairs. Jack walked up to the balcony window alone.

The tall window was designed to look like a firing aperture on an old castle. Jack peered carefully. He brushed the curtain back a few inches. Far below, the Hudson River was a bright ribbon in the moonlight. The big country homes nestled on the east bank of hills under a cloudless sky above. Patches from an earlier snow looked blue in the moonglow.

Jack sighed. *How many times have I done this? Looked out there. Right there is the other world away from West Point that promised so much. God, I hated this place. Now, I'm back. Trapped like a rat. Worse. Again.*

Jack walked over and plopped down on a couch, another relic, on the balcony. Sleep sneaked up without warning. The steps from conscious thought to fade to black rest were so tiny as to not even be noticed.

When Jack woke up the room was totally dark. Someone had covered him with a wool Army blanket. For the foggiest of seconds, he couldn't remember where he was or how he got there. Before fear grabbed him, the details washed up in his mind like shells in the receding tide. *It sucks to be back at West Point. But, I'm still alive.* He had to urinate badly. Slowly, he fumbled to find the door his memory recalled.

West Point, NY
December 8th, 2012
Saturday

Jack's eyes welcomed the morning light. Ever since Jack's childhood deathly fear of the dark, he exalted in light over the darkness, no matter what. He remembered fear rising as his bedroom door closed down the radius of light in his room to a tiny few degrees. Everybody else was sitting at the battered conference table. A platter of food waited there. *Why didn't they wake me up?*

"Ah, Jack, Good morning, Sir," said Bubba.

'Good morning, Jack' rang around the Amigos. Ruth and Ish were in private conference again. Pablo looked cheerful. Naomi smiled kindly at Jack and offered him a plate.

"Ish and I had quite a meeting with our host, the good Lieutenant Colonel," Ruth announced. Jack heaped on the bagels and fruit. "The attack yesterday on the DEA is big in the news. We lost fourteen people in the attack. Sixty more are in the hospital. Two of the attackers were killed."

"Those numbers seem low," said Bubba.

"The bombs caused most of our casualties. But the bombing was not indiscriminate. They could've taken down the whole building. But, they only went for a couple of select places. The gunmen searched the building for specific targets. The object of all of their effort was us," said Ruth.

"The NITs must know more about Rosetta than we suspected. They're targeting the cinquefoils hard. This is out and out cyber war now," said Ish.

"Ish and I were reported dead. Three unidentified persons were declared dead, also. But we don't think that story will fly for long," said Ruth.

"It seems that Lieutenant General Larry Trento made some decisions on our behalf. They're implementing some sequels we have as contingency plans," said Ish.

"I wouldn't characterize his decisions as such. The decisions are being made over our heads. Without due consideration," Ruth's crow's feet framed the narrow squint of her eyes.

"We're to stay here until Rosetta 6.2 is good to go," said Ish.

"Here at West Point?" asked Naomi.

"Here in this room," Ruth shook her head.

"In this room?" asked Naomi.

"Yeah, the plan is to keep us right here," Ish replied.

"Why?" asked Pablo.

"When the DEA was attacked, in the open, in daylight, with bombs and a bunch of assassins, that put any idea of safe houses under DEA out of the question. Too much is compromised. We can't be sure about what isn't compromised within the DEA," said Ish.

"How about Camp Peary and the CIA?" asked Bubba. Decades ago the newspapers printed what the locals already knew. Camp Peary was not a Navy base, it's the Central Intelligence Agency 'farm'. Camp Peary was close to Bubba's home and Barbara.

"No go. We lost confidence in all safe houses, even those run by the CIA. West Point is a closed post. The Army is determined to have a drug free zone where the soul of the Army is nurtured. The Great American Public, is welcomed to walk the hallowed ground in awe, but that's it. The Great American Public is watched very carefully. There won't be any surprises here."

"No kidding," said Jack.

"The computer facilities here at Thayer Hall support the Academy. They've got a good Department of Computer Science. But, they also do other work. It's a storage facility for other things." Ish pointed to the outside wall, "This building is made of granite and snuggled up against more rock, so only a direct hit with a nuke can take it down. Some very classified work is done here. There are many computer firewalls to allow very compartmentalized work. We can access the entire military system. It isn't traceable to here. The same is true for internet work."

"Internet work can always be traced," said Bubba.

"Maybe. Maybe not," Ish grinned wickedly. "Here are the rules of engagement for our confinement. When the cadets have to go back to their rooms at eleven, we have free reign of the building. Until then, we need to stay in here."

"When do they come in in the morning?" asked Bubba.

"Staff can be in as early as six a.m. The building has an automatic locking system that runs everyone out by eleven and doesn't let them in until six," said Ish.

"Oh, joy. I get to live the Diary of Anne Frank in my own country," said Ruth.

"We'll be able to work on remotes in this room during the day. But we really can't wander about," said Ish.

"Or go outside?" asked Bubba.

"Not yet. Maybe we can figure a way later, Bubba," Ish's smile was his sympathy.

"This will get cozy," said Pablo.

"It will get better. Our lieutenant colonel is getting things for us. In fact he will get everything. He will work out food from the messhall, so it looks like chow for a guard detail. He will get more clothes. He will work it all out," said Ish.

"It's unbelievable," Ruth started a smokeless cigarette.

"It'll be bearable," said Naomi.

"It'll be unbelievable," said Jack. *Four flights. Four refugees. Each time is less freedom. More prison. How long can this go on? But, I'm not dead yet. Ah. It could be worse. How long can my luck hold out?*

The Amigos divided the room into work and rest spaces. Respectful people bent over backwards to be solicitous and kind to one another. Jack did his best to check out the room for security as his specialty. The window had a small attenuating device. The attenuating device created vibrations that bounce against the window to garble the normal vibrations that could be picked up by a sensor. *Thayer Hall has to have this? What goes on in this academic building?*

The light from the single window bounced off the walls to brighten the room throughout the day. When night came running as it does in December, the darkness couldn't be dispelled. It looked like the dimly lit recesses of an exclusive men's club with individual reading lamps spread around the room. The room kept the musty odor of dust despite a day of serious scrubbing. This eventide, after the Group ate together at the old conference table, Bubba offered some commentary.

"And the evening and the morning were the first day. So it is written. So must it be," Bubba's face sagged under its own weight. "We're brought to this place for a purpose. In all things, even in hardship and during despair, we're to give thanks because God's mercy is great. God's love is great. God is great and His Will be done in this world and in the next. I know that we're moving downscale in our living accommodations." He smiled at Ish and Ruth, "Your safe houses were more than adequate, thank you. But, I know, I just know…that something very good is going to come out of our time here. Something very good, maybe wonderful is going to come out of this place. I don't know what that is, but I wanted to share that with y'all." The Amigos nodded politely.

Jack couldn't see goodness in this promontory of cold gray stone. He searched his heart memories for some sense of goodness. The only thing that warmed even one cockle was the friendship of his classmates. *This is the place of my band of brothers. My fellowship of the Ring.*

Jack didn't want to face the inquisition he knew his mind would make of his heart if he left his mind unoccupied. He knew to stay busy just to be busy and feel the fulfillment of rest that comes with utter fatigue. It kept the demons of questions that can not be denied away for another night. Jack read until he fell dead asleep.

West Point, NY
December 11th, 2012
Tuesday

Quickly, Ish got the equipment they needed to go to work. A new Rosetta 6.2 ops center was set up in the old storage room as its own stand alone system. The only clue that it existed was the e-mailbox. Ish said, "I'm worried about trace-ability. So class whaddya gonna do?"

Ish wrote his big bullets on a whyteboard. "Consider these."

- How can we use the DOD system without being found out?
- How can we use commercial systems without being found out?
- How can we continue with the end-to-end test?
- How can we defend/replace the Rosetta Cinquefoil icons being destroyed?
- How will we know that Rosetta 6.2 is ready to go?

Ish stood back and crossed his arms on his chest. He lowered his head and stuck out his lower lip. Jack smiled. *Ish's trademark thinking pose.*

Jack searched his mind for the answers. He was on the edge of an answer, but the words didn't shape for him. *There's got to be a simple answer that ties all togther.* The solution lay just beyond the darkness in his mind.

Bubba spoke up, "The distinction between DOD and commercial is mute, Ish. Both have high security sites."

"Right you are, Bubba," Ish nodded his head with increasing vigor. "But, I think the distinction remains in terms of the execution of Rosetta 6.2. Rosetta gets kicked off from DOD systems. Then, all of the feedback loops, battle damage assessment if you will, come back to DOD systems. Our command and control primary link for DEA is from the Pentagon. I need to change the words." Ish erased the first two bullets and wrote:

- How can we maintain Rosetta C4ISR fusion on DOD systems?
- How can we insure Rosetta operability on commercial systems?

"Better?" asked Ish. He recrossed his arms.

"What is C4ISR fusion?" asked Pablo.

"Command, control, communications, computers, intelligence, surveillance, reconnaissance fusion. It means everything that information has to do in a system of information systems to serve the military commander. Which, by the way, is exactly what information must do for Rosetta 6.2."

"Isn't Rosetta 6.2 just a military operation? Isn't Lieutenant General Trento going to be in charge?" asked Naomi.

Ish placed his hands in front of him in the unfolding flowers motion he used when teaching. "Rosetta 6.2 looks like a military operation in specific phases. It uses the military forces and resources in a big way. But, it is, quite clearly, the implementation of public policy on behalf of the President of the United States of America to break the back of the NITs in our country. War is always an extension of politics."

Eyebrows raised and chins dropped across the room.

"Rosetta 6.2 employs the total power—military, economic, legal, police, information, and moral—of the Government of the United States, good ole' GOTUS, to achieve goals approved by the Chief Executive of the United States of America."

"Then we had better get it right," said Pablo.

"You're so correct. We must get it absolutely right," Ruth made a knife jab with her hand. "Rosetta is going to save our country in a campaign. It'll be blow after blow against the NITs until we win, or all is lost and the criminals and terrorists win. The criminals will take over the country like the criminals called Nazi's did in Germany. Like they have around the world since the end of the Cold War. And the terrorists will have free hands."

"Criminals like Nazi's run the U.S.? I worry more about Hillary," scoffed Naomi.

"Both sides worry about the other in domestic politics. My job, Naomi, is to fight the NITs. But, you're right, the criminals don't run all things yet. Not just yet. Criminals destroy the rule of law when they corrupt the police and courts. The justice system is worse than a joke when it's for sale. You know how much the People have lost confidence and trust in justice. The judges are tyrants. The judges subverted the law to liberal politics. They make the laws up as they like. So, its criminals and tyrants together. You're right about that. Same difference eventually. One becomes the other over time," Ruth read their reactions.

"Rosetta 6.2 will operate under a to-be-signed Presidential Decision Directive to seize and maintain the initiative against the NITs. We'll go for their center of gravity and drive to the hilt to kill this beast. How am I doing, Ish?" Ruth's smile smoothed the hardness from her brittle features.

"You're doing great, Ruth," said Ish.

"Ish taught me all about planning and ops. He is the chief planner for Rosetta 6.2, as you know, and I am the first approver. I presented Rosetta successfully to the final approving authority," Ruth paused for effect.

"I have an idea about that. About how to make Rosetta ready," Jack found his idea. "Look at your fourth bullet—Protection of the icons. Let's not do it. Let's not protect the icons. Let the bad guys destroy all of them. Let the druggies get rid of every Rosetta Cinquefoil icon they find. We watch and see which ones they find and which ones they miss. That'll tell us something about their search capabilities. As long as we have a master somewhere, then we wait and at the right time, we re-populate the Cinquefoil icons and activate Rosetta before they can hit. It's a deception."

"Great idea, but I have the only complete copy of the five hundred twenty three Rosetta Cinquefoil icons," Ish pulled a thin black disk from his shirt pocket. "That would be risky to go down to only one copy residing at this one location only."

"Ish, I have a copy of all five hundred and twenty-three at my study carol in the stacks of the library and here," Pablo pulled a thin black disk from a pocket protector.

"Uh, Ish, me too," Naomi looked sheepish, "I made a copy on the net server in DC at the UMW and here." She reached into her purse by her chair and pulled out a thin black disk.

"So much for my configuration control!" laughed Ish.

"We should go with Jack's idea. Let the NITs take out every Rosetta Cinquefoil icon they can. We get ourselves ready. When we need to act and act fast, we will," said Ruth.

"Yes, ma'am. That's the way to go. We can play needle in the haystack for a couple of months. We might have to make the whole world our haystack."

West Point, NY
December 15th, 2012
Saturday

The week blurred with work. Jack and Pablo became running partners in the evening. They emerged when the building was empty and cleared for the night. The men ran hard. They went up a flight of stairs for a quick lap of one floor and then up another flight for another lap for four stories. They ran until sweat soaked through and through and they were breathless.

They raced past the Winter Holiday decorations papering the hallways. The symbols of Christmas abounded in flora, color and context, but the word Christmas was nowhere to be seen.

"Look Pablo. No Christmas here. West Point is politically correct too," gasped Jack.

"Ah, I noticed. Would that they were historically correct," gulped Pablo. They picked up the pace.

The runners staggered back to their cell. They joined everyone for a midnight snack. Naomi offered them hot apple pie a la mode. They smiled like little boys.

"You know I have good news about our loved ones on the outside. I know how much it hurts to be here for Christmas," Ish looked at Ruth, "and Hannukah. But I have the good news that everyone is safe and sound. I mean everyone."

"Can we get through to them?" Naomi's voice cracked.

"No, I'm sorry, we can't. We just can't do that, Naomi. It will put them at too much risk. The NITs didn't buy the story that we were killed."

"Some Christmas," said Jack.

"Jack. Guys. I'm really sorry. But our families will thank us when this is over. When we win," said Ish.

"What do our families know?" asked Bubba.

"They were told that we're no more," Ish sighed.

"What? What? You said that was a temporary story! That's terrible! That's too terrible a burden on them! How could you? My sweet Bar," Bubba's face was red.

"Oh no," Naomi held her face in her hands. She sobbed, "my babies, my babies".

"Ish that was too far," said Jack. *My baby angels think I'm dead. How is Maude handling it?*

"You told my mother that I'm dead?" Pablo looked wounded.

"Yes, because we had to. It was in their best interest to stay alive. It'll be in your best interest ultimately. Don't you get it? The NITs weren't buying our death, but they know our families think we're dead. If we're so out of touch then it's like we're actually dead. They can't be sure that what they do to our loved ones would get reported to us, let alone leverage against us. Vengeance without profit isn't their style. At least, not for now," said Ruth.

"You couldn't give some secret message? C'mon folks," Bubba drained pale as fast as he flashed beet red.

"It was my decision. I know it causes concern, but it is the safest way," said Ruth. Naomi kept crying. Pablo's eyes moistened. Jack kept his head bowed.

"Ruth, please. When did you make this decision? Why can't we let the truth get through? Just to our spouses, huh?" asked Bubba.

"It was my decision the day after we got here," Ruth lifted her chin.

"It was my idea, friends. It includes lying to my wife and family, too. It's the best way," said Ish.

Bubba shook his head.

Pablo ventured the tiniest of smiles. "I know, I know, I think I know. We'll pray and give the message to the Holy Ghost to tell our loved ones that we're well."

Jack rolled his eyes, "Great. More prayer. Just what we need."

"Yeah, it's what we need. God refuses nothing in His Will from his beloved. The Holy Ghost will deliver the message," said Bubba.

"And comfort," said Ish.

"No. They'll get the real deal. The message, a real message will be sent and they'll get it. And they'll know," Naomi breathed deeply.

"Let's do it now!" said Bubba.

Bubba knelt before the long couch like it was an altar rail. Ish, Pablo and Naomi lined up beside him on their knees. Bubba said, "Oh Lord, Father God, Abba, Abba, Abba."

Ruth and Jack looked at the row of praying petitioners and then at each other. Jack saw the deep curiosity in Ruth's eyes. They finished their treat in silence as the rest of the Amigos prayed and prayed. Finally, they rose, reluctantly, from their knees to reheat their cold food and eat with enthusiasm. *They sure look happy.* Jack and Ruth retired to their corners to read alone.

West Point, NY
December 20th, 2012
Thursday

The work on Rosetta 6.2 slowed. Creativity might be coaxed, but it can't be commanded. Ish interrupted each day on a irregular basis with what he called his 'Rosetta 6.2 Tutorials'. So, the Amigos sat with rapt attention after Supper in the chill early winter evening that was as bitterly cold as the heart of winter. The cold permeated the stone walls, despite their several feet of thickness, so they ceased to act as insulation, but acted as conductors for biting cold. The Amigos bundled in borrowed sweaters and sipped hot beverages.

"Okay, Amigos. Yesterday we discussed the idea of center of gravity and culminating point. The center of gravity is the long pole in the enemy tent. Pardon the mixed metaphor. Take it down and the tent falls down around your ears. The culminating point is where the enemy has had all he can take and it's all over for him. His center of gravity is about to go when he reaches his culminating point. What would be, then, the center of gravity and the culminating point for the NTs?"

"There's always been a supply and demand argument for drug use. The old war on drugs sought to cut off the supply of drugs. The policy of the past fifteen years is to work more on the demand of drugs through education and propaganda. Neither way worked. Look what happened to Columbia. Venezuela. Bolivia. Peru and now Africa," said Jack.

"Good. But, the supply and demand metaphor is the argument that drugs is about economics. That assumes that everything is subject to market forces. It doesn't allow for a vertical demand curve. Everybody up on their micro-economics? Supply and demand curves? Regardless, it's the wrong model," Ish paused.

"Consider another idea. Drugs are a form of poison being

smuggled into the country. The poison is very valuable, so it's moved along supply routes because of the lucrative freight tariffs that each person in the chain of custody can successfully charge. I know that that still sounds like an economic model. Consider this then. When the poison gets to its destination it's used to kill people. Like a terrorist attack. Then where would we go for a center of gravity?" asked Ish.

"The narco-terrorist leadership?" asked Naomi.

"Maybe," said Ish. He stood tall with his heels together. "But, if the NITs disappeared tomorrow, then there would be new NITs the next day. What's the key to drug use?"

"I would venture to say the users, but you have already dismissed that option—the demand side. So, if it isn't the bosses and it isn't the users, I mean the targets for a chemical attack, then it is the means of attack. That's the ways the drugs get to the users or the drugs themselves. Aha!" Pablo smiled, "That's it! It's the drugs."

"Bingo! That's exactly it. The drugs are the poison weapon. The drugs are the chemical weapons. Get rid of the chemicals and then you can't have a chemical war," said Ish.

"Isn't that really hard to do? The quantities are so small. They're located everywhere. They can be hidden anywhere. Some can be made at home. How are you gonna do that Ish?" asked Jack.

"It t'is hard. But, not impossible. Switch metaphors for a second with me. If there were a batch of bad honey on the shelves that was poison, then what would happen?"

"Every jar of honey in the stores would be taken down," said Naomi.

"And if the poison problem was nationwide, not with some local distribution of a bad batch?" continued Ish.

"Then, every jar of honey in every store would be taken down," said Bubba.

"But honey in stores is easier to get to than drugs in nooks and crannies under the control of bad guys," said Jack.

"Both problems are finite. Large numbers, grant you, but still finite. If you had to eradicate honey from the face of the earth then what would you have to do?" Ish's eyes narrowed.

"Seize all the honey in all the stores. Seize all the honey in the hives. Smash the hives. Kill or neuter the bees. Pull up flowers, especially the clover, or neuter the plants," said Pablo.

"You could consider killing all the queen bees," said Bubba.

"Hmm. The bees are not the users, the people who buy the honey are the users," said Ish.

"The queen bees are the NITs!" said Bubba.

"The NITs, like bees, have stingers enough," said Naomi.

"And honey has been around as long as alcohol and drugs," offered Pablo.

"Then, what is the center of gravity for drugs?" asked Ish. His smile played his bright white piano teeth.

"Seize all the drugs, everywhere and destroy all the queen bees and kill or neuter as many bees as you can" said Naomi.

"Yeah, absolutely so! That is what Rosetta 6.2 is going to do."

"How?" asked Pablo.

"Rosetta 6.2 is going to activate every police officer, every security officer that is straight, every soldier, sailor, marine, airman, coastie, state trooper, county mounty, school crossing guard, you name it, in this country to scoop up every ounce of drugs in this country," said Ish.

"Every ounce, really?" asked Jack.

"Trust me. Is there any doubt in your mind that the cops in any town in this country could sit down and make a list of almost every place drugs are sold, who sells them, who buys them, etc. in their town?" asked Ish.

The Amigos looked at one another. No one would argue.

"The fourth amendment rights of search and seizure, will make it difficult," said Jack.

"They could. They would. But, Jack, when Rosetta 6.2 kicks in, things are going to happen very, very fast. Rosetta 6.2 harnesses the power of the Omni to gather all the information we need. Rosetta will gather more than all the information that we need. Believe it or not, we can do it. No. You can do it. Your work on Rosetta is going to make this all happen. We're going to pull up all the data on every ounce of drugs in this country and put it to work."

"The data is time sensitive, Ish. The drugs are consumed and brought into the U.S. at a certain velocity. Furthermore, that velocity has high volatility," said Pablo

"Sure, the honey is in production, in transit and in use at the same time," said Ish. "But, our reach is going to be the longest arm of the law than you ever imagined. It's going to be the biggest arm of the law that you ever saw. We will get a lot of volunteer help. So much happens when Rosetta 6.2 kicks. Assignments go to every police station in the country. Every active and reserve unit in the military gets a mission. Every federal officer gets an assignment. Every private security service gets a task we trust them with," said Ish.

"What about the corrupt ones in the police and military?" asked Bubba.

Ish grew grim in a flash. "There's a very specific plan for those people. We will talk about that later in detail, because the plan needs fine tuning. Maybe a new direction."

"Rosetta 6.2 is going to coordinate the power of millions of persons in manpower to seize the NITs and all the druggies."

"The users?" asked Pablo.

"The users and the drug dealers will be swooped up."

"How many people is that? Altogether?" asked Naomi.

"Fifteen million minimum. Thirty million tops," said Ruth forcefully.

"Thirty million. That's how many undocumented workers there are. No one can handle that. That's why they aren't deported," said Pablo.

"You mean, illegal aliens," said Bubba.

"Whatever you like. No one can handle those numbers politically," said Pablo.

"That is a pretty broad spread in the estimate," said Jack.

"As Omni comes on line, we will know within short order, exactly how many it is."

"If there are over three hundred million people in America, then almost one in ten or one in twenty is going to be affected. That's before you touch the one in nine that are illegals. So twenty per cent of the country may be against you from the start," said Pablo.

"Everyone, Pablo, everyone, is going to be affected by Rosetta 6.2," said Ruth.

"Not all of those people will be put in jail," cautioned Ish, "but they'll all be affected. Their drugs are going to be taken from them and destroyed."

"Wow!" said Bubba.

"Wow is right," said Ish.

"Then what? Won't they just come back because you missed one queen bee somewhere? How does this center of gravity lead the enemy to a culminating point?" asked Jack.

"First, seizing and controlling all the honey for six months or so will bring the enemy to a culminating point. The terrorist collaborators will be desperate for money. Then other things kick in from Rosetta. Like we make it awful to even want honey. We make honey seem bitter, not sweet. We make it odd and socially beyond the pale, and I mean for everyone, any one, to want to consume honey. We make it really, really shameful."

"Double wow," said Pablo.

"Me, too, wow," said Naomi softly.

West Point, NY
December 25th, 2012
Tuesday

Christmas broke without a sound. There was the usual stirring of bodies slipping sleep of their bodies and rising from the cots and couches. The realization, though, that this morning was Christmas indeed, opened like a present in their minds.

"Hey folks, Merry CHRIST-mas! Rise shine and give God the Glory this CHRISTmas day!" Bubba almost shouted the 'Christ' of the word and fully pronounced the last syllable as 'mass'. He sang the hymn he greeted so many mornings "Holy, holy, holy."

"Lord, God almighty," Naomi, Pablo and Ish joined.

"Early in the morning, our song shall rise to thee."

"Holy, holy, holy."

"Merciful and mighty."

"God in three persons, blessed trinity," Bubba's eyes twinkled with tears. He started the song again. They joined hands in a circle and sang through three times more. The beauty of the harmony of their hearts was too much for them to stop too soon. They hugged and said 'Merry CHRISTmas, Brother and Merry CHRISTmas sister'. Naomi hugged and kissed Ruth on the cheek. Bubba grabbed Jack and pulled him into a bear hug. Much to Jack's surprise, Bubba kissed him on the forehead. Bubba hurried out to fetch the breakfast trailer. He rolled it in with a flourish. The breakfast was overboard in its plenty. It was like a brunch on steroids.

Bubba chirped gleefully, "Hey, y'all look at your computers. Boot 'em up and take a look see." The Amigos indulged him. They chuckled at the images that popped up. Bubba created quite a display and personalized each one with touching kindness. Each graphic show was a variation on 'Twas the Night Before Christmas' where the jolly old elf, who morphed to look like Bubba himself, left a big red sack of presents. The red sack was the treasure trove of delights. The presents may have been virtual, but they were all things dearly enjoyed by the recipient. Smiles warmed the room. Laughter made the old storage room sparkle.

Naomi rushed to give Bubba a big hug and kiss. "Thank you so much. You're too sweet! Where did you get those pictures of my babies?"

Bubba blushed. Ruth walked and kissed him lightly and elegantly on the check. "Thank you, Bubba. You are such a thoughtful gentleman. I love the Channukah memories."

Pablo and Ish slapped Bubba on the back and hugged him in turn. Jack was dumbstruck. The red sack presented photos of his family, his old home, his job, his family—including his departed parents—and, even better still, cards that his kids might have given him this Christmas. The cards looked so authentic, it was uncanny. There were other virtual presents of West Point and Army memorabilia and Virginia historical bric-a-brac. There were photos of the kind of houses and land that Jack might dream of buying some day. There were books he wanted to read and food he liked to eat. The presents seemed to touch every thing of interest that Jack and Bubba shared over a couple of years on the job and the intense past few months.

Ish grumped, "Bubba you've been off the job a bit, haven't you?"

Bubba's face dropped faster than a scolded beagle, "Not much." Ish's stern black mask cracked into a smile.

"How did you do this?" Ruth hit 'did' with inflection like a drum.

"Truth is," Bubba looked around the room like he was checking for spies, "I used some of the Rosetta capabilities."

"Ah."

Breakfast lingered over more and more coffee. Eventually, the Amigos found their individual spaces a few feet apart and quiet gathered over the room. They went back to their individual presents from Bubba. They played with the images and sounds. Bubba had a lovely unfolding of the Biblical CHRISTmas story in pictures and special effects. The rest of the day wound itself out like the long chains of a grandfather clock being pulled by their own heavy weight. Naps, reading and quiet talk took turns. Yet, the feeling of the day remained special.

The Christmas feast arrived well after dark made its closing call to pull the curtain on the day. Christmas was just the afterglow in the heart. Pablo asked to light the advent candle centerpiece. He spoke lovingly of the four weeks leading up to CHRIST-mass. Pablo thanked God for Jesus and Mary and for all the blessings they brought to a suffering world. He concluded in Latin and translated into English, 'let there be peace on earth, good will toward men'.

The meal was sumptuous. The strong smells of bread, meat and gravy warded away the cold and dark as much as any fire could in their granite cave. The cinnamon touch to the hot cider and apple pie added an authentic Christmas scent. The holly scented advent candles filled their nose's memories of Christmas.

"We've come a long way since Thanksgiving, haven't we?" asked Bubba.

"How so?" asked Ruth.

"Well," drawled Bubba, "it is always a long ways from Thanksgiving to CHRIST-mass. We're finally here, so it has been a long while."

"Huh? It's only long if you're a kid. Or a captive," said Jack.

"Plus the couple of hundred miles from NoVa to New Yawk is like a million miles from God's country to Sodom and Gomorrah," said Bubba.

"Sodom and Gomorrah are 50 miles south of here down the Hudson. This is just Hell here," offered Jack. Everyone obliged in smiles.

"Christmas has come and gone and our families are fine and still they live," said Bubba.

"Or, so we know now," said Jack. Jack watched Bubba's forehead wrinkle at the comment.

Bubba shrugged, "We've come a long way emotionally. We actually went through a CHRIST-mass without our People and lived to tell about it."

"No little accomplishment," said Naomi.

"More than that, believe it or not we just celebrated a CHRIST-mass without possessions. We celebrated Christ first, foremost and last," said Bubba.

"How about the presents you gave us?" asked Ruth pleasantly.

"They were virtual," Bubba's blue eyes didn't blink.

"They were real enough for me," said Naomi.

"Me too," said Ruth.

"Thanks, ladies, but you know when the jewelry is real or not," Bubba chuckled at himself.

"We celebrated CHRIST only this CHRIST-mass in loving one another as we love God. That's been so special for me. I may recommend it to Barb when I get home, that we do it this way some year when the grandbabies don't come home."

"And when would that ever be? No grandchildren at your house?" asked Ish.

"Oh yeah. Not much chance of that. Least, I hope not."

"Not much chance you'll be alone with the missus, brother Bubba. But, I know what you mean. I felt it too. I felt a specialness this Christmas here," said Ish.

"It was special, because it was a sanctification," said Pablo as he reached for more pie.

"You became saints?" asked Jack.

"No. We became purified in our time here. Our celebration of CHRIST-mass was pure love," said Pablo.

"I agree," said Naomi. All heads turned to the power of her voice. "This time, as painful as it was, was a cup that couldn't pass. We had to drink from it. And when we did, we became as sanctified as I have ever felt in my life."

"Huh?" Jack poured a cup of coffee.

"We did what we didn't want to do, like Jesus went to the cross when He didn't want to do it," Naomi said with authority. "Course, now, we aren't Jesus, and this room itn't the cross. But the pain we bore was at the Father's bidding for the Father's will."

"I thought the U.S. government was hiding us out here," said Jack.

"We are sanctified for a purpose. We'll find out what that is in due time," said Pablo. Bubba, Ish and Naomi nodded their heads in agreement.

"So, you're trying to find pleasure in some pain?" asked Jack. "Is this the stuff of martyrdom? Useful fictions?"

"John-James, did you not feel the special spirit of yesterday and today in this place and with us?" Bubba motioned to his friends.

"Yes, but I always feel the Holiday," said Jack.

"Not the holiday, the Holy Day. The feeling you feel every year may be a piece of the spirit. But, say, didn't you feel something special with us?" asked Pablo.

Jack searched his own heart. *I do feel different. I don't know what it is.*

"I miss Christmas with my family," Jack's voice cracked.

"I felt something special. I felt a warmth of friendship, no," Ruth gathered herself for a second. "The comradeship. That was indeed special."

"Thanks. We're talking about something even better than warmth. Although a real warmth is part of it all," said Naomi.

"Thanks, Ruth. Jack. I'm glad that you felt something different. Both of you look at us a great deal, but maybe you don't see what's really happening inside of us. Both of you dear hearts have listened to much, but you don't understand. Really. Jesus said that you should know the truth and the truth will set you free," said Ish.

Ruth stiffened.

"We've had the most remarkable experiences of our lives. It isn't all this near death excitement of almost being killed. Running for our lives and hiding. Being hunted. The most important things happened inside of us. It happened to us individually and very personally. Intimately. And, still, it happened to all of us at the same time. I know better than to preach in the workplace, but this is our home for now. And I have the right of free speech, even to my boss," Bubba, Pablo and Naomi nodded in the affirmative to Ish.

"We're changed people, even though you can't see it. Maybe you can't hear it or watch it yet in our actions and words, but we're more transformed than we used to be, to be the men and women that

Jesus wants us to be. We are sanctified for purpose. You could understand everything I'm saying, if you had a personal relationship with Jesus. Until you do, you'll see through a glass darkly and never know what we know. All of these trials will work to good for the believers in Christ Jesus. They should work good for you too, but they'll work great when you believe. We know we're part of a really big purpose. Beyond Rosetta 6.2," Ish was radiant.

"Amen," said Bubba.

"Amen," said Pablo.

"Amen and amen," said Naomi.

"I'll take that under advisement," said Ruth. She smiled graciously.

"I'll see what I see," said Jack.

"Jack, I'm so confident that you'll see all someday. Please pass that pie, Sister Naomi," said Ish. The meal, like the day, wound down and was done.

West Point, NY
December 26th, 2012
Wednesday

The morning after Christmas was unique because it held the day before as a memory. That awareness walked in everyone's mind, first thing, as gently as natural light wakes a sleepy head. Jack couldn't wait for Ish's plan to get out and about. The day after Christmas, while the Cadets were on leave, the Amigos would walk around like residents on the post. First, the Amigos had to map out every security camera and possible long-range surveillance shot from across the Hudson. Rosetta 6.2 provided the software tricks to save them. They borrowed a friendly virus to screen and delete their images from every camera up-linked to any unblinking satellite, cell tower or network.

It took awhile to set up their security properly. Finally, they bundled up against the bitter cold. The Amigos exited Thayer Hall in twos to taste the air outside. A heavy new snow provided a blanket a foot deep. The sun flashed on the whiteness stinging unprotected eyes.

Pablo kicked his feet as he walked. The powder of snow splayed out to catch the light so the tiny crystals glimmered and sparkled. It looked like pixie dust.

"Like it, huh?" asked Jack. Pablo blazed a trail around the Plain towards Trophy Point. The snow before them looked like the clean unbroken icing of the perfect cake.

"Yeah, don't you?" Pablo waved at Ish and Bubba and Naomi and Ruth as they took the plowed paths back towards the barracks and the Hotel Thayer.

"Yeah, I do," Jack kicked his feet like Pablo to push out a bigger snow wake as he walked. He looked back at their trail. The trail marred the beauty of the smooth snow, but only by making the ugly scar of a trail could they enjoy the pleasure of the plowing the snow field. When they reached Trophy Point, Jack moved ahead around the rows of old captured cannons wrapped in a blanket of white. He walked and skidded a few feet down the steep drop of the amphitheater hill. Pablo followed him. Jack tried to drink in the cold through deep gulps. He pointed to his left.

"Storm King," said Jack. The mountain stood as a shoulder to the sky. It framed the specatacular view of the Hudson valley. The rock outcroppings looked black against the stark white of the snow. The Hudson River flowed directly at them with huge blocks of ice floating in its dark blue waters. A hundred feet below and out of sight the river made its dramatic ninety degree turn to create the west point of the Hudson. More hills on the right held the river in place. *I never tire of seeing this. Never.*

"I used to come here when I was a cadet," said Jack. Pablo nodded 'go on'.

"As much as this place could suck, this spot here, is always beautiful. Every season is great."

"It is beautiful," agreed Pablo.

"At night you can see the lights of towns upriver. I used to wonder about all the normal things going on up there, when I was here in fantasy land. I thought about families having meals together, watching TV, guys with their own rooms, instead being in the rat race here at the West Point experimental psychology lab."

"Makes sense to me. You were away from home," said Pablo.

"Yeah, I thought a lot about home then," said Jack. "I felt like

I could be at home, sometimes, when I just looked out at this and thought about my family."

"You were lonely, really lonely?"

"Yeah. It really sucked. I wanted to be home so badly, that I really felt like I could be transported there."

"I know that feeling," said Pablo.

"When you went to college?" asked Jack.

"Some, but more now," answered Pablo.

"Now?"

"Yes, I miss the sacraments so badly," said Pablo looking afar and away.

"Communion? You miss communion like family?"

"Yes, very much so. I'm hungry for the closeness to God that only comes in the sacraments," Pablo's brown eyes looked hurt.

"I don't get it, Pablo."

"Many don't, but some do. Like Ish said last night, the biggest things in our lives are what happens on our insides. You can't see the earthquakes, the volcanoes, the storms inside the human being."

"I still don't get it."

"The unity of the physical, the spiritual and the mental," Pablo added emphasis, "for me, is the communion bread and wine that is a sacrament to me. Jesus is physically present to me."

"Isn't that cannabalism?"

"Not to us, to me. No, it satisfies a hunger within me that nothing else can do. I haven't had it in weeks now."

They walked back up and around the high winding road up past the chapels. Jack couldn't figure Pablo out. *Odd hunger for communion. Like it's real life. But my Trophy Point, that's a place of peace. Sweet peace. Every season. Any hour day or night.* Jack made a new snow plow path back to Thayer Hall. More work waited each short day and long night.

West Point, NY
December 31st, 2012
Monday

New Year's Eve was bitter cold. The wind gusts rocked and as fast and furious as a temper tantrum. Bubba cut short his walk because of the battering cold. After supper, Ish announced that he procured the beverages and hors d'oerves of their choice, or he hoped it was their choice, because it was too late to change it now to celebrate the New Year.

The conversation meandered through the evening in pleasant circles of no consequence. Ish actually did what he promised. There was cheese and bread, fishy things, meaty things with sauces, vegetables with dip, salty crunchy and gooey chocalatey to match every individual desire.

"I don't know if I can make it to midnight," moaned Bubba. His eyes sagged at half mast.

"Sure you can," said Naomi.

"This's been quite a year. I don't see why I have to carry the durn thing to its bitter end. It's wore me out enough as t'is."

"It's been quite a year," agreed Naomi. Everyone nodded sagely.

"Wait until next year. This will be a year for the history books. A red letter year," said Ish.

"Your confidence is encouraging Ish," said Bubba.

"Next year is in minutes. I wonder when Rosetta will kick in."

"I wonder how it will all end," said Jack.

"It'll end well. Rosetta will be ready in a month or so. It'll kick in soon after Omni is ready. If there are no major glitches between then and now for either Rosetta 6.2 or Omni."

"Then what?" asked Jack.

"Then, there is a plan and you know what happens to plans. They all go to squat upon first contact with the enemy," said Ish.

"So what does that mean to Rosetta?" asked Naomi.

"It means that we have a plan and a timeline for Rosetta to work in phases. What will change is the actual timing of the phases. Some may take longer or shorter. We will, certainly, have to adjust actions within the phase to counter-attack the enemy's counters. Also, we may have to start phases concurrently rather than moving sequentially. Depends on the situation. Most of all, we will have thought out all of our options and the enemy's before we hit obstacles. We call it planning all the branches and sequels," said Ish.

"Yeah or before we get hit. It all depends on the Mission,

Enemy, Terrain, Troops, Time and Civilian rules of engagement[1]. METT-T-C," said Jack. He chugged another German beer.

"The phases for Rosetta 6.2, if you haven't figured them out yet on your own, are," Ish paused and looked at Ruth. She raised her eyebrows, but nodded 'yes'. "Are as follows: one is Information Control. We get our word out and prevent the other from talking. See first. Decide first."

"Seize and maintain information dominance," interrupted Jack.

"Yes, but more than you're used to hearing about. We're going to also influence public information in unheard of ways. More on that later as I always say."

"As you always say," said Jack.

"The second phase is the attack orders for physical and information attacks. Attack First. Attack more often. These attacks continue until we bring the enemy to a culminating point and utterly defeat him. Finish Decisively."

"How long will that take?" asked Pablo.

"About six weeks. Depends on what the enemy does. Then, we go to phase three which is to win the hearts and minds of the American people."

"I have heard that before. Vietnam. Iraq," said Bubba.

"Shouldn't the hearts and minds be won before the action?" asked Naomi.

"In a perfect world, maybe. We're going to have to act when it's time to strike. The Omni is vulnerable."

"Window of vulnerability. Now, I heard that before too, Cold War," said Bubba.

"Right. But history isn't going to repeat itself here. We'll learn from history, not fail in its metaphors. So, here's one more idea. The final phase is 'de-nazification' or 'de-baathist'."

"Hope it goes like Germany, not Iraq," said Bubba.

"I could have called it 'Reconstruction', but that period was too flawed. De-Nazification of Germany was very effective," said Ish.

"Especially since some Southerners never got properly reconstructed," smiled Bubba.

---

1. Rules of Engagement. Instructions for soldiers on what is allowed or not, like when to engage with what weapons. Known as ROE. This information is included in every operations order.

"That and other things," said Ish.

"Jury is still out on Iraq. It'll stay undecided for decades or longer," said Bubba.

"This is the most important phase, because it'll determine if we win or lose. We are directing a revolution. Like all revolutions it's really a civil war. Most revolutions destroy the revolutionaries and discredit their ideas. It's like riding a huge wave cresting and most revolutionaries fall and drown. For Rosetta 6.2 to be a success, drugs will never be looked at the same in our country. It's about a transformation of the heart."

"Well, that worked for slavery and segregation but not because of government. Reconstruction after the first Civil War didn't fix anything. Just made it worst. Jesus won the victories," said Bubba.

"It has to work faster, with more people, and more effectively to win the war on drugs," said Ish.

"I kinda had a feel for this. But, I still don't have all the details. Can't believe the government is going to sponsor a civil war that leads to a complete revolution."

"It's about winning the current civil war and completing the revolution. The federal government isn't neutral. We either uphold and defend the Constitution or die. This is all about preserving the Constitution before it is absolutely worthless paper. You'll get it, Bubba, you will. I know I keep saying this, but you will. Next year. Next year, will be something indeed."

"Hey, this year was more than I ever dreamed. I never expected to live to see tonight."

"It seems like a lot more than a year since September. The time I missed from my family seems like forever. I can't imagine how long we will have to wait next year," said Naomi.

"The time will go by, just like this year did. No matter what you do, it will go by. The chaplain here at West Point told my class on Day One, 'this too shall pass' and it did," mumbled Jack.

"I praise God we will have a next year. That there will be a next year for us and others. Praise Him," said Pablo.

"Thank you, Pablo," Ish and Ruth chimed together. Ish raised his glass to toast.

"Hope is life. Life is Hope. Cheers to Hope."

"Cheers to Hope," they all chorused.

Pablo looked at his watch and counted in a loud voice, "Ten, nine, eight, seven…"

The rest of the Amigos checked their timepieces too.

"Three, two, one, Happy New Year!" said everyone.

"Happy New Year 2013! Lucky thirteen for us!" shouted Bubba.

The men kissed the women on the cheek and shook each other's hands and patted their backs soundly. Ruth and Naomi hugged. When Jack leaned forward to kiss Naomi, he stumbled in his haze and she caught him at the edge of her lips. Their lips brushed on the way to the cheeks.

"Happy New Year, Jack," said Naomi. Jack felt his cheek branded with the fire of her gentle kiss. He sat back in the numbness of alcohol to feel nothing else.

The Amigos sang an off-key first chorus of Auld Land Syne. Bubba excused himself to go to sleep. Ruth did likewise. Jack felt his head spinning. He laid down to feel the firebrand on his cheek and enjoy its sweet stinging. 2012 was gone to history and memory as soon as Jack closed his eyes.

2013
West Point, NY
January 1st, 2013
Tuesday

"Jack, come here please," Naomi asked evenly. She sat at the window looking down the dramatic fall to the Hudson River. In the last moments of the day in Winter the lights shifted from golden to pink to blue as the sun fell behind clouds at the edge of the earth. The last waning light illuminated the snow in the blue glaze that is brilliant in moon glow. The moon was already up, full and ready to hand off the light of the sun to the snow below.

"Jack, you need to take some breaks. Everything's going great on Rosetta 6.2. You need to find a balance in work and rest," Naomi patted his forearm.

"You mean I look bad? Is something wrong?" Jack blushed. *My father's heart disease showed up at my age now.*

"No, no, honey, you look fine," Naomi laughed softly. She called everyone 'honey'. "I just know that you're working too hard. You need to find a balance."

Jack sighed long and hard. He stared out of the window and then up at the ceiling. "I can't. I can't, Naomi."

Naomi leaned forward. "Tell me, Jack."

"I can't find the balance. I had to get a divorce to leave the Army."

"Divorce?" asked Naomi.

"Yeah. The Army was like a wife. I was totally dedicated to her."

"I truly loved the Army. Even though, I think I hated West Point, I loved the Army."

"Think you hated?" asked Naomi.

"Think I hated. I dunno. I'm not sure about that. I can name all the things I hated. Like the hypocrisy of elitist ideals and bull, uh, BS reality. But, whatever that means, I still had to get a divorce to leave the clutches of the institution to begin a new life."

"Are you happy in that new life?" Naomi smiled hopefully.

"No, no, I'm not. Not at all. But, I can't go back."

"Hmm. Maybe you aren't supposed to go back," said Naomi.

"I know this. West Point is an insular institution. The Army is an insular institution. They are inwardly-looking and inwardly-breeding and inwardly-living. Living in Officer housing is like communal living without the sex," he tried a smile and looked back again at Naomi. She was listening with her whole body. "But, I liked the intensity. I got good at that. Intensity, that is. I loved the intensity. You know I felt like West Point and then the Army was this cocoon."

"Intensity in a cocoon?"

"Yeah, not like in biology, but figuratively. To live in the cocoon for me was to live with an intensity that excluded all other things, so it was like being in a cocoon. In its separateness from the world. You know, cut off."

Naomi nodded.

"Now, I am a good husband and father. When I wasn't at work, I gave one hundred per cent to my family. That left nothing for me. I still had time for other passions. Uh, with Maude you know," Jack blushed again.

Naomi smiled her whole face smile, "I know. I don't doubt that you're a good husband and father."

"I had to leave the cocoon. Now, I kinda feel like I am back. I like the rush of what I call 'Kombat Krazy'. I like the intensity, Naomi. I really like it. You know I used to love being in the field. Playing Army."

"Maybe you're back, Jack, for more time in this cocoon. This room sure seems to fit the description. But, remember that a cocoon is about metamorphosis. West Point and the Army changed you. You were a boy and now you are a man. If this's a cocoon then you'll come out of it a changed man."

"Not a butterfly? I wanted to be a butterfly."

"You'll come out of this cocoon different. Perhaps, as Bubba said the other day, we all will."

"What will change?"

"I'm not sure, Jack, I'm not sure at all. Dealing with this Christmas away from my family, and this lie about our death, is changing me."

"What?" asked Jack.

"I don't know what. I do know who. God uses the Holy Sprit to physically work on us on earth."

"Oh," Jack was disappointed.

"I know we are all dealt with by the Holy Ghost. Right here, right now. I can feel it, Jack," Naomi squeezed his forearm with both of her hands. "But, I don't know why. I don't know what kind of butterflies we will become out of this cocoon."

"Or even if we get out of this cocoon."

"Oh, we'll leave here, John-James. We'll leave here fine. I know this at least, John-James," Naomi squeezed his arm again and walked down to chat with Ruth.

The Hudson River looked angry in a growing wind with whitecaps. *Maybe this is a cocoon. I'm ready to be a butterfly.* Jack imagined flying free and lightly with joy and peace in a field verdant and warm and abundantly alive in late Spring. *I wish.* The image soothed so he closed his eyes to rest in it.

West Point, NY
January 8th, 2013
Tuesday

The Amigos worked hard long hours every day. Before they could digest a day and its import, it was past. And so was another day and another day and so on. Ish handed out assignments with very short suspenses. He huddled with Ruth to work on their presentation for LTG Trento. LTG 'Laser' Larry Trento was going to sneak in after his lecture to the graduating seniors. The annual Ops lecture was a chance for every Army DCSOPS to make an impression on one class of West Pointers. Ish said he could write the speech right now. "He'll make the most of the opportunity to preach the virtues of the combat arms by telling graphic stories of the vices of war. He repels the weak and solicits the strong. He wants the risk takers who will make success at any cost choose bloody combat arms—infantry, armor, artillery and aviation—at their branch selection.

"He'll talk about the brotherhood of war, the manly strengths of character and brutal physical challenges of close combat. It pumps him up. LTG Trento considers his career as damaged goods—over, since his infamous, intentional widespread use of battlefield lasers was reported—just when he was at the top of his form to serve the United States Army. So, he'll just cut lose and have a good time calling it as he sees it."

It was almost 9 PM when LTG Larry Trento waltzed into their room. His face flushed with success. LTG Larry Trento took of his bemedaled jacket, pushed his seat back from the table, put his feet up, pulled out a large cigar and lit it with relish. "Ish, what've you got to tell me about Rosetta 6.2 tonight?"

Ish turned on the computer slide projector, "Welcome to our humble abode and workplace, Sir. We have Phase I of Rosetta 6.2 in the can. We need to get your take on it. And we'll see what else we need to do to make it good to go."

"Let me remind you that we have all the executive authority we need to proceed," said Ruth. She slipped into the seat next to LTG Trento.

"Phase I is the takedown of drugs domestically. We attack

sources and lines of communication externally. We round up of associated persons around the world. We seal the borders—all of them," Ish ticked off the first bullets.

"Around the world? You go into Indian Country in Afganistan? Columbia? You'll have to shoot your way in."

"Roger. On order, Rosetta 6.2 sends the taskings down to every public police or security organization, every private organization and the military."

"Every single one?" LTG Trento's cigar smoke clouded the storeroom.

Ish nodded to the affirmative. He pointed to Pablo to turn on the other projector. Ish walked over to his computer and typed. A large silver metallic rose cinquefoil appeared on the wall next to the screen with the briefing. Rosetta 6.2 was written in an English gothic font below the 3-D cinquefoil. He pointed a thin laser stylus at the screen. A list of agencies, CIA, FBI, FEMA, ATF, Secret Service, etc. started scrolling.

LTG Trento leaned forward on his elbows and puffed hard on his cigar. Ish double underlined FBI with his stylus and the list changed to show every office in the agency. As Ish scrolled down on that list and double underlined the Harrisburg, Pennsylvania office. The screen showed a menu that included maps, personnel information, information management profiles, communications architecture, specified instructions, on-call missions and on and on.

Ish opened a few more boxes to show how much more detail was available. Each new chart displayed a three dimensional color-coded graphic to show how reliable, current and perishable the information was.

"So, youse guys pick up my Uncle Louie from the Harrisburg office?" LTG Trento smirked and pushed his nose to one side to signal a mafioso 'wise guy'.

"Only if he's on our list. He won't be on our list if he isn't involved in drugs."

"You can get out orders to everyone at the same time? Really?"

"Yes," Ish opened an icon labeled 'Orders Refresh Rate Tests'. "We've been working out that for some time. The orders will be sent on time."

"What makes you think they will be obeyed?" asked LTG Trento.

"We have all the proper authorizations in the can. We just get what is needed for every organization's authentication."

"That includes the court orders. The court orders will be signed just before the execute order," said Ruth.

"How long does that take? What about crooked judges? Something will leak."

"Every signature authentication is ready to go now. We'll only need the final execute authority of the Chief Justice of the Supreme Court."

"The Court is in this? They're involved? That's new to me," confessed Larry.

"Yes. A majority of the SCOTUS[2] is read on to Rosetta."

"Risky business if you didn't read them all on," said Bubba.

"We know that. But, remember that the Court isn't Mount Olympus. They're not gods. They're the third political branch of government. If a majority approves, then a majority wins. Always."

"I'm surprised that they would go along without a full hearing with all members," said Jack.

"We began at the top with the Chief Justice. Thank God for him. He knows who will share the plan with the wrong person and leak it. He knows who won't. He knows how important it is to save the Country to save the Constitution."

"Isn't that backwards?" asked Pablo.

"No. The Constitution is the first law, the supreme law of the land. It provides the structure and process for our Nation. The Constitution provides opportunities for persons of good will to do right, but it can't enforce anything. It is a piece of paper. We, the people, are the sovereigns," Ruth looked around the room like a tiger. She was a thin, angular tiger, but fierce. She knew well what she knew.

"Lincoln put the Bill of Rights on the shelf during the Civil War and didn't get a peep out of the Court until after the war was over," said Pablo.

---

2. SCOTUS. Acronym for the Supreme Court of the United States. Other acronyms are POTUS for the President and GOTUS for the Government.

"Roosevelt interned the Japanese-Americans in their own country and got away with it. Course, we'll never hear the end of it now," said Jack.

"So, what if some orders aren't obeyed?" asked LTG Trento.

"We have two ways to deal with that. If Rosetta gets feedback data that actions aren't being taken as intended, then a new set of orders gets sent out. They're options. It could be a different unit taking action, going around an individual in the unit or referral to the Star Chamber."

"Star Chamber?" asked Pablo.

Ruth put her hands on the table, "Star Chamber is the name for the routine sub-process in Rosetta. Ish named it. The Star Chamber, as you know, was the English court of law that started as a speedy and flexible way to dispense justice. Then, it became abused by the Stuart kings as an arbitrary means to enforce royal privilege."

"That is an unfortunate choice of terms isn't it? Star Chamber means abuses by secret proceedings," said Pablo.

"We didn't want to call it the Judge Roy Bean court, because we don't know that we're going to hang everybody," said Ish.

"Our Star Chamber is first and foremost a list of suspect persons in government. The list will be referred to a panel of judges as needed. The judges give us the authority on a case by case basis to remove officials from any branch of government for the duration of Phase I of Rosetta 6.2."

"There's another issue, too," said Ish.

"The Star Chamber may consider removing some officials with prejudice," said Ruth.

"With prejudice as in with death? Capitol punishment?" asked Bubba.

"Yes, that is what is being looked at by the High Court," answered Ruth.

"I really can't believe that the justices will go with that," said Pablo.

"They're looking at it. We have real problems with it. We think that may be going too far."

"Yes, you are, that will make it another Star Chamber and history will hate you," said Pablo.

"Depends. Depends on what you're doing. If you're at war

then anyone resisting the forces engaged can be killed for their resistance. The distinction we make is in the few seconds that lie between being shot and surrending," LTG Trento stubbed out his cigar. "If you are engaged in law enforcement instead of warfare, then it is exceedingly bad form to kill the accused criminals. So, what is it? Law and order or war?"

"It's war," said Ish.

"War," said Ruth.

"I know something about war," LTG Trento stood up and pulled on his jacket with its rows and rows of ribbons. "Let's finish this tomorrow. I'll be back in the a.m." The goodbyes were made and the night closed.

West Point, NY
January 9th, 2013
Wednesday

The next morning bustled with activity as Ish scurried to tie together every last detail possible before LTG Trento returned. Ish didn't have long to prepare.

"Glad to be back," LTG Trento announced as he entered. He worked the room with a glance and poured himself a cup of coffee.

Ish turned on the computers. He quickly ran the General back through all the steps of Phase I. "What are your questions about Phase I?" asked Ish.

"Let's look at your information ops. In paragraph three of your mission order you mention the commander's intent for all information operations to support the plan of maneuver. What are the details?" asked LTG Larry. Ish used his handheld system to pull up the Operations Order, the background Executive Order, and the Information Operations annex key pages. He framed the subjects on a split screen three by three presentation.

"Very soon we'll be prepping the battlefield for our information operations. This prep is aimed at the psychological operations we planned under the overall umbrella of information operations," said Ish.

"Here's a key point. We discussed earlier how thinking is

expressed in language. If we can change the language, we can alter the thinking. If the People use our language they will be closer to seeing our thoughts. So, we have articles ready to go out to all the media and plant the seeds to change the terminology," said Ish. LTG Trento stared through him. Jack saw the same intensity he had seen in the tactical operations centers. *So, they call him Laser Larry for a couple of reasons. Blinding enemy soldiers is only one.*

"We're going to change the paradigm from drug abuse to drug slavery by changing the language first. Additionally, we're going to make the drug words an anathema. Drug abuse is going to become taboo, kapu—as the Polynesians call it, in this society," said Ish.

"The society we call America is not homogeneous," said Pablo pointing his finger in the air like an objection.

"Right. Popular culture is multi-faceted, but it remains pervasive. We'll send the message in every venue of popular culture. TV. All channels. Hip Hop. Rap. Country. Nascar. You name it."

"Diversity works," mocked Bubba.

"To the degree that popular culture is very diverse—along whatever lines the diversity is drawn—we'll send the messages that communicate to every person in each group you can find. We'll make the linkage between drugs and slavery explicit. Drug-slaves will become one word. Also, the drug pushers will become drug-snakes. One word, too."

"I like that. Every culture has negative connotations for the snake. Some have positive ones too, like snakes have wisdom, but for the most part, snakes are disliked," said Pablo.

"Disliked? How about hated? Spiders, too," said Naomi.

"Drugsnakes will be something to be avoided. It'll be a norm in society. It gets better," said Ish.

"Drugsnakes sounds pretty cool. Powerful stuff," said Bubba.

"It gets better because when Rosetta kicks off, the seeds we planted in language will take root. This is really neat. We have a virus that is going out to every word processor in the country and beyond. Everywhere. That virus won't allow the word processing programs to write some terms and forces it to write some other terms. For example, every mention of a 'drug dealer' will be modified to read 'drugsnake'. The word 'drug dealer' may appear for a few weeks in parenthesis, but then only our term is allowed. If a programmer tries to fix it, the word processing program will self destruct at the code level."

"So much for free speech," said Pablo.

"So much for free speech for Phase I of Rosetta 6.2. Abe Lincoln would understand. Every newspaper, every teleprompter, every internet site is linked to a word processing program in a computer. We have the virus implanted in every one. Right now."

"Every single one?" asked LTG Trento.

"We think so. A stand alone system that hasn't been connected to a LAN or the internet for the past three years might not have the virus. The emphasis is on 'might'."

"Geez, Ish, you planted this virus in word processing code at the factories three years ago?" LTG Trento laughed with his eyes. "Sounds illegal."

"Yes, sir, we have. No harm, no foul. It wasn't illegal, but it was impressive. This sort of thing has been done before, like engineering phones so the government can tap them."

"Unbelievable. What's next?" asked LTG Trento.

Ish continued outlining the details of the information operations for a couple of hours. Jack found it a fascinating weave of messages, finely crafted and tuned for mass and more tailored audiences. The messages were ready to go in all media—video, print, music, web postings, and audio. They only needed a few details and an execute message and they would be cut, processed and produced to flood the markets and keep on flooding with wave after wave of information. Ish took pains to show how he had tapped the staffs of defense and other government agencies, as well as private contractors and advertising agencies to have the right talent ready to go.

"You know well, that over 60 years ago the D-Day invasion of Normandy was planned for over two years in every detail. On the second day of the invasion the plan was useless. But the thinking that went into that detailed plan made it possible to deal with every contingency that followed. They had thought through every problem in the planning. I submit, sir, that we have tried to do the same," said Ish.

"Tried Ish? Or done it all? Buddy, you'd better hope you have it as right as Ike's staff did in W-W-Two," said LTG Trento.

"Ish masterminded something incredible. This planning has

been ongoing for a number of years. Some of the key pieces were approved and launched several years ago. Rosetta 6.2 brings it all together in an executable form. Omni makes Rosetta possible. If it is compromised then Rosetta is impossible."

"How did you get stuff approved during this last Clinton Administration?" asked Jack.

"They saw it as a tool for domestic security against their enemies. They were happy to have the tool. They planned on using it in a big way," said Ruth.

"Against us," said Bubba.

"Right, against us," said Naomi.

"Well if I was to choose anyone to be a mastermind, it'd be Ishmael. I'll get back to you if I think of anything while I am back at 'the building'. But before I go, I must share a message from the President-elect. President Kyle wants to know that when Omni is ready, that you will be ready. Absolutely. She wants to know how soon after the Inauguration that might be. Also, she wants to know, specifically, what it will take to make it happen, whatever that means."

"I know what that means. I know exactly what that means," said Ruth.

LTG Trento looked at her expectantly.

"Rosetta needs a political or social event that is the catalyst. If none appears, then we can create the circumstances that are close, but we would really rather not do that. We're looking for the event that might serve as a spark. Until then, the President will be working from the day after Inauguration to build up the kindling for the bonfire. Sort of like Franklin Roosevelt pushing us into World War II against the Nazis. Then, thank God, the Japanese attacked Pearl Harbor and the Germans declared war on us."

"We'll be in touch," said LTG Trento.

"We'll be working here," said Ish. Ruth stopped LTG Trento at the door for a whispered tete-a-tete. He nodded his head emphatically.

West Point, NY
January 21st, 2013
Monday

The Martin Luther King Jr. holiday arrived before the Inauguration. The holiday was a normal working day for the Amigos in their little crucible. The mess hall sent over one of their commemorative cakes with 'I have a dream' written in frosting. Ruth proposed a toast to Martin Luther King, Jr. All rose, toasted and took their seats again. All eyes fell on the one black person in the room—Ish.

Ish leaned back in his chair and crossed his arms over his chest. "It's really nice to have your undivided attention. I feel like Bubba in his better moments."

"All my moments are better," said Bubba.

"Ahem," Ish cleared his throat and rocked forward, interlacing his fingers and outstretching his arms on the table. His white sweater stretched across his ample shoulder muscles. "I can't add anything to that fine toast of Ruth's. Thank you, Ruth. But, if you will indulge me like we did Bubba on his birthday, I might give a short soliloquy on being black in America."

"All four hundred years?" asked Bubba.

"No, just the past forty-two years of my being black in America."

"So, you were something else at one time, other than being black? Or other than being in America?" asked Bubba.

"I'm connected to the full four hundred years, but I won't do a chronological account for the sake of brevity. Just for you, Bubba."

"For the sake of sanity, thank you."

"But I will begin before my birth. I must tell you about my grandfather—George Washington White. My grandfather was a porter in the pullman cars on the railroad. To my father, the late Mohammed Ali Shabazz, that meant that grandfather was a baggage boy for the white man. My poor, poor father," Ish shook his head.

"Grandfather stood six foot two inches tall. He was lean and when he dressed in his Sunday best he looked more dignified than any man I have ever known. When I was a kid, everyone addressed him as Mr. White and called him 'sir' wherever we went. He died when I was 12, but he has been with me all of my life, every day, since I can remember," Ish's eyes misted.

"Grandfather was a PROUD man. He was active in the union. He knew A. Phillip Randolph well. In fact, older folks said Grandfather looked like Mr. Randolph."

Ish took a drink.

"My Grandfather told me that if a man was on his knees to Jesus, he could stand up to ANY man. My Grandfather told me how it took fifty years to become a 'Negro' in the eyes of most whites instead of the 'N' word. He was incredibly proud to be a Negro man. He was almost as proud of that as he was to be an American. And he was almost as proud of that as to be called a Christian man.

Grandfather White knew that he was a Christian, an American and black in that order. He never faltered in that. And he didn't care what others thought. Except my father, his son, was one who thought differently. My father thought he was a black man first and foremost. He renounced Christianity soon after my Grandfather's and Grandmother's deaths and became a Black Muslim. Dad changed our names from White to Shabazz. I went from John Washington to Ishmael Ali Akbar. My father was ashamed that his father was a porter. My father hated being discriminated against so much that he learned to hate everything. My father hated most of the things that my grandfather loved. We lived in Northeast Washington DC. We did every trendy thing of color you can think of," Ish's lips almost curled.

"My father divorced, got into drugs and alcohol, then out again with Allah's help or so he thought, and then back into it again. He died with his health broken by drugs when I was 25. My parents divorced before I got out of high school. My mother is still alive, God bless her. She has had too hard a life."

The Amigos sat stunned at his emotional nakedness. Jack squirmed in his seat.

"I went to Stanford to study Afro-centrism studies. I did the usual college trip. I had a white girl friend and then a black girl friend and then too many girls I called my 'hos'. Mostly I had my father's anger ringing in my ears. I got the shock of my life when I found out in my sophomore year that my dad had spent the last of my Grandparent's savings. My grades weren't good enough to have Stanford pick up the ticket, so I was desperate. Much to the surprise of everyone, and I mean everyone, I enlisted in the Army Reserve to get some money for college.

Much to my further surprise there was a war in the Middle East and I got called up. I shipped out as an augmentee to the active component units. So, I became part of the extra staff, a complete, second shift in the tactical operations center of the Second Battalion Fourth Cavalry. That is the divisional cavalry squadron for the 24th Infantry Division. My boss, the Operations Officer was Major Larry Trento. There in the desert I learned more about race in the Army than I ever did before. Anywhere. I learned that race mattered little when men were men with a mission to do."

Bubba and Jack nodded their heads to the affirmative. Pablo smiled encouragingly.

"I also saw a man, my commander, who was tough, intelligent and a devout Christian. Lieutenant Colonel Thomas Lane was a West Pointer, a Harvard graduate, and a born-again Christian. He broke my stereotypes more than anyone. He was a made-for-Hollywoood tough, but fair leader. He didn't care that I was black, but he cared so much about me." Ish touched his own chest, "Me. My health. My mind. My soul.

The diversity of colleges and public education is such bull. The Liberal holy trinity is race, gender and class. What bunk. I learned the real Holy Trinity is Father, Son, and Holy Ghost.

Anyway, when I was released back to civilian life I had a lot of questions to answer. I finished Stanford better than I started and won a fellowship with the Institute of Politics at the John F. Kennedy School of Government at Harvard University. There I became an educated man. I skipped the lectures and sherry and hors d'oevres and spent my time underground in the stacks of Widener library and in the reading rooms of Lamont library. I did a terrible thing for a liberal… I read the books. I read the canons of Western Civilization. I read the newspapers and first hand accounts from the American Revolution to the present then. I studied other civilizations and history. I studied war and economics. I studied other belief systems. Islam. Hindu. Buddhist. Existentialism. Secular Humanism. Indigenous Paganism—all the native religions, you name it. You name it."

Ish sighed, "When my father went off on one of his binges, his live-in girl friend kicked him out. She sent me a box of his belongings. She was at least that proper. I found my Grandfather's Bible. The pages were dog earred and his handwritten notes filled the margins. It was fascinating. I was touched to see that, but still not convinced of anything. So, I started to read the Bible with a caustic and critical eye. I started in the New Testament and found plenty of things that seemed to be contradictions. I wasn't convinced, as I said, but I found the writing compelling. I felt a sense of love that was quantum leaps beyond the Koran. Then," Ish gulped.

"I read the 8th chapter of Romans and the part about we are more than conquerors, through Him who loved us, for I am convinced that neither death nor life…" Bubba, Pablo and Naomi began to mouth the words softly in unison with Ish, "That neither angels nor demons, neither the present nor the future, nor any powers, neither height nor depth, nor anything else in all creation, will be able to separate us from the love of God that is in Christ Jesus our Lord."

"Amen, Amen brother," said Bubba. Tears streamed silently down his red face.

"As I sat to ponder what that meant, I flipped my Bible forward and it opened to the Book of Isaiah. I looked at the page and Isaiah 59:21 was underlined. My name and the names of all eight of my first cousins and our parents were written in my Grandfather's neat hand along the seam of the page with an arrow pointing to this passage. It read," Ish closed his eyes and lifted his chin like he was looking up to something on the ceiling directly above him.

"It read…" Ish stopped, swallowed, breathed deeply and started again. "As for me, this is my covenant with them, says the Lord. My spirit who is on you, and my words that I have put in your mouth will not depart from your mouth, or from the mouths of your seed, or the mouths of your seed's seed from this time and from evermore, thus saith the Lord."

"Amen!" said Naomi.

"I thought about what I had read a second before—the part about through him who loved us—and then I looked back at my name in my Grandfather's handwriting and I saw his eyes. I saw those brown, brown eyes. I felt their weight. It was like someone was standing on my chest," Ish opened his brown eyes and looked lovingly at every one in the room in turn. A tear coursed a glossy black line down his cheek, but his voice held.

"I felt the weight of the past, the pain of color in this country and the pride of success all at once in his eyes. I just kept seeing them and feeling them. Then, I knew what I had to do. The standards were set before me. I couldn't betray them or him. I felt a pain of pride earned at great cost and it made me feel brave to be of his blood.

I knew that passage in Romans referred to him that loved us as Jesus, but I knew that him who loved me like Jesus was my Grandfather. Grandfather showed me Jesus after all those years since his death. I understood. I understood that the covenant with Isaiah was a covenant my Grandfather held as his own. All of this happened in a flash. I felt like a warm air was blowing into me and then I just said it. I said what I had heard Colonel Lane say night after night when he counseled men outside the TOC. I asked Jesus to come into my heart. I said I believe that You, Jesus, are the Son of God and my Savior and You died for me. You rose from the grave and You are alive now."

Naomi cried. Pablo beamed. Bubba cried. Ruth and Jack stared.

"My life has never been the same since that moment. Things are the same, but I am not. I changed and am changing today. And that my friends tells you what you should know about Dr. Martin Luther King Jr.'s birthday."

"I don't get it," said Jack blankly.

Ish laughed with his whole body. "Of course you don't. Martin Luther King was a Christian. What I share with him is Jesus. The color I share with him matters less than the religion I share. All of his writing, protesting, leadership was based on being Christian! The holiday is either about his ideals—which are fundamentally and profoundly Christian—or it's about his color. For many of my fellow Negroes," Ish accentuated Negro in separate syllables. "and for me religion trumps race everyday and twice on this holiday. Get it? See, I'm a man of color or a man of God. I chose Christ as God as the truth. I saw Jesus Christ in Grandfather White. I chose truth over Islam."

"Oh, okay. For many people, race trumps religion," said Jack.

"You got it, brother," Ish slapped Jack hard on the shoulder.

"I never heard the whole story, Ish, thank you," said Ruth in restrained but genuine gratitude.

"Ruth, you haven't heard a tenth of the whole story," said Ish.

Bubba bear hugged his friend. So, did Pablo. Naomi kissed Ish's cheek and hugged him too. Jack shook his hand, but he didn't really know why, it just seemed like a time of congratulations. Ruth smiled and shook his hand politely. The holiday was done well and completely.

West Point, NY
January 22nd, 2013
Tuesday

Inauguration Week in Washington is always special. West Point enjoys some reflected glory. Two regiments of the Corps of Cadets lead all the military since the Army is the senior military service. The Amigos spent most of Inauguration Day mid-morning and afternoon lolling before the large screen projection of the TV across the back of North Auditorium. They enjoyed a modest break.

"Jack, did you march in an Inauguration?" asked Naomi. She radiated good health.

"No," Jack almost whined, "it wasn't my regiment's turn. I sure would've liked to go. My parents were right there in Arlington." *They'll always be in the Arlington cemetery.*

"Hey, look at President Maggie Kyle, itn't she something?" asked Bubba.

"This was a watershed election," said Pablo.

"How's that?" asked Bubba,

"It's the change of worldview for the ruling elite. Not the national elite," Pablo smiled and pointed at the TV wall. "Definitely not the media elite! But, this election is more of a big deal than '04 or '08 or '00, you name it."

"I agree, the leadership of the House, the Senate, half of the Supreme Court, and the new White House have the same worldview," said Ruth.

"What would you call it? Christian Conservative, I'm sure. All the top leaders before were Christian. So what's the difference?" asked Jack.

"The difference is really Conservative and really Christian," said Ish.

"The Conservatism is the old Edmund Burke view that some things, like institutions, like West Point are worth conserving," said Pablo.

"But it includes an appreciation for change and managing change that makes it positive in its view and in its message," Ish picked up the thread.

"And it, I mean we, care about the things that all people do—like families, fairness, clean air, land and water—so it is populist through and through," said Bubba. He reached for a piece of fruit.

"I realized how all the pieces fit together only recently. Really and truly. I thought that the religious right was a bit of a tangent to the mainstream of America. Then, gosh this is going to sound like Ish's speech," said Pablo.

"No way you can top mine," said Ish.

"Let him try. He's better looking and in better shape than you," said Bubba.

"Okay. As I was saying, I found out that there was no mainstream, but two courses of rapids pulling to the left and the right. The channel that cut the deepest and which drew the most water, was on the right," said Pablo.

"That's new news?" asked Bubba.

"Yes, for me and many of my brothers it is. The issues of life and death, the ones at the beginning and the end of life should have defined it for us, but our love for the poor and justice, made one side seem appealing still. They still sound right sometimes," Pablo looked so young when he looked sheepish.

"My sympathies have always been Liberal. I would love to be Liberal today, but to do what must be done, the worldview of the Right must win for awhile. We have to do what we have to do. My side won't or can't fight it for all the wrong reasons. But things will change through time and the pendulum shift from right to left again, like it always does," said Ruth.

On the big screen, an Air Force officer holding a briefcase spoke in the ear of the President as she walked off the speaker's podium. She stopped and then she cupped her mouth with her hand closely by the officer's ear. The officer lagged behind the President until he was no longer on the screen.

"Wonder what that was about?" asked Bubba.

The spider phone on the conference table rang.

"Hello? Uh-huh. Uh. Uh-huh. Yes. Yes. Got it it. Thank you," Ish folded down the antennae slowly. "There was flash traffic from the President of the United States to the Superintendent, United States Military Academy. We're to get Rosetta and ourselves ready for transport ASAP.

This morning three of the developers of the Omni working out of NSA were reported missing. All three were read on to the highest levels of the Omni special access program. They didn't come home last night. They were working on different sectors of Omni, but they really know too much about the whole system. The Omni could be compromised in hours." Intensity thickened the air.

"We're going out in teams of two to populate the icons separately. We execute on order. Ruth, you and Pablo will go to Ft. Lewis, Washington. Bubba, you go with me to the Defense Logistics Agency depot in Memphis, Tennessee. Naomi and Jack, you two are going to Ft. Leavenworth, Kansas."

Before the questions could come running, Ish said, "That's all I know."

The Amigos scurried into action. They checked and double checked and checked again the disks they would carry on their persons. The Amigos packed their meager clothes and toiletries into Army green 'kit' bags. Jack looked around the room for what he might have forgotten to pack, and, unspokenly, for what must be remembered.

They hurried out the door and down the stairs to the waiting van. The van took them over Storm King mountain to Newburgh and the National Guard side of the field. Three J-model C-130 transports waited with their big blades turning. The farewells were hurried into a blur. They became three teams of two safely strapped into cloth troop seats winging away into the deep Winter night.

Chapter 5. Limbo

Covington, TN
February 2nd, 2013
Saturday

Each twosome had a special mission based on their location. Pablo and Ruth were in the Pacific Northwest to be close to the source code and key people for the software that makes the world go round, as needed, if needed. Jack and Naomi had access to the military nets through the communications center at Ft. Leavenworth. Ish and Bubba were close enough to Federal Express to make sure that the physical distribution of Rosetta's outpouring of information CDs, DVDs, videos, audio, print media, etc. was set up properly and responded as necessary.

As far as the NITs knew the cinquefoil icons were gone. Since they abducted the Omni experts, the NITs had to know how far along the Omni was. Ish knew they would be shocked to find out nothing about the connection between the Omni and Rosetta 6.2. *Those poor guys are going to be tortured for nothing. There's no way to connect the dots from Omni to Rosetta. We're the only ones who can make it happen. We'll make Rosetta rock the Omni!* A voice broke Ish's line of thinking.

"You know this place itn't really Covington?" said Sheriff Jared Bringle. Ish and Bubba were staying at the safe house on his farm. "This place actually can be found on a map, some maps. This here is Bride, Tennessee," he smiled broadly. Jared was a thickset man in his late 30s with a shock of black hair that was about to grey early on the sides. He was the sheriff of Tipton County, Tennessee, a position he held in august respect.

"What here is here?" asked Bubba. They sat outside under a large catawpa tree waiting for Spring. Two farmhouses and a country store were divided by the road splitting into a 'y' just beyond the high hedge of Bringle's frontage.

"Yessir, this's downtown Bride," said Jared. His green eyes twinkled and cut deep laugh lines for early crow's feet. The pre-spring Southern warm spell let them 'set a spell' outside.

"When do we take the tour?" asked Ish.

"You can take the tour pretty much from where you are sitting. There used to be two stores here. My great-granddiddy had one right there on the corner," Jared pointed with a flick of his wrist like he was shooting a basketball.

"So, this is downtown Bride, huh?" asked Bubba.

"Yep, you oughta see it at rush hour," said Jared.

"What grief do you get from the NITs in Memphis?" asked Ish.

"They push their products here. I do what I kin do raise the bar on how hard it is for them to move stuff in and out of Tipton County. I take care of the locally grown marijuana my own self. Little bit ago, they moved a lot of money into one of our local banks. Ah'm corncerned about that. If they bring in too much money then this County is in real trouble," Jared's eyes narrowed.

"There isn't that much drug money here now?"

"Nope," Jared chewed gum with his lower jaw rotating like it was the 'chaw' of tobacco that his wife had made him quit using. "The money and the monsters that live off of it go down to Meaphis." Jared picked up a twig. He broke it in two with a loud snap and threw away the smaller piece. He casually reached into his pocket and pulled out a pocket knife to whittle. "Ah'm the law in this County. The State's district attorney, the County judge and the Tennessee district judges and I've an understanding of who does what in these parts."

"Different from other places?" asked Bubba.

"Not different like ill-legal. But different than some I suppose, cause it works well," Jared's cowboy hat with a sheriff's star shaded his eyes.

"You know long ago in England, the Sheriff in the shire was

the King's law. He and the magistrate just about did it all. They figured out if a crime had been committed. Then, they set about to keep the King's justice by administering the King's law. But then y'all would know that if you're lawyers. Y'all aren't lawyers are you?"

"No, but isn't your county filled with lawyers like everywhere else?" asked Ish.

"More civil than criminal. But lawyers don't pay mind, unless people pay them."

"So, how is Tipton County different?"

"If I don't keep the lid on drugs and crime then the folks here sure will."

"Vigilantes?" asked Bubba.

"That's such an ugly word Mr. Bubba," Jared spit sideways like he still chewed tobacco. "The folks here look like farmers, but they think like frontiersmen. West Tennessee wasn't opened until the 1820s when it was stole from the Indians. It was frontier when what little there was was destroyed in the War of Northern Aggression," Jared looked closely at Ish. Not even an eye flicker broke the black granite of Ish's face. "It whatn't rebuilt much until the TVA money come in and the Second World War brought Millington Naval Air Base. This's more wild west than most places in the South. Bet you didn't know that. If the law dodn't right wrong, here, then the people will. They'll get their brothers and cousins and do whatever it's to be done," said Jared.

"Black and white the same?" asked Ish.

"Both, unless they's on drugs, then all bets is off."

"What do drugs do?"

"Drugs make people more crazy than likker. Children kill children. Momma's kill babies. Daddies don't act like fathers. And men aren't men, they're fiends from Hell or wuthless as teats on boar hawgs."

"So, your county is clean, Sheriff?" asked Ish.

"Not clean, just under some control, but not by much. That new Sin drug is tearin things up. It ate up our usual hard core users. It went from the High School into the Middle School in weeks. It's worse than anythang I've seen."

"How would you really know that you have control?" Bubba zipped his jacket to his chin against the slight breeze.

"I got eyes in the back of my haid and up there," Jared pointed his stick at the sky. "Aerostats."

"Anchored helium balloons, dirigibles, used for sensor and comms packages across the U.S. southern border. Picks up every aircraft, boat, and truck crossing our border," Ish informed Bubba.

"That's how you got this real safe house," Jared pointed at the tiny green farmhouse perched on cinder blocks.

"And some house it is."

"That's built by my people with their own hands. My Great-grandfather got his first indoor plumbing in h'it."

"No offense meant. I'm grateful to have it," Bubba blushed.

"None taken. I get a down link from a bird up there at forty thousand feet. Every vehicle on my roads has its license read and reported to my ops center. We keep track of whut is whut in near-real time."

"Can you use the aerostat as a relay out?" asked Ish.

"Of course."

"Then, could we send some traffic on your net and not raise any attention?" asked Ish.

"You kin go through my net as me in my Fraternal Order of Sheriffs Association. Or you kin be me in the Sons of Confederate Veterans network," Jared looked evenly at Ish again.

"I'll take the Sons of Confederate Veterans cover," Ish unbarred his teeth in a smile rather than a grimace.

"You got it, Bubba. You too, Bubba," Jared nodded to the actual Bubba and got up from the metal rocking chair. He took off his hat and wiped his brow with his sleeve.

As soon as possible Ish contacted the Amigos. Using iconic language, Ish gave out new assignments for the Amigos subject to Ruth's approval. Ruth concurred with every item.

Fort Leavenworth, Kansas
February 14th, 2013
Thursday

Naomi and Jack had adjacent rooms in the VIP guest quarters

near the Army's Command and Staff College[1] classroom. They were a short block to the converted stable that serves as the School of Advanced Military Studies[2]. Its underground entrance lead to the communications center. Ft. Leavenworth also held the military prison and sat squarely next to the Federal and State penitentiaries.

Those security demands lead to the installation of the latest in image 'fuzzers'. The image fuzzer blurred the visual images and multi-spectral signatures of heat, light, audio or motion from long-distance systems. The neat aspect of the fuzzer for the military was the ability to fuzz the images to everyone else, but not to your acquisition systems. The success of the fuzzer meant that Naomi and Jack could walk around Ft. Leavenworth with few restrictions.

Walking around at midday was welcome exercise for Jack and Naomi. The wind rocketed over the plains to blast them regardless of the direction of their hike. It didn't dampen their joy to be out and about in the open air and among other people. Jack lead the hikes up and down Leavenworth's hills hard by the mighty, brown Missouri River. The great old deciduous trees stood their barren watch as sentinels for Spring. Their huge, uplifted branches cracked as they banged together in the wind. Their strength was undiminished by their dark nakedness. *"I wonder which of these trees are native. Which ones were lovingly planted by soldiers' wives when this outpost was the western rampart of the United States of America and Western Civilization?"* Jack liked to think of phrasing things in his head.

Naomi was new to the Midwest. The large rolling hills weren't much by the standards of hills in her West Virginia, but they gave a vista for the eye that undulated to a far horizon.

"Look beyond the ridge of this horizon and imagine more of the same for hundreds of miles to the south and a thousand miles to the Arctic north," said Jack.

---

1. U.S. Army Command and Staff College. Mid-level school for officers. It's focus has changed over the years since it was created following the Spanish-American War in the Root Reforms. Credited as an unsung, except among professional officers, key to success in WWI and WWII. An important institution to cross-level understanding and achieving quality across the officer corps as preparation for higher duties.

2. U.S. Army School of Advanced Military Studies. 1980s innovation to create a cadre of well-trained officers schooled in the operational art of war.

"Okay. Speaking of frozen. I'm ready to microwave lunch," said Naomi. They ended their walk in the VIP Quarter's tiny kitchen.

"The target list is driving me mad," said Naomi. Her brown eyes didn't look upset.

"Huh?"

"We have almost forty million Americans in our database. We have another twenty or is it thirty million, who knows, illegals and their data is so flaky. There're over thirty thousand primary target places."

"Disaggregation," Jack took a bite of his piping hot sub sandwich. Reflexively, he spit out the burning bite as soon as it hit his tongue. "Excuse me."

Jack blew on his food, "Just keep breaking it down into smaller pieces, put someone in charge and hold them accountable."

"The numbers are still too big. How do you know that the important targets are taken care of?" asked Naomi.

"Centrally manage the hi pri's, you know—the high priorities, and decentralize the execution of everything else. Manage by exception," Jack tried to take a bite again, but it was still too hot. "We need to check the targeting plan for two key things. First, what're the 'gotta have' targets from soonest to last? Second, what're the select forces, like DEA agents or Army Rangers that are in short and specialized supply? They get sorted against the targets that only they can do," Jack set down his food. He unfolded the paper napkin for paper.

"If I remember correctly, our priorities are as follows:

- Internal security
- Our communications
- Their communications
- Enemy agents
- Weapons
- Caches

After those national priorities, then the forces in each region go after:

- Finances
- Physical Assets
- Individuals"

Right? But maybe we have to change the order, depends on the situation," Jack cocked his head like a collie questioning his own words.

"What is the difference between internal security and communications again?" Naomi pointed to the bullet. When she leaned forward across the table to point, Jack smelled her cologne. She still had the scent of 'old girl friend' that triggered such memories, but he couldn't place the name of the perfume or the girl friend.

"Internal security is people and communications are hardware and software."

"What does people mean?"

"It means making sure that our people are reliable. We take out anyone who is suspect on our side."

"The phys assets include what?" Naomi pointed again.

"The physical assets include cars, boats, planes, and houses and computers."

"What if there's a family living in the target?" asked Naomi. She poked her salad.

"I'd have to go back to the rules of engagement, but I think the target is secured and the family is moved out to some holding area like a school gymnasium or something like that set up in the local area," said Jack. He touched the gooey open end of his sub.

"That won't make for good TV when so many families are moved. It'll look like the internment of the Japanese-Americans in World War Two."

"From what I heard from Ish, I don't think there will be too many TV pictures going out. Those that do will have the right story—positive and upbeat. Anyway the families of drugsnakes will be released to go home in very short order after their homes are vacuumed by our guys," Jack fell into using 'drugsnakes' with ease.

"That control of images will be hard to do with all the digital cams in this country."

"Pictures will be plenty, but broadcast mediums are fewer and controlled."

"Including uploads on the world wide web?" asked Naomi.

"Harder to control, but doable. Ish's spiders will be out checking the millions of websites looking for video uploads on fast refresh rate. Rosetta 6.2 will zap any unauthorized upload fast. Incredibly fast."

"The web is a big place, Jack."

"Yeah, but I can't find too many things Ish hasn't already thought about. I think we all have made some improvements to his plan. And we can still do more. I'll check this list against what we have in the targeting plan. The thing we need to work is the target nomination process. We've a lot to do." Jack folded the napkin and stuffed it under his pale blue sweater into his breast pocket.

"Anyway, we have the internal, national targets nominated by the police and state police of more than seven thousand jurisdictions. Then, we have the FBI, DEA, ATF, INS, CIA and Secret Service nominations[3]. The nominations are dumped into a database and sorted by Ish's program. The output of that program is the daily target/mission list that goes out. The reorganization of intelligence services in 2005 under Porter Goss helps. Of course, it didn't help him when he got canned. Ish was on the inside when all the information architecture was tweaked," said Jack.

"How many lists is that again?" asked Naomi.

"By jurisdiction or by number of days?"

"Days."

"There are one hundred and eighty mission days pre-planned. Of course, the volume of missions goes down exponentially after Day Thirty. The place holders are there for repeats and alibis," Jack used Army rifle range terminology for 'do-overs' from scratch—alibis, and 'do-agains'—repeats.

"One hundred and eighty days, a half a year, for targeting," Naomi said softly.

"It'll take at least that long," said Jack.

After they made a quick cleaning of the kitchen to brighten the day of the kitchen staff, they bundled against the blast of Canadian air rocking the big trees outside the glass front door. The door

---

3. Acronyms for Federal Bureau of Investigation, Drug Enforcement Agency, Alcohol Tobacco Firearms, Immigration Naturalization Service, Central Intelligence Agency

banged out of Jack's hand. He shut it with a snarl. Naomi turned around as she walked, her parka hood pulled up around her head and drawn tightly. "Oh, Happy Valentine's Day," she called back to Jack.

"Uh, Happy Valentine's Day to you," Jack said clumsily. *"I didn't know that. Hmm. Valentine's Day with Naomi. Or with Maude. Hmm."* The wind won the quarrel for his attention.

Fort Lewis, Washington
February 20th, 2013
Wednesday

Ruth stepped into the crystal light of sunrise and sighed. Mount Rainer captivated her every time she saw it. She knew many great peaks from the Northwest, California, and the Rockies to the Andes and Alps, but this domination of the sky demanded her eye. Like checking a disturbing reflection in the mirror over and over to see if what we see is still there, she kept glancing over at Rainer. Ruth was in spandex and running shoes stretching for a morning run.

Pablo was a few feet away swaying in his languorous warm up. Across the runway troops were running by in formations. Their frosty breath echoed with their throaty 'jodie' cadence. Their movement at a distance looked like a huge, many-legged bug, making a rhythmic accordion motion.

"How far today?" asked Ruth. She knew exactly how far they went yesterday, so she knew exactly how far and how long they would go today. She wanted to sound polite and encourage Pablo to get going.

"How about an hour?" Pablo looked at his watch. His body was the lean and sinewy figure of young men who don't give a care about what they eat and drink for a decade or more. Ruth admired the cat-like ease that guided his walk. It was graceful without being feminine.

"Now, this is the place to have an office," she smiled at the great evergreens around her.

"Let's go."

After the run Ruth walked for her cool down. She was glad to be out of the bunkers of the Army Rangers' staging area. *Winter doesn't mean much in this land of evergreens.* It was chilly. Later in the day it might be wet again, but it wasn't the bone racking cold of the mountains or plains or the East. *If I could ever leave the political game in Washington, this place certainly might be nice. But, I don't know if I could ever leave D.C. It's Rome. How does one live away from Rome when all the World lives under the power of Rome?*

"How about my Mama's enchiladas tonight?" Pablo asked Ruth as they met at the security door to their quarters.

"Great," Ruth spoke flatly. *I'm glad he cooks.* The day's work was spun in the separate solitudes of their concrete bunker offices.

That evening Pablo laid out all of the ingredients for cheese, fish and beef enchiladas. Ruth poured the wine to go with a light appetizer of quacomole dip.

"Beer would be better with this," Pablo overloaded a chip with green dip.

"Maybe. What did you mean in that email today about unleashing change?"

"Oh, sorry to not get back to you."

"No problem, why can't we predict what has to be done to follow through on Rosetta 6.2? We must manage change. Otherwise, all of our work may be undone in a few years."

"Let me introduce the thought," Pablo kept his eyes on his chopping and preparing.

"Okay, Assistant Professor."

"When I was in college and then in seminary, I wanted to understand more about the Protestant Reformation. I wanted to know why so many people would leave the warm bosom of the true faith," Pablo fake laughed.

"I read about the conditions of the time. The money grubbing efforts of the church hierarchy had gone too far. The claim that souls could be bought out of limbo and hell with the clink of a coin was too much. It was too much for some thinking people who loved God. Also, it was a temptation for many people to gain some of the physical wealth and possessions of the Church."

"I looked at Martin Luther. He was no great genius. He wasn't like the Apostle Paul, the brilliant Jew, formerly Mr. Saul of Tarsus, you may recall. But, Martin Luther expected to be put to death in a week, literally, burned at the stake, for what he wrote. He accepted the idea, but he was compelled to speak the truth as he saw it. And that is it," Pablo threw the lettuce into a strainer with a flourish.

"Martin Luther articulated what others were thinking. He brought the back of their minds out into black and white on the Church door at Worms. When people read his ninety-five theses the ideas they held privately, exploded in front of them in public."

"The impact of what appeared as revealed truth was incredible. Monasteries and convents that were old, that looked permanent to men because they'd been around for almost a thousand years were abandoned in a few weeks. Priests and nuns married. It was the old saying about an idea whose time had come. The same thing happens in some revolutions. Look at the end of Communism in Europe after Nineteen Eighty-Nine."

"So we need an idea whose time has come," said Ruth.

"Exactly, then we can predict that there will be certain reactions. But we can't predict for certain all the final outcomes."

"Like?" asked Ruth.

"If one of the ideas is an end to fear for our physical safety and an end to fear for children being lost to drugs, then maybe we will get the reformation or revolution you want. But, when that passion is over, then a new idea must take hold where the old was. There must be an idea about drugs and the Islamist terrorists that is more compelling than their enticements for the body and the billfold and what is PC."

"You have thought about this a lot, Pablo. I can see. What's the new idea?"

"I'm not so sure. Probably anathema, like Ish suggested. You know the root word in Greek for anathema is anti-God?"

"No, but I'm not surprised."

"Like I said, I'm going to make these enchiladas California style, like Mama, not Tex-Mex," said Pablo.

"Fine with me. Tying drugs to snakes and slavery doesn't seem like enough to me," said Ruth.

"How about making it the moral choice?" asked Pablo.

"Morality only works with consensus values. We have a Culture War about values, haven't you heard?" Ruth didn't mean for her tone to be a touch too sharp.

Pablo stopped cold, "Then it's time to take sides, Ruth. The one side or the other will have moral ascendancy in America. One side or the other can make drugs a thing of the past. Like slavery, or de jure segregation, like child labor, like abuses of workers and women, you name it, they're past and they aren't coming back in this country, unless America stops being America. Whoever wins the Culture War can dictate the terms of peace and that will include the status of drugs."

"So, you are a fan of Martin Luther?" Ruth asked lightly.

"I learned to appreciate him for what he was. I really admire one of his writings. I liked it so much that I memorized it. Martin Luther defended teaching and writing and that's more than okay by me. Besides, Vatican II made us all Protestants. Now, I didn't really say that. Got it?"

Ruth dipped the quacomole delicately. *Why does he have to defend writing and teaching? Ah, celibate priest and manhood issues?*

Pablo cleared his throat, "Martin Luther said, 'Workers with brawn are prone to despise workers with a brain such as city secretaries and school teachers.

The soldier boasts that it is hard work to ride in armor and endure heat, frost, dust and thirst, but I'd like to see a horseman who could sit a whole day and look into a book," Pablo played the actor.

"It is no great trick to hang two legs over a horse. They say writing is just pushing a feather, but I notice that they hang swords on their hips and feathers in high honor on their hats.

Writing occupies not just the fist or the foot while the rest of the body can be singing or jesting, but the whole man. As for school teaching, it is so strenuous that no one ought to be bound to it for more than ten years. Ta-da," Pablo bowed low.

"Bravo!" Ruth clapped. *He's so bright! It's good to laugh like this again.*

Fort Leavenworth, Kansas
March 6th, 2013
Wednesday

It looked like an uncertain Spring. March is still winter for the most part in the Midwest. This year was full of false starts. Early warmed days made promises of sultry hours to languish, but gray clouds and cold rain or snow would chasten to a harsher reality. Spring on the Great Plains would take hold and warmly invite the Summer, but only when it was time, truly.

Jack felt trapped by time. The news on Omni during the month of February was slow and steady progress towards completion. The drug 'Sin' rampaged without any sign of abatement. The Global War on Islamist Terrorism smoked and flared at every flash point.

The aftermath of the election of '12 was beyond ugly. Hillary charged massive voter fraud like the bank robber yelling 'thief!'. Her allies organized protests. They demanded a re-election. Judges considered their claims seriously although nothing in the Constitution supported 'do overs' if your side lost. Just like abortion, racial quotas, and a right to sodomy the Judges could see words in the shadows of the Constitution which are invisible to the peasants, The People.

Meanwhile, Jack and Naomi worked long hours refining the target lists. Time plays humans like musicians play their pieces. *A month ago I was just glad to breath. I expected to die any second and every day. Wow. Now, I'm bored. I want to go home. I want Maude and the kids.* He was more than ready to get on with some other kind of life. Or go back to his former life glittering in his forgiving and lapsed memories.

"Jack, look at this please," Naomi backed away from the screen of her computer so Jack could see. The underground Special Compartmentalized Information Facility (SCIF)[4] anteroom wasn't much larger than some of the cells over the next hill at the military prison. The low lighting did little for the beige painted cinderblock.

Jack swiveled around in his chair and scooted a few inches forward. He saw the full face of a hispanic male in his late thirties.

---
4. SCIF is Special Compartmentalized Information Facility. A special room or building meeting exacting standards to handle TOP SECRET information.

The man's full cheeks suggested that he was becoming overweight. His black hair was receding. His eyes were large, brown and warm, almost meek. There was nothing sinister in this face.

"This is him. This is Pablo Ponce de Leon of Columbia," said Naomi.

"The face of the enemy," said Jack.

"I was looking at his target folder. Did you know that Rosetta has three cruise missiles programmed for his big ranch complex? Then, the U.S. Army 160th Special Aviation guys and then lots of Army Rangers sweep? A Columbian Army Ranger Battalion is going for his warehouse complex? The National Police raid on his bank and a composite DEA—US Special Forces team hit on his beach house?" asked Naomi.

"No, I didn't remember all the details, but it looks like this guy is going to get nailed."

"What about his five kids?" asked Naomi. She touched the mouse to flip through pictures of his family on screen.

Jack took in a deep breath and blew it out like a trumpet player. "They're probably going to be schwacked in the attack."

Naomi's eyes met his and made their accusation.

Jack averted his eyes to the flashing screen images of grandma Ponce de Leon, aunts and uncles and their children living on the compound. "This is war, Naomi."

"War against women and children?"

"Innocent people get killed in wars. Happens all the time. Look at Iraq. Afghanistan. Nine Eleven."

"I don't see why it has to be done this way."

Jack swallowed hard, "The hit has to be certain, one hundred per cent, or it fails."

"There has to be better way, Jack," Naomi's eyes filled with tears.

"I wish there was," said Jack. His emotional gears tightened in compassion for Naomi, not for the faraway, foreign targets.

"I don't want to be part of this," said Naomi. She swiped a tear drop as it made a run down her cheek.

Jack wanted to reach out to her, but dared not. *I don't know what to say. Again.*

"Do you know how many more there are of these? These

attacks with what you call limited 'collateral damage'?"

"Lots. I know."

"They're all around the world," Naomi fidgeted with the files until the master overseas target list popped up.

"Drugs have gone around the world. The Islamists are everywhere too. The drugsnakes have big production operations in Africa where they can just about buy entire little countries. They corrupted enough officials in Asia and whole countries in Latin America for years. They established distribution systems throughout Europe and North America. We have to hit them all."

"Look at this guy's family, Jack. Do they look evil? Like they ought to die? Does this man look evil?"

"No, he looks normal. He looks like us."

"Oh Lord, he doesn't look scary at all."

Jack pulled down a menu and opened a small file from an insert box.

"Here's his known, likely and suspected crimes and activities list. Hmmm, he's killed two hundred people outright. He killed a dozen himself. Muy Macho. Oh, one hundred fifteen were in the turf war to get him to his present position before age 40. And he has ten per cent of the cocaine market coming into the USA. So, a half a million Americans get that poison from him."

"Still doesn't look like a monster."

Jack scrolled to other tabs. "Look at this. Pablo was involved with the El Salvador gang, and he is Columbian which is a big deal, MS-13 from their very first contact with Al Queda."

"MS-13. I've heard of them. They are monsters."

"La Mara Salvatrucha. Bunch of murdering, raping, roping animals, big in Boston, Chicago and other El Salvadoran immigrant places. Working hand in glove with murdering Al Queda."

"But, still, what about his family? I need a break. Let's get out of here."

Outside clouds played peek a boo with the sun in their race across the sky. A cold, bracing, but not bitter wind whipped the bare sticks of trees to a chattering knocking. They walked along the road on the bluff. The old bell tower for the Command and Staff College stood proudly with its yellowish beige against the blue and white checkerboard of sky.

"I forgot my gloves today," said Naomi absently.

Jack pulled his right glove off and gave it to her. He reached and took her left hand in his. They interlaced their fingers, but kept walking and looking ahead. Jack meant nothing untoward. But her hand felt warm and wonderful. Her grip was strong and even against his. He pulled her a little closer as they walked. She moved over willingly. They walked in silence.

As they turned away from the cliff over the Missouri River and passed in front of the military prison, Naomi said, "I can't believe that cupcake man is a drug lord."

"I thought you had all of the answers for life."

Naomi looked at him quizzically.

"You know. Your faith seems to tell you so much." The wind blew fresh in his face.

"I don't understand all things, Jack. I can't stomach what's going to happen to all the innocent people," Naomi's tears came quickly glistening her eyes. Her lips pouted. "I just can't believe that that man would do what he does to other people."

"Really? After all since 9–11? You don't see the ugly things in war? I see it, but I haven't figured out evil myself. I've tried though, Miss Naomi."

Jack squeezed her hand. She squeezed back.

"I know there is evil in the world, Jack. But, I hate it whenever I see it for real. It scares me, Jack. I don't want to do wrong."

"Scare you? You wanted to fight!"

"I do want to fight them. I will. I must. But I am still scared. A lot."

"I don't like to look at evil, Nay," Jack shortened her name. "But, sometimes we have to, I guess. That's why I am okay with those target folders. We have to do what we have to do."

"I guess we do, too," Naomi's breathing changed.

A necessary silence fell like a weight. They walked back to the VIP quarters. They passed the visface and usual security checks. Jack stood at Naomi's door and gave her room to open it and walk in. He followed. They paused for a second facing each other and locked in one another's eyes. Jack took off his coat. He draped it over a chair. Naomi turned to hang hers in the closet. She stepped back and faced him.

Jack tasted the dry cotton mouth of fear and excitement. He felt his heart pounding and his face flushing red. Wordlessly, he reached for her waist, put his arms around her and pulled her close for an embrace. She turned her head to lay flat against his sweatered chest. As he hugged her towards him, he felt her flatten her hips and press hard against him. The press of her bosoms against him was like Maude, maybe even more full and hard.

He turned her chin with his hand so her face looked up from his collarbone. Her eyelids opened wider and wider like a flower opening with a pulse. Her brown eyes stared at him intently with a fierce certainty. Jack lowered his head and kissed her on the lips. Her mouth opened to his. They kissed into each other. Then, she turned her head against his chest. She pulled him tightly across his back. Jack tried to reach her face with his to kiss her again, when she suddenly pushed herself away with both hands.

"I can't, Jack. I can't. I won't."

Jack was surprised. He took a step forward reaching. She curled backward.

"Okay. Sorry," Jack grabbed his coat and let himself out. He hurried to his room.

Now what? This is terrible. My Maude. I'm married. She's married. Oh, I want to go back to her room. I don't want to stop. Uh, I feel sick. The nausea washed past him fast and left him dripping with his desire for Naomi. He paced his room in the swirl of his emotions. He sat on the bed and turned on the TV, flipped the channels and turned it off again. He kept thinking through every second of their encounter. He replayed it in his mind so quickly over and over. Jack went into the bathroom. His face was flushed. He splashed cold water on himself. Jack thought he heard something. *Is she crying? It's so wrong. I will be so ashamed. Why doesn't she call me?*

Fort Lewis, Washington
March 13th, 2013
Wednesday

Pablo tapped at the plastic Cyclops called computer. He tapped at the writing pad on the desk to his side. Pablo was on the verge of an answer, but wasn't quite sure he had it. He needed a sounding board to challenge him if he was close, tease him if he was wrong and applaud him with just a few easy questions if he was really right. Pablo missed Brother John and Father Tony from Georgetown University. His frustration came to a head, so he hopped up and walked to the next office and knocked on the door.

"Come in," Ruth's voice was weak and out of focus.

She looked up from her grey metal desk and took off her reading glasses. Her eyes were red and puffy.

"What's wrong Ruth?"

"Nothing, Pablo, nothing. How can I help you?"

"You can help me first by telling me what is bothering you."

"Nothing, Pablo, really," Ruth feigned a smile.

Pablo sat down in the military office metal chair and scooted it to the side of the desk in the tiny airless cinderblock office. "Not really is not really right. Is it these working conditions?"

"No, it's not this military interrogation box called an office, although that seems to me to be reason enough to be upset. It's not the workplace."

"Then, it is something about work," Pablo smiled disarmingly.

Ruth froze her face into her best bureaucratic game face.

Pablo knew his fishing line hit. "What are you working on?"

"The Star Chamber."

"I haven't looked at that in awhile. What is the problem?" asked Pablo.

"Its the idea that we will have people taken out and shot. Here in America. That is what the communists do. That is what the Nazi's did. It's what the Islamists do. The Taliban, Al Queda, all of them."

"Do we have to do it? Really?" asked Pablo.

"I don't see another way around it. If we arrest them and put them in our court system, then they'll go free. Or they will get out in just a few years. They will continue to operate from inside the prisons," Ruth's words dripped disgust as much as frustration.

"It has gotten that bad?" Pablo folded his hands into the lap of his best pastoral counseling pose.

"You know it has," Ruth cursed softly.

"If they were different men, they would respond to something short of death."

"They won't even respond to a death threat," said Ruth.

"Don't want to kill them. Can't scare them. Can't reform them without Jesus. And that takes time and all won't choose to reform. But you have to get rid of them," Pablo ticked off the options as he saw them.

"Get rid of them. Yes! Get rid of them!" Ruth's face lit up. The hard lines of her face rounded into softness. She clinched her fists in victory. "Oh, Pablo, you dear, that's it. Get rid of them! Ah."

"Glad to help, Ruth, What did I do?" Pablo's gentle face became kinder by degrees.

"Hey, you gave me the right idea for getting rid of them. We'll literally get rid of them. We'll launch them into exile."

"Internal or external?"

"Maybe both. Maybe the exile could be an extreme exile. Like we drop them off in the old Russian gulag," Ruth looked relieved.

"Better have an army to guard them. The Russian mob will have them out in no time. Lock them up at home."

"You can't just keep them locked up. Habeas Corpus, remember? Americans won't stand for it. We've had freedom from being locked up for nothing since the Habeas Corpus Act of 1679 established the rule of law over men."

Pablo held up an index finger point of order, "Nope. Wrong on history. Sorry. We suspended the right here in our country during the Shay's Rebellion in 1787, the year of our Constitution, by the way. Then, again, in 1861, Abraham Lincoln suspended it by proclamation during the Civil War. Some states have suspended it, that is the courts suspended it, under periods of martial law during strikes. Now, you have the Patriot Act holding citizens as 'enemy combatants'."

Paulo took a wind up breath, "And, remember, that the whole Habeas Corpus Act came about because of the abuses of the Star Chamber and the Privy Council. The Star Chamber was abolished in 1641 in the Long Parliament. The stupid Star Chamber was the problem, not the answer then, why should it be the answer now?"

"Wow! You know your history. Mr. Assistant Professor Brother Pablo. Point taken. If we go against four hundred years of legal tradition and truth, then we will become the bad guys, no matter how good our cause is."

"Almost. If the situation is perilous enough to the State, and obviously The People, then you can get away with it for awhile. But the window of opportunity is small indeed. Rights of law can be replaced by rule of men only as long as there is genuine fear among The People that it must be done. The danger is never returning to the rule of law, not men. If we lose the law to corruption, we aren't free anymore. It's over. The Great Experiment fails."

"Ha. That's why the NITs are destroying this country. We gave up freedom after freedom in the name of security. Years ago, I would've screamed bloody murder at the idea that the Omni was even being considered. I hated the idea of Big Brother."

"With Rosetta 6.2, you're Big Brother, aren't you?"

Ruth looked startled. "No," she leaned forward with her hands on the desk. "Rosetta is the necessary instrument. It'll be used through the necessary evil of revolution and war to create and maintain real freedom. Freedom from fear. Freedom from corruption. So there can be a real system of laws, including prompt Habeas Corpus," Ruth got lost in the thought for a long moment. She asked, "What did you want to tell me when you came in?"

Covington, Tennessee
March 22nd, 2013
Friday

Jared's rooster crowed while it was still dark. That nocturnal wakening always astounded Ish. Ish wasn't used to the country. Ish lay still to pray and ponder for just a few more minutes until the rays of first light lightened the window. *"Oh Father God, precious Abba, Lord Almighty, thank You,"* Ish gave praise and let it linger. *I give thanks. Let me feel the love of Jesus warm me.* He needed more warmth to rise this chilly March morning. Ish was so tired from the strain of thinking, waiting, working at a distance from the others. LTG Trento kept pinging him for more new work and more and more details.

Ish smelled bacon and coffee. He remembered the joy his Grandfather White would share when he would rise before everyone and make a huge breakfast for the house for no special reason at all.

Grandfather would kiss, hug and pat everyone in turn as he gave encouraging words for the day. *Oh Lord, let me see the children of my children growing in health and love and with a love for God. Please Father, Lord Jesus.*

"Hey brother, juice or coffee?" Bubba yelled from the other side of the door. Ish rose fast.

Bubba's blue eyes were alive, the brightest blue-gray. He looked proud of his breakfast productions.

"Juice first, then lots of coffee, always! Why are we off of our diet today?" Ish slapped his thick middle.

"I just feel good. Something tells me that this is going to be a great day! So, we will rejoice and be glad in it. Look, good ole fried salty country ham and bacon."

"We rejoice and are glad for everyday He has made," said Ish. Ish and Bubba spoke in Bible phrases, bits and pieces with key words. What sounded like code communicated full thoughts.

"And we will eat and give thanks today. Anything we eat with the right attitude of gratitude will add to our health and not hurt us."

"Unless we eat three helpings!" said Ish. They laughed together.

Bubba offered a short prayer and the men ate with gusto. His red eye gravy wasn't half bad and his grits weren't lumpy. Ish commented favorably on all accounts.

"So, today is going to be a great day?" asked Ish.

"Gonna be sumthin good, gonna be sumthin good."

The security light above the panel at the kitchen back door flashed green.

"Jared's coming," said Bubba. He took a huge bite of biscuit and fresh honey.

Jared knocked politely. He knew they knew he was coming. He installed the security systems himself.

"Mornin' fellas," Jared tipped his cowboy sheriff's Stetson.

"Morning Jared."

"Morning Sheriff Jared. Cup of coffee? Biscuit?" asked Bubba.

"Coffee, thanks," said Jared. His eyes had the slightest slant to them.

Ish read his face. *Maybe, he is part-Indian. He is definitely Irish and something else, Maybe a little horse-faced English.*

"Fellas, I got a problem in town. In Me-phis."

"Memphis, we have a problem," Bubba deadpanned.

"We do. The Omni terminals at the Defense Logistics Agency depot are fried."

"We'll check it out," said Ish. *How does he know so much about the Omni?*

"You can't do it from here. There's no connectivity with the Omni during these Beta test phases. There is only one link in all of Me-phis," said Jared.

"The depot should have several commo links on stand-by for hook up after the Beta testing."

"Those links can't be hooked up. 'Sides, seems someone's been messing with them too. The only link is at a neighborhood station we have in the city. It's an old house that we rent and use as an ops center."

"Why do you have operations centers away from the downtown metro police headquarters?" asked Ish.

"It's not THE ops center. It's one that gets most of the info traffic that I care about routed to it. I have to make sure that it's good to go," said Jared.

"Good to go? What's wrong with the main office center?" asked Bubba.

"Why're you fellas in a safe house? My safe house at that?" Jared let the question burrow as he drained his coffee cup. "Some folks can't be trusted. The trick is to know who to."

"Wanna come with me into town?" Jared asked.

"Sure," said Ish.

"Yes sir," said Bubba.

A few minutes later Jared drove up in a huge black sports utility vehicle. The black one-way windows hid the occupants.

"Looks like a druggie wagon," said Bubba.

"It was," Jared smirked.

The drive from the countryside downtown seemed substantial to Bubba and Ish and all too short to Jared. New housing developments were hawked on signs for this development of hundred estates or that coming development of some olde english-looking acres.

"La-ti-da," said Jared.

As they drove past the center of the city, they passed the high rises of the riverfront downtown. The car was silent as they surveyed block after block of buildings scarred and made ugly by a pox like war.

The 'Beirutization' of America came so suddenly. A new generation of barbarians in an increasingly de-based culture divided cities into warring factions. The mix of random and planned violence came from criminals and terrorists by turns. The attempts to control made movement difficult like tribal Beirut was in the 70s and 80s. The few black people on the streets glared at the SUV in a seething anger.

This town is as black as Africa. There is a middle class somewhere in gated communities. How many black folk have to live in these war zones? Ish's pain painted his face.

"It didn't used to look like this, Ish. Back when the people here was called colored, these places did not look like this. It went to hell after integration. But integration didn't do it. Drugs did this. The break up of the family opened the door, but the drugs's what did it. No fathers in families destroyed the civilization."

"Too few fathers is right. Need real Fathers," said Ish.

"You know what Frederick Douglas said? To make a contented slave, it's necessary to darken his moral and mental vision, and, as far as possible, to annihilate the power of reason. He must be able to detect no inconsistencies in slavery, he must be made to feel that slavery is 'right', and he can be brought to that only when he ceased to be a man."

"You quote Frederick Douglas, Sheriff?" asked Bubba.

"I just did, Bubba," Jared looked again to see how Ish took it.

Ish scooted up in his seat so his face was between Bubba and Jared in the driver's seat. "What do you know about slavery?"

"I see it every day. It's a sin against God."

"Did your family own slaves, Jared?"

"Most were too poor, Ish. But they probably wanted to. Farm work was pretty hard back then. But, I'll say this, there's a lot of black Bringle's running around, so someone owned somebody. The old ways and thoughts are gone out of our hearts. Southern white Christians have had the biggest transformation of the heart in American history, but you knew that," Jared smiled broadly.

"Praise Jesus," Ish hiked up one corner of his cheek in a sardonic half-smile. Jared passed the race test. He didn't weasel in guilt that demonstrates inner shame at his own feelings.

"Do you think drugs are slavery?" asked Ish.

"Absolutely," said Jared.

"Then consider this from Frederick Douglas: Does a righteous God govern the universe? And for what does He hold the thunders in His right hand, if not to smite the oppressor and deliver the spoiled out of the hands of the spoiler?" said Ish.

"Amen," said Jared.

"Amen, brother," said Bubba.

Jared pulled up to a one story white-siding house on the corner. The street sign read Waverly Ave. There was an eight-foot cyclone fence around the back yard. Heavy metal bars guarded the windows. The neighborhood was shotgun houses with full front porches and a long, narrow run of rooms to small back yards. An alleyway split the spine of each block. The neighborhood was in its prime in the Nineteen Twenties and decent until the Nineteen Seventies. Now it was just another war zone.

Jared's radio squawked, "Stay in your vehicle. We've a situation developing there. Leave now. You can make it. Turn right and left and go." Jared obeyed automatically. When Jared turned to the right and then left, they saw a band of doctors marching around the corner. Their audacity was astounding. It was daylight and they were about to assault a police neighborhood station.

Shots rang out. The doctors' automatic weapons made the little pop-pop-popping sound. It's so familiar to too many neighborhoods nationwide. A few rounds pinged off Jared's armored SUV. In seconds the men from the country were safe and free of danger. Jared gave some curt orders to his guys on his radio thirty miles to the north.

"What was that about? Omni or us?"

"Omni. They were going for the terminals there," said Jared.

"How do you know that?" asked Ish.

Jared popped a piece of gum into his mouth, "I just know what the targets've been past few days. 'Sides, those kids, those doctors, were followin orders. They were high. Super high."

"Jared," Ish looked at Jared's eyes in the rearview mirror, "Red rose colon havoc slash mall slash drums blue blue blue."

Jared's eyes twinkled, "Blue colon execute slash assembly slash zero ten hundred central."

"You! You're Blue Elvis twenty six!" exclaimed Ish.

"Yes, sir, Ah am," Jared grinned ear to ear.

"Blue Elvis?" asked Bubba.

"Code name. One of the best Rose Cinquefoil developers there is. One of the best!" said Ish.

"Thank you, sir" said Jared.

"You're a programmer?" asked Bubba.

"Nope, I'm an operator. I did some of the proof of principle evaluation from the police perspective."

"Some of the best, Elvis," said Ish.

"You can still call me Jared."

"What was the code you were talking?" asked Bubba.

"It was the code for instructions to begin the Blue Movement in the streets. Ish gave the execute order. I gave the response that demonstrations were going to begin in shopping malls at 10:00 AM. I, ole Blue Elvis, helped develop that part of the program."

"Blue movement?" asked Bubba once more.

"Yes, the Blues. Remember Rosetta 6.2's political movement for demonstrations to end the drugsnakes in America? The movement has a color and all sorts of other trappings to give it identities across the country. We thought about 'Right Reds' for the 'red' states, but that would be too political in your face and divisive. The overall movement is the 'Blues'," said Ish.

"Oh. Right, I wasn't thinking."

"So, Blue Elvis, how do we get our people, the huge majority of the people out in the streets? What is the political catalyst for us to kick off the military operation under Rosetta 6.2?"

"It'll take an awful lot to get people out of their safe zone," offered Jared.

"Yeah, those doctors could intimidate a lot of people," said Bubba.

"They could intimidate me. So, it must be something big to get people out and active."

"Out and active and angry more than they are scared," said Jared.

"That'll take an outrage," said Bubba.

"Yes, it'll take an outrage. What outrage would do? Half the country lost heart to fight Islamists a couple of years after 9–11."

Washington, D.C.
March 29th, 2013
Good Friday

The preparations for the massive anti-drug rally looked frantic, but it's always frenetic when a big event takes place on the Nation's Capitol Mall. The Park Service permits narrowly limit the set up and take down time of even the largest gatherings. The people's Mall must return to normal fast. The awesome concentration of police and firepower around the Mall made it appear like old-fashioned normal with a freedom of movement and freedom from fear.

As busy as ants, the workers made a stadium-size platform, jumbo speakers and screens rise to multi-stories from the grassy ground at the foot of the Capitol. The President's people convinced the Evangelical Association of Churches and Ministries to expand and enhance their Easter weekend rally on the Mall. The church folk agreed, reluctantly at first, to have something called the True Blue Kick-Off Rally start on Saturday, cede back the podium on Sunday for sunrise and mid-morning worship, then let the True Blues come back and parade speakers to talk to the masses the rest of the day until five in the afternoon. The President of the United States would speak briefly at two on Saturday to make the evening news and Sunday morning shows. All was set for her capstone speech at the closing ceremony at 2 PM Easter Sunday afternoon. That speech should make the Monday night news if it had any news legs at all.

Recently, news was all bad for the NITs. The kidnapped Omni people talked, but said nothing important, until they were tortured to death. The Omni could be only days away from being up. President Maggie Kyle pushed hard for completion. The NITs knew something was happening. If the President was assassinated, the uproar would delay work for certain. Pablo Ponce De Leon's organization might make sufficient progress with some technical people, moles, at the National Security Agency[5] to make Omni impotent by exception. Pablo Ponce De Leon would have to relish the thought that Omni could gobble up his competitors and leave him alone.

The innocent looking family man, whose photo image troubled Naomi so, decided to kill President Maggie Kyle with a bomb. It would look like Islamists did it. The chemical tracers in the explosives would lead the investigators back to the Mid-East where the explosives were purchased. There were members of fringe Islamic organizations in the employ of the Mall concession companies. Their unfortunate death in the explosion would have all the appearances of a suicide bombing.

Pablo's lieutenant assured him that the Semtex[6] explosive would not be found by the bomb dogs. Hundreds of the four by four lumber struts and braces for the Mall's speakers' platform were purchased from their lumber company. The four by fours were hollowed and loaded with Semtex. The boards were soaked in a chemical compound that the drug laboratories insisted would mask the Semtex with a chemical bonding. The bond changed the chemical composition of the interface between the plastic explosive and the wood without changing the explosive qualities.

Pablo liked the plan, but worried about the clean up. Only a couple of guys in the lumber yard, the truck driver who delivered the Semtex to the yard, and the guy who did the final wiring would have to be cleaned up permanently. Pablo demanded that their bodies never be found He feared the advances in forensic science. The guy setting the detonation was a trusted fellow. His name was Frank Martin.

---

5. NSA is National Security Agency. The eyes and ears of the U.S. government intelligence services located at Ft. Meade, MD where the world-wide sensors dump their data for analysis.

6. Semtex. A European plastic explosive preferred by terrorists. Pablo wanted to make sure that the deed was done. He knew from his Machiavellian political warfare in Columbia that regicide must succeed even if he couldn't spell Machiavelli. The penalty for failure was as extreme as it was certain. They used five thousand pounds of explosives throughout the podium. It would have the effect, if not the exact signature, of a truck bomb.

Washington, D.C.
March 30th, 2013
Saturday

Frank Martin wasn't such a bad guy, really. He liked to get high and he resented anyone trying to keep him from getting a hit when he wanted it. For twelve years since he dropped out of college he held a job, or a steady stream of jobs. He got up in the morning and got to work, so whose business was it if he got rocked with alcohol or marijuana or cocaine or a designer drug when he felt like it? It was his body and he should have the freedom to do what he wanted to do with it. Wasn't that what being an American was all about anyway—freedom? And a little shot of 'sin' drug?

Frank read enough political hate speech from liberals to know he hated President Maggie Myriah Kyle. Besides, he was making big, big bucks for this job. Connect a few wires and set a timer and that was that. President Kyle would speak at two and finish by two twenty. If he set the timer for two-ten, it would be 'good to go, and she would blow'. The huge combined children's choir would be off the stage by one-thirty. Just Maggie and the filthy Christian Right hypocrites that wanted to stand behind her on TV would be boom-ba-boom. He'd make sure those Christian bigots didn't steal anymore elections.

The cops wanted him to hurry up with the line to the jumbo speakers he pretended to fix. He heard some speaker droning on and on above him as he worked. Then he heard thousands of little feet, children's voices and occasional adult admonitions as the two thousand voice choir of churches nation-wide ushered onto the broad layered podium.

Frank didn't check his watch when he was done. The hit of 'sin' he took just before he began his work made him jubilant in his work. But he was more careless than he ever would have thought. By the time he finished wiring under the podium and set the timer under the jumbo speaker monkey bars he was in a euphoric state. After he set the timer, he remembered in a flash that he had to adjust for daylight savings time. He was certain that this was the weekend for daylight savings time, so he had to like spring backwards this weekend.

Man, he was so glad that he was so smart. Frank set the timer for '1:10', shut the utility box door and padlocked it. As he walked, he phoned his live-in girl friend to see if she was home. *"This will show those pious religious bigots."* If he had looked up to at the jumbo screen directly above his head, he would see the running clock in the lower frame of the picture. It was '1:05' EST.

Chapter 6. Revolution

Washington, D.C.
March 30th, 2013
Saturday

    Washington's latitude places it at mid-field where late Northern Winters and early Southern Springs compete for possession. This March ended with the South holding a picture perfect Easter weekend. The cherry blossoms flowered a little earlier as if on cue. This Saturday was breezy and warm in the seventies like the best of days should be.

    The 'Third Millenium' children's choir moved like a huge herd of cats to their places on the podium. The Evangelical Association planned this rally for over a year. Every state and territory of the United States of America was represented by children wearing frilly colored cottons. Most of the two thousand children were between the ages of six and twelve. A few teen choirs and a more adorable groups of very little children were placed in the back and the very front respectively to add the balance of mature voices and precious little faces. Every race and ethnicity smiled and teased and frowned in turn among the assembled babes. As the camera crews from all the networks set up to record the President, they rolled good lead-in footage of the children.

    Cameras captured test pictures when the babes started singing 'Jesus Loves Me'. One network closed in on a four year old boy whose wispy blonde was blowing in the breeze as he stopped singing and leaned his head against his older sister's shoulder. She continued to sing with gusto. Another network focused on twin boys who sang heartily, but with that faraway look of children watching the world watch them. The twins' black cherubic features were brought out by their bright white shirts. All of the children stopped singing at ten minutes and three seconds after 1 PM Eastern Standard Time.

The bomb made a flash of intense orange that moved horizontally across the field of vision of the cameras like lightening. Then a cloud came roiling towards the screen like the rush of volcanic ash in an eruption. Except this cloud was not volcanic subterranean gray, it was the brightest pink. It seemed so incongruously pretty for the tenths of seconds it took to fill the whole view of the camera. As soon as the pink cloud smothered the cameras, the mist condensed like rain and ran blood red in droplets down the screen. And in the instant the pink covered the whole eye of the cameras, the sound blasted into the receivers. The sound was a long sharp crack. Then, a lower, longer echo of boom. The cameras well beyond the blast recorded the flash of pink cloud followed by a much larger black and boiling cloud that climbed past the museum roofs and spiraled up until the winds bent it to their direction.

Most of the hundred yards of humanity around the podium was gone. They vanished in the cloud and crack of sound. For several hundreds of yards the crowd was pelted with fragments of wood, metal and parts of human beings. Many of the red masses were, clearly, parts of children.

The wounded shrieked in terror and pain. The crowd of almost half a million people screamed in fear and moved away looking for shelter. There was little space to move. The people who were not physically injured surged backwards then forward to the place of impact. Then, within the long, nightmare walk of one second-hand sweep of a minute, the full realization came upon the uninjured mass of the crowd.

"The children! The children! Where are the children? Ahh-yi!" the tapes of the cries bore true testimony of the most terrible noise. Above the bedlam of vehicle and building security systems activated by the blast, the sound of the tens of thousands of voices rose and fell in a wailing crescendo. The first camera to move closer to the carnage fixed on a young mother frantically going from body to body. Her brown hair was matted on one side of her face with her own blood. Her dress on one side was tattered. She was grasping a child's jacket in both hands. Desperately she rushed and paused, looking for her missing child, calling her name, and rushing on to see if the next lifeless form might be her child and her alive. Her face was crazed with fear. The camera could not leave her and she never left the consciousness of everyone who saw her that day.

The sound of so many people crying rose above the shouting for loved ones and help. The crying became a wailing, groaning of human suffering. The sound sent shivers up the spine of people watching. Within seconds the whole world was watching. The distant cameras kept rolling and came in close to capture the hell on earth of evil unleashed on innocents. Every network carried the scene live.

People around the world were shaken. Americans were horrified and outraged.

Pearl Harbor, President Kennedy's assassination, the explosion of the Space Shuttle, the death of Princess Diana, the Columbine school murders, and the Islamists attacks after the Iraq War of '03, and of course, 9–11, were just warm ups for this emotional gathering of the American village. Within minutes the police, soldiers from the Old Guard at Fort Meyer and the Marines from the Washington Marine barracks helped Washington police frantically secure the entire area around the Mall. The new President insisted on going over to the Mall.

President Maggie Kyle carried an armful of towels and a first aid kit. She jogged over across the ellipse and up the rise of the Washington Monument. She was swallowed by the crowd for long minutes while Secret Service elbowed their way up to her. They tried to drag her out. She said sharply, "Either help here or get lost, guys!" They fell in behind her and administered first aid.

President Maggie Kyle moved slowly up the mall for over an hour. Some people begged her to go back to safety. Most just wept at her presence sharing their suffering. Maggie hugged and kissed and cried. The stunning white ladies' power suit she donned for her speech was covered in blood and dirt.

Some media waited when President Kyle made her way around to the front entrance of the White House. No one had ever seen a President of the United States look like a battle-weary Florence Nightingale, drenched in the blood of her people. Her National

Security Advisor pulled her by the elbow to turn her back on the cameras for a second as he whispered in her ear. She turned around tight-lipped and grim-faced.

"My fellow Americans, we have been attacked. Again, many, many of our citizens, our people, have been killed in a despicable bomb attack. This is murder. Most of the victims are children," President Kyle opened her bloody, muddy palms to the cameras.

"We do not know if there are other attacks planned as yet. The nation's armed forces and security forces are mobilized. I am returning to the White House to confer with leaders of Congress and the Chief Justice of the Supreme Court on the issue of martial law," President Kyle breathed deeply the burning anger from her gut.

"We know the source of this attack. This was not an act of war by some foreign power against the United States. This was an act of wanton massacre, the murder of children, by the most despicable of the anti-Americans, the Drugsnakes and Islamists among us. The Narco-Terrorists did this."

"How do you know Madame President? How can you know so soon?" shouted all the reporters.

"The Omni is up. We knew who did it immediately," President Kyle walked away with her shoulders squared, ignoring the shouted questions bouncing off of her back.

Covington, Tennessee

Bubba and Ish fixed lunch that red letter Saturday with the TV on as background noise. They wanted to hear President Maggie Kyle at the True Blue Rally. Both men committed to eat healthier and exercise more, as usual, after breakfast, so they shared the tedious duties of cutting fresh vegetables. They stood over cutting boards an arm's length from each other when they heard the crack and boom. They jerked their heads erect like deer hearing a twig break. The instant their eyes meet, they both bolted for the TV. Their collision in the doorway could have been comical. Bubba plopped down on the footstool in front of the black faux leather over-stuffed chair. His hands hung limply in front of his pot belly. Ish stood tensely, his fists on his waist like he was about to make some defiant public stand.

They saw the pink mist, the red drops and, after long seconds of dead time, the mother searching for the child to fill the coat in her hands.

Bubba looked like he was going to swoon. Then, he fell forward from his perch to his knees. He pulled his hands up under his chin like a little boy in prayer. His murmuring was broken by huge body wrenching sobs. Tears ran freely down his red face. Ish grabbed the back of the other chair. He thought his knees were going to give. He eased himself into the chair and stared with his mouth open.

Ish absorbed what was going on. His 'totally alive' mind started to ask itself questions. *Bomb. No doubt. No, the President wasn't on the podium. A lot of people, especially children, are slaughtered. But why would they blow up kids? Anyone who did this would have to know it was such an outrage that it would enflame the people. An aroused American people is a terrible thing to consider. Ah, an outrage indeed.*

Suddenly Ish realized, *I gotta see the information traffic.* Ish opened a window on the terminal in the other corner. Ish monitored the Army Ops Center and the J-3 NORTHCOM[1]. He was already forty messages behind when he opened the window. He read breathlessly as the iconic translator worked as fast as it could. Ish couldn't believe what transpired. Even though he knew the best efforts of his life constructed these very fast-breaking actions, it was unreal that now was the time. For real. Ish read:

- Homeland Defense: DEFCON 2
- Threat Color Red

The United States is at Defense Condition 2—war is imminent, hostilities have begun.

- OCONUS: DEFCON 1

CENTCOM, SOUTHCOM at Defense Condition 1—war is ongoing in theater.

- Presidential Emergency Powers Act stages One through Five.

The coordinating messages for the military commands were in a flurry. The 'pock-pock' sound of message titles filling up the screen

---

1. J3 NORTHCOM is the Joint Operations officer for the Northern Command Headquarters.

sounded like the rapid fire of a computer wargame.

Bubba called for Ish to see President Maggie Kyle as she spoke in front off the White House. They were startled by her mention of Omni.

"The Beta works! It's up and running. Praise God, praise God! Thank you, Father. Oh please, now, let Your Will be done. Work Your good will from this terrible tragedy," said Ish.

"Messages are fast and furious," said Bubba.

Ish felt the knots in his stomach doubling over themselves. He felt nauseous, *"I hate this. It's like being in the TOC[2] when the 4th Cavalry Squadron was closing in on the Iraqi Republican Guard in the middle of that freak rain storm."* Back then, he was terrified that he would pass out in front of everyone as his blood pressure spiked. Fear of failing physically in front of his buddies was worse than a missile screaming through the command track and blowing him to bits.

Ish called to God silently again, *"Father, now please, now. Take the anxiety and cast it away. Oh, Lord, make me like David into a mighty man of Israel. Give me strength to rise up like an eagle. Make my feet strong, not clay. Let me ignore any pain or panic I feel. God, I know you will provide the health I need and no more—if it is in Your Will."*

Ish saw the Martial Law orders. One message entered the cue and the cue stopped. A 'personal for—eyes only' for Ruth and Ish sat blinking, waiting to be opened. Ish made the correct authentication and read carefully.

"Bubba!" Ish shouted. Then his voice dropped to the controlled sang froid LTG Trento expected to hear over the radio in combat, "Rosetta 6.2 is activated. We're a go."

Ish and Bubba looked at the screen and then at each other. Rosetta 6.2 was as serious business as either man contemplated in his life. It was going to be momentous for the country and the defining act of their lives. They both knew it. Bubba saw Jared's shadow fill the window frame on the front door before he heard him pound on the door.

---

2. TOC is Tactical Operations Center.

"You fellas have a military jet waiting for you at Millington[3] within the hour. Time to go. I'll be back in ten minutes," said Jared.

"Make it fifteen," Ish ordered. *"I have to make double sure that I've got the right files on disks I carry on my person. Can't make a mistake."* Ish presumed they were going some place close to the heat of the decision making, so if a fire on Rosetta 6.2 needed to be put out the right firemen would be there. Ish tapped the thin disks in his pocket several times before they stepped out of the house.

Two deputy's vehicles pulled up in the yard as Bubba and Ish emerged into the glorious Spring day. Their light jackets felt too hot immediately. Jared squared his cowboy hat with sheriff's star and they headed out in a three car caravan.

"I need to stop by the bank on the way," said Jared.

"The bank?" asked Bubba.

"Yeah, the bank," said Jared. He reached into his jacket, pulled out a thin strip of paper and waved it at his passengers in the back. His deputy, a thin, young black man, looked straight ahead. "I've got ta pick up five men before midnight tonight. There's another ten I've ta secure in anuther twenty four hours."

"Who are the signature authorities on these warrants?" asked Ish.

"I got this order from the State Attorney General. It's countersigned by the National Guard Adjutant General for Tennessee. We're going by the bank for the first boy on my list."

"He'll be at the bank on Saturday afternoon?" asked Bubba.

"Yes, sir, he's the president. We got a fix on him being here right now. Hey, we're here." The three cars squealed into the parking lot of the small bank. The thin deputy pounded on the door until a fat, doughy man in his late forties ran inside the dark glassed lobby to let them in. Ish and Bubba absently followed Jared.

"Hey, hey, I got it!" the man shouted through the glass. The deputies kept pounding.

Jared turned his head and spoke lowly to Ish and Bubba, "This guy's the biggest money launderer in my county. He's 'bout ready to buy the county. He refused my deputy a loan for a house, but he suggested that my man and he could work out some other kinda deal."

---

3. Millington is the location of the Naval Air Station between Covington and Memphis.

"Why, Sheriff Bringle, what do you boys need?" the bank president smiled unctuously.

"We need to talk, Jim. Your office," Jared's curtness changed Jim's demeanor.

When they entered the office Jim hurried to his high backed chair. He was a bank president again behind his massive desk. Jared stopped at the door and signaled for Ish and Bubba to stay outside. Jared looked at the back wall camera eye and nodded to his deputy. The deputy leaned against the door and pulled a long silver gun from his holster where his service revolver should be. The gun was a hand held laser. Its thin red line burned to scorch optics. It could blind a person. The deputy fried the eye of the center camera. He moved, cat-like, to lase the cameras in the corners and, finally, the small one at the corner of the desk. Jim was too shocked to speak. The blackmail video cam was gone.

"Hey Sheriff, what's goin' on here?" fear crept into Jim's voice.

Ish stuck his head in the room.

"Hey, Jim, what exactly is going on here?" Jared raised his voice to dominate hidden still-recording audio tapes. "Jim, put down that laser, you'll hurt someone. Freeze. Keep you hands out where I can see them."

Jared and his deputy moved fast. Jared slid a snub-nosed .38 caliber revolver towards Jim across the desk. In a natural response, Jim took it. He held it limply.

"Jim, you're threatenin' an officer of the law!" Jared shouted loudly. Jim was too confused. His eyes were wide.

"Gun! He's got a gun!" the deputy yelled.

"No, Jim, no! Put down that weapon!" Jared shouted as he drew his .9mm automatic out and engaged the red laser dot on Jim's chest. "Put it down, drop it!"

Jim raised his hands and looked down in horror and disbelief at the red dot on his silk shirt when Jared emptied his clip into Jim. The impact threw the chair against the wall. Jim's dead eyes and mouth were frozen open. His body stayed in the chair. There was a small red hole about an inch in diameter oozing blood onto his expensive shirt. The wall above him showed what tumbling high velocity projectiles do to humans and chairs. The backs were blown out of both and embedded in the wall in a spray pattern several feet wide.

"We've got ta go now," Jared said to his deputy.

"What in the Hell was that?" demanded Ish.

"It had to be done, Ish. No man is goin' to corrupt the law here."

"Then what was that? That was murder!"

"This's justice. Let's go."

Ish caught Jared's elbow as he got to the driver's door. He spun around.

"You murdered a man. That wasn't justice!" Ish yelled in Jared's face.

"We're following orders. That man was on my list. He resisted arrest. He is a category 'Zulu' fugitive[4]. You know egg-zackly what that means, don't you?" Jared was pumped with adrenaline. His nostrils flared.

Ish knew that Category Zulu's were to be apprehended with weapons drawn and exposed. If the subject blinked aggressively, the rules of engagement allowed automatic 'defensive' deadly fires. No further questions asked. "You know what you did," said Ish.

"I did what I had to do," Jared climbed in his black sports utility sheriff's mobile command post.

"We will come back to this, Jared," said Ish. *If a good guy, a Christian, like Jared did this cold-blooded execution, what would others do around the country?* Ish felt the knots in his stomach churn.

"When this is all over, Ish, you can come back here and do anything you want," said Jared.

"You'll never be able to fake out the forensics, Jared," said Bubba. He was huffing for air.

"The county coroner will come the right conclusion. The case'll be closed," Jared looked in the rear view mirror at his passengers, "long before you boys come back to my county. If you'n ever do."

They rode in silence for a few miles. Jared said, "I've known Jim all of his life. I know his family. I know what he's done for the

---

[4]. Zulu fugitive is one of the special categories of fugitives developed under Rosetta 6.2. It gives 'shoot on sight' authorization.

most part. He'd get the best lawyer money could buy in the Mid-South and walk away from any trial. He got the Tennessee justice he deserved. If you was me, you'd do the same thang."

Ish listened. *God help me. I'd do the same, or worse, if it was my county.*

"Thou shalt not kill, Brother Jared," said Bubba.

"I didn't hate Jim when I shot him. I just executed him, Bubba. Execution itn't murder," said Jared.

"It's murder without a judge and jury," said Bubba.

"Technicality that's overlooked in martial law. This's war. I did what was needed to be done. I done it and I'll answer for it when my time comes."

Nothing else was said. The men shook hands and looked hard into each other's eyes when Jared handed them over to the Marine military police at the Millington Naval Station air terminal. Ish and Bubba were ushered into the communications center where the military transportation system terminals were connected to the Transportation Command (TRANSCOM)[5] worldwide network.

Ish sat down at an operator's terminal. He reached into his pocket and pulled out his first disk. In the time it took him to make the mouse movements and keystrokes, the Rosetta Icons coursed their way at the speed of light to their locations throughout the military C4I world and beyond. The little PC terminal where Ish made the entry made copies of Rosetta. Ish packaged and launched an email to the Federal Express headquarters a few miles away in Memphis. Soon, Rosetta icons would be re-populated world-wide. As he left, Ish warned the Officer in Charge of the site that he should keep his people away from that terminal for the next week. The terminal had a high probability of exploding. The officer looked confused. *How simple it was. How quick. Now it's over. Just like I planned it to be exactly so.* They climbed into the military executive jet and learned their destination was Dulles Airport outside of Washington, DC.

---

5. TRANSCOM is the Transportation Command Headquarters. The Joint Headquarters for moving the military around the globe.

Fort Leavenworth, Kansas

Naomi wanted to watch the True Blue Rally from start to finish. It kept her occupied in an uplifting and positive way. The sacred music reminded her of what was right and wrong. Since Jack was a room away every night, she had to keep right and wrong clear in her head all the time. She looked right at the TV when the pink cloud came boiling towards her view. The color was so confusing. It took a little time for the boom and the distance shots of the black explosion mushroom billowing skyward for her to understand. She gasped. She gasped again. She crossed her arms protectively over her bosoms. "Oh my God, Oh Lordy!" she gasped.

She rushed and banged on his door. "Jack come here! Hurry!"

Jack heard the urgency in her voice. When he opened his door, she was already back in her room. Naomi stood in front of the TV and pointed at the screen. She put her hands over her mouth.

Jack looked at the TV intently. He got the picture, "Where was the bomb?"

"The True Blue Rally," Naomi choked.

"Oh, no! The President!"

"No! The children! They killed the children!" Naomi burst into tears and stood close to Jack. She pulled her hands and arms close, hugging herself, as he wrapped his arms around her back.

"The children? What children?" Jack asked.

"The children's choir was singing when the bomb went off. There were two thousand babies out there. Maybe more."

"Two thousand children?"

"They're gone, Jack, they're all gone," she cried harder. Naomi unfolded her arms and pulled him tightly across his upper back.

Jack held back tightly and started to rock back and forth gently. "There, there, Naomi," he said gently. He held her for a minute. The TV announcer urgently read the updates flashing in front of him. "Naomi, we need to go to the SCIF. Now."

Naomi nodded her assent. He led the way to the SCIF. When they logged on, they were way behind on the message traffic. Jack stopped scrolling when he saw a message in from the Army Ops center with Jack's code name and an 'eyes only' heading. It decoded swiftly and read, "Stand fast. Populate Rosetta 6.2 from your station. Execute same. Further orders follow. Trento."

Naomi smiled wanly, "I guess it begins, doesn't it, Jack?"

"Yes, it begins," Jack felt a rising excitement. He was ready to go into action. Soon after Jack finished his first mission so swiftly and efficiently, a message came into the cue and froze the screen. The iconic language message sat there at the top of his screen pulsating different colors. After it flashed its long sequence of colors, it hesitated in its original form as a grey, metallic rose cinquefoil and slowly disappeared.

Fort Lewis, Washington

Ruth worked in her solitude at 10:10 AM, Pacific time, when the bomb went off. Pablo was in his room reading all morning. Neither had a TV, radio or personal communicator on. There was a lot of hustling and bustling in the hallways. The troops were coming in for a mission. Maybe it was another alert. No one came to tell Ruth about anything special, so she continued to work. She didn't turn on the TV until it was almost time for the President's speech. Ruth got an eyeful in an instant. She switched to the message window. She went through the same machinations as Jack did half a continent away. As she read the messages, there was a sharp knock on the door.

A strapping Ranger buck sergeant stepped in and handed Ruth a message. "There is an aircraft warming up for you. It'll be ready to go as soon as you are, Ma'am."

"Thank you," Ruth read the message and tucked it in a waist pocket of her sensible slacks. Rosetta 6.2 was initiated. She walked briskly to Pablo's room and knocked on the door. "Pablo, it's time to go."

"Go where, Ruth?" Pablo got up from his reclined reading, book in hand.

"I don't know yet. But there was a terrible bombing in Washington. They bombed the True Blue Rally," Pablo grimaced as she spoke.

"Who did the bombing?" asked Pablo.

"The NITs did it. They did it," said Ruth.

Leesburg, Virginia
April 8th, 2013
Monday

Rosetta 6.2 performed admirably while its creator and chief designer, its prime advocate, and two of its artisans moved under cloak and dagger regimes of very secretive travel. Four amigos went to the estate astride the high hill on the western outskirts of Leesburg, Virginia. Driving out from Washington, D.C. it is the first blue hill, the right flank on a map, one sees of the mountains of Virginia. It had a straight line of sight to the highest points in downtown D.C. It could shoot back to the west to the communications tower at the old presidential bunker hideout and up north to Camp David, Maryland.

Ish, Bubba, Ruth and Pablo were thrilled to see one another. There were waves of emotion at their reunion. But, there was no time to pause. The work began that night, continued through Easter Sunday and stayed at a breakneck pace.

The first week of the Rosetta 6.2 Revolution launched, simultaneously, the large scale physics of several wave motions in human dimensions. The outrage of the pink mist brought the American family to an emotional peak. The War on Drugs was wrapped into the War on Islamist Terrorists. The World War IV (World War III was the Cold War), the Global War against Islamists, exploded in every home again. Control for illegal immigration seemed a serious possibility. Martial Law made all of it real and personal.

Martial Law is foreign to Americans. So, Week One, Phase One, of Operation 'End Fear' imposed the gravity of the situation upon the people. Better to prepare them for the severity of the solutions coming down the road. Martial Law limited flight for fugitives among a whole nation that is constantly on the move. Air, train and ship passenger travel was shut down. There was only emergency travel for ninety-six hours. Road blocks set across the east-west and north-south axises along riverlines and interstate highways dissected the country into huge grids. In the Rocky Mountain states the checkpoints set at mountain passes created the same effect. The borders were closed effectively. The Nation became a grid of Areas of Operation (AO)[6].

---

6. AO is the Area of Operations.

The grids covered the mapscreen in the large meeting room of the mansion. It looked like a Leavenworth Command and General Staff College class joke on "How to take over the country—the Leavenworth Way". Ish wasn't amused as he laid out the papers for a pre-briefing to LTG Larry Trento. LTG Trento wanted to get ready, really ready, for a tough meeting with the Joint Chiefs of Staff and their Ops Deputies. It was going to be another hard-nosed meeting in the 'tank'[7].

The Chiefs, the foremost constellation of four-star generals, already were peeved that a three-star was hand-picked by the President as the Joint Task Force Commander. The four-star admiral commanding Northern Command should have lead this Operation in Homeland Defense. Moreover, the Chiefs stayed worried about conducting military operations at home. The Secretary of Defense accused the Chiefs of cutting him out of the operational details. He was sitting in the policy meetings with the President, but was forbidden by the President to manage much in these first few phases. He blamed the Chiefs and they passed his heat onto LTG Trento.

LTG Trento barged in with an entourage of note-takers just as Ish finished the set up. LTG Trento and Ish had a second, when they bear-hugged. "My old RTO[8], still hangin' in there," said LTG Trento.

"Trying to keep you straight."

"First slide," LTG Trento commanded. No more pleasantries today.

The first slide opened up on the screen—'Objectives'.

"Let's go to the objectives for Week One. We can skip the campaign objectives for now because we went into such detail on Easter Sunday and Monday in the tank," said LTG Trento.

"Sir, as you know the seventy two hour period of maximum curfew was completed at 1600 EDST on Wednesday. During this period you can see how many subjects were pursued and apprehended. We are presently at 96.3% effectiveness for arrests."

"What about key people? Any of the big fish still out of the net?" asked LTG Trento.

"Yes, sir, three key narco-leaders and fourteen Islamists are

---

7. Tank is the name of the room the Joint Chiefs of Staff meet.

8. RTO is Radio Telephone Operator, the soldier who operates radios and communications for the Commander.

still out," Ish deftly opened a hyperlink to show the list by priority of 'still outs'. "We have leads on two of these characters, but we have absolutely nothing on Pablo Ponce de Leon. He has vanished. The Islamists are the same guys we've been looking for a long time before the Easter attack."

"I thought we hit his place in Columbia on Day One," said LTG Trento.

"Pablo and his family were gone. The problem is that all of our indicators read that he was on-site until the last minute."

"How can that be?" asked Bubba. He wasn't supposed to interrupt.

"The sensors read all right. The messages came in wrong. That means we have a dirty operator or someone has gotten to our software," said Ruth.

"The Omni software is compromised? Or is Rosetta 6.2 corrupted?"

"No sir. We don't know what is or is not compromised. It could be one sub-routine. It could be the local sub-system of systems," said Ish.

"The J-2[9] and the director of the NSA are working it hard. There are no other indications of system compromise, yet. Your Intel Deputy was selected this morning, as you know, to head a tiger team to find and fix the problem."

"Let's look at the execution matrix for Phase I and II in Week One. Phase One began on order of the President of the United States at 1701 EST, Saturday, March 30th, 2013. Phase One was in force six hours with all missions assigned—initiated. We achieved missions complete at N plus eight hours. The delay was getting the comms secure, set and fully operational down the AO Task Force Commanders," said Ish.

"Martial Law was declared at 1600 hours EST, Easter Sunday, March 31st. We were well into Phase I in every area except those that couldn't begin until the formal declaration by 1600." Ish pointed at the tree branch of activities that occurred at 1600 with an old fashioned wooden pointer. The branch was an exponential curve moving up and away as it moved right through time on the matrix.

"The seventy-two hours for Phase I was long enough for us to

---

9. J2 is the Joint Staff officer for Intelligence.

establish the inter-agency, Joint Task Force for every AO. We restricted the travel and flight of the truly key people we scarfed up. The period wasn't too long to create economic disaster, but it did cause enough disruption nation-wide to have the desired psychological effect on friendlies and the enemy and the illegals."

LTG Trento nodded 'continue'.

"Most of the personnel raids were conducted during the hours of darkness while the curfew was in effect. This kept our casualties down and lowered the collateral damage. It scares a lot of people. Arresting people at night. It's sending the wrong message to many," said Ish.

"At the end of the seventy-two hours, we reached a point in our build up of combat service support for the majority of our forces to be out of their barracks and operating from their Task Force AOs. The combat service support logistical build up continues from Phase II to prepare for the security, safety, health and welfare of the detainees we're going to take in. We initiate those search and seizures when we move into Phase III tomorrow. The Blues break out soon and it will complicate what we're doing immensely."

"Why is this Blues movement going to go into the streets in Phase III? This doesn't seem right in Martial Law, having demonstrations, now does it? Every liberal organization in the country is ready to break out demonstrations as soon as they won't get shot for being in public. The illegal aliens have nothing to lose by demonstrating. How are we going to sort that out?" the edge in LTG Trento's voice was close to a growl.

"Sir, this operation is all about politics. The military operations, as you know Bismarck said, are just an extension of politics. Every military task has a political objective. So much is not under our direction at all. The Blues Movement, works in concert with our military operations to have the desired effect," said Ish.

"Who's in charge?" asked Bubba inappropriately again.

Ruth answered, "The President of the United States, the Commander-in-Chief essentially declared war with her imposition of Martial Law. She's waging a war on drugs and Islamist terror that will win. It will end the one war for good. It'll set the conditions for the decades it'll take, maybe centuries, to win the second one, the World War on Islamists. The military strategy she is employing is to conduct an internal revolution." The word 'revolution' captured the room. The silence was absolute. "It's an internal revolution within the boundaries of the Constitution to protect and preserve the Constitution against domestic enemies. Your duty in the Army, is the same as it was in June 1775. You're to win your part of the revolution. With the support of the other Armed Services, of course. You knew where this was heading months ago."

"I understand. But, Ruth, I'm charging you personally responsible to keep me informed on any Constitutional questions the political part of this operation brings up. Before it happens. Let's wrap up the rest of this briefing," LTG Larry Trento pointed his finger at Ruth Weinstein.

Fort Leavenworth, Kansas
April 17th, 2013
Wednesday

A glorious early Spring day swept the American prairie from Texas north to Canada. Jack missed light for several days. He moved an Army cot into the closeted facility to stay next to the beeps, buzzes and rings that telltale military information traffic. He stayed there day and night. He awoke to a gentle shake of his shoulder. The weight of accumulated fatigue made him slow to rise. When his eyes unblurred he saw Naomi's pretty and kind face smiling at him. The bright bank of neon lights above her head made it hard for him to look at her. These days he found her face to be more and more beautiful each day.

"Sleepy-head, you'd get more sleep if you left this place for a few hours," said Naomi.

"I might miss something important," Jack propped himself up on one elbow. Jack pulled back the sleeping bag and swung his legs around to the floor. He wore his wrinkled khakis and a T-shirt as his sleeping attire. His bare feet awakened to the cold concrete.

"Coffee?" Naomi held out a large steaming styrofoam cup.

"Hoo-ah. Thanks, many thanks," Jack looked at his watch before he reached for the cup.

"Ish wants you to talk to him about some targeting priority.

Also, LTG Trento wants to speak with you. I think it is about the same thing," said Naomi.

"Hmm."

"Your beeper went off, but you didn't hear it," said Naomi.

Jack looked at his belt. The red light was on. The alarm button was on too, but had long since done its duty. "Guess my staying on station didn't help this time. Who called first?"

"Ish," said Naomi.

Jack put the message through to Ish. He looked at the small mirror near the pencil camera over his work station. He needed a shave badly. His blood shot eyes looked terrible. *"Oh well, better to get the word soonest. I can clean up before I call LTG Trento. Stupid cameras."* Rosetta 6.2 operated the visface pencil cams at every commander's laptop. The commanders had face to face communications anywhere they went. For decades commanders in the field trained to listen to the voice in voice-to-voice communications and judge on the fitness to lead. Now, the early fielding of some Future Combat Systems[10] technologies allowed commanders to read the faces of their subordinates. It was back to the future for leaders to lead—face to face.

Ish looked stern as only Ish could do. His jaw set his purple-black skin squarely in a face that brokered no nonsense. "Jack, I want you to look and see if there are any anomalies in our BDA[11]. Are we having trouble with any specific area of the country or overseas? Are we having a problem with misses or no-go's for any block of time? Is there any type of target that is especially tough? Are we getting conflicting reports on BDA? Check the targeting problems by location, time, type of target and BDA."

"Roger, Ish, got it. What're you looking for really?"

"Don't want to tell you right now. It may set you to look for a certain pattern and overlook something. Just do a sort of the data and let me know what you come up with."

"Is this why Trento called?

"Yeah, I think so. I'll call to confirm. You get to work. If I don't clear things up for Larry, then he'll call you later. Questions?"

---

10. Future Combat Systems is the Army modernization program began in 2000 to capitalize on the Revolution in Military Affairs for the next era of warfare.

11. BDA is Battle Damage Assessment. The estimate of damage after any attack.

"No, Sir," said Jack. Jack made a point as a civilian to not 'sir' as excessively as an Army guy, but 'siring' Ish came naturally now.

"Naomi, did you catch that?" asked Jack.

"Yes, I know where to start," said Naomi.

Jack padded back to the men's room to clean up. His mind was full of cobwebs. Oddly, he remembered the fluttering of butterfly wings back at Langley NASA before the world exploded in fire and shrapnel. Jack thought of the moment after when he would be dead. He felt the dry mouth of fear. He hated the nothingness of black unconsciousness. He wouldn't even know he was gone. *"Naomi is convinced that she's going to a place of warmth and light with her consciousness intact. No. Enhanced. All memories alive in her mind will stay alive. To live, to keep living after death, that would be nice. How could that be? It's just too good to be true. It'd really be something if it was. Naomi thought it was. How can she?"* Jack shaved another long stroke up his neck to his chin.

Late that evening Jack collapsed into the overstuffed black chair in front of the big screen TV in his room. He couldn't believe how much was happening out there in the country. *"I can't believe how my handiwork plays out. I can't believe I'm not out there in command somewhere."* Jack watched the speakers strut across the stages of the TV screens and thought smugly to himself, *"I could do better than that. I did better when I was a company commander speaking at a formation."*

There was a knock on his door. Jack knew the weight of Naomi's footstep on the creaking polished hardwood floors and the volume of her knock. "Coming."

Naomi held a pot of steaming 'Russian' Tea. She looked as fresh as a vase of just cut flowers. Her brown hair reached her shoulders. She pulled it back in an upsweep that highlighted her long neck and firm jawline. She was radiant. It took Jack's breath away.

"Want some tea? It's the kind you like," she said. Outside, the gorgeous day before blew itself into blustery cold evening.

"Sure," Jack breathed the fragrance of the tea more than her perfume. 'Russian' tea was the concoction of instant tea, lemonade, cinammon, sugar and some other spices that warmed a cold day 'in the field' playing Army.

"What's up?" asked Naomi. She poured Jack a cup to the brim.

"More demonstrations. Some people started going house to house to search and seize drugs. They say you are True Blue if you let them in. It looks like they have hand-held chemical detectors calibrated for drugs. So, it must be us," he smiled.

"We're doing a lot aren't we? Think about how many chem detectors Ish and Ruth said they ordered for years and stockpiled! I can't believe how much they anticipated and how much they prepared."

"Yeah, but there is always the 'for the want of a nail' thing you forget."

"Oooh, quoting Shakespeare, I like that John-James."

"Actually it was Ben Franklin if you look on line. Naw, I'm just quoting e-Shakespeare[12]. What a super blogger! I remember a great piece some years back, when I was in school, on the whole for the want of a nail, shoe, horse, kingdom was lost thing."

"Do you think our Bubba penned that one?"

"No. Besides no one pens anymore. They icon. They text message."

"How are the searches going? Really?"

"Mixed bag. Some are going great and some are turning into riots. It gets really complicated, apparently, when outsiders come to your neighborhood. Organized opposition, political stuff, is building up. But, the bonfires and bands look like a real hit. Did you hear the band last night outside the gate?"

"Yes, faintly. It's a long way from here. Where do you think they ever came up with the idea of door to door True Bluism?" Naomi took a long sip and wet her lips.

"It's all, Ish. All Ishmael. I think he came up with that one based on what happened during the American Revolution. He said the revolution was carried door to door in Georgia and New York. A mob of patriots or tories went to each house and banged on the door. If you were on the wrong side, you were threatened, beaten, or hung. Sometimes they ransacked your house and sometimes they'd burn it. It depended on the mob and the moment. I remember reading about that too."

"Tory or Patriot mob?"

---

12. 'e-Shakespeare' is name for quality anonymous writing found on the world wide web. Several bloggers vied for the title with their excellent writing.

"Yup. Both. The difference was determined later by who won the war. A lot of former Americans became Canadians pretty soon after the war was won by the noble patriots."

"But, they were noble, Jack. Just like these True Blue folks are."

"I'd like to see with my own eyes. I feel pretty useless here."

"You don't feel good about what you're doing everyday? You're at the epicenter, ground zero, for Rosetta 6.2 happening."

"I'm at the point for the targeting cell. But, Naomi, ground zero is out there not in here. I'm a staff guy here," Jack motioned with a jerk of his thumb.

"Jack, we can only be in one place at a time."

"The motion is out there. The really important stuff is hanging in the streets. The revolution will be won out there, not in here," Jack jerked his thumb again.

"What you're doing is important."

"Was important."

Naomi shook her head slowly, "There'll never be an important enough Jack. No one, not even President Maggie is important enough to do all or be all or be everywhere."

"Huh?"

"You're looking for something you'll never find in your life. There'll always be something else going on that looks more important or vital."

Jack stared.

"What you're doing is important in its own way. You'd want to be back here, if you're out there."

"We're just sitting here, watching history on TV. We're doing a job that someone else could do. But, only the people out there are taking chances enough to change history," said Jack.

"You'll always be frustrated with your circumstances."

Jack's eyes flared.

"Your frustrations, Jack, come from the outside in to your way of looking at it. But truly, you can only be content from the inner man out."

Jack squirmed. *Maude. How many times has Maude made a burden of her affection and ravage of her afflictions in our marriage? How often?*

"Every day is yours to live or not. You choose what you think, say and do. Even when you're working so hard and so well on an important mission like ours, you make choices. How happy you are, Jack, is a choice. How frustrated you are is your decision. No one can make that different for you."

"Okay, I guess."

"John-James, you make eternal decisions daily. Every day is an eternity if it's your last. One day will be the last step into eternity for you. You decide it all."

Jack averted her eyes. He looked in his orange red cup as he sipped. *"Church talk coming. Evangelical church lady words."*

Naomi smiled a beautiful but enigmatic, contented sigh. She patted his arm. She stopped speaking. They sat silently and watched the dynamic news of the day. They drained her teapot and she left for the night.

"I can't believe I'm just sitting here," he spoke out loud to hear the words better. "I'm just watching history instead of making it. I should be doing more."

Jack let that thought stand as he paced the tiny space in front of his TV. "I should be so much more."

Leesburg, Virginia
May 11th, 2013
Saturday

"Ready to go?" Ish asked rhetorically. They were ready an hour ago, but he insisted on re-checking everything before they went out into the open to see the dynamics of a Blues rally first hand. It was time for a close, personal look at what was off mission for Rosetta 6.2. Ish foresaw there would be unforeseen problems. Now he needed concrete answers. They climbed into a black Land Cruiser.

Ish cleared his throat, "As we briefed many times before. Rosetta 6.2 was developed as the program to fully implement the awesome new capabilities of the Omni computer. The projects were developed in parallel, but apart, clearly. Rosetta 6.2 pulled together all of the assets of the nation to decisively defeat the NTs in a swift campaign. Additionally, Rosetta 6.2 reinforces the political will of the government, the military and the people to execute a real revolution without changing governments."

"That's hard to do," said Bubba.

Ruth took over, "We saw a lot of anger at the pink mist massacre. There's a lot of passion that something is wrong and something needs to be done, but there is no conviction that these past two weeks will have a lasting effect. We might have a bunch of revolutionaries out there, but we might not have a revolution. And there's a counter-revolution that thinks the Christian Right is pulling a coup. It started with the Liberal lies about the election being stolen, but it's worse now."

"Maybe it takes time, like a steam engine, to build up a head of steam," said Pablo.

"You may be right," Ruth wagged her finger at Pablo. "But, what if you are wrong? We don't get seconds and thirds at this. It has to happen now. Where is the Revolution? What stops the counter-revolution before there's civil war?"

"It's coming, ma'am, it's coming," Ish answered.

"How do I know that? The polls are all over the place," said Ruth.

"Maybe it is hard to digest it all so fast. The turn around on crimes caused by drugs wasn't that long ago. The crime rate and everything were going down for a long time, then they spiked back up," said Pablo.

"Yeah, and overall drug use was down, but the use of hard drugs at younger and younger ages was going up. People didn't put together what was happening. This generation grew up just when the corruption rotted all the way through government, when whole countries like Columbia and Venezuela went under the criminals, and when the drugs got better chemistry. It all came together in five or six years. It hasn't sunk in. The Islamist connection was cooking for a long time. It came together tightly in the past few years. The Islamists attacks don't have Narco fingerprints."

"People want peace, not a revolution. They want security and stability," Pablo said.

"If the people still love liberty, then they will want a revolution," said Ish.

"Hey, excuse me. But, how can we go from almost absolute,

world-class, most-wanted fugitive isolation to go out and walk in the open air again?" asked Bubba.

"The truth changed. The drugsnakes are busy surviving right now. The Islamists want to take advantage of any civil disorder. The Illegals are simmering in fear and anger."

The security detail parked Land Cruisers just south of the old railroad line bisecting Leesburg. They walked up and down the steep hill to the county courthouse. The True Blue Rally was a 21st Century event starting in the 19th Century center of town, marching around to the High School and ending in a 20th Century strip mall parking lot. A pimply high school boy ran up to them and gave them each bright, light blue armbands.

They heard the drumming from far away. It was magnetic in its pull, just as Ish planned. He knew when a time of decision came—for all past thousands of years—the people gathered at bonfires for the tribe, then the village, then the city. The normal rhythms for sleep at night were disrupted. The people would gather, listen and proclaim. The gathering gains a rhythm of its own, accentuated by drumbeats, to let people know that this time is different. Ish enjoyed the sound. *It's working. They're thinking what we wanted. This time is significant. Everyone's involved in this gathering in person, at home on TV, on the Internet. This will be considered one of the special 'times' of this generation's life. We know that we must be there in order to someday say we were there. We must be there tonight as it happens. This True Blue Rally has it all.* Trucks and cars carried blue banners across their hoods and held blue flags high on makeshift guidons. People of all ages, especially young people, crowded the beds of trucks. They waved their flags, honked horns, and called out loudly.

The Amigos smiled at one another as they jostled apart and together by the crowd flowing like water to its own level. They felt the intensity of the moment flush like the cool night air on hot cheeks. Ish nudged Ruth to point out the clumps of sullen men and women on the edge of the crowd. They stood, stooped shouldered with their hands thrust in the pockets or waist bands. They did not look happily at the rally or its message. A few people wandering around were high on drugs or alcohol. A number of poorly dressed people looked sullen and wary.

A high-pitched young man rambled, enthusiastically, about the cost of drugs to his generation. He was followed by a middle-aged woman who was introduced by the sturdy fellow acting as the de facto master of ceremonies. High School bands formed in the narrow street in front of the courthouse yard. The woman's few remarks on Islamist terrorism, the wars in Afganistan and Iraq were unremarkable. The band started up. The parade started south on U.S. Route 15 and wound through the center of town. It took a little less than an hour to reach the parking lots of the strip mall shopping centers straddling the road. Here was the closing event.

A truck with the portable speaker's mike waited at the center of the lot near Wendys' fast food. A man in his fifties with the unmistakable signs of greying, thinning brown hair, thick bifocal glasses, midriff bulge pressing on paunch and the casual, clumsy clothes of a man married long enough to not dress to impress the other sex, hopped up to the cab. He paused to catch his breath.

"I want to say something that we all should hear, together, tonight, in this public place," he spoke clearly. His voice was accented with the Middle Atlantic hard over O's and was northern enough to be Baltimore or central Pennslyvania. The crowd craned necks and murmured to see who this fellow was.

"I'm your neighbor here in Leesburg. I've been here almost eleven years. My wife and I are raising our three children here. My wife is a nurse at Leesburg Memorial. I work in the Department of Homeland Security." Some people nodded and pointed in the crowd as they made some connection with the speaker. "I live right on Route Seven in the white house with the big pines in the back. You've seen my garden grow for a decade.

Friends and neighbors, I love Leesburg. I love Leesburg!" he shouted. The High School band tooted and banged. Some in the crowd cheered.

"This is my home. This is our home. No one can take that away from us. No one can come in our homes, unwanted and hurt our families. No more 9–11s. Never again!" The crowd perked up. This man's voice reached to the edge of street.

"Or not? Or is that a lie that we cling to in our fear? Someone comes into our homes against our wishes and despite our fears. Someone comes in to hurt and kill. And what do we do about it?

What happened on 9–11? What happened this Easter?

What happened two years ago two houses up from my house? You know what happened. Ed Jones died from a drug overdose. Ed, the only son of that fine family started messing with alcohol and drugs late in his senior year. But, he wasn't a bad kid. You know that. He was a great kid. He was the friend of my children." The crowd was quiet.

"He even stayed home and worked right over there in Food Lion to help his family when he went to NoVa[13]. But, he started running with the wannabe cool guys. He spent the night at a friend's house. He got high and died."

"He was just experimenting with drugs and he died. We went to the funeral. We shared the pain with his family. We know the unspeakable fear. That could have been my child. Or, your child."

"But nothing happened. You may say it was the responsibility of the child who took the overdose. Yes, he was at fault, but who brought the poison to him? Who provided the poison? Who provided the place to take it? Who said that kids will be kids? Who looked the other way about alcohol and marijuana? Who covered it all up? Why is Ed dead and his so-called friend driving around town in a new car, still doing drugs and encouraging others to get high?" passion rose in his voice.

"Where is the law? Where is the justice?" he changed tracks.

"Who wants a woman or a girl to go out to the store after dark alone?" he paused.

"Why not? Why can't all the citizens of this great town have the right to walk to any public place at any time and not be in peril of robbery, rape or murder? The NITs prey on people like a pack of wolves on innocent deer. Where is the law? Where is the justice?

Why are middle school kids getting stoned on alcohol, marijuana, cocaine, heroine, ecstasy and now 'sin'? Why can't drugs be kept from children? Aren't toxic chemicals that hurt the environment kept under lock and key? Aren't medical toxins controlled? But a toxic poison can be given to one of your children and you can't stop it. The police can't keep it out of our schools, our homes. Where is the law? Where is the justice?" The people became agitated.

"Let me see a show of hands. Who knows someone who has

---

13. NOVA is the nickname for Northern Virginia Community College and the Virginia region around the national capitol.

ruined their life with drugs? Do you know someone who is a drugslave?" Most hands were raised.

"Who knows someone who has died? Who knows a family destroyed by divorce or loss of job or abuse spawned by the demon seed of drugs?" The hands became fists pounding the air.

"Who bought expensive security systems for your house? Your car? Your family?"

"Who among us does not know the fear that some drugsnake will attack some member of our family? Who knows someone who was robbed? Who knows a child who is intimidated by the gangs in schools? Who sees the drugsnake gang graffiti around town?" He lowered his voice, "Friends it isn't graffiti. It's pornography shoved in your face."

"Who came to kill us on 9–11? Who killed again and again? Who murdered our troops in Iraq? Who beheads captives? How are these terrorist snakes different from the drugsnakes? Who bombed innocent babies on Easter? They're allies. They're the same enemy. The terrorists sell drugs to the drugsnakes and weapons too. They are all NITs. They're Satan's brothers!"

"Where is the law? Where is the justice?" he shouted.

"The President of the United States of America declared martial law. The war, the real war on drugs, is our war. But, what are we do to? We can rally and march to show support, but what can we do for the law? For justice?" He breathed out 'jus-tice' in two powerful syllables.

"We are the sovereign of the nation, the state and this city and county. We are the people! The law is ours. Justice is ours to claim." The crowd looked for direction.

"We can clean our own house. We do every day for dirt. But, we must clean up every home for poison. We demand that our neighbors who support the drugsnakes, who sell their poison, who are the drugsnakes, stop. Stop it now. No more drugs in Leesburg. Drugs are poison. Poison kills same as a bomb does. Drugs are different bombs."

"No drugs, now!" he started a chant. He let it build to a crescendo and waved his hands to stop it. "No more drugs in Leesburg, Virginia. If not here, where? If not now, when?"

"I say for me and my family, no more drugs nowhere. Now.

Out with the poison now! Let's go door to door and demand the drugs. Bring it back here and burn them. Now." The crowd buzzed.

"Come to my house and search it. I will come clean. Then, you can put true blue paint on my white house. Paint a blue check or a cross or a fish, whatever, write okay. And let's go on to my neighbor. Who will say no? If someone refuses, then they have something to hide. The time of hiding and harboring drug poison and drugsnakes is OVER! The police can't go door to door. There aren't enough of them. But there are enough of us! We are The People. Let's clean out all the drugs!"

"Remember Ed! Remember every violent crime! Remember 9–11! Remember your fear for your family and why it's there!" An accomplice in the crowd tossed him a can of blue spray paint. He held it high and lead a cheer.

"As for me and my family the revolution against drugs is now! Let it begin here, in our town, tonight, with us! If the drugsnakes fight back I don't care! I will not be afraid any longer! No more! Give me liberty or give me death! Death to the NITs! Give my children a life without drugsnakes, Islamists and fear! We are free! We will be free at last! Follow me!" the speaker shouted until he was breathless. He jumped down from the truck and bulled his way towards his home. The crowd surged and followed.

Ruth spoke in Ish's ear, "He wasn't Winston Churchill."

Ish furrowed his brow and drew Ruth into the privacy of his reply. "Let's go see how it works. This guy added some wrinkles of his own. You're right, he wasn't Patrick Henry."

"You did the script?" asked Pablo.

"Rosetta 6.2 puts out a lot of good ideas. A lot of good ideas," Ish smiled faintly. The sullen faces were gone from the crowd. "Where did those other people go?" Ish asked no one.

Leesburg, Virginia
June 6th, 2013
Thursday

Ish sat on the eastern porch facing the mushrooming city of Leesburg below the hill with the countryside tumbling beyond. He listened to the radio as he ate his lunch to stay connected with the public news, but he ached to just rest. *Oh Father God, if I could just lean back in this warm breeze and sleep for a few hours. Maybe the whole afternoon. I'm bone-deep tired, Jesus.*

Ruth walked up when Ish gave into the demands to rest his eyes in the healing sun.

"Ish, it's so nice out here isn't it? Mind if I join you? The counter-demonstrations are really gaining strength. Have you seen what is happening to some of our systems?" Ruth set her simple salad and bottle of mineral water on the table. She sat and knitted her hands at her waist.

"Yes, I have. The NITs are working the counter-information campaign hard. Rosetta icons are attacked almost as fast as they're posted. The attacks on the military systems are spotty at best. But they're a recurring threat. The bad news is how much this is shaping up like the civil war we hoped the Culture War would never be," said Ish.

"I have some other news. There are more reports of kidnappings. In New Jersey, Virginia, Maryland and California. All of the kidnappings are engineers who've worked on the Omni project. Did you know about that?" Ruth's face was set in hard lines of intensity.

"Yes, I did, Ruth. But, I don't know what to make of it. I did some checking to see if I could find a common thread or a single vulnerability. And I can't find one."

"I think the problem is Pablo Ponce de Leon. We need to get to him, before he can get to the Omni. We have a sophisticated enemy here. They have some incredible rumors fighting for public opinion. Christians are told that the time of the Anti-Christ has come. President Maggie is the beast with '666' tattooed on her skull, etc. Liberals are told the Christian Taliban is rising to create a theocracy. National Rifle Association members are informed that the raids and True Blue house searches going on around the country are to collect private citizens' weapons. Illegals and legal immigrants are going to be shipped to concentration camps and then deported. Anyone with a foreign accent will be arrested."

"Information Warfare isn't new. You can read about the ancient Greeks using it. Thucydides wrote about it. Sun Tzu knew."

"The media, the speed and volume of messages is different.

What is happening isn't random. This isn't some odd ball reaction to Martial Law. You can spot them in a second. We're opposed by an organized force."

"Who do you think it is?" asked Ish.

"Pablo Ponce de Leon. He is as powerful as Al Queda in this hemisphere."

"Nothing is coming in to the current intel ops cell. He has totally vanished. We have nada," said Ish.

"That tells you something right there. It means this guy can operate outside the boundaries of the Omni and Rosetta 6.2. Or, he has compromised one or both."

"He may have compromised the Omni code, but he hasn't gotten into the Rosetta 6.2 program. I'll bet my life that no one, no one, has compromised Rosetta 6.2."

"You already have, Ish. Get with Jack at Leavenworth and get a fix on this guy Ponce de Leon. I want him found ASAP. I want him nailed, Ish," the fire burned in Ruth's eyes. Then, Ruth uncharacteristically reached over and patted his arm, "Ish you are doing a great job."

"Thanks, Ruth, thanks a lot. I'm doing all that I can think of doing," Ish's large black bags under his eyes were a shade different from his purple-black skin.

Pablo strolled over to their table. He carried a plate full of so much food that only a young and vigorous man could consume it all. Pablo walked with the confidence of unchastened youth. His smile was bright even against the noon Spring shining sun. He plopped down, prayed quietly for a long minute, genuflected, and dove into his food. "Great day, isn't it?" His buoyancy was contagious. Ruth and Ish smiled back.

"Pablo, are we winning?" asked Ish.

"Sure, we are. We are going all the way."

"Why are you so confident?" asked Ruth.

"God is in Heaven, Trento is in command and Ruth and Ish are making it happen," said Pablo. Bubba led the laugh.

"Is it time to go home, Pablo? Are we done here?" asked Ish.

"No, almost. But not quite," Pablo took a huge bite of steaming lasagna.

"We need to see how far we are off the mark in making the society want to be drug-free," said Ruth.

Bubba ambled over and plopped down heavily with his lunch. Ruth looked up and said, "We have to complete the job. I know all about drugsnakes. I hate them more than all the other NITs." Her eyes welled with tears they had never seen before.

"When I was in college my boyfriend used drugs," Ruth looked out and away. There was no warning that her emotional pot had boiled to overflow. "He overdosed and died. He died in my room. He died in my arms. I bought the hit. We were supposed to get married after graduation," Ruth continued to gaze outwardly as her innermost past found the words to ride out of her.

"I got pretty messed up. I took an overdose, I suppose, I knew it was. I woke up in the hospital. They told me that I was okay, but I lost the baby. I didn't know there was one growing in me. I didn't know for sure. Not until it was too late. I hate drugs. I hate them so much! I hate them!" Tears ran down her cheeks, melting makeup in their path.

"I know you do, Ruth," Ish said tenderly. *I had no idea, Sister Ruth.*

"Excuse me, I have to go the ladies room," Ruth hurried away.

"I never knew it. I never knew why. I always wondered where the determination and fire came from. I never knew," said Ish.

"I never would have guessed. But, I knew she had the passion for right," said Pablo. A long silence followed.

"Remember our field trips? The crowds didn't seem too repentant or be concerned about their drug status," said Ish.

"They aren't. They want drugs. They want to alter their moods chemically and they haven't found a substitute. They could abuse alcohol if they can't get 'sin' or other drugs. They think this is a bunch of religious nuts taking over the country and about to spoil their fun. Make them go to church. I dunno," Pablo shoveled more food.

"So, if we wean them off other drugs they go back to the oldest familiar drug?" asked Bubba.

"These people have a God-sized hole in their heart," said Pablo.

"We are dealing with a mass problem. Look at how many people are in here from just this community! We can't wait on the change of one heart at a time," said Ish.

Fort Leavenworth, Kansas
June 23rd, 2013
Sunday

Jack agreed to go to church on Post with Naomi. He wanted a few minutes to be with her and not be eyeball deep in work. There seemed to be nothing other than work and a little scarce time for eating and rest. The blossoms on the trees exploded with the full blast of their potential. Green leaves, whole and complete in their newness, weighted the branches to sway beautifully in every warm breeze. Every graceful uplift of their skirts by the gentle wind was like a blush at the fulfillment of Spring's pregnant fertility. Jack wanted more and more of each second of warmth, light and color. The new grass was humid as the dew cooked away by the sun. *I'm alive. So alive.* He remembered the feelings from his long Autumn walk and the brooding cold of his sojourns in Winter at West Point.

The light from the chapel's stained glass windows of warriors, apostles, and a crucified Jesus was many splendored. *It's pretty. Historical and artsy. I like the warm light of the sun on my bare arm. Wouldn't it be better to worship outside?* Naomi was in her prayer mode. She seemed oblivious to his presence close by her side.

The service droned for Jack. His mind wandered with his eyes among the singing, reading, and speaking. He missed the cues that others knew to say the Lord's Prayer or the sing the Doxology from memory. He mouthed words when he had to fake it. Towards the end of a longish sermon on something called justification, Jack considered the alternatives of faith again.

If I'm wrong about Christianity and don't get 'saved' I would die like a bug. If I get 'saved' and the Christians were wrong, then I still die like a bug. If I get saved and it's all true then I would live, really live. No way. It's gotta be fake. Wishful thinking. How could these people be right and people from every other religion be wrong? Maybe the New Age people are right when they say that all religions are right paths to finding God. Maybe they're all off and there's no God.

Then a thought came into his mind like a flash, "Death is not a nothing, a no-thing. There is a light and a warmth on the other side.

There is some-thing because I Am."

Jack sat up and looked around. Where had that come from? His heart pounded. He heard nothing else in his head. He kept re-playing the words in his mind.

When church finally ended Naomi looked at him for the first time in an hour. Her smile was hopeful. "How was it?" she asked.

"Fine, thanks, fine," Jack smiled insincerely. They meandered along the way back to the VIP visiting quarters. *Naomi seems to enjoy the celebration of life around us as I do.* They walked back to the VIP Quarters. *What happened to me in that church?*

"Lunch?" asked Jack. He felt like he was piano wire being tightened. He tried to look calm.

"You need rest, Jack. Take a nap and then we'll go back to work. See ya around four," Naomi went into her room alone.

Jack kicked off his shoes and did a back flop on his bed. He spoke out loud for the company of his voice. *What was that thought?* He re-played the words his mind. His heart kept drumming. *I Am.* He had heard that phrase somewhere else. *What was that all about?*

I Am what? Jack wondered. *If there was nothing then there would be no God, no thing, no nothing. But if it is not true, then what some say is 'nothing' is 'something'. If it is something, if there is a some thing that is God, then He has to have an identity. Hmm, then, God would say, 'I Am', wouldn't He?*

Jack looked out the window up through the branches of trees heavily laden with new life in green leaves. The blue sky beckoned in moving patches between the brushing leaves. *But there is some thing. There is something out there in nature. If there is some thing or some things, then there can't be just nothing after all this. It all can't be for nothing. Or can it, life, all be for nothing?* Jack propped himself on his elbows. Then he sprang to his feet and paced.

"If there is no nothing, then there must be something. Some-thing for sure is nature. But, is that all there is? What could be the other some-thing? Where did that darn thought about 'no-thing' and 'I am' come from?" Jack felt an odd sense of anticipation. "If there is something more to this life and death, then it must be something real." He wondered what light and warmth was in that thought that flashed like lightening—whole, dazzling, as a brief bolt of clarity.

Naomi came to get him promptly at 4 PM. They marched back to their bunker, "John-James, Jesus is going to change who you are."

"How? To what?"

"The Holy Ghost is going to make you a Christian," she answered.

"How? I thought that was up to me," Jack mumbled.

"It is. The last step is. You will come to a place, John-James, where you will think about whether or not Jesus got up on that Easter morning with a transformed body and walked out of the grave or not. Either you look in your mind and see Him lying there on the stone shelf rotting or you seem Him radiant and walking. Soon enough, you will look and see Him walking. Then, you will say, 'I believe'. From there on out the Holy Ghost will take over."

"What does Naomi mean? Why is she talking to me about a dead or alive Jesus when we've got these golden moments of opportunity together?" Jack turned his mind back to his mission, "Yeah, sure, I'll think about it, Naomi. First, I gotta find Pablo Ponce de Leon. Then I'll look for Jesus."

Chapter 7. Civil War

Leesburg, Virginia
July 4th, 2013
Thursday

The President's big speech meant everything to Ish. His Amigos worked their hearts out for weeks. They polished and re-polished their input. President Maggie Myriah Kyle's 4th of July address to the American people was crucial. The Nation was at the tipping point for one side or the other. Revolution and Counter-Revolution competed for the people in the middle. Once again the citizens with no mind for the mess of politics had to choose one side or the other. Just like 1776 and 1861, but the issues had different names. Judeo-Christian Civilization or Pagan Human Secularism Civilization? Individual rights or group rights? Rule of law or tyranny of judges? Capitalism or Socialism? Freedom of religion or from religion? Drugs or no Drugs? Fortress Defense or Strategic Offense? American Civilization or Multi-Cultural PC?

Ish's heart rate accelerated like he was climbing a cliff. He was sitting at his desk. He couldn't let go of the events that were still unfolding, even though they were totally beyond his control. Ish held himself personally accountable for the unrealistic perfection of his work and, unfortunately, events which were way beyond his reach.

My anxiety shows a lack of trust in God. I'm so weak here. It's my only weakness in my relationship with you, Lord. Ish got up to take a walk. He knew his blood pressure was up into unhealthy numbers. *I should lie down. Maybe a walk will help as well.*

A thought came to him before he reached the door. "You can't give it up, because you aren't doing it for the right reason."

Ish kept walking. *Ah. The right reason for working is to glorify God. I'm working to glorify me, despite the selfless service I lived since my awakening to Christ in the Army. I still want success for me. My selflessness in my duty is one of my boasts to myself, to my inner pride.* Ish was out in the bright, hot heat.

I want my work and my side to succeed because I want to win above else.

But, the first Commandment is love God with all of my heart, mind, strength and soul, so when I put all my heart, mind, strength, and soul into my work I'm worshipping by my actions a false God of work. Unless my work is for God.

If my work is for God and not myself, then I can do it and let it go. I can trust in Him. I must trust in Him. I must be obedient to Him in my work. I must give God my all and all and hold nothing back. Worry about the work denies God's sovereignty.

For the umpteenth time in his Christian maturity, scales fell from his eyes and he saw the familiar words from the Bible, sermons, songs and prayers take shape as new and freshly alive concepts for living. Words that he thought he knew well and lived in his life, were shown to him in a new light. The words infused a new meaning, a new texture and detailed application in his life.

I must give every ounce of my work in my daily life to God. How? Every ounce.

Dedicate the work to God, not Ish. Do the work in God's name, not Ish's. Ask God to give me the light to see how to do the work for Him and not for my reputation in my puny mind. Puny stood out as an appropriate insult to his own pride of self.

Ish strolled about the grounds to have more of this time alone with his God. Ish spoke softly under his breath, "Father, this is the demon, the desire, I haven't defeated. I know my sin of pride. How can I do this really?"

"Love Me," came as a thought in his mind.

Ish protested, "But, I do love You so. I try hard to love You so much."

"Then give Me your work," the next thought arrived in a flash.

"Focus on Me as you pour yourself into your work. I poured

Myself out for you in blood."

Ish wondered where his own thoughts began and ended. He paused and listened to the black silence of seconds tick by in his mind.

Ok. Think about Father God as I work on my work more? I thought I already did that. All the time. This will be a distraction.

"No, it will be a focus," the thought rang out.

"I'll try. No, Father, I will do it," Ish said. He walked with his head down staring at where his steps were next on the ground. The green, green grass rolled briskly under his limited field of vision. Ish was startled. He bumped into Pablo.

"Excuse me!" Ish reached out to catch Pablo.

"Excuse me, Sir," said Pablo reflexively.

"I'm sorry Pablo. Didn't look where I was going," Ish confessed. "I was praying."

"Me, too," said Pablo. They looked at each other with surprise although each knew that the other was a praying man. "I was praying about the President's speech."

"Let's continue, Pablo," said Ish. He dropped to his knees on the shiny green grass. Pablo quickly followed. Ish reached over and put his hand on Pablo's shoulder. Pablo overlapped Ish's arm with his own to put his hand on Ish's shoulder.

"Oh, Lord, bless and guide President Maggie Kyle as she gives the speech," said Ish.

"Father, let the speech be a huge success for Your will, not mine," said Pablo.

"Holy, holy, holy Father God, please use the speech and your servant, Maggie, to do Your will." Humidity draped them like a wet wool blanket.

"Dear Abba, let Your infinite Will shine through all of our work like a bright light for others. Do not hide Your instruction from us whether we need to see the light or be chastened by the rod."

"Forgive me for my sinfulness. Please guide me to pray to You with a pure heart for Your will, not my selfishness," Ish's voice broke.

"Father, forgive me of my sins as I must forgive others. Please keep me from the temptations. Deny me my pride."

"Please let our work be the words that hasten an end to war in this country, our country, and bring peace in Your name." The bugs hummed as background.

"Please lead us to Your peace."

They fell silent. They left their communal realm and retreated into their private sanctuaries to listen and speak one on one with the Lord. The Living God communed with them individually, yet simultaneously, as only God can do. Their minds then answered the urging of their inner hearts. It felt like a pregnant pause to a casual observer. To the praying men, the time flew with the urgencies of their concerns.

Ish took his hand back and lumbered to his feet. Pablo got up a second later lithely.

"I wouldn't think you would be praying against pride," said Ish.

"Nor I, you," said Pablo.

"We all have our private demons, don't we?"

"Yes, I guess we do. But, we can give it all over to the Father." They left the Summer cooking day outside. They went back to work in the richly air conditioned mansion on the hill overlooking Leesburg.

Leesburg, Virginia
July 16th, 2013
Tuesday

"When are we going to see Jack and Naomi?" asked Bubba.

"I dunno, Bubba," Ish didn't look up from his spread sheet. He didn't want Bubba to see the growing irritation he had for that question. Jack and Naomi were re-deployed the week before to the National Reconnaissance Office (NRO)[1] in a high rise at nearby Tysons Corners to set up an alternate command post for Rosetta 6.2 operations.

"Seems strange for them to be so close and we still haven't seen them. I just feel so close to y'all, like my children, that I want to know that everyone is okay."

"Your children? Loan me twenty bucks, Dad?"

---
1. NRO is the National Reconnaissance Office. The NRO is responsible for the satellite-based intelligence.

"Son, you'll have to do your chores first. Now, go fetch your brother and sister from Tyson's Corners," Bubba's blue gray eyes spoke to Ish.

"Okay, Bubba, got it. But, seriously, just give it up for now, all right?"

Ish read the numbers on the report. The revolution transformed since President Maggie's 4th of July Declaration of Freedom from Drugs and Fear. The American people were pushed off the fence as planned—as hoped. There were no spectators now. What was expected to be contained as a narrow counter-Narco-Terrorist cultural revolution had widened. Culture War was Civil War. It was the life-or-death struggle of two sides pushing and pulling on the fabric of the nation. It was a tug of war for the flag itself.

Ish worried about unleashing these dogs of war, despite all his planning. He looked out the window for a break and some answers. This Summer day was a hot, wet, grey wool day. The humidity and heat were measured as twins in the 90s something. The air outside felt heavy to breath, heavy on the shoulders and heavy on the heart.

The lone surviving drug lord—Pablo Ponce de Leon—knows revolution and civil warfare well from his Columbia. His drugsnake atrocities against the police, the military and their families were finely pointed exercises in the application of terror to provoke an over-reaction by the government. He's playing the Islamists. He's using the Illegals as puppets. They aren't playing him. Pablo Ponce de Leon knew what he was doing then. He knows what he is doing now getting others to soldier for him and they don't even know they're being used. The Islamists, eco-terrorists, other radical Liberals and Illegals are being manipulated. Ish concentrated his thoughts.

The Islamists lack central direction. They're just a collection of cells and fanatical individuals that will be policed up when they show themselves. Likewise, the Liberal extremists lacked leadership. They have their hatred of Christians and Jews, but no organization for real combat. They make a good mob. The Illegals are just fighting anyone in a uniform. They know and fear government oppression.

Ish looked at the press reports on an Operation Rose. Alternatively, the media called it Op Rosy or Rosetta. The media only understood small portions of what was really happening. Rosetta 6.2 was censoring less to see what explosive steam had to be let out the closed kettle. The news and blogs claimed conservative, Christian 'extremists' were trying to overthrow the government and institute a theocracy as one big story.

Any element of truth in a lie gives it legs. The NITs fanned matchbooks into prairie fires hoping for a national firestorm. The story of the pink mist murder of innocents, martial law and several months of the Blues Movement was recast. New story lines appealed to the worst of fears and the most tightly held Liberal biases. Demonstrations were designed to create martyrs. But, there was no indication how the resistance could stop Rosetta's actions. That troubled Ish. *I can't see where they are going. What's their plan? That's what worries me.*

Rosetta 6.2 couldn't keep Ish's version of events, his truth, as the only truth. Contrary claims were zapped like a video game, but clearly there was a ground swell of controversy. Like all things human, it was very complicated. There were many perspectives. All were held in diametrically opposing passion as the absolute truth. *This hurts my head.*

Ruth walked behind Ish and dropped another spread sheet in front of him. She patted his shoulder in an unusually warm affirmation, "They came back better than we thought."

"Rule One, Ruth, never underestimate your enemies," said Ish.

"I thought Rule One was have a plan."

"Ah, you finally caught on. There are a lot of Rule Ones. And they're all priority one."

"If you mess up anyone of them you are screwed. Right?" Ruth came around and stood with both fists on her narrow hips.

"You got it boss lady. They're coming back big time. But, we should note that it isn't a 'they' out there. There is only old Ponce de Leon in this country organizing and planning. He is behind all of this," said Ish.

"He is not running all of it. No one man could possibly be behind all of these attacks."

"No more than one man could be behind all that we do. One enemy is behind the strategic direction, to the extent there is any. One enemy is planning the new operational phases, like these attacks on Interstate Highway bridges near state lines and blaming them on gun nut militias. One enemy is planning and executing key tactical missions against us. One enemy drives the agitation in the demonstrations."

"Who is sending out all these confusing messages on prohibition of alcohol? Or tobacco is an abused, illegal drug?"

"I'm not sure. Some of that was Pablo dis-information. Some of it is a bogey."

"Who is behind the attacks on abortion clinics and churches?"

"Same dynamic. Some of the attacks are pegged to Pablo. Some are by crazies out freelancing now that their actions can be blamed on someone else. The Illegals are going a hundred directions at once."

"So what are we going to do, Ishmael?"

"We're going to hit back harder than they do. At least that is what I am going to tell Laser Larry when he shows up in a few minutes."

"Good answer, Ish. It will do," Ruth smiled. Ish walked back to his desk by the great French doors.

Ish felt the blast before he heard the explosion. Then, he couldn't hear anything. The explosion was huge.

The first cruise missile slammed into the steep hill a hundred yards below the mansion where they worked. The power was terrific. The shock wave shattered all the glass on the eastward frontage. The rain of glass and powerful push of the highly pressured air made a shambles of the beautiful working spaces and dining areas. The security alarms went mad. Confusion compounded with each ensuing crash.

Ish woke up looking at smoke gathering on the high ceiling. The smell of cordite was pungent. Ish was groggy. His vision was blurry and he couln't hear anything except the loud ringing in his ears. He saw Ruth a few feet away lying still. When he started crawling he noticed that his left leg wasn't moving. Ish looked down. There was a pulpy red mass and dusty black skin hanging from the gaping hole in his trousers. He felt with his hands. It hurt to touch, but there was no arterial bleeding. *Good. Thank you, Jesus.*

Ruth stirred and moaned. "Not again." She slowly pulled herself to up to lean against the huge oak table. She was shaken but not hurt. The table took much of the blow for her. There were pieces of glass in her hair, but she wasn't cut. She looked around the room at the residue of an instant of destruction. The room was destroyed. The human survivors were slowly responding to recover. The dead were silent among the other debris of violence.

"Ish, you're hurt," Ruth's voice was choked with dust. Her head was ringing, but she could hear some. Ish looked at her lips.

"I can't hear you. I'm okay. Wounded. Okay. Are you okay?" said Ish. Ruth couldn't hear either. She looked at his lips.

"I am fine, Ish, fine. Can't hear. But, we're still alive. I can't believe that they blew us up again. Like November, we got bombed again," Ruth cupped her ears.

Another roaring blew by right over head. A few seconds later a blast shook the house from the west. The ear splitting roar followed. Ish felt the shaking even if he couldn't hear the noise. *Missiles. Maybe cruise missiles.*

Pablo rushed to Ish. Bubba hurried there too.

"Just stay down on your back, Ish. Let me check you before triage gets here," said Pablo. Pablo motioned to Ish with his hands.

"I'm fine. It's just a scratch," said Ish. He couldn't hear himself speak.

The medics were on site in minutes. Ish was carried outside and plugged up to an IV. He saw a Blackhawk helicopter swing low in a circle over Leesburg and then come in a beeline for the mansion. At the last second it banked sharply, the nose came up and the helicopter came in like a belly flop a few yards away. The helicopter doors opened and the hawk profile of LTG Trento emerged. Jack and Naomi were on his heels.

LTG 'Laser' Larry Trento cupped the back of Ish's head in his hand. He patted Ish's wounded arm lying on his stomach with his other arm. "Ish, you old warrior, looks like you caught one. Too bad it didn't get you in the butt. You never would have felt a thing. Or in the head. Woulda bounced off."

Ish smiled weakly at whatever LTG Trento said.

"Cruise missile?" mouthed Ish. LTG Trento nodded vigorously.

"Cruise missiles, Ish. Probably Chinese manufacture. Came off commercial ships in the Bay and some off shore Atlantic," LTG

Trento spoke slowly so Ish could watch his lips. "Roger, Ish. Yes. Cruise missiles."

"Hey, we saw all three of them run right past us in flight," said Jack.

"Big attack?" asked Bubba.

"Really big," said LTG Trento.

Ish felt shocked eyelids grow heavy until they were pulled closed by their sheer weight. The black rush of sleep swept in as fast as his eyes could close, faster than any tide Ish had ever seen.

LTG Trento walked around in his shirtsleeves helping for long minutes. He frequently spoke on his personal communicator. His short sleeve green shirt was stained with soot and other people's blood. He directed the Amigos to his helicopter. When all were on board he gave the 'wind it up' signal with his hand. He jumped into the middle seat behind the pilots. He motioned for everyone to put their head sets on. The helicopter lifted off and headed back towards DC.

"Ok, everybody hear me? Listen up, I was going to bring Jack and Naomi up here to put our heads together about an impending attack I was expecting. My timing was off. Jack and Naomi set up an alternate CP[2] at the NRO. They did a great job doing it in a classified facility in Tyson's Corners. It's at one of the defense contractor's buildings. You will be going there by ground transport after we go to the Pentagon. This is a new level of war. We need to get you up to speed on the post-attack. Then we'll move on," LTG Trento paused to collect his thoughts.

"There will be an extra security detail with Ish in the hospital. As soon as he is moveable, we will get you guys together. I thought a new attack was coming. But, frankly, the cruise missiles were a surprise. I'll have to fire the Two[3]."

"Who launched the missiles?" Bubba figured out how to work the headset.

"The NITs. Islamists like Al Queda would do it on their own if they could. But, trust me. This was the NITs. They have the money for the missiles, the geeks to make them work and the shipping to

---

2. CP is Command Post.

3. The Two is the S-2, G-2, J-2 Staff Section at different levels of command is responsible for Military Intelligence.

move them. No brainer. Listen Bubba, Pablo, when you get back to Tyson's, I do NOT want you to go on line. You will take the comms only on my personal command. Got it?"

"Yes, sir," said Bubba. Pablo nodded.

"I'm getting reports that this was a two hundred fifty plus missile attack. They went for military comms targets by and large. Hit some cities. It was like missile rain at Fort Meade."

"The NSA got hit?" asked Bubba.

"Big time. Most of their above ground is gone. This was more than a terror attack. This was a C4ISR main attack. They're trying to get at Rosetta. They must know somethings doing with the Omni. They're targeting to see if one system is the linchpin," said LTG Trento.

"How is Rosetta 6.2 functioning then? Where is all the data going?" asked Jack.

"It's functioning. Ish had a plan for a catastrophic attack. He's incredible," LTG Trento clicked off the internal aircraft speaker and switched to external channels. The Amigo's headsets went silent for the rest of the ride.

Vienna, Virginia
July 18th, 2013
Thursday

The nation was truly shocked to discover that there was no national defense against missile attacks. The missile defense against China wasn't built yet. It wouldn't have helped anway. The attack was from cruise missiles on mobile launchers strapped to the decks of commercial ships. It created a terrible new sense of vulnerability for the public. But, the NITs overplayed their hand. They launched a dozen missiles into key population centers to rub the military's nose in excrement. This exercise in machismo enraged the American people. The Amigos struggled to leverage the anger and fear. They worked long hours in their alternate command post high in the Booze-Allen-Hamilton Tower in Tyson's corner.

As the long day came to a close in the late Summer evening, Bubba approached Jack at his work station. "Jack, Ruth arranged for me to get a van to run up and see Ish in a few minutes. But, I have to beg off. I just can't go. My body is too worn out," Bubba looked very pale.

"Sure, I'll go. When do I go?" gulped Jack. The ride was an hour both ways.

"In about five minutes. Naomi and Ruth were going to go, but Ruth needs to stay here with Pablo for some new tasker they got LTG Trento. Naomi still wants to go. Is that all right?"

"Sure."

Naomi chatted on the ride up as Jack brooded for his desires. The evening's sun faded fast behind the overcast low clouds. They felt the oppressive heat and humidity of a normal, killer Washington, DC summer day as they walked to the hospital entrance.

Ish was asleep in a private room at Loudon Memorial Hospital. He was minutes below the destroyed mansion in beautiful, quaint Leesburg. His black features were presented starkly on the blistering white hospital pillow. He looked noble in his sleep. His face was thick and lined in the right places for a man in his forties. Jack smiled at him. *He's a black lion. Lion heart.*

Naomi took his hand in both of hers. An IV dripped a clear liquid into Ish's arm. Jack cautiously laid one hand on Ish's shoulder. Ish blinked his eyes open. He breathed heavily.

"Hey," said Ish in a crackling voice. He didn't try to rise. The room stunk of disinfectant.

"Hey, Ish, how are you?" Naomi leaned forward and kissed his forehead.

"Howya doing Ish?"

"I'm fine. They have me mainlining antibiotics. I've got a lot of painkillers."

"I'll bet. I saw your hip. Bad slide into third base, buddy."

Ish smiled. His eyes opened and closed slowly like slow rolling window shades going up and down rhythmically.

"What do you need, Ish?" asked Naomi. She looked around for something to do.

"Nothing. Need more rest. Gotta get back to work."

"No, you don't. We'll be fine until you get out. Then you can chew us out and set us straight," Jack spoke loudly.

"Do you want something to drink?" asked Naomi.

"Water please."

"You need to rest until you are one hundred per cent."

"You mean I'm not one hundred per cent, now?" Ish teased weakly.

"Here, Ish," Naomi helped Ish lean forward to sip the small cup of ice water. "Anything else?"

Ish waved his right hand towards the nightstand. "Read for me." Jack looked on the night stand. There was nothing there. He opened the drawer and saw a Gideon Bible.

"Is this it? The Bible?"

"Yes," said Ish. Jack offered the Bible to Naomi to read. She waved him off and held Ish's hand with both of hers. "What would you like me to read?"

"Psalm 51:1," said Ish.

Jack fumbled to find the right place, "Have mercy on me, O God according to Your unfailing love according to your great compassion blot out my transgression. Wash away all my injury and cleanse me from sin." Jack looked up.

"51:17, please."

"The sacrifices of God are a broken spirit, a broken and contrite heart. O God You will not despise."

"Oh, God forgive me. Romans 8:31, please," said Ish weakly.

Ish needs forgiveness? Whatever for? Huh? Then what do I need?

Jack hunted the right pages again. "What then shall we say in response to this? If God is for us, who can be against us?" Jack smiled.

"Like that, huh?" asked Ish.

"Sounds self-righteous, but powerful, Ish."

"It is so. It's powerful."

"Romans 8: 38, now" said Ish.

"For I am convinced that neither death nor life, neither angels nor demons," Ish and Naomi mouthed the words softly as Jack read. "Neither the present nor the future, nor any powers, neither height nor depth, nor anything else in all creation will be able to separate us from the love of God that is in Christ Jesus our Lord." Naomi eyes glistened with tears.

"Thanks, Jack. How about John 14:2?" asked Ish.

"Okay. Got it. Do not let your hearts be troubled. Trust in God. Trust also in me. In my Father's house are many rooms," read Jack.

Ish and Naomi chimed out loud with the next verse. "If it were not so, I would have told you. I am going there to prepare a place for you." They smiled an unspoken confirmation at each other.

"I will come back and take you to be with me that you also may be where I am. You know the way to the place I am going," Jack paused.

"Thanks, brother. Continue with six."

"I am the way and truth and the life. No one comes to the Father except through Me. If you really knew me, you would know my Father as well. From now on, you do know Him and have seen Him."

"Jesus is the way," said Naomi looking at Jack.

Why is she looking at me?

"Jack, read those passages again. But, don't do it not now. Later, to yourself. Jack accept the Lord Jesus as your savior. You've read all you need to know to make your decision," Ish's eyebrows furrowed his brow with earnestness.

Now what? Do what? How?

"You need more rest, Ish," Naomi kissed Ish's broad forehead again.

Jack patted Ish's forearm, "See ya later, Ish. Good night." They went quietly to the car.

The cloud cover made the night pitch black for the ride back. Jack broke the silence, "Ish looked really tired. Beaten up."

"He did, John-James. He certainly did." The van gave a high pitched whine as it sped down the blackened path called road.

Jack felt Naomi's hand reach his on the bench seat. Her fingers intertwined with his. Jack started to move his body closer. Naomi pushed him away with the same hand glasping his.

What does she want? Hold my hand but not come closer? Huh?

No one spoke. When they got past the motel road teeth right off Route 7, Naomi released Jack's hand. They said good night to the driver guards and walked silently to the second floor of their gated motel hideout. Jack followed Naomi the extra steps to her door.

Naomi spun on her heel. She grabbed both of Jack's hands tightly. In the safety light on the landing, Jack saw the searching intensity of her probing eyes.

"John-James, you *are* a good man," Naomi kissed him softly and quickly on the lips. Her eyes opened to his. She sighed deeply and turned to stab the door with her keycard. The light lock turned green and she entered quickly.

Jack stood like a statue. Then, he slowly padded back to his room.

Vienna, Virginia
August 2nd, 2013
Friday

When Ish returned to limited duty, the work in the office tower gained a routine. It was a tough, demanding schedule, but everything seemed under control again with Ish in charge. Even if he was only part time. The bright light streaming in through the high rise windows was like the former mansion in Leesburg with great shafts of light in its paneled rooms. That building was no more. That very morning two commericial trucks laden with explosives were used to blow the gate and totally destroy what was left of the building. The drugsnakes were determined to destroy Rosetta control wherever they suspected it might survive.

Jack looked out from the office tower. Great cumulus clouds, the working material for any imagination, marched in magnificent banks at a stately glide across a deep blue Summer sky. Jack's eyes returned to a black screen. He clicked the power off and on. Nothing happened. He tried it again. Nothing responded. He looked to see if the lights were still on. He hadn't seen a flicker. Jack went to the next private office and looked in at Naomi. She looked perplexed.

"System down?" asked Jack.

"Totally," she fussed with her keyboard to make it better.

Jack barged in on Bubba, Pablo and Ruth in turn. Everyone faced a black screen. Jack rushed to Ish's work station and tried to log on with no luck. The Amigos gathered in Ruth's office.

"We're totally down," said Jack.

"Anything else down?" asked Ruth.

"Phones work," said Bubba. "Fax, too. I called Army Ops immediately. They're not having system problems."

"Call them back, Bubba, and see if that is still the situation. See if the secure lines and the open commercial lines are open, please."

"Yes, ma'am," said Bubba.

"This is intentional, not accidental," said Naomi.

"I agree," said Ruth.

"They are pretty good to find us and take all of our systems down," added Pablo.

"They've been really good. We knew they kidnapped some priceless help. Also, we've lost some people who have chosen the other side as their own."

"Jack, would you call Ish? See if he feels like coming in early today," asked Ruth.

"If you will excuse me, I'll retire and read for awhile," said Pablo.

"Read about how to fix this mess," said Ruth.

"I'll do my best. Let me know if I can help. I don't see anything off hand here. I'll offer some powerful intercessory prayer. It's my specialty. I'll rebuke Pablo Ponce de Leon and bind him as an agent of Satan," smiled Pablo.

"Okay," Ruth raised her eyebrows to make her exclamation.

"How can I help you? Besides praying like Brother Pablo?" asked Naomi.

"Keep me company, thank you. And keep me from jumping out of the window if we can't fix Rosetta 6.2. No, help me jump out a window if we can't fix Rosetta 6.2."

"How about some tea instead?"

"I would love one, please," Ruth sat down hard and swung around in her swivel chair to look out to the far rim of the first Blue Ridge.

About a half an hour later Jack reported back, "Our systems are crashed, but the supporting communications backbone is good to go. It's staying up and carrying a lot of traffic. So how did our individual systems get crashed?" There was a surprise thump at Ruth's door.

Ish rolled into the office in a wheelchair, "Have you found the culprit? Is it a virus? Power spike? Was it a logic bomb?"

"If it was a logic bomb, it wasn't planted recently. Maybe the logic bomb was already there. What Omni files did we download on every system with Rosetta 6.2?" asked Naomi.

Lights came on in every person's head.

"We downloaded the communications protocols and the Omni translator software, because the Omni uses its own system language," said Bubba breathlessly.

"The communications protocols for Omni are updated weekly, right?" Ish knew the answer.

"Yes, those changes are made at Ft. Meade, at NSA," answered Jack.

"Exactly. Fort Meade is totally destroyed. So, where does the contingency plan say the backups are made?" demanded Ish.

"Ah, then the last bunch of our guys kidnapped are still alive. They're helping the NITs fight Omni and Rosetta 6.2," said Jack.

"I'll check on the comms protocols. I'll look at the recovery annex and see who is doing updates," volunteered Bubba.

"I'll check the rose cinquefoils and targeting," said Jack.

"I'll help Jack," said Naomi.

"Get Pablo, please," said Ish.

"Sure, Ish," said Ruth.

In a few minutes Pablo sauntered in. He looked perplexed to be summoned from his solitude, "Hey, good morning, Ish. Yes, Ruth?"

"Pablo, sit down please," Ruth invited him with her open hand. "We think we have a logic bomb planted in the Omni communications protocols by the kidnapped Omni code writers. How can we reboot all of Rosetta 6.2 and not let anyone figure out what we changed? I need you 'Mr.-out-of-the-box' to think, classically, whatever, if you will."

Pablo took a deep breath, stood and walked slowly in a figure eight in front of where Ruth and Ish sat. Pablo looked at the carpet and the ceiling in turns. He made occasional eye jabs at his audience. He followed a path of thought that lead him, slowly, to words. "Our memory is tagged by our senses. Specific memories are filed in our brain by sight, smell, taste, touch and sound. Moreover, the very language we use creates a particular understanding—a perception if you will—that is placed in a unique spot in our mind."

Ish and Ruth sat patiently listening to the exposition.

"Furthermore, simply thinking about something, recalling a memory from any of those catalogs I mentioned from the perception of senses, changes the thoughts and, when the thought is placed back in memory, the act of thinking changes the memories. The amino acids of cells are broken up and recombined in slightly different combinations and bonds. Perhaps the changes are insignificant by some measure of memory effectiveness, but change happens and is continuous. I know Ish put this level of sophistication in Rosetta 6.2 to perceive data through different sensory inputs. So, Rosetta has a living capacity to perceive data differently depending on the sources, right? And if the Omni does more than read data, then is it not possible to have multiple perceptions—data files—of the same event? Isn't it possible to recall the data and then re-file it in a different place?"

"Yes, oh my Lord, yes," said Ish.

"What? Like, you can have different memories of 'rose'?" asked Ruth.

"Exactly. If someone understands how Omni perceives information, then someone can alter the inputs to change reality for Omni, or they can change the algorithims for perception itself or they can change the filing of data after its use," said Pablo.

"Or call it two memories. Substitute the new memory for experiencing a rose for the old one?" asked Ruth.

"Which means that someone could make the computer schizophrenic. There could be two minds, as much as the computer is a mind," said Ish.

"Someone could be inside using the Omni at the same time that we are and we wouldn't know about it," added Pablo.

"The kidnapped code writers could do this, couldn't they?" demanded Ruth.

"Yes, they probably could. They must," said Ish.

"Are we totally dead?" asked Ruth.

"I don't know. But the enemy is inside the gates. The enemy has the keys to the gates. We have to see what the communications protocols hold in more detail. Somewhere in that software is a lie, a big lie, that hides a logic bomb," said Ish.

"The logic bombs will keep coming," said Ruth.

"You have to change perception of old inputs to store them in new memories. The new memories have to be under our control," offered Pablo.

"We could use Rosetta icons with a slightly different chemical interface. You know, we had a prototype icon with a different interface. They have a one cell thick density interface with a different carbon-silicon alloy," said Ish.

"How does that work? Refresh my memory," commanded Ruth.

"The interface changes the resistance of electricity flowing through the icon at just enough of an offset on the sine curve to make every system fail to read the data. That is why we couldn't use them in the first place. We could program these icons to handle anything with the communications protocols," Ish smiled stronger than he felt.

"They crash every system?" asked Ruth.

"Yeah. But, we could send an e-spider to every system in the world to act as a rectifier. It would convert the signal to the precise frequency so the system functions normally."

"If you only have two sets ready to go, you have to place the icons directly on an Omni hard drive. If you load them any other way they will be discovered as anamolies," cautioned Pablo.

"How long will it take two new sets of Rosetta cinquefoil icons with five hundred and twenty three separate icons to reach out and touch every system already affected by the billions of Rosetta 6.2 icons already out there?" asked Ruth.

"Let's figure that out," Ish used his hand held, pocket PC to work through the Computer Science Department at West Point. He ran the analysis on his old model there. He read out loud, "Lapsed real time looks at ten days, one hour, forty minutes, and ten seconds."

"We need two sites for insertion of the new Rosetta 6.2 cinquefoil icons," said Ruth. They searched for the best locations. They settled on the satellite down link hub for the NRO at another office building in Tysons Corners first. The second was a house in nearby Arlington. The Omni liaison officer to the White House Communications Office was kidnapped from this house, his home.

The place was still isolated and safeguarded as a crime scene.

"The kidnapped fellow had a PC there operating on the Omni system as one of the links to the drugsnake Pablo Ponce De Leon. He must have been on the take before he was kidnapped or went over to their side," said Ish.

The upload had to be timed with the next release of communications protocols. Ish planned for Jack and Bubba to do one upload while he and Pablo did the other. Ruth and Naomi would monitor from the alternate command post as Rosetta 6.2 repopulated itself. It took a week to get the programming right.

NRO Office, Tysons Corners, Vienna, VA
Near Midnight, August 11th, 2013
Saturday

Jack and Bubba rode in an unmarked van the few blocks to the NRO office. Summer dumped humidity and heat on NoVa like so many loads of concrete to cover everything in a hot, wet, sticky, grey mess. The nighttime grey clouds glowed pink orange on their underbelly as they reflected the lights of the megapolis back on itself. Once in the office, Jack took a seat directly in front of the computer that acted as the server for the NRO LAN[4]. Bubba took a seat a few feet away to Jack's right at the back-up machine. A communications specialist, a dark-skinned fellow, definitely a descendant of the Indian sub-continent, thirtyish, with a short haircut sat down on Jack's left to form a small semi-circle. They faced large flat monitors and deep-chested metal boxes that hummed and beeped without respite.

Bubba made small talk, but Jack barely nodded and smiled in response. Jack practiced the physical play-by-play in pantomine to make sure that his part went smoothly. Bubba had the single back-up disk in his front breast pocket. Jack pushed the disk in at the stroke of midnight and clicked to open the file and move its contents. The shadow of the file folder fell open to the appropriate file folder on the hard drive. But, nothing happened. One second became five and by ten seconds it was clear that something was wrong.

---
4. NRO LAN is the NRO Local Area Network.

Bubba coughed like someone slapped him on the back. He said, "Oh my," and held his forehead like it hurt. He slumped forward and fell flatly to the floor. He didn't move.

"What's wrong? Bubba, what's wrong?" Jack looked at the running clock on his hand held. He pushed eject for the disk. As soon it popped out, he slammed it back in. He moved the mouse to transfer the files. His hand shook so badly, he could barely control the mouse. "Help him!" Jack yelled at the communications specialist.

Bubba lay on the floor. He tried once again to breath in deeply. But as much as he sucked in air, nothing happened. The air wasn't going anywhere. The tingling he felt in his shoulder and arm a few minutes before became a searing fire. A huge weight was on his chest, crushing, crushing, crushing. His head hurt like it was smashed by an anvil. He felt his strength ebbing away as fast as a tingling tide of darkness rushed up from his toes and fingers to his brain. He wanted to speak, but couldn't. He knew exactly what was happening, but it seemed such a surprise to be this particular moment. Like a thief in the night, the resounding end of his life happened with incredible swiftness. *How fast it goes. How fast it comes.* He saw Barbara in his mind and felt love. The image was lost in the swallowing darkness. He peered into the darkness to see his expectation. The utter blackness of impenetrable depth and volume lasted a split second before the burst of wonder. He saw and felt a warming light.

Jack finished a second later. The Rosetta 6.2 cinquefoil icons were booted, up and coming on line around the world. Jack saw Bubba lying on his stomach. He was lifeless. His blue eyes looked brighter than ever, staring at some distant point of wonder and surprise. The communications guy was at Bubba's side looking for a pulse.

"Call in 'green'. We're good. I'll get him now," Jack threw himself down to Bubba's side. Bubba felt so heavy when Jack rolled him to his back. There was no pulse and no breath. Jack cursed himself for not knowing CPR perfectly. He tried a few strong breaths into Bubba and some shoves on his chest with both hands. There was no response.

"Did you get through?" Jack yelled.

"Yes, sir."

"Call 9–1–1"

"They won't be allowed in here."

"Call 9–1–1! Call our back up to help us carry him to the door!" Jack continued a rhythm of breathing and pushing to no avail.

Bubba is dead. I can't save him. Jack was overwhelmed by the helplessness. He breathed short breaths broken by pleading sobs. "Oh, please Bubba. No. Not now. No, Bubba. Live man, live. Bubba, live for Barbara. Live for the grandbabies. Oh, please Bubba."

Jack's pleadings seemed so small compared to the enormity of reality. "Not now, Bubba. Please live."

Jack shouted, "Oh God, oh God, help him! Make him live God! Oh, please, please, God, I beg You. He loves you so. Oh, please God, make him live! Please God," Jack felt desperate, frenzied fear. He grasped, "In the name of Jesus, please God, oh God, let him live! Please God!"

Bubba lay dead on the floor.

The guys from the security vans thundered into the room. They elbowed Jack aside and swooped Bubba up into strong arms and hustled him down to the entrance. The ambulance siren was closing in. When Bubba was loaded on the gurney and slid into the back of the ambulance, Jack tried to follow. The communications expert thrust his fist, still clutching his mobile communicator, to Jack's chest to stop him in his tracks.

"No, sir. We have to continue the mission, sir."

Jack opened his mouth to argue, but the words were denied. He knew to finish the mission regardless of the cost. Jack stood slackjawed with his arms weighted to his sides as the ambulance sirened away. He went back to his mission crying.

NRO Contractor Office
Tysons Corners, Vienna, VA
August 15th, 2013
Wednesday

Jack wiped his eyes as he walked down the hall to Ruth's office. The tears just came without warning since Bubba died. *God, I feel so sad. I can't shake it.* Jack walked with his eyes down. He entered Ruth's office without knocking, without thinking. He was startled to hear her speaking in Hebrew.

"Yeetgadal v'yeetkadash sh'mey rabbah. B'almah dee v'rah kheer'utey v'yamleekh malkhuei, b'chahyeykohn, uv'yohmeykhohn, uv'chahyei d'chohl beyt yisrael, ba'agalah u'veez'-man kareev, v'eemru: Amein[5]."

Jack stepped back against the wall quietly. Ruth had a shawl over her head and shoulders. She was rocking back and forth. Her back was to Jack and the door.

"Y'hey sh'met rabbah m'varach l'alam u'l'almey almahyah Yeet'barakh. Y'hey sh'met rabbah m'varach l'alam u'l'almey almahyah. Yeet'hbarakh, v'yeesh'tabach, v'yeetpa'ar, v'yeetrohmam, v'yeet'nasei, v'yeet'hadar, v'yeet'aleh, v'yeet'halal sh'mey d'kudshah b'reekh hoo L'eylah meen kohl beerkhatah v'sheeratah, toosh'b'chatah v'nechematah, da'ameeran b'al'mah, v'eemru: Amein."

What is this all about? What is she saying? It'd be too embarrassing to disturb her. He stood so still that he hoped he could become invisible. Ruth's thin shoulders shook under the shawl. She was sobbing. From her deepest inner depth up through her bowels and chest to howl out of her mouth

"Y'hei shlamah rabba meen sh'mahyah, v'chahyeem aleynu v'al kohl yisrael, v'eemru, Amein."

"How do I get out of here?" Jack edged back to the door. Her Hebrew became more mumbled with each racking, chest heaving, pulling out each sob.

"Oseh shalom beem'roh'mahv, hoo ya'aseh shalom, aleynu v'al kohl yisrael v'eemru: Amein."

---

5. Mourner's Kaddish: Glorified and sanctified be God's great name throughout the world which He has created according to His will. May He establish His kingdom in your lifetime and during your days, and within the life of the entire House of Israel, speedily and soon: and say Amen.

May His great name be blessed forever and to all eternity.

Blessed and be praised, glorified and exalted, extolled and honored, adored and lauded be the name of the Holy One, blessed be He, beyond all the blessings and hymns, praises and consolations that are ever spoken in the world; and say Amen. May there be abundant peace from heaven, and life, for us and for all Israel; and say Amen.

He who creates peace in His celestial heights, may He create peace for us and all Israel; and say Amen.

It's not worth it. Then, she was done. Ruth let out one last lingering, long moan. It was the sound of a groaning ache, more than a grimace. Pain from the soul is far worse than pain in the flesh. Her eyes opened to the floor and caught Jack as they swept up with her head to Heaven. She jumped back a foot.

"I'm so sorry Ruth!" Jack held up both palms in surrender. He leaned back towards the door.

"What are you doing, Jack?" Ruth pulled her prayer shawl from her head with one hand. She balled it in her fist.

"I'm sorry, Ruth. I didn't notice you until I was in the room. Then, I didn't want to disturb you."

"How long were you there?"

"A minute. Just a minute" Jack blushed. Ruth caught his eyes and locked them in her clear interrogation. He knew, instantly, that she knew he had no ill will.

"It's the Kaddish, Jack. I was saying the Kaddish. I'm supposed to say it in the temple or within a quorum of temple. But, I went ahead and did it here and now."

"The Kaddish?"

"Yes, the Kaddish. The prayer for the dead. You say it for the soul that died."

"I didn't know you spoke Hebrew. What are the words in English?"

"I don't speak Hebrew so well. I pray it pretty well," Ruth smiled and her face cracked from her temple to chin in small wrinkles. "Essentially it praises God and says may there be peace."

"You were doing it for Bubba."

"Yes, I was. I was doing it for Bubba," but Ruth had prayed and cried a flood of tears for others besides Bubba.

"Thanks for doing that. For Bubba. I came in to see if you wanted to hear about an idea I had."

"Yes, sure," Ruth reassumed Ruth.

"First, let me ask you a question since you were praying for the dead. What do the dead do? I mean, what do they know? I wish I could ask Bubba, or my parents, where are they? Do they have memories? What are they doing?" Jack blurted out what he normally kept to himself.

"I don't know all the details, Jack. I must say, my parents, grandparents and dearest friends are gone. I think they are in a better place. But, that knowledge is based on my senses, not my intellect. It bothers me," Ruth allowed her truth.

"I got it. The emotional seems to rule the intellectual when we wanna. But, you can't say Ish or Pablo aren't intellectuals."

"Ish wouldn't like you calling him that. At least not to his face. He thinks he is still a soldier," Ruth smiled at the picture.

"But, he knows he is a genius or near it. He's gotta know. His faith in a heaven must be intellectual. He and Pablo make a mockery of people who think they are too smart for God. Bubba for that matter. He just played the country bumpkin," Jack looked out the window. *There are so many things I still want to ask Bubba about. Darn.*

"Then ask Ish when you get a chance. What else is on your mind?"

"Oh, yeah. This civil war thing is getting bad. The other side is organizing its coalitions. They say its all an over-reaction to the children being murdered at Easter. The Liberals say that the President's authority is illegitimate. Their go-to guy and gal judges are in protective custody. That won't last forever. They will rule that everything happening with Rosetta is illegal. Then what do the cops do? What does anyone do?"

"Ish said this would happen. I remember. He talked about the Civil War and how complicated it was. He said in some people's minds Maryland, Kentucky and Missouri seceded. Different groups of people claiming to be the legislatures declared different things. Lincoln arrested the Maryland General Assembly before they could secede."

"Okay, what does that mean now?"

"It means we need to do what Lincoln would do."

"What's that?"

"Lincoln would do whatever had to be done to save the Union. No matter what. Anything."

"Ah, now I get it."

"Here's another example. The U.S. Constitution specifically says you can't make a state out of an existing state. But, that is what happened when they made West Virginia from Virginia in 1862. No one ever went back to change it."

Jack grinned ear to ear, "Then how about abolishing the Federal Judiciary System. All of it. Either by martial law decree or get Congress to do it. Either way. Create new courts for drugs. New courts for terrorists. New courts to do what the old courts did, but divide the labor and geography differently. Hey, new courts for immigration. Whatever President Kyle will buy."

"That was always one of Ish's branches for possible actions."

"No way."

"Way, Jack, yes way. I thought you would've seen it in the contingency annexes for Rosetta," Ruth's voice was cold with ice.

"Missed it. I skimmed the legal sections," said Jack sheepishly.

"Why don't you check it out? Then, see if the conditions we posited have been met. But, see if the conditions are still valid. Maybe the circumstances demand we move out on this option. Set up a meeting with the Solicitor General, White House counsel, Trento's military head counsel, oh what's his name, and the Attorney General. And whoever else ought to be there."

"Yes ma'am," Jack straightened up his back. He almost came to attention with his thumbs on the seams of his trousers. *Can't believe that she is orchestrating this high a meeting. This is White House stuff. Ruth is doing it. Herself. Under the President's authority. Wow! I love making this happen at this level. This is so cool. I wish I could run the meeting.*

Tysons Corners, Vienna, VA
August 22nd, 2013
Wednesday

Pablo was the first to join Ish in the sunny, bright motel dining room. The aroma of coffee, bacon, ham and biscuits made his stomach turn over in anticipation. He saw Ish looking at his pocket PC.

"Good morning, brother. Getting smaller, huh, Ish? The target list is getting smaller? Isn't it?" asked Pablo.

"God's morning to you, Brother Pablo," Ish snapped his device closed and stuffed it in the breast pocket of this bright open-necked summer shirt.

"Peace be with you," Pablo replied genuinely.

"Juice or coffee first?" Ish tilted the plastic mug towards Pablo.

"Both first," laughed Pablo gently.

The men sat for a second to savor the first fresh sip. The air conditioning of the dining room gave enough chill to have the hot coffee make sense. Outside the sun was going to scorch the earth this day.

"Why are we going so late tonight?" Pablo asked.

"There is going to be a Blues demonstration in the neighborhood. If we go in before hand, we walk into the enemy observation that is checking out the demo site. I'm frustrated to death that we have to go do this re-booting again," said Ish.

"Doesn't coming in during a demonstration set us up for another ambush?" asked Pablo.

"Yes and no. We need another on-site boot of the Rosetta icons directly on an enemy Omni station. The lab guys have some very minor, but maybe really important tweaks that may help us find your cousin Pablo," said Ish.

Pablo looked startled, then amused, at Ish's comment. A more sensitive soul or, rather, a more polarized hyphenated person could take offense. Pablo didn't do so, "Pablo. My cousin or brother in Christ some day, God-willing Pablo. Pablo Ponce de Leon and Jesuit brother Pablo named for the Apostle Paul, huh?"

"Yeah, like that will happen. I think you and he have had almost as many brushes with death as the good Paul," said Ish.

"Funny you mention that. I have thought about it myself a number of times. Be right back."

Pablo returned with a young man's full plate of food heaped with steaming good things to eat. "I thought it odd, almost comical, like the perils of Pauline. Ha, another choice name, right?"

Ish laughed in a good natured sharing.

"Anyway. I considered it somewhere between comedy and tragedy that so many attacks came our way. Then, I remembered how many times the Apostle Paul was attacked and beaten. Then how many times is any one person shipwrecked? Never. It's a big deal to be shipwrecked and survive once. But, no, no, Saint Paul, my real brother Pablo, gets shipwrecked twice! Can you believe it?"

"Brother Paul, Brother Pablo?"

"Oh yes! My brother in Christ, of course. But, really so much my brother in the parts of myself I see in him."

Ish looked at the ceiling for an answer to the obvious question of Pablo as Paul. "You're both very bright. And you are both celibate."

Pablo laughed so hard that his white milk came out of his nose. "I always hate it when I do that!"

Ish threw him his napkin while laughing.

Ruth walked up and put her hand on Ish's shoulder. "Am I missing something here? Bawdy jokes with the boys?"

"No, we are starting those in a minute. We expect your best, too, Ruth," Pablo shot back from under the napkins shrouding his face.

"Actually, we're discussing the perils of Pauline, Pablo, Pablo and the Aposte Paul—the good Saul of Tarsus," Ish stood as a gentleman should upon the arrival of a lady. He pulled out a chair for her.

"Thanks. But, let me get my food first. I'm starving too," Ruth's eyes were on Pablo's overflowing plate.

She returned with bird's portions of food. "So, continue with the story of similarities. I want to see you blow milk through your nose from the start, Pablo."

Pablo almost did it again. He showed his bright white teeth. "I'm comparing myself favorably and not so favorably to my namesake, the thirteenth apostle."

"Lucky thirteen, hmm," said Ruth.

"Yes, you bet. He was a monumental hypocrite in his youth."

"I thought he was very devout always," said Ruth.

"He was very devout. Yes, but that was just it. He was a super Jew. He was the best at living to the letter of the Law," Pablo spoke more rapidly.

Ruth looked startled at his gaffe to speak ethnicity to the ethnic.

"Saul loved the Law because he loved God. When Jesus spoke to him on the road to Damascus, Saul realized that he was persecuting the followers of the very Messiah that he had begged God to bring to the world in his lifetime. And knew the scriptures of the Torah and the Prophets by heart. When he saw Jesus and felt the warming, overwhelming glow of His love, he was thunderstruck."

Jack wandered in and silently took a seat. Pablo continued in growing intensity.

"I understate the case, how it was so significant for Saint Paul. Paul was slapped hard with the realization that all of the scriptures, all predictions from over eight hundred years past had come true and he had blown it. He, who loved the truth and knowledge, had hated the greatest truth and knowledge in the universe when it was presented to him. Jesus was in a form that he didn't think was right. I may be interpolating a little here, but I think not. Furthermore," Pablo drew a long breath.

"The Super Jew became fulfilled with love just as God had fulfilled the scriptures in Jesus. Suddenly, Paul knew what the primary commandment to love God with all of your heart, mind, strength and soul and the second Commandment to love others as you love yourself meant, because the word love took on a whole new meaning."

Ruth sat silently eating and listening.

"Love gained a whole new meaning, because Paul experienced the love of God personally and his understanding of love changed. It gained a breadth, a depth, a timelessness, a power to endure, a strength to return hate with love, a rejection of evil, a desire to deny self, an urging that could not be denied, a passion, that he had never known could exist."

"Some love," said Ruth.

Naomi joined them as Pablo listed love's new attributes for the Apostle Paul, "All those things about love are in his letters. Romans, Ephesians, and Corinthians, all of them. Love is patient, love is kind, love does not envy."

"Love does not boast, it is not proud," Ish interrupted.

"Love is not rude, it is not self-seeking," Pablo picked up.

"Love is not easily angered, it keeps no record of wrongs," Naomi looked at Jack when she spoke.

"Love does not delight in evil, but rejoices in truth," said Pablo.

"Love always protects, always trusts," said Ish.

"Love always hopes," said Naomi with another quick flash of her eyes to Jack.

"Love never quits," Ish, Naomi and Pablo chimed in unison.

"If I have faith that can move mountains, and it can, but if have not love, then I have nothing!" Pablo practically shouted.

"And now these three remain: faith, hope and love. But the greatest of these is love," said Ish.

"God is love," said Naomi.

"Jesus is Lord," added Ish.

"And He is risen. He is alive!" said Pablo.

"He is risen indeed!" said Ish.

"He is risen indeed!" said Naomi.

"Oh, Lord, I miss Bubba!" said Ish. He sobbed. They all cried. The tears flowed without sobbing. It was the sweet release that was too, too overwhelming. "See, Jack, we laugh and smile and joke and cry at the same time grieving. God is good. No matter what."

Ish, Naomi and Pablo reached for one another's hands across the table for a quick squeeze. They shared the bonding energy. They reached out to Ruth and Jack. Ruth smiled tolerantly. Jack let his mouth gape in wonder. *What was this?*

As they left the table. Ruth remarked to Pablo, "I can see your passion like the Paul you describe. But that is precisely why I don't see you as a Priest. You have so much to live for as a young man."

Pablo looked wounded. He spoke softly, "The passion you see led me to seek truth and knowledge." He paused for a long second. The others stopped in their tracks to listen.

"Much to my utter surprise, the greatest truth and knowledge for the whole universe from the greatest to the tiniest of all things and all time, was found in what I used to mock to myself and my super smart friends. I found the purest and most complete truth in the faith of my Mother and my peasant grandparents. Christ is the complete revelation of God to man. Once I met Him and came to know Him, I was moved by the same passion for the truth to serve the truth with everything I have. I came easily to the Mother Church and the priesthood. Now, becoming a Jesuit is not so easy. It's work!" Pablo smiled like the little boy he once was.

"Well said, Brother Pablo," Ish clapped his hands.

Pablo took Ish aside. He whispered, "I hate it when someone says I'm too young, too handsome, too manly, too smart to be a Priest of the Roman Catholic Church. It's my choice for my passion, my intellect, my whole life, my everything. And just like the former hypocrite Saul, it's the balm for my former hypocrisy too. Yet, the love that commanded him and the love that filled him by the grace of God, denies me such critical comments in public, brother. My words can't wound more than they illuminate the darkness with the light of truth, so I keep to himself. Help me explain this to Ruth. She's not a believer."

"Okay, Pablo. We will figure out a way," said Ish.

Jack saw the two men whispering and walked on. He was confused by the reaction Ish, Naomi, and Pablo shared about Bubba's death. But, something was powerful and comforting about their dealing with death. Their peace was strength. *I want what those people have. I want it now. God, give me what they have.*

Ish insisted the Amigos split up into two man teams again to boot up the Rosetta icons. The change in Rosetta 6.2 was just a few more degrees of capability for the icons, which were really microscopic hardware chips, to perceive data as well as read only data. The icons could discern a micron more in differences in data inputs than the earlier icons. That should be good enough to find Pablo's lair.

Ish and Jack headed to the house on North Kenilworth Street in Arlington, Virginia. Pablo and Naomi were sent to a radio station a mile or so away on Lee Highway. They had a new point of entry to get into the digitized medium world directly. Ruth would stand watch at the NRO office at Tysons Corners until all of the little eagles returned home to the nest.

1610 N. Kenilworth St.
Arlington, VA
9:30 PM, August 22nd, 2013
Wednesday

Jack's heart thumped before this second booting mission. He sat in the vehicle with the air conditioning running against the heat a blistering day banked into the night. The moon and the stars fuzzed behind the big city night haze and light pollution. Jack waited for the 'execute' signal. Ish stepped outside against his own orders to breath the night in before they tried one more tricky cyber attack on the enemy.

Jack leaned back and closed his eyes. Suddenly, he saw the familiar nightmare of his dead body and nothingness closing in from all sides. This time he didn't go back to wallow in his life and dread of death. He was alone in the vehicle, but he didn't want anyone to hear any of this. He thought of Bubba. *Dead Bubba, where is he? My parents? Everyone?* He spoke out loud in a husky whisper, "What must I do?"

"I want what they have."

"Okay God. Are you real or not?"

"Oh, Lord, tell me if I can believe. What do you want anyway?" Jack put a few seconds of silence in between his words.

"Okay. I'll do it. I will say that I believe. Jesus, You are Lord. You are the divine Son of God. You died for my sins on the cross. Forgive me of my sins. Save me. Please. Save me?" He heard the hum of the air conditioner.

"Tell me, God, is it true?"

Jack tested the idea in his mind. As clearly as he could see the black moonscape of eternity with his dead body on an unearthly desert, he tried to picture the tomb outside of Jerusalem. It is the first Easter morning. *What is there?*

A picture of a whitewashed stone sepulchre from a book Naomi showed him at Leavenworth. He looked into the opening. He saw nothing in the dark but felt the cool, dark space like a wine cellar.

Jack saw himself, or found himself, suddenly standing outside again looking at the entrance. The man brushed by him quickly, oddly, like he was a shadow of light of a man's figure. Jack smiled ever so slightly. He felt his eyes well with tears.

The tomb is empty. Now Jack, and his inner John-James, felt it. Then there was enough light on the inside to see the empty bench where the body should lie. The tomb is empty! Jack felt a warmth like a shawl around him.

"He arose. He really arose," Jack sat up as straight as an arrow.

"Jesus is alive! It IS true!"

One word repeated itself in his mind. *"True, true, true, true."*

Jack ran through the mental test, the visualization of the tomb, again.

"He arose. He lives. He is alive now!"

A thought he didn't think came into his mind came quickly, "I Am I Am. I love you, son."

Jack swallowed hard and breathed deeply through his mouth. He ran the exercise a third time. The tomb is empty! He felt an unbelievably quiet, calm assurance. *It's all true. All real.* Jack laughed out loud. A rolling chuckle. His eyes stayed filled to overflowing with tears. He felt a well-spring of joy bubbling up across his chest. A peace like a warm wind filled him like a balloon. It felt absolutely wonderful.

Jack cried in free flowing tears and smiled at the same time. He felt more overwhelmed than he had ever been in his entire life. Jack started to cry so hard his body shook with each cleansing sob. He wasn't sad and he didn't feel guilty. He was overcome by the joy, the disbelief of actual believing and feeling so sure of it, like a criminal receiving a last minute pardon. *I can't believe it. It's true. He died for me. He rose again so I will too. Jesus is alive now.*

He felt at once bonded to God and free from all things that cause pain. He didn't want the moment to end. It felt so good; good to believe. *I'm free. I'm saved. I'll live forever.*

"Thank you Lord Jesus. I am Yours. I'm gonna be a Christian man. Like Bubba. Like Ish. Like Pablo. Be like You, Jesus." Another wave of overwhelming gratitude washed him. He couldn't resist the tears that came. He felt the tears were cleansing him.

I've gotta get a grip. We've got a mission to do in a couple of minutes. He had to stop crying, but he didn't know if he could. Jack was surprised by the simple joy that he felt. "I love You, Lord Jesus," Jack said with a salty tear-stained grin in the darkness.

He heard a thought like a quick, but painless thunderclap in his mind, "I love you, too." It was a small, clear, soft voice.

After a few more minutes of grins and sobs and circular thoughts of joy, peace, and thankfulness, his tears dried. Ish knocked on the window. When Jack jumped out of the vehicle. He couldn't contain himself.

"I believe, Ish. I accepted Jesus as my savior. I believe He is alive. I'm saved! Jesus is my Lord and Savior."

Ish cocked his head so hard his chin hit his chest. He tried to catch enough light to see Jack's face better. He put his nose close to Jack's and whispered. "I knew it would happen. He is risen indeed.

Jack, I knew the Holy Ghost would get you. You're too good of a man to be left out of the Lord's Army. Praise the Lord. Thank You, Jesus," Ish pulled Jack with one arm and said, "Now, follow me."

They hurried in to do their mission. Only two blocks away the drums of a Blues rally carried Rosetta's call through the humid air. The rebooting of Rosetta 6.2 was over in a few minutes. The installation was easy. As they waited for some initial feedback the leader of their on-site security team rushed in. He was a stocky Asian guy, Chinese-American, to Jack's eye.

"Sir, did you know that one of the targets for tonight is only a couple of blocks over there?" the agent pointed.

"Yes, Agent Chin. There are a lot of targets tonight."

Ish's PDA vibrated, "Ruth? Roger. Got it. Something big is happening. Is it in the Blues Rally or near the Blues Rally? You're breaking up."

"Listen to this," the agent held his personal communcator up to Ish's ear. Ish heard a popping sound a second before he heard it with his naked ear. Then high-pitched voices walked on each other over the same frequency. Ish heard clearly the excited exclamation, "Yes, yes, roger, it looks like Pablo, it looks like him."

"Saddle up, soldiers. It's a block away. We're going over there," Ish commanded. Jack and Agent Chin followed obediently.

Around the corner of a hill from Kenilworth street were the 'garden apartments' built during World War II for the influx of government workers. The tiny boxes of brick had charm once. In recent decades they were the home to succeeding waves of the poorest immigrants moving in to grab the droppings from the table of new imperial power in the world—Washington. The neighborhood's good old Virginia name—Westover—was incongruous with its international melting pot flavor. No adult in Westover spoke English as a native.

The Blues march in Westover was disrupted by the authorities. The local Blues' drums had called the people to witness a moment and share an experience. But, chaos reigned instead of the passionate intimacy of the planned rally.

The sudden rush of vehicles and the loop swoop of helicopters was a shock to the Blues. Heavily armed men rushed one of the apartments. More vehicles roared in to close off the streets. There was the pop-pop-popping sound and it was all over. The men quickly put out a single wire barrier around a large area. The wire shone with a luminescent light and had a very painful shock for the fool who tried to cross it. Some of the residents, Blues and others, screamed to be allowed back into their homes. Many Blues marchers milled around in confusion.

Ish arrived as the medical team sprinted to a ground floor apartment. Ish went in right behind them. The burly arm of one of attack team caught him in the chest like a punch. "Not so fast. Halt," he said gruffly.

Agent Chin was one step behind Ish. He grabbed the fellow's arm and showed him the badge on his chest. "Scan it," Chin commanded.

The big guy took a penlight scanner from his armored vest. In a second the answer came up in the head's up display in the full face visor. They saw the reflection of green light. 'Highest access authorized. No stop. No reclama.'

"Proceed," grunted the big guy.

Ish, Agent Chin and Jack filed past. Two dead men lay at the door. A dead woman was broken and sprawling across a large leather chair. Blood splatters covered the walls. In the far corner before a wall of computer gear racked and stacked to the ceiling was the body of a Hispanic man in his late thirties. The medics prodding and tested for life. An athletic soldier stood over them with his helmet off. His shock of short blond hair combed to one side. He recognized Ish was a man of some authority just to be given on-site access.

"He's dead, sir. It's him all right. We whacked Pablo Ponce de Leon."

Ish peered over the shoulders of the medics. He studied the dossier too many times for any doubt. "How long until lab positive ID?"

Jack strained to see. *It's Pablo.*

"Couple of minutes, sir. We printed him. Launching the data now."

In the next room women and children screamed and wailed in Spanish.

Ish went back out into the night of flashing lights, loud voices and very warm breezes. Jack and Agent Chin followed and stood in a small circle with him.

"I can't believe he was so close. He was doing exactly what we expected him to do. He was hugging us physically as much as in cyber space. He wasn't hiding out in some palace redoubt," Ish waved his hand back at the modest apartment.

"Good job, Ish," said Jack.

"We got him! Thank you, Lord. Thank you, Jesus. It'll all come crashing down now, Amen. We won. Thank God and God bless the United States of America, we won," Ish smashed his fist into his open hand.

Jack gave him the ultimate accolade of one American to another. "Way to go, Ish." He extended his hand.

"Way to go, Sir," Agent Chin shook his hand too. Ish beamed even though he looked very tired. The long race was over and it was won. Or, it would be won, totally, very soon for sure.

Agent Chin pushed his ear phone in with one hand to hear better. "Sir. LTG Trento is inbound." Jack saw the running light of the helicopter over the houses.

The helicopter landed in the parking lot of Westover Baptist Church across the street corner. The old bricked Swanson Middle School stood a silent sentinel on the other corner. LTG Trento hustled across the street in a trot. Ish smiled at the joy of remembrance seeing his old boss in full combat gear. The old warrior lieutenant general acted the young stud Army officer running to the sound of the guns.

Almost automatically, Ish drew himself to a tight position of attention and saluted LTG Trento. Ish pointed to the apartment and said, "This way, Sir."

LTG Trento returned the salute while still at the double time. *That's a minor faux pas of military etiquette.* Jack didn't crack a smile. LTG Trento made the same quick inspection like Ish. The medics were bagging Pablo when the good general interrupted their work. They proudly zipped down to show off their catch.

LTG Trento went outside to almost the exact same spot Ish halted. It was time to pow-wow and to bring closure on the hard kill. LTG Trento slapped Ish hard on the back several times and grabbed his hand for a hard pumping handshake, "Way to go, Ish. Way to go, soldier."

After a moment's discussion on what to do next, LTG Trento took a step backward and saluted Ish. He held his hand salute conspicuously until Ish returned it as a senior might do to a subordinate. LTG Trento did an about face as sharply as he would on the parade field and jogged back to his helicopter like a young company commander going back into the fight.

Ish, Jack and Agent Chin stared until the Blackhawk helicopter lifted away into the dark skies. Ish gave a quick salute of his own to the machine as it banked to go away. "Let's call it a night. We can tell the Amigos all about it back at the NRO."

"What a night!" said Jack. Jack felt the wonder of the fearful darkness of death dreams gone. Every thought of his fears, even the old enemy failure, seemed to be washed in a bright light. The fears fell silent and harmless before the simple, almost silly sense of joy Jack felt. *We launched the Cinquefoils. Pablo Ponce de Leon is dead. I'm saved! Thank you, Lord Jesus.*

Fort Myer, Virginia
September 2nd, 2013
Sunday

Rosetta 6.2 triumphed. The one man with the will to lead the NITs in Civil War was killed. No one else had the ability or will to lead so fiercely, so well. And will is the essence of war. Now, Ish's will, living through Rosetta 6.2, led to victory.

The ideas and energy to resist flattened, like the air going out of a punctured tire. An individual might decide to do something, but nobody contra-Rosetta 6.2 was capable of coordinating anything. It seemed to most Americans that Rosetta, even if they didn't know it by name, was working and winning. It looked like the President's plan was going forward. President Kyle went before the Nation to boldly proclaim the beginning of the end of the War on Drugs and the start of a new, more sustainable phase of World War IV.

LTG Trento honored the Amigos with a Trento signature touch event. A farewell brunch was the capstone of their debriefings and return to civilian life. It was safe to go home now. LTG Trento knew ceremony spoke to important human needs. Years ago LTG Trento heard from his underclass buddies how the returning hostages from Iran in 1981 got grounded for a couple of weeks at the Hotel Thayer at West Point. He planned to bring the Amigos home from this war at the Ft. Meyer Officer's Club above Arlington Cemetery.

The reception room was resplendent in the flags of the military services, the bright red general's guidons with their great white stars, all the flags of the states and territories of the United States of America, and a huge Old Glory herself. The windows of one wall overlooked the club pool and the old stables of the horse-mounted soldiers of the Old Guard, the 3rd U.S. Infantry. The Old Guard provides the Honor Guard for the Tomb of the Unknown Soldier as LTG Trento pointed out to Naomi. He had an eye for beauty as well as duty.

Ruth and Ish stayed close to one another to share the victory together. They were melded in the fires forged of many, many months long before the Amigos showed up. Pablo befriended everyone there. Naomi flitted by the window after LTG Trento's quick tour. She kept looking to the western sky. Soon enough, she would fly back home just to the West of this blue horizon. Jack felt ill at ease now that it was finally over. Jack wanted to speak privately with Naomi.

LTG Trento called everyone to take their seats. The farewell brunch was elegant. He had a head table set up with the Amigos and the Chairman of the Joint Chiefs and his wife alone. The other generals, their wives and assorted guests were seated in an egalitarian jumble.

LTG Trento followed the blessing from the Army Chief of Chaplains with a brief introduction of guests. During the meal, the chamber music group from the Army Band played.

When the meal was finished, LTG Trento introduced the Chairman of the Joint Chiefs of Staff. The Chairman spoke gruffly about Duty, Honor, Country and the defense of the Constitution against all enemies foreign and domestic. His remarks were heartfelt, but predictable, until he reached into his breast pocket and pulled out a five by seven card of stiff, elegant White House vellum stationery. He cleared his throat and put on his reading glasses.

"The White House. September Second, Two Thousand Thirteen," the room fell to the quiet of shallow breathing.

"To the persons known to themselves as 'The Amigos'," The Chairman chuckled and the room echoed. "They are," he read their full names.

"On behalf of the grateful nation of the American People, our Republic, the United States of America, I extend my deepest appreciation and admiration for your invaluable contributions to defend the United States of America in the most recent time of peril. Your courage, skill and self-sacrifice was above and beyond the call of duty for any American patriot.

Thank you for all that you have done so bravely and wisely. You served at great risk so that your fellow citizens may live without fear, without drugslavery and Narco-Terrorism, in a nation which cleansed itself from the cancer of corruption. May God Bless you and your families. May God Bless the United States of America. Maggie Myriah Kyle, President of the United States of America."

LTG Trento was the first to spring to his feet. It was a thunderous standing ovation. The room filled with the clapping. LTG Trento lead the 'here, here's', 'bravo', and the few throaty old 'huzzahs'. The accolade took long minutes to subside. Every one of the Amigos felt the warm eyes of tears rising, but they held their composure in alternating faces of surprise, pleasure, disbelief, embarassment and thrilled joy. Finally the Chairman enjoined the Amigos to rise and take a bow. They did several times and sat back down.

The Chairman was red faced, but dry-eyed when he blew his nose noisily into his handkerchief. "I extend my personal thanks on behalf of every member of the Armed Services of the United States of America." More long applause and another standing ovation.

"I must comment that the classified nature of the Amigo's activities and the ongoing sensitivity of operations they have been affiliated with will preclude more public recognition for some time into the future. But, we know what you did. We know we couldn't have won without you and your Rosetta 6.2." Everyone exchanged knowing glances. The Amigos and Rosetta 6.2 would stay hush-hush for a long while.

"I ask the Group, you Amigos, to please share a few words with us." The Amigos stood up unevenly and awkwardly. Jack, Naomi, and Pablo looked to Ish, then Ruth, to speak first.

Ruth began, "Thank you all for this wonderful brunch. Thank you, Larry, for your special efforts today and especially for your leadership through all of this. You know what Rosetta 6.2 means to American history. You contributed to a great victory that re-established a future of our country. Thank you for honoring our Amigos so beautifully this day. Allow me to give the floor to the author, the architect, the genius behind Rosetta 6.2," Ruth let brevity take this day.

Ish took a long measure of the men and women around him before he spoke. "I will be eternally grateful for the opportunity I had to serve. I must mention our fallen comrades. Specifically, I must speak for a man named Bubba," he stopped and got control of his voice.

"My friend, Bubba Holland, comrade in this trial, and brother in Christ Jesus would have loved to be here and speak to you," Ish smiled. The Amigos grinned at the inside joke. The room smiled too, despite the obvious pain Ish bore.

"In fact, Bubba would be the first to tell you how no one else could speak for him as well as he could." Ish opened his mouth to say more, but nothing came out. He raised his glass, "I propose a toast to our fallen comrades."

Everyone rushed to comply. "To our fallen comrades," they thundered. Applause broke out and silent tears lined Ish's jet-black cheeks. Ish raised both hands like a master of ceremonies summoning a crowd's attention. "I neglected to mention one thing. I'm going to Poquoson, Virginia with a death notification team to visit Ish's widow. Then, with the support of the Chief of Staff of the Air Force, I will accompany Bubba's widow, Mrs. Holland, and an honor guard to a graveside ceremony in Arlington Cemetery." The room applauded heartily and the Air Force Chief smiled appreciatively.

LTG Trento gave thanks again and asked for the benediction.

It was time for everyone to go their appointed ways. The Amigos nervously avoided saying good bye to one another until they were all out on the covered-sidewalk entrance. A single file covey of government vans waited.

The Amigos cried through the hugs, handshakes, and kisses good bye. They groped like a family farewell after a funeral. Then each person broke to make a separate way with an escort at the elbow. Ruth was the first to force herself to go. Pablo followed. Ish kept talking even as he closed the door on himself to leave. Jack spun around from his to catch Naomi on the arm. He looked into her laugh lined face with longing one last time. "Good bye, Naomi." He hugged her hard.

"Good bye, John-James. You're such a good man," she kissed his cheek and withdrew from his embrace. He didn't have time to respond in word or deed. Jack wiped his eyes with the heel of his hand. The other vans pulled away. When he could see again, he was alone with his escort.

As Jack's van drove across tiny Fort Myer, he asked the escort, "How much slack time do we have before the plane takes off at Andrews?"

His escort, a crew cut grey-haired officer some years his senior answered, "The plane leaves when you get there. Whenever that is, Sir."

Jack pondered a second. "Okay, then. Swing down through Arlington Cemetery. Go down Hap Arnold street," he ordered.

"Yes Sir," the escort officer gave the orders to the driver.

Jack leaned forward in his seat looking for landmarks. September's sun didn't know yet that Summer was waning. It was hot and humid with a bright, blue sky dotted with cotton white clouds. Moody breezes blew the full green branches this way and that in uneven fits. Recent rains rejuvenated the browning grass to a brilliant, wet and alive green. When Jack knew he was close enough he commanded, "Stop here."

As he got out of the vehicle, he said, "I'll be a few. Give me a coupla minutes."

"Yes, Sir."

Jack walked the rows to his parents' gravesite. The heat sucked most of the oxygen from the air. He loosened his tie. His thoughts and their emotions were too many to sort out. When he saw his father's name, he walked around to stand directly in front and read his name again. Then he stepped gingerly to the other side to read his mother's name. Jack bent one knee and leaned on the simple granite stone with one hand. He rested his weight on the warmed rough surface. Jack let every ounce of the world he carried fall off his head and shoulders and down his arm to the supporting stone.

He thought of the song his friends in the Group sang over and over. Jack sang in soft tenor, "Praise God from whom all blessings flow."

His eyes welled with tears for another unbelievable, unbearably bittersweet time that day, "Praise God from whom all blessings flow."

He sang as the tears flowed without restraint, "Praise God all creatures here below. Praise Him above ye heavenly host."

"Praise Father, Son, and Holy Ghost."

I have so much to tell you. I wish we could visit. Talk. Hug. Kiss your old faces. See the love in your eyes. Hug and feel your hugs with the joy we had. My Momma. My Daddy. Oh, Lord, My God, I love them. They are Yours.

Jack wiped his face and cleared his throat, "Momma, Daddy, I'll see you again. I'm going to Heaven. I sure hope you're there now. Oh, Lord please let it be so. I'm saved. Your son is saved by faith. I'm a Christian man. I'm gonna be a good Christian man." The tears of overwhelming gratitude took him again. Jack regained his voice as he regained his strength to stand up like a man again. "What a great day! You shoulda been here! You would have been so proud!"

His mind turned home. *I've gotta share it all with Maude. We've got to do over. In love. In Him. I love my babies!* "Thomas, Mary, Nathan, your Daddy is coming home!" he exulted. He remembered Bubba. *Where's Bubba buried?*

Jack looked around this quadrant of graves. Jack took a few hesitant steps up the smooth grade of grass and graves on row by row towards the Tomb of the Unknown at the top of the hill. He paused and took a few more paces at an odd uncertain urging. He scanned left and right. The corner of his eye caught fairly fresh earth and a word that summoned him before he could read it. He saw the Holland name. It was Bubba's grave.

Jack patted the stone like an old dog. Jack surprised himself with his strong voice carrying a laugh in it, "I know you're not here either, Bubba. Thanks, Bubba. Thank you so much." Jack stepped away to give the stone a solemn hand salute. He made a sharp military left face and jogged back to the van, his home and new life. Another of Bubba's songs came to his memory in Bubba's soothing bass. *"Because He lives, I can face tomorrow. Because He lives…"*

Beckley, West Virginia
September 2nd, 2013
Sunday

Naomi went back to the familiar helipad at the Pentagon for a helicopter ride to a very isolated Special Operations Forces training hideout in West Virginia. She rehearsed what she would say in person to her family over and over on the flight to the safe house in the Appalachian mountains. Nothing seemed right, though. She asked Ruth to notify her family of her 'non-death' in an unusual moment of weakness. Naomi couldn't bear to break the news herself. She couldn't handle the feedback of pain and joy she would awaken in the very hearts she loved beyond words in this world.

Naomi kept hearing Pablo's pointed short comments at the brunch. He explained from his perspective as a historian what the message from the President meant.

Pablo said, "The President and others like LTG Trento will make the history books. Others might be asterisks, perhaps. Decades from now, history students will ferret out the unsung heroes and place them in small print in the less widely circulated history tomes. These weighty works would be written after they're all dead when the documents are declassified."

What will I live to see or not in the rest of this life? I don't need fame. I need my family for as long as God will grant me breath.

The helicopter made its final approach in the tiny clearing of the barnyard. She saw her family on the other side of the tired wooden gate. Arnett and Winona held the children back by the shoulders. Pete looked clean and handsome. He smiled, no, beamed at her helicopter's approach.

It was scant few feet from the edge of the Blackhawk blade to the fence standing between the members of the one family of love and blood and faith. That fence was no barrier to the love that knows no boundaries of time, space or things of this earth. The bug-helmeted crew chief slammed open the door, helped Naomi to gracefully alight in the mud and pushed on her shoulder to encourage her to crouch walk away from his aircraft. Naomi saw nothing once she gained her feet on ground except the faces of her babies. Her smile meet their squeals. Six arms reached for her with six little hands grasping for their own Mother. The helicopter blade was beating to a stop, but still going fast, when she reached the fence. She reached to them over the wood slats as Pete swung the gate open. Naomi hurried around the edge of the gate. Sarah, Ruth and Joshua broke free from aged hands and ran the few child steps to Naomi's outstretched arms.

She plopped down on both knees in a mud puddle splattering her bright sundress.

They tried to kiss her face and cling to her at the same time. She pulled them close like a beloved brood under the wings of a bird mother. She kissed them over and over. She moved her head to kiss each child, a loving peck to each head of hair. Their little arms reached around her as far as they could stretch.

She said huskily, "I love you, I love you, my babies," over and over.

Kiss, "I love you, darlin' darlin'."

Kiss, "I love you, precious."

Kiss, "I love you, sweet angel."

Arnett and Edith patted her shoulder waiting their turn in tears to kiss and hug like there was no tomorrow. Pete stood close by smiling. He cried, too, honest tears.

The children all spoke excitedly at the same time.

Lil' Bit Joshua pulled his head up to face squarely into his Mother's face. He scrunched his chin and lips in his most adult scowl, "Don't ever leave again, Mommy! Mommy, don't ever go away again! Don't never!"

Naomi gave Lil' Bit a big kiss on the check and pulled him up to hug her neck. She rocked all of her children back and forth from her knees.

"I won't dear, darling. Praise the Lord our God. I won't. Oh, thank You Jesus! Thank you Lord! Oh, praise God! Thank You, Abba. I love YOU!"

Poquoson, Virginia
September 3rd, 2013
Monday

Jack leaned back in his chair and closed his eyes. The sun was so warm on his face. It felt good. Everything still felt wonderful. He heard the kids high pitched chatter a few feet away playing in the yard. Being with Maude as man and wife again was great. Feeling the joy, the slight uplifting buoyancy of sensing, throughout his body and mind, the love of God through Jesus was refreshing. Not being afraid, cautious, but not anticipating violent death and fearing it for his family every day was intoxicatingly high. *Life is good. God is good. All the time No matter what.*

"Jack! Jack!" Maude called from the kitchen.

"Yes, honey, I'm out here watching the kids," Jack cupped his hands to project his voice back to the house.

"You're sitting on your butt reading the paper. Are you ever going to help me?"

"I'll be there," Jack rose quickly and looked carefully if he could leave all three kids alone for a few minutes. No sharp objects nearby. No critters bearing watching.

"Take the laundry out of the dryer and fold it. Put the wet stuff in the washer in the dryer. Two shirts need to be hung up. Read the labels. And then I'll tell you what else," Maude sat at a card table surrounded by coupons clipped from magazines, a shopping list and a stack of her personal notecards.

Please. Of course, you meant to say, 'Please Dear'. Jack did as he was told. He smiled. *I can do all things through Christ Jesus. Oh, I love it when those Bible verses just come to me when I need them.* He read the Bible every morning and evening now. More and more the Bible words hopped into his thoughts. It comforted him as much as it pleased him.

"Hey Maude, some of these shirts don't have laundry labels."

"Can't you tell?"

"No."

"Oh, Jack. Can't you do anything right?"

Jack clamped his jaw like a trap. *I can maybe help change the course of American and Human history with Rosetta 6.2. But, other than that, I can't do much right.* He chuckled to himself. *Husbands love your wives as Christ loves the church. Okay.*

Mary opened the sliding glass door to the den howling, "Mama, Mama! Thomas hit me!"

"Jack! Jack!" Maude opened her arms to little Mary. "Jack get Thomas in here. Don't leave Nathan out there by himself!" she shrieked.

Jack met Thomas coming in. "I didn't hit her. I threw her the ball. She missed it," Thomas edged beyond his mother's reach. He looked sad.

Jack scooped up Nathan sitting in the sandbox and oblivious to all. He rocked Nathan back and kissed his fat cheeks. Nathan squirmed and giggled. Jack walked back inside still nuzzling Nathan and biting his ears gently while making doggie noises.

"Thomas, you're too rough. You're always too rough. You're clumsy. Mary is just a little baby. You're a big six," said Maude sharply.

"I'm not a baby," Mary's tears stopped in an instant. Thomas hung his head.

Jack handed Nathan to Maude and scooped up Mary and put her high on his hip. He turned Thomas' head with his free hand and said, "Let's go out and try again. C'mon team."

"Jack, I'm not finished," said Maude.

"I got this. Love Nathan. See if he has sugar on his tummy." Nathan squealed in anticipation. He lifted his shirt to look at his stomach.

"Jack." Jack closed the glass door and the fussing behind him. He put Mary down.

"Thomas, wanna play ball with me and Mary or wait and play big boy catch with me with your baseball glove?"

Thomas brightened, "I play catch with you, Daddy. I'll play cars now."

"Mary won't want to play ball long. Get your glove and baseball, son. Be ready, okay?"

Thomas ran to fetch. Mary already had her big plastic ball in both hands. "Play ball, Daddy."

"Yes darlin'. Roll the ball to me, please."

Mary threw the ball with all her strength. It tumbled out of her hands early and flopped a few feet forward. Jack came closer to stand only a few feet from the barefoot angel in the little sun dress. *Thank you, Lord Jesus. Thank you for these precious babies.*

"Throw to me Daddy. Throw to me."

"Okay. I got the concept, babe." Jack rolled the ball back to Mary. She fell over reaching for it in the grass. She jumped up smiling. *I've got to remember this moment. I've gotta burn this in my brain.* Mary's grin couldn't be any wider. The joy was frozen on her face. They rolled the ball back and forth. The grass, which Maude mentioned really needed mowing, swished in the wind as much as Mary's curls cascaded back forth across her face. *It doesn't get any better than this. Thank You, God.*

"Hey Daddy, I'm ready," Thomas held his ball, two gloves and a catcher's mask and bat.

Jack smiled broadly. "One minute, son. Just another couple of minutes, okay?"

"Okay." Thomas dropped everything to the ground. He went to his cars. Jack looked to see if Thomas was disappointed. Thomas looked focused as usual, not hurt.

Maude came outside and plopped down in Jack's chair with Nathan. She started a game of patty cake. After each 'cake in the oven' tummy tickle, she kissed Nathan's lips with a big smack. She was better. Over her fit.

Jack rolled the ball to Mary. *Lord, Father God, Holy Ghost, Sweet Jesus, I will do whatever You want. No matter what. Just let me have my family grow up in health and live to know You. I'll do anything.* Jack listened in his mind as he kept playing ball. He looked one to the next at each member of his family.

This moment, like many others recently, lingered as it happened. The excitement of homecoming after such a time changed time. Jack still felt like CHRISTmas is to a child. There were reality checks at work, at home, and in his heart when he thought of Naomi. But, nothing diminished the love he felt he drew like an endless well of water. Living water. He poured out love for Maude and there was more to spare. More to share. *Fathers, provoke not your children to wrath, but bring them up in the nurture and admonition of the Lord. Willco. I will do this.*

Maude smiled at Jack. She rubbed foreheads with Nathan. *Husbands love your wives as your own bodies. Be holy and without blemish. Love your wife as you love yourself. Hooah!*

The End